Eighty years ago, the unimaginable shattered our world. Will history dare repeat itself within the next twenty *or even tomorrow? Genesis Revisited* sweeps across a century of seismic change—from the fiery dawns over Hiroshima and Nagasaki, through the shadowed years of the Cold War and the promising leaps of the Space Age, *right up to the present and uncertain frontier of artificial intelligence then beyond.* This is not just a novel – it is a clarion call, a labyrinth of questions and razor-edged answers that none of us can afford to ignore. The time for complacency is past. The moment to act, to question, and to shape what comes next, is now. *Turn the page .... and hold your breath ....*

"The year of this book's publication (2025) has shown us some of the darkest sides of humanity, with nuclear-armed countries involved in different conflicts and civilians suffering abominable atrocities. Some of these same states are spending staggering amounts on the modernisation and expansion of their nuclear arsenals, still believing that these weapons will keep them safe, when in reality, they threaten not just them but all of us with annihilation. At the same time, the majority of countries strongly oppose nuclear weapons, with the support of much of civil society, academia, and the financial community. *The UN Treaty on the Prohibition of Nuclear Weapons* demonstrates that humans are entirely capable of cooperation to prevent our own destruction.

"Genesis Revisited is a timely reminder of the interconnectedness of humanity and nature and the need to guard against threats to both, and will hopefully guide its readers to think about their legacies for the generations to come."

– **Melissa Parke,** Executive Director of the
International Campaign to Abolish Nuclear Weapons *(ICAN)*
For further information, visit: https://www.icanw.org/

Praise for Genesis Revisited

"*Genesis Revisited* increases our awareness of a critical question - will future generations survive and thrive, or will they be victims of catastrophic global conflicts? A nuclear war would be an unthinkable occurrence, but it is one which has risen to the surface of concern for many of us today. We must ask ourselves, what happens in the collective minds of government officials when invading other nations seems like a plausible option? When countries go to war, is it due in good part to the leaders of the provoking nation having acquired a sudden malicious and extreme aggression which has exceeded all limits? John Pescitelli's *Genesis Revisited* answers these questions and more than that – it is an extremely interesting and thought-provoking novel which keeps you turning pages and I sincerely believe it will help motivate its readers to better understand that, with appropriate advocacy, we all can play a part in preventing nations from using aggression and violence as an alternative to peace and cooperation."

– Robert C Bransfield, MD, DLFAPA, Author

"For the sake of future generations, we must take decisive steps today to alter our course and safeguard our world. Our survival depends on the choices we make now, and we must embrace global cooperation, and prioritize peace and innovation. *Genesis Revisited* is a one-of-a-kind, action-packed, and highly well-developed novel – it is the book we need right now in order to start this necessary conversation. The time to act is now, before it's too late."

–Nickolas Harold Potter, Screenwriter

"Read this roadmap for humankind's future within these hallowed pages, brimming with suspense, intrigue, and astonishing originality. Dive into the gripping tale of how two former presidents might have averted mankind's extinction and be swept away by a narrative rich with action, wisdom, and warning. This electrifying masterpiece is my favorite book of the past two decades."

–Michael Carona, Historian and Manager

"No doubt, *Genesis Revisited* will give every reader a lot to consider. The Prologue serves the purpose of setting the stage that is relevant and important to the story and all that it addresses. What makes this book so captivating is that it successfully mixes romance, politics, history, and science in a way that will satisfy readers across strict genre lines. The writing is full of intricate details, the characters are extremely believable, and the plot leads to an ending that is both surprising and unequivocal. Within the story, the issues that are tackled are just as real today as they were many years ago, and that is what will challenge the reader's perspective and provide opportunity for reflection for those readers looking for a book with something to say. The story will pull you in and keep you wondering just where the plot might go. Admittedly, there are some tough-to-read, emotional moments, but there are also sweet and charming characters to cheer for along the way, and it is this blend that makes *Genesis Revisited* worth the read."

–Elizabeth R. Burton, Writer/Editor, Teacher, Mother

"An action-packed novel about what has been prepared ahead of time to save humanity from Armageddon. This book is absolutely mesmerizing from start to finish. Already happening today, this cautionary tale is brilliant - a must read before things get worse than they already are...."

–David Francis, M.Ed., Account Manager

"Surviving our very own existence might be our biggest challenge since mankind's aggression knows no bounds. but have we prepared for what's to come, or is it already too late …? *Genesis Revisited* is a fast-paced adventure with so many ties to current political hijinks that it will give you nightmares. But do humanity a favor and read it, but more importantly, live it…."

–Brad Jacques, Film Director

"John Pescitelli's *Genesis Revisited* is a solid, thought-provoking book that I genuinely enjoyed digging into. It takes a hard look at how we humans tangle with technology and violence, and it's the kind of read that makes you stop and think about where we're headed. The story is serious, a bit heavy, and full of questions about why our bright ideas so often end up in dark places. That's what makes it so valuable for anyone curious about the bigger picture. The book's real strength is its tough, no-nonsense view of our future – it doesn't pull punches, and I respect that. Pescitelli sketches out a world where we might just trip ourselves into a mess, but he leaves a sliver of hope, like he's nudging us to figure it out. It's not a perfect wrap-up *(or is it?)*, and it doesn't pretend to have all the fixes, but that raw, unfiltered take keeps it real and sticks it to you. *Genesis Revisited* is a strong piece that adds something worthwhile to the conversation about *what's next for us*."

–Igor Rivilis, PhD

"When the final war erupts, engulfing the earth in an all-consuming nuclear inferno, an exquisitely trained American astronaut and a brilliant Russian cosmonaut and surgeon must rise above the chaos. Their love and unity become humanity's last hope. Armed with every meticulously planned resource provided by an agreement between Ronald Reagan and Michael Gorbachev decades earlier, they embark on a mission to rekindle life on the charred remains of our planet. Will they succeed in rewriting the fate of mankind or succumb to the remnants of destruction that threaten to engulf them? You will be glad and extremely enlightened after you have finished reading this book. *Genesis Revisited* is a masterfully crafted, action-packed thriller that you will not be able to put down...."

–Rosanne Centineo-Fischer, Executive Assistant

"A one-of-a-kind original story with characters the likes of which you would want to have on your side when things go wrong. The scenes are so vivid – *would make a great movie!* This novel has everything you could ever hope for in a historically accurate, very well researched, thriller. The ending will knock your socks off and the entire story keeps you on the edge of your seat."

–Anthony Grieco, Retired Administrator

∞ ∞ ∞

GENESIS REVISITED

By John Pescitelli

Genesis Executive Order Number One Publishing
90 Matawan Road, Suite 100
Matawan, NJ 07747
(732) 410-7588
info@genesisrevisitedbook.com

Genesis Revisited

Library of Congress Cataloging-in-Publication number:
ISBN: 979-8-9995942-1-1

Printed in the United States of America

To my wife, our daughters, and granddaughters, whom I love with all my heart!

Through this book, I hope to raise awareness that now is the time, as a global community, to ensure the survival of our glorious planet Mother Earth and the future of us all!

Table of Contents

Foreword

By Robert C Bransfield, MD, DLFAPA

∞ ∞ ∞

Genesis Revisited by John Pescitelli increases our awareness of a critical question - will future generations survive and thrive, or will they be victims of catastrophic global conflicts? To answer that question, I believe we need to first look at two other questions. The first question: are humans fundamentally flawed with violent tendencies? The second question: will advancing technology be used to deter or to magnify humanity's potential for violence?

The first question has been asked many times before from ethical, religious, and scientific perspectives. In the early part of this novel, there is a discussion between Ronald Reagan and Mikhail Gorbachev which takes place in 1986. Those two presidents had control of nuclear arsenals, and both were eager for a discussion to work out their differences. Especially, however, they worried that something could go wrong in the future which would cause an extinction event for humanity, and so they developed a plan of action. The novel proceeds from that meeting. Presently in 2025, there are nine individuals in control of over 12,000 nuclear weapons. Will these nine individuals and the people who come after them always act in a responsible manner?

History has demonstrated cycles of cooperation and growth versus cycles of conflict and decline. During cycles when cooperation and growth are dominant, safety and quality of life are improved. The cycles when conflict and violence are dominant result in a decline in security and individual well-being.

Aggression is not always violence, but it can be a precursor. Although well-focused aggression is innate and can be adaptive and constructive, that is not the case when it degrades into violent behavior. The two most deadly cycles of violence in history were World War II that resulted in the deaths of 70 to 85 million and the Mongol invasions and conquest from 1207 to 1405 that caused 20-60 million to be killed. The War of Three Kingdoms, Taiping Rebellion, and Manchu Conquest of China resulted in the deaths of many millions of people in China.

A nuclear war would have an even much higher casualty rate. We must ask ourselves, what happens in the collective minds of government officials when these cycles of violence spike? The interplay between compassion and collaboration vs. competition and aggression constantly occur in both mammalian and human functioning. Extremes of competition and aggression are normally restrained by opposing social bonds and social structures that support collaboration and cooperation. When countries go to war, it is due in good part to the leaders of the provoking nation having acquired a sudden malicious and extreme aggression which has exceeded all limits.

Violence has greatly impacted mankind's history throughout all ages, with periods of advances and declines in civilization associated with cycles of collaboration and conflict, respectively. Collaboration, compassion and empathy are a part of human functioning that allows us to collectively experience great achievements and a better quality of life. However, at different times in history, and in different geographical locations, conflict, violent behavior, and a decline in quality of life are more prevalent.

What explains these episodic increases in violence? This is a subject which should be studied with as much vigor and support as any other areas of scholarly pursuit which include analyzing disease, criminality, economics, and human suffering. *Genesis Revisited* is such a study in itself and provides a much more comprehensive outlook about the role of human nature itself, *and it presents a good argument.*

How will advancing technology impact violent behavior? My second question above addresses the impact of technology upon potential human violence. In today's age, weapon technology is more advanced than mental health technology, and the mental stability of the individuals controlling these weapons is of grave concern. Trillions are spent on technology that counters violence by developing even more technologically advanced weapon systems. Could some of this money be better spent developing technology which can help us to further understand and then prevent mankind's penchant for violence in the first place?

With our modern AI-driven systems, the need to understand the root causes of our violent tendencies has never been greater. Instead of just fueling an arms race, directing resources toward preventing violence could harness technology's true potential. *Will we create more tools of destruction, or will we seek to understand and mitigate the very triggers of violence?* As a psychiatrist I have evaluated and treated violent individuals over a span of 50+ years and strongly believe this is the path we must now take. Research and prevention can potentially transform our understanding, offering hope that we can alleviate the violent impact of our very own dark impulses.

I thank John Pescitelli for drawing awareness to these critical questions in *Genesis Revisited.* I find the book extremely interesting and thought-provoking, and I sincerely believe it will help motivate its readers to better understand that we all can play a part in preventing nations from using aggression and violence as an alternative to peace and cooperation through advocacy. We are all winners once we embrace a better understanding and prevention of violence, but we are all losers from any furthering of the arms race.

– Robert C Bransfield, MD, DLFAPA

∞ ∞ ∞

Preface

∞　∞　∞

From the time I was a young boy growing up on what was known as the "Lower East Side" of Manhattan, New York, I remember living in the shadow of an apocalyptic nuclear attack by what was then the Soviet Union. This end-of-time possibility permeated our daily existence. It even extended into the classroom, usually a safe haven, in the form of Civilian Defense air raid drills which required children of all ages to hide underneath their desks when the shrill of an air raid siren sounded. It was traumatic and, obviously in retrospect, a useless exercise. This trauma followed all of us who were children at the time even into our living rooms on a Sunday evening when the family gathered around the thrilling invention of the 20th Century, the television set. As a family, we would watch *The Ed Sullivan Variety Show* which presented wholesome, age-appropriate entertainment for adults and children.

However, at some point in the show, a public service announcement would advise parents to have their children leave the room, a feat that was nearly impossible in my family because we occupied a small three-room tenement apartment. Then came the Civil Defense video clip in which a nuclear explosion followed by an ominous mushroom cloud filled the screen. It then showed the effects of the bomb's shock wave and accompanying radioactive fallout, decimating trees and finally a small house and its occupants in its all-encompassing path.

This was the beginning of the Cold War that was to impact my thinking for decades to come concerning the Divine experiment called "Human" beings on this earth. As I got older and learned about the "Human" experiment and all its wondrous achievements throughout recorded history, including the archeological discoveries of scientists like the Leakeys and pioneers like Margaret Mead, I began to form my own negative view of our self-destructive, glorious species.

This atomic terror escalated into paralyzing fear in October of 1962, during the Cuban Missile Crisis, which brought the United States and Soviet Union to the brink of World War III. I was a high school sophomore who was determined to become an astrophysicist, having decided upon this career path as a ten-year-old in 1957 after the Russian launch of Sputnik, the first manmade earth satellite. So motivated was I to become a scientist that as a high school freshman, I chose to study the Russian language, which I did for the next five years to prepare myself to be able to communicate with what I hoped would be our Russian allies in space. Ironically, both of my high school language courses required us to translate two accounts of historic wars, Julius Caesar's *Gallic Wars (De Bello Gallico)* and Leo Tolstoy's *War and Peace (Voyna I Mir)*. For me, these were both just further commentaries on the prominence of human aggression and violence against their fellow man. The Cold War continued, and eventually I took a different path, utilizing my scientific training in the business world.

Following the works of Isaac Asimov[1] and Nobel Laureate Konrad Lorenz[2], I decided that it was time for a cautionary take on man's apparently inexorable march into the abyss. This sense of urgency reached a compelling high point approximately 35 years ago when President Ronald Regan and General Secretary Mikhail Gorbachev were in power. Their summit in Reykjavik, Iceland had resulted in a dire message about the proliferation of nuclear weapons to all inhabitants of the planet that we call Mother Earth! Consequently, I strongly believe it is time to take notice lest we all perish. Thus, it became the impetus for this book, **_Genesis Revisited._**

∞ ∞ ∞

---

[1] Asimov, Isaac, and Frank White. *The March of the Millennia: A Key to Looking at History.* New York: Walker, 1991. Print.

[2] Lorenz, Konrad. *On Aggression [1st ed.].* New York: Harcourt, Brace & World, 1966. Print.

Prologue

A Final Hope

∞ ∞ ∞

"Henceforth, the only outcome of an all-out war will be that both contenders must lose."

- Henry Kissinger, from his book, *Nuclear Weapons and Foreign Policy.*

August 6, 1945 - Dawn

In a quiet neighborhood perched on a hill overlooking the heart of Hiroshima, Japan, a thirty-year-old husband and father by the name of Takashi stands before a bathroom mirror in his one-story house, meticulously preparing to depart for work. Carefully adjusting the cap of his black Kokumin-fuku, the civil uniform mandated for working class men ever since the war had started, his eyes reflect a mixture of determination and concern, and he can't help but wonder if he looks too similar to a Japanese soldier, whose basic, loose-fitting uniforms were not all that much different than his except for their lighter color. He does not like the look of these uniforms at all, and he misses the Western style suits he had worn before this miserable war.

Beyond his reflection, he glances at the rooftops of the houses below which stretch out like a patchwork quilt, showcasing an array of traditional Japanese designs with graceful curves and sloping eaves, each one bearing the weight of history within their wooden beams and tiles. Hiroshima had been spared all along from any attacks by the Americans, and so the leaflets the Westerners had passed days before warning them all to flee and to overturn their present government seem like propaganda. Most of the citizens had long since stopped heeding the air-raid sirens. Whereas some still flock to the bomb shelters, customarily the "all-clear" alarm would sound, and everyone would go about day-to-day business just the same. Takashi has worked hard to keep this house, which had been in his family for two generations, and he and his family are very comfortable and happy here.

He walks to the front of the house where his wife, Aiko, is standing in the living room watching through the large window as their two daughters play in the front yard. She is a vision of serenity and beauty, and he notices that the soft pastel shades of her old "work" kimono, though now quite faded and worn, still match the vibrant hues of the even row of bright pink oleanders blooming along the eastern edge of their meticulously tended garden out front. He had carefully trained these shrubs over the past seven years to grow as single-trunk trees almost three meters high, and he can smell their sweet fragrance as it now dances in the air, carried by a gentle breeze into the house through the open window.

Their daughters, Hana and Mei, play in the yard, their laughter intertwining with the song of morning birds. Hana is nine years old with a cascade of ebony curls framing her cherubic face, and she is busy carefully tending to one of the oleanders, her fingers delicately touching the flower petals as if encouraging their life. Mei is seven with bright, twinkling eyes, and she is frolicking behind her older sister, gathering fallen blossoms and placing them in one of her mother's old straw hats.

Coming to stand beside Aiko, Takashi gestures towards a half-built stone barrier near their welcoming front porch, "Will you be working on the wall today?" he inquires, a subtle worry creasing his forehead as he glances outside and up towards the sky where the sun promises a warm day. "The sun will be unforgiving."

Aiko nods, taking note of the steam rising from the evaporating dew in their yard. "Yes, we can use it to dry some of the vegetables in the direct sunlight there." She turns and looks at her husband with a thin smile. "Miyuki will be dropping off Osamu for the first part of the day. She must attend to her duties at the factory until after lunch, so I'll be watching over the children and managing the wall at the same time."

"My wife is remarkably skilled," Takashi says, a mixture of admiration and love in his smile as he traces the delicate outline of her face with his eyes.

Just then, they see Miyuki hurrying up to their house from the road, together with Osamu, and the little girls eagerly welcome their cheerful friend. Osamu, a lively young boy with a contagious smile and playful eyes, immediately joins them, matching their excitement with his youthful energy. The three children are soon running wildly through the yard as Miyuki carefully steps up to the porch landing. "Good morning," she calls out. "Sorry I'm late!"

Takashi and Aiko walk together to the front of the porch to greet Miyuki; high above, the slender shape of an aircraft pierces the morning sky, its intentions veiled by the gentle dawn haze. A low hum resonates, reaching their ears first as a soft echo, and then expanding into a nearing rumble that hints at possible violence. The air-raid sirens sound and they all freeze for a moment, even the children stop in their places and look back at their parents.

Their eyes follow the aircraft but especially zoom in on the bay doors on its underside. As it passes over the city for several tense moments, the doors never open and nothing is released. The aircraft changes course and heads back out to sea, and a minute later, the comfortingly familiar "all-clear" siren announces another false alarm. Miyuki, turning her eyes from the aircraft back to her friends, stands with quiet resolve, her dark work uniform seeming a size or two larger than it should be. She gives a polite bow to Takashi and Aiko, who respond with their own bows in return.

"The Americans *know* they have already won, and yet they continue to spy on us,"

Miyuki remarks, her face etched with both determination and sadness.

"Do we leave them any choice?" Takashi asks.

"What a mess we've made of this planet. At least the war is nearing its end," Aiko reflects, the morning sun's gentle caress enhancing her timeless beauty. The trio shares a solemn, silent moment of agreement. "No more death. No more pain. I don't care who's right or wrong anymore. Nothing is worth what this war has brought."

Miyuki takes a deep breath and gazes respectfully at Aiko, all the while nodding in agreement with her every word.

4

Takashi nods at his wife as well, puts on his shoes, then gently kisses Aiko before stepping down onto the porch landing. For just a brief moment, he allows himself the small pleasure of breathing in the sweet aroma of the oleander blossoms once again.

"Better get moving. Can't afford to be late," he then says with urgency, throwing a quick glance over his shoulder to Aiko, who smiles back at him despite her emotional weariness from the war. With determination, he strides down the pebble walkway, tossing a grin towards the children, as well, as he goes.

"Wait! I'll come with you!" Miyuki interjects, rushing to catch up with Takashi as she looks back once more at Aiko and shouts, both gratitude and relief evident in her tone, "Thank you so much for watching Osamu today! I owe you!"

"Don't worry about it. Both of you have a good day!" Aiko calls out, the faint smile which had been adorning her lips quickly fading as she looks once more towards the sky.

∞ ∞ ∞

More than a thousand miles to the southeast across the Philippine Sea, at the Allied Air Base on the Island of Tinian in an empty hangar, sits an American Naval Pilot named Captain Rocco. Thirty-three years of age, his uniform disheveled and untucked, Captain Rocco supports his back against the base of a workbench, drinking a Budweiser. Behind his cheap, bottleneck eyeglasses, he wears the look of a puzzled student who just can't grasp his science lesson no matter how hard he has tried understanding it. He's drunk, with several empty beer cans scattered around him. His hand rests on a pistol as he sweats profusely, and he seems to have the weight of the world on his shoulders.

Sean Ryan, a twenty-two-year-old American with a sort of boy-next-door innocence adorning his comely face, enters the hangar with audible footsteps. He is a low-level crew member with a heart of gold and had formulated a quick but deep friendship with his captain from the first day of assignment here on the island. "Captain Rocco, there you are! Everyone is looking for you, Sir." He comes to within a few feet of his friend and takes a closer look. "Sir, are you drunk?" He puts his hand on his forehead and then scratches determinedly. "What's the matter? *Are you alright?"*

Coming out of his stupor, Captain Rocco has to squint even in the low light of the hangar to see Sean Ryan, but finally, focusing on the voice of his friend, he knows who has come to find him, and Rocco immediately becomes enlivened. "Sean Ryan! Sit down and have a drink!"

"I'm on duty, Sir. I can't drink." He hates having to confront his captain but realizes the consequences will be very severe if he doesn't do something quickly. "And I think we better get you cleaned up, 'cuz you shouldn't be drinking either, sir."

Captain Rocco barks defiantly, "Sit down! *That's an order!"*

Ryan looks around the dimly lit hangar and finds that the entire place is deserted. He sits and Captain Rocco uses a can opener to poke two small holes in the top of the steel can of beer and hands it to him. The crew member tentatively takes a small sip. "Tell me what's wrong, Sir." He feels a deep pang of pain in his heart seeing his captain so out of sorts. He thinks he knows why the captain is so terribly upset, and in his characteristically innocent and kind voice, he asks, "Are you upset they took your wings when you didn't pass your eye exam?"

The captain turns in his direction and his face seems like a pile of unformed and yeasty dough. "You know you don't have to call me *Captain,* or *Sir* when it's just us." Rocco furrows his brow and becomes introspective for just a moment, then slowly starts to shake his head. "My wings? They can have 'em. I'm *Intelligence* now, don't you know?"

Ryan looks with concern at someone he's clearly very fond of; it is unsettling to him seeing this man so broken for whatever the reason may be. "Then what is it, Roc?"

Rocco looks into Ryan's eyes and his face softens. He then places his hand affectionately on the back of Ryan's neck, cocking his head a bit to really study the young man's eyes. He is captivated with the awareness that no matter what, they always seem to emit an ember of warmth reaching from deep within Ryan's soul. Ryan rests a hand on the captain's arm as he waits patiently for words to come from his lips.

"You're the best man on this whole damned island, you know that?" Rocco says. "But they won't let you make the big decisions, will they? You'd get them right. And that's what they'd be afraid of." Ryan doesn't say anything, just listens and tries to comprehend the message from his friend. "You're better off if I spare you the details."

"Is it about the bomb? Has something gone wrong?"

"Depends on what you mean by *wrong.*" Rocco takes his hand away from Ryan and reaches into his pocket for his ration pack of Lucky Strike cigarettes. He lights one and offers the pack to Ryan, who shakes his head. "It won't be long now, and Baby Boy is going to erase a city - *and everyone in it.* Mostly civilians, women, children – babies, for fuck sake!" His eyes become wild with rage suddenly, but then he calms himself and takes another drag of his cigarette. "The war will be over soon. I'll save you the suspense: *We win!*"

With that he sneers and drains the bottom half of the beer he had been drinking. He tosses the can out into the center of the hangar where it clanks and then rolls for another ten seconds before coming to a stop. Ryan is confused and doesn't know how to take Rocco. The captain takes off his glasses, places his face in his hands, and starts sobbing. Sean Ryan is at a complete loss. Not knowing what to do he scoots closer to his friend and puts an arm around his shoulder.

"Hey, Roc, that's a good thing, right? Us winning the war, I mean. I don't understand why you're so upset...."

He speaks through his sobs. "Should be. Should be a good thing. But the end of this war is the beginning of more wars and bigger wars in the years to come." Rocco then mumbles something, his emotions continuing to deteriorate, until Ryan pulls him nearer, encouraging his head to rest on his shoulder.

"You're not making sense, Roc. Just think about it - there'll finally be peace! And that's what we all want, right? We want peace and now we'll have it." He rubs his head against the captain's as he had during some of their times together during furlough and he thinks of all the joyful times they had spent together these past twelve months. "Come on, now. Cheer up!"

Rocco sniffles loudly and gets himself under control. "There'll never be peace on this planet, Sean. Never. We ain't built for it."

"What do you mean?" In the silence which follows, Ryan fears that his friend is suffering from some form of emotional disorder. "Roc, I'm worried about you. Battle fatigue, maybe. Maybe you need a lot of rest. Maybe a little help sortin' things out...?"

He is surprised by the captain's response. "Can you keep a secret?" Overhead, they hear the roar of a loud engine from a plane passing too close to the ground.

Once it is quiet, Ryan plays along, "I guess so. *Sure, Roc,* I'd never spill a secret you gave me. You know that." They share a knowing, familiar look. Notwithstanding his state of intoxication, the trust between them is solid.

Rocco then speaks, his tone deathly serious. "In a few minutes Baby Boy is gonna fall from the Enola Gay above Hiroshima."

Ryan nods gently. "I know that."

"What you don't know is how it's gonna play out, see? You don't know the choices we've made in the name of peace. You can't imagine the blood we're going to spill. *You can't* - I don't know if anyone can imagine it!"

Rocco suddenly lifts his head from Sean Ryan's shoulder and the young serviceman turns to face him, looking his friend hard in the eyes. All at once, there is more than just a hint of fear in Ryan's countenance as he senses he is about to learn something he probably doesn't want to and now has no choice but to listen in spite of his trepidation. He starts to protest. "Maybe I'm better off …."

Rocco cuts him off before he can say another word. "We set Baby Boy *not to go off when it hits the ground*, but above ground, see?" Ryan gives him a baffled look, not following the reasoning. "Listen to what I'm saying, Sean - *the bomb is a sphere.* They wanted to make sure that no radiation was wasted going straight into the ground. Going off above ground, fire the likes of Hell itself comes out of every point on that sphere because this way it potentially penetrates a living soul. More damage. More death. *There's no reason for it, damnit!* They'd make their point just fine letting it hit the ground."

That's when Captain Rocco picks up his pistol and Sean Ryan's eyes go wide. "Whatcha doin' there, Roc? *Is that thing loaded?* Maybe you better give it to me for now. You're a little drunk and we don't need an accident."

"It's not loaded."

"Just the same -"

"I said it's not loaded!"

"OK, Roc." Ryan eyes Rocco's hand that is holding the pistol and is relieved that, for now, none of his fingers are on the trigger itself. He thinks of making a move to take the pistol away from him but realizes the danger of this given Rocco's current mental state.

Resting the pistol on his lap, Rocco continues. "You know what else?"

Ryan responds with exaggerated interest, as he would to a puppy that wouldn't stop playing with a toy already shredded beyond recognition. *"What Roc? What else do you have to say about all of this?"*

Rocco eyes the last can of beer he had taken from the canteen in the paper sack beside his feet. "They made other choices, too." Finally, he reaches for the can and quickly presses two holes in it, then drains half of it before taking the pistol in his hand once again. Ryan had a moment when he might have grabbed the pistol from Rocco's lap, but it had been lost before he could commit to that course of action. "For maximum blood. Revenge, I think, for Pearl Harbor, but it makes no sense. Two wrongs don't make a right."

"What do you mean now, Roc? You're making me a nervous wreck, so please, let's get this out and over with and move on, okay?" Ryan takes the pack of Lucky Strikes from Rocco's shirt pocket, along with the flip-top black crackle metal Zippo lighter there, and lights himself a smoke. "See? You got me smoking now and I can't even stand the taste of tobacco."

Rocco speaks with a quiet and reserved authority, one thus far unfamiliar to Ryan. He finally makes a point which hits Ryan with precision. "A warning shot in the Bay of Tokyo would've shown off the power of Baby Boy just as well. Or out in the country … farmland, maybe, or way out in the wilderness...."

Exhaling his second puff with a raspy cough, Ryan's eyes go wider as he's beginning to get the point. *If the Japs knew we had this powerful bomb, of course they would have relinquished and surrendered.* At least, now, he feels like he understands why Captain Rocco is so despondent. "You're probably right, Roc. I think I see your point. They're just killing innocent civilians for the sake of killing and for no other reason. *A capricious and arbitrary decision* like you used to say to our regiment if we did something stupid when we first got here!" And with that, he suddenly shares his friend's sadness. "Why couldn't they make the decision to do any of those other things you mentioned? The war would have ended, and many lives would have been spared."

Captain Rocco looks at Sean Ryan and his face softens for his young friend even more, realizing that evil things simply don't occur to him. "It's because we're blood-thirsty, Sean. *The whole damned human race.* That just occurred to me this morning when the Enola Gay took off from the airstrip." He finishes his beer, crumples the can and tosses it. He then takes a cigarette and lights it, reaping the rewards of a healthy puff. *"And we're cowards!"* He spits out into the center of the hangar. "Baby Boy is gonna kill *tens of thousands* of innocent people today, *needlessly.* And from then on, the world will be living under the constant threat of utter and total obliteration in the form of a lightning-fast strike which gives way too little warning and no hope of escape."

Ryan smashes his cigarette into the cement floor and shakes his head, his eyes glistening with fresh tears and newfound anger. His mind can't ponder the correct words to formulate a response or even a valid question.

Rocco continues, dazed and forever withdrawn into a world he can no longer abide by, knowing there will never be an adequate response to the embodiment of the truth which seemingly he alone has foreseen. "Naw, there'll never be peace on Earth again. I'm sure sorry you're going to have to live through it, buddy. But not me ...." Rocco changes the grip he has on his pistol, his index finger slipping onto the trigger.

Ryan immediately notices and tenses up, and he fumbles for the correct words and tone to use. Finally, he settles on a soothing tone. "Take it easy now, Roc. Watch what you're doing."

Rocco smiles at him. "I'd tell you to toughen up for your own good but being tough will only get you so far. Better advice is to get smart. *Think about what peace really is.* Get out of this God-forsaken war business and go to college. Put your mind to work and not your fists. *Will you do that for me?"*

"Sure, Roc. Yeah. Of course." Ryan lifts his right hand towards the pistol but stalls. "You know, we could do it together. How about that? We could still see each other after our service to our nation and that way, we –"

An old, gruff voice suddenly bellows into the hangar: "Rocco, where the hell are you? *You're on duty, you son of a bitch!"* Both Rocco and Ryan turn toward the direction of the voice. His decision having been made and having found the right moment, in a split second, Rocco lifts the pistol beneath his chin. Ryan senses his movement, turns in time to see him, and immediately, he knocks the gun away *just as it fires.* The bullet goes into the workbench behind them with shards and splinters of wood flying in all directions at once, some falling over them.

"Roc, what the hell are you doing?!" Ryan finally makes an effort to confiscate the gun from Rocco.

12

The officer who had just bellowed into the hangar and several other soldiers come running upon them as Ryan wrestles with Rocco who is determined to put the gun back under his chin and fire. With four arms flapping and one of those holding a weapon of death, Ryan yells, *"No! Stop it, Roc. For God's sake, quit this nonsense!"*

As two of the officers begin an attempt to subdue Rocco, the gun fires again and they jump back. Rocco begins screaming, *"Get off me! Lemme go! They're gonna put me away! I'm done with this, Sean, don't ya' see?"*

Ryan finally gets Rocco's arm that is holding the gun under his control. "No, you're not! *And no, I don't see!* Gimme the gun, Roc. Please!" But Rocco's determination is boundless, and he uses his free hand to push into Ryan's eyes, forcing Ryan to turn his body away until his grip on Rocco's arm is loosened. Rocco immediately places the pistol again beneath his chin as Ryan reaches back for Rocco's arm one more time, *"Gimme the damn gun!"*

The pistol fires a third time as Ryan's hand comes just in time to knock it away again. The bullet pierces Ryan's arm and suddenly his blood and flesh exit from a bullet hole in his uniform. Seeing this, Rocco is suddenly horrified, and he finally stops the struggle. *"Shit!* Sean, are you OK? Oh, God, I'm so sorry!"

Ryan wields his good arm into a solid uppercut to Rocco's jaw, instantly knocking him out. He then quickly takes the gun from Rocco's limp hand. Panting hard, and with tears streaming down his cheeks, he shouts, "Better they put you away than you put yourself in the ground!" Suddenly overwhelmed, he collapses to his knees. *"Damn you, Roc!!"*

The officer and other soldiers circle around Rocco and look down at his unconscious body. Captain Rocco lies in a bloody mess with his mouth gaping open and several of his teeth broken. The Officer, using his boot, carefully rolls Rocco's head toward the workbench to make sure he's out cold. Completely detached and devoid of any empathy, he says, "I knew the son of a bitch was losing it. I saw the look on his face this morning after we had initiated what will surely be our greatest moment of superiority over the enemy." He looks at the empty beer cans and then back at Rocco's disjointed and troubled face in disgust. "This kind of sympathetic thinking sickens me. Get him out of here and clean this shit up, got it?"

He turns and starts to walk away but first stops beside Ryan. "Good job, son. You got yourself a good flesh wound there. Report to the medical unit and they'll get you patched up." He then storms out of the hangar as if nothing has happened, leaving Ryan to process the entire ordeal. He looks helplessly at his friend as the other soldiers pick Captain Rocco up like a sack of potatoes and cart him away.

Wiping the tears from his cheeks, he breaks down further, suddenly shaking violently and sobbing uncontrollably. He is no longer as much disturbed by the sequence of events that have just transpired as he is now fully aware of the murderous rage of his fellow countrymen, leaders he had respected and a government of good, *all now a shambles of faulty and disillusioned beliefs, reasoning, and propaganda.* He knew nobody would care if he were to speak his mind to the chain of command, nor would they ever admit things could have been different had their intentions been beneficial rather than malevolent.

Somewhere deep within his soul, his heart begins to break beyond repair, and his weary mind grapples to make sense and order out of the remnants of all of these miserable pieces of decayed military whimsy. His wound is nothing compared to what will follow momentarily to an entire city of people. He feels his gut wrenching and looks outside of the hangar for some evidence that the bomb has hit but finds only a hazy blue sky and birds whistling in the gentle breeze. *But life will never be normal again!* He suddenly vows to himself that his life will bring meaning from Rocco's words, and even if it were to somehow kill him, *he would do all within his power in order to get the word out to the masses.*

∞ ∞ ∞

A Final Hope

Chapter One

Beginning of Time, Start of Something Worse

∞ ∞ ∞

We were told science and technology would be used for, *and would do us all,* extreme good. Genetics would be used to enhance our lives and defeat illnesses. Nuclear bombs would be limited, and war would have no place in the future of mankind. Nations would cooperate to feed the hungry, and clean drinking water would be in abundance. Yet, looking around, we see corruption, disease, famine, war, surging nuclear proliferation, and angry mobs. In fact, we have grown quite a bit more hostile and hell-bent on rageful episodes during the past thirty or so years, not less so.

Truth be told, mankind's innate aggressive tendencies have never been quelled and have proven to be the downfall of many cultures throughout our entire history. As humans, we are fully alive and fully aware of our place within the hierarchy of animals. Unlike everything else that only runs from death, our species excels at survival, and yet, humankind seems to take for granted the power of peace. We excel at survival but at the cost of violence against one another. Therefore, we mostly wind up lusting after death. One culture's survival seems to threaten other nations who fear dwindling resources or who envy land. *Why is this so?*

Looking at the history of humanity, an objective read shows that, for the most part, groups scream out for peace but do so even as their leaders run to a show of power and might instead. As time marches onward, it is becoming painfully apparent that what the group wants does not matter in the end - only land, resources, control, *and the finer things that life can offer those who lead and who want to live a life of luxury.* Meantime, the rest of us get to wipe the daily sweat off our backs to support those we love.

Before going forward with my cautionary tale, it may be helpful for us to review the history of mankind's relationship with weapons, since whatever culture had the most powerful weaponry in any given era ultimately had the power to stay in control and to conquer other cultures and lands. I will do this in nine short, historically accurate, vignettes which follow at the start of this Chapter One before we pick up with the story. At first a necessary tool for survival against the elements and predators, mankind's weapons soon developed to control and conquer other groups of people. War became a means to an end, and once that happened, humankind went to endless means to have the most powerful weaponry.

Due to faulty reasoning and the lust for control… derivations of survival of the fittest, instead of cooperating, we competed against each other. The riches which came from resources became the ultimate goal, and it was no longer merely about survival, but something far more nefarious….

∞ ∞ ∞

I

Another night falls upon the savanna as the insects' songs begin to rise and the last golden rays of light stretch up from an eternal horizon. The moon bears a mere crescent of light and stars have begun twinkling in their nightly dance.

The ancestors of humanity, these standing ones, have tasted most of the available flesh. Standing has begun to erase their fear of the dark because it affords greater sight. Each new day offers abundance, but they have eaten their fill, and now the large, biting flies swarm. These prehumans are alive and still, while everything else runs from death, and in death do these walking ones find their treasure. They dress in feathers, fur, and bone, and they seek survival most of all. Across their brows and around their necks are pearls of teeth from prey, while stiffening pelts of small beasts now rest upon their shoulders. Those present without treasure kneel in supplication, while those with jewels stand tall.

Tonight, all lie curled up inside their cave, except one whose troubled mind keeps sleep away. Standing, the awakened one watches over them all, his wiry frame quivering in the cold air. He remembers when the giant had come, massive limbs falling upon them like tree branches from the sky. *Those arms of stone could not be stopped! The giant will take all the jewels and furs, leaving us all to become food for the prey!*

The frantic eyes of this awakened one dart across the earth before him. He ponders their safety and finally his eyes catch upon a stone as big as a head. A head of stone. Lifting with every muscle, it is a struggle, but soon the head of stone is hoisted into the sky. Now he believes that he is as strong as the giant, and this thinker knows his arms of stone rise to protect those who dare to sleep, who would otherwise succumb to the arms of the giant and fall one by one ....

Believing he has solved his quandary; he silently walks towards the giant's den within the thistle. His arms grow wearier with each step until finally, his eyes settle upon the sleeping giant, who thus far has never needed to worry about a predator. So many treasures lay strewn about the cruel limbs in front of him. The awakened one remembers the pain, the peace disrupted. But now, the impossible problem will be solved. His solution held high, the dreamer paces without a murmur and stops when he is right above the giant. Now facing the fear which had caused so many sleepless nights, he releases the headstone.

In silence, swift justice is served. The giant stirs no more. Their treasures no longer belong to the dark force. The dreamer stands triumphant, the power of the stars coursing through his veins. He has now become a leader, and he has ushered in a new era of strength and survival for the tribe. The night is no longer a terror, but has become a canvas of victory, painted with the light of a million stars.

∞ ∞ ∞

II

Upon the cave walls, painted animals dance in the flickering firelight. The tribe huddles in a circle close to a tiny fire, gnawing on bones from their last meal. Starvation is near, but the blizzard has finally cleared. A collective thought emanates from their eyes as they glance at one another: *we must hunt the mammoth or die.* The oldest among them traces the river in the dirt, marking the mammoth herd's drinking area.

The tribe's memory of scavenging a fallen mammoth urges them onward, and with their obsidian tools, they sharpen stones to pierce the mammoth's hide. Two are sent to find wooden branches. When they return, the tribe binds sharp stones to the wood using dried reindeer gut as string. *These will pierce the mammoth's hide and heart from afar. These will save us.* One is assigned to remain awake to watch over the tribe, and the night passes in a ceremonial sleep for most, furs pulled tight around their bodies.

Before dawn, the tribe moves toward the river. The journey is arduous, the cold biting, but they press on. By midday, they reach the flowing river with its frozen edges. Here, they wait, hidden in furs as all eyes watch the horizon. As dusk falls, the ground begins to vibrate, and they glance at one another. Soon, the mammoths arrive, kneeling at the river to drink. The herd begins to sing a song of contentment, unaware of the danger.

Counting fifteen, including four calves, the tribe focuses on the largest mammoth, its tusks curving skyward. They edge closer as their fear now mixes with determination. Night falls, enveloping everything around them within a shroud of dark anticipation. Finally, protected by the wind and the vibrant whispers of rushing water, the tribe stands and silently tiptoes toward the herd.

They encircle the master mammoth with spears raised and pounding hearts. This is the moment for which they had planned, and in unison, they strike, the first spear piercing the beast's hide. The mammoth bellows, rising to its feet, but the tribe does not falter. More spears fly, each finding its mark. The giant's cries echo through the night, but the tribe's resolve is unyielding. They close in on it and then, with a final, mighty thrust, they each deliver spears directly into the flesh of the beast and the mammoth falls. Victory is theirs.

The herd flees, leaving their fallen leader. The tribe stands triumphant under the starlit sky, their faces streaked with red ochre and the blood of their conquest. The tribe's hunger will be sated. They gather around the mammoth, offering prayers to the spirits….

∞ ∞ ∞

III

She kicks the spear across the hut's earthen floor, feeling mocked by its uselessness. *Why were they only made to be used by men, our men who have never returned from a tribal meeting across the jungle many moons ago?* Only women and children now remain in the village.

Adorned with colorful ancestral jewelry around her neck and wrists made from bones, shells, feathers, colored pebbles, and animal teeth, her anger grows as she paints her skin red. She bends over her sleeping children, feeling the weight of responsibility. Once she used to sew, cook, and teach, but now she weeps alone, as the village's food supply has dwindled to almost nothing.

Distraught, she wonders how she might throw the spear, since their village has been left unable to hunt with the men now gone. She grips her sewing thread until it cuts into her fingers, her blood staining the ground. Grabbing the spear, she storms out and immediately endures laughter from her mate's sister. In the village center, she attempts to break the spear against a boulder but fails and is thrown back. Rising from the ground, she hears more laughter from the rest of the women.

My shame is here for all to see. When she had been thrown back, the obsidian tip of the spear had broken, and now its many pieces lay scattered across the ground. Wailing in rage,

22

she jumps up and grabs the spear again, thrusting herself at the rock. The spear again bends, but this time when it throws her backward, she is ready, catching her fall with her hands and sliding backwards across the ground.

How strange! The spear swallows my rage and spits it back at me. It takes my forceful thrust and throws me with my own power. How can such a thing be possible? Does my husband's power remain in the spear? Does my husband's force keep the spear straight when I try to break it?

She understands that, for whatever the reason, the spear has innate power. Simply bending it loads this power. She pulls herself to her feet and picks up the spear, walking back into her hut. Her youngest child begins crying. She sets the spear down onto the ground and goes to pick up her baby, and that's when an immediate thought comes to her. *My baby won't be as helpless as I am. She will hunt, and I will teach her.*

With her spool of thread in hand, she tightly wraps one side of the spear. Sitting atop the wrapped side, she pulls the spear into a bend with all her strength and quickly winds the thread around the other end of the staff. The staff falls to the ground, curved and secure.

Her oldest child wakes and approaches, his eyes drawn to the bent spear. He picks it up and plucks the thread, producing a beautiful sound. She takes the staff from him and plucks the thread again, hearing a strange song - a whisper which informs her that *the staff of the father will throw the staff of the son by the thread of the mother.*

Thrilled that her husband's power remains in the spear guiding their future, she fits the tightened thread into a notch at the end of her son's smaller spear and walks outside. This time ignoring the hysterical laughter rising from the other women, she glances at them all with a look of triumphant courage, then

23

she stretches her arms apart and releases a new power for all to see.

∞ ∞ ∞

IV

The arrows sling outwards over the city walls, falling onto the farms adjacent to the city and missing their intended marks. Now under siege, the city's gates remain tightly closed to prevent the enemy's impending entrance, trapping the citizens within the prosperous city of Uruk. The unknown invader camps at a distance, but their arrows continuously rain down from the wood's edge, completely cutting Uruk off from the outside world. Farmers outside the city walls retreat with their surviving livestock, seeking refuge in the outer fields.

Within a stone gazebo at the heart of the city's safest point, the ruling council now gathers. Their rich robes and intricate braids signify their status, and their golden bands and copper trinkets glint in the sunlight as they frantically wave their arms debating a solution. "We have posted our own archers atop the walls day and night," proclaims the white-bearded man in yellow robes, *"and our arrows cannot reach them!"* He pounds both his fists upon the wooden table in front of them, demanding, *"We must send men out to meet them and drive them away!"*

The man in the green robes opposes, fearing their soldiers would be ambushed by the enemy, who are fully ensconced within the forests surrounding the city. The youngest urges a sacrificial charge to the gods of all newborns, but the chief priest, his blue and purple robes elegantly shimmering as he stands forward, calls for a divine plan. "Anu does not wish for his children to be sacrificed," the priest declares. "I have been given a great vision. We will send our men out with speed, protected from the arrows."

Not far from where they hold their discussion, the city's great limestone, three-tiered, spiritual ziggurat protrudes into the sky. Its outer walls and stairwells are all plated in hammered copper sheets which are now gleaming in the midday sun. It had taken generations to build, but the copper sheets could be dismantled in mere days. The priest points a ringed index finger towards the temple and reveals his plan. "The copper plates of Anu's temple will be used to armor our men from head to toe. Thus protected from the enemy's arrows, we will use our horses to pull harvest carts full of bowmen, *who will fall upon Uruk's enemies as messengers of the sky god himself!*"

While slaves strip the temple of its copper, blacksmiths toil through the night, shaping the divine metal. As dawn breaks, the city gates swing open. With copper plates over their chests and backs, and helmets atop their heads, the archers stand tall in chariots and now resemble the gods painted on their temple walls. Howling a battle cry that pierces the world, they charge through the open plains and into the forests, *ready to meet their heroic destiny.*

∞ ∞ ∞

V

He watches their metal shields glistening in the sun in a spastic pattern, carried by men fully sheathed within bronze breastplates and helmets. The noble young boy scowls as he peers at the soldiers, their march resembling drunken elephants. *This is the rotten fruit of the Republic.*

He had been commanded by his father to march to the northern campaign, and he understands the necessity of the

25

order. *We must observe the enemy*. Inside an opulent carriage, he grits his teeth for the last time, as it once again tilts violently. With a sigh, he pushes through the velvet curtains at the side of the carriage and leaps out. "I'd rather walk than be rocked about by a fool," he proclaims, storming away.

Walking alongside the rock ledge which flanks the gravelly road, he eventually reaches a cliff and stops to glimpse the water. Standing tall and contemplating the sea for several moments, he suddenly feels a tickle. He looks down to see that he has placed himself over an anthill, and a line of red ants has already reconnected its highway and is marching over his sandaled foot otherwise completely undisturbed. He smiles and watches them. *Why do Roman soldiers not move as these ants do? Rome has given so much power to the individual, but how can we expect to conquer the world when we cannot even control our own masses?*

Looking closely, he realizes that most of the ants carry something in their arms, and from down the line they bring along the carcass of a dung beetle, a dozen of them working together to maneuver its large black body over the sand towards their dune home. *These are the minds of true soldiers, obedient to their master at all costs. The queen ant in the hill is larger by far, and all the lesser ants fear her and so she gets the most out of each one of them.*

And then, a succession of thoughts come to him, culminating in a new vision. *If we were to train our own soldiers to move so obediently, they could carry the savage enemies of Rome back out into the wilderness from which they came.* The boy steps backwards and brushes the ants from his foot. He then crouches, reflecting on his uncle's teachings as he watches the ants marching down the hole at the center of their mound. He finally understands why Romans must practice a higher ethic than their enemies, and now he knows how they will do it.

He envisions soldiers as obedient as ants, nothing stopping or deterring them from their commanding officer's mission and orders. Rising from his crouched position, Julius Caesar once again admires the anthill, smiling as his new understanding of how to properly train the Republic's soldiers forges within his thoughts.

∞ ∞ ∞

VI

From the heights of their mountain monastery, the foreign warriors appear as mere ants. The abbot and monks had watched the cities below burning for weeks, knowing that interference in worldly affairs was not their business. Things changed with the arrival of a messenger from the emperor's palace, demanding an audience with the abbot. "The emperor has heard of a secret power held by the monks," the messenger declares. *"Reveal it, or face death."*

The abbot, understanding the gravity, bows and says, "There is nothing we would keep from the emperor."

These invaders, clad in formidable armor, had brought turmoil to the empire. The emperor's archers, whose arrows once fell like divine wrath, found their weapons useless against the invaders' shields and breastplates. The emperor feared an endless battle was afoot, and they would be driven to attrition.

Two days earlier, a highly motivated penetration agent for the empire overheard a lively conversation between two monks who were discussing a new discovery in a community courtyard. The monastery alchemists had long been experimenting with powders from the earth to find healing properties within them, but in so doing, they had stumbled upon a formula which created a striking reaction. According to what the agent overheard; this formula somehow awoke the raging spirits of fire itself. When the monks had finished their conversation, he concluded that *the secrets learned by the monks of the monastery might determine the fate of the kingdom.* He immediately reported this information directly to the emperor, who dispatched the messenger without haste.

Presently, the abbot escorts the emperor's messenger to the basement halls of the monastery, through a bolted wooden door, and into a dark, stone-walled room. They come to a large table whereupon the abbot takes two small vials, mixes their powdery contents together in a clay crucible, then stands back as he discharges a spark from a flint of iron pyrites aimed at the mixture. Suddenly, the messenger witnesses that the monastery's alchemists had indeed discovered a fiery formula, *a magic that could turn the tide of war.*

From their courtyard two weeks later, the monks gather and watch as hundreds of flaming packages are launched by the emperor's catapults into the air towards the invading army, blazing like tiny meteors in the afternoon sun. Brimstone rains down from the sky, and they soon observe craters full of dismembered bodies in the wake of the fire's golden aura. As the invading soldiers fall, those who do not die are severely injured, confused, and absolutely demoralized. Those who can do so cast off their heavy plates and retreat into the forests and mountain gorges, but the divine emperor's mounted archers give chase to finish the task.

The abbot watches these enemy ants very carefully, and his eyes fill with tears. *They were not to involve themselves in the outside world. Is this still the will of heaven?* A few decades later, this magic invention of the Chinese monks would come to be known as *gunpowder.*

∞ ∞ ∞

VII

The 3-masted galleon vibrates under their feet as the cannons explode. Upon the shores of the island, a village of natives receives its punishment for spilling the blood of God's messenger. Boom after boom erupts from below the decks as iron balls descend like God's own fists, and where each one lands, it levels a hut or encampment where once a rich human landscape had existed.

Dozens of small boats have been issued from the galleon, covered with animal hides to protect the crossbow armed soldiers within, and now the warriors hidden within those boats line the shore. Using winches to draw back the strings of their weapons, they depress their crossbows' small levers which trigger the release of short and extremely sharp bolts which can pierce metal, if need be, and which have a very extensive range.

Now, the beach has become the bloodied tapestry of an indigenous culture that made the wrong decision. As the thundering of the cannon fire comes to an end, the conquistador grimaces. By his side, an old priest in black robes proudly arches upward and gazes into the sky. With clasped hands that are shaking, his tongue starts chattering excitedly in a mysterious language.

"Does it please God to see men destroying other men, Father?" the conquistador asks with a sad voice as he casts a dismayed look at the priest.

The priest turns to him with a scowl. "*These are not men, my dear boy.* They do not live as men do. They do not cultivate the lands and create order, as men do. *They live as beasts,* and it is our burden by the command of the Almighty God to serve as stewards of the wild beasts." The priest chances a slight grin as he continues to eye Conquistador Juan Rodríguez Cabrillo. "Why? Have you begun having moral quandaries, Conquistador Cabrillo?" It is a rhetorical question, and there is no need to wait for a response; the priest is ready to deliver his point precisely as he hoped. *"God's kingdom on Earth does not kneel before the spears of angry Indians."*

Cabrillo recalls the horrors of his long campaign sailing north and south along the California coastline. They had come upon many local populations at varying degrees of civilization, some not unlike the rustic peoples of Europe. And yet, the conquistador and his men had done many terrible things to them. When the natives had welcomed the mysterious visitors, their men and boys had been captured and forced into labor in the gold mines, while the women had been given to the sailors as slaves to do with as they pleased. In cases where the native people defended themselves, their tribe no longer existed in any form.

Now looking at the island before them, they see that the village has caught fire. Thatch roofs burn to ash in seconds, and the wooden walls and floors have begun to combust. The surviving natives are in disarray on the beach, casting sand onto their heads and wailing their pain into the waves. Their Eden has been taken from them, and their homes collapse inward upon themselves one-by-one as the insidious delirium spreads.

∞ ∞ ∞

VIII

A flash of fire explodes over the New Mexico desert, and early dawn is instantly transformed into the middle of the day. In the profane silence he wonders, *can the soul be destroyed, or does it continue on no matter what?* Before an answer can come, the roar of the bomb shakes them to the marrow. Dust suddenly lifts from the earth and flies over the bunker, and the earth spasms beneath them; they watch in awe as a gigantic fireball hurtles heavenward like a comet which had just plunged through the center of the planet and was now soaring back into the universe in order to annihilate other worlds.

Most of the scientists present, holding clipboards and dressed in suits and lab coats, are completely still, their mouths agape. In camouflage and military dress, the military men erupt into congratulatory activity: *hooting and swearing, laughing, and clapping each other on the back.* Some of the more decorated officers grin and shake each other's hands. Oppenheimer is the first to remove the goggles from his eyes, nodding his head slowly but painfully. His lips are pursed and his eyes glisten.

The scientist is shaken from his trance by a heavy hand on his shoulder. "It worked perfectly, didn't it?" When he gets no response from Oppenheimer, the gruff voice of the General demands, *"Well God-damn it! Didn't it, Robert?"*

Oppenheimer turns slowly to meet the eyes of the General. "Yes, exactly as designed sir. We will need to analyze the results from the ground, but it looks like the bomb performed as expected."

"What ground?" the General laughs, slapping Oppenheimer on the back. "This'll show those Jap and Nazi bastards not to fuck around with the land of the free, *am I right?"*

"Quite right," Oppenheimer manages a wry smile and turns to another scientist at his side. He speaks in a subdued monotone. "Let's get to work parsing through this data, shall we?"

Turning back to the general, he says, "If you'll excuse me, General." Oppenheimer gives a shallow bow and follows the rest of the team out of the bunker as they make their way toward the lab. When he steps outside, he pulls the wide brim hat atop his head a bit lower and takes a deep breath.

He immediately realizes that the other scientists are all gawking at the sight before them, and so he lifts his head to see what is commanding their attention. It is a giant smoldering cloud that resembles a parasol mushroom, rising from where the fireball had just traversed. As they continue watching, the top of the mushroom's crown becomes ever more gargantuan and begins leaning into the Jetstream as it reaches the upper atmosphere.

Oppenheimer watches a few more moments, then turns back towards the lab with a sinking heart. *Have we just destroyed our own souls? This weapon that we will wield against the fascists of today... will it not eventually fall into the hands of tyrants who will eventually threaten and then destroy us all?*

As he pushes open the doors of the lab and paces towards the counters with their multitude of machines on top, each of them beeping, flashing, and spitting out reams of paper with arcane script, his fingertips soon begin to pour over the symbols being printed. He fumbles with the figures as the great gears of his mind try to force together some hidden logic. *I am a scientist, and this is wartime. This is what my country has demanded of me. Yet, in trying to find a way to defeat the enemy, now I have become death, the destroyer of worlds ....*

∞ ∞ ∞

IX

"You're doing God's work, gentlemen," the lieutenant yells over the chugging diesel engines. The submarine crew throws their hands forward in a Nazi salute as the officer ducks through a hatch leading to the captain's chambers. This mission is unparalleled. Though the war ended two years ago, the Germans have kept U-boats for special operations. Now, just below the surface, they traverse the Mediterranean, shuttling cargo and VIPs between Italy and Greece.

At dusk, onboard an American surfaced submarine, the radio crackles to life. Officers scramble up the ladder and spread out across the deck, dressed in ornamented navy uniforms with black leather trench coats offering slight protection against the frigid marine layer. A white light flashes three times from the tower of their submarine. In the distance, the officers witness a light on the surface of the water flashing back three times. This repeats every few seconds as the light from the water grows closer. Twenty minutes later, The U.S. Gato-class submarine pulls up alongside the U-boat, and officers aboard each vessel throw lines to each other to secure them together.

The ocean is calmer in twilight, but the rocking still poses a challenge. The Gato-class bangs against the U-boat, jostling the men. Stabilized a minute later, four newcomers jump from the U-boat to the American sub, and the American officers help to steady the Germans as they land onboard. The lines are then released, and once all are below deck, the deck hatch closes. The lieutenant leads the four newcomers past the officers to the captain's quarters, closing the thick metal door behind them. Alone for now, the officers burst into animated conversation.

"Do you know who they are?" one asks wide-eyed, already knowing the answer.

Another scratches his head and exclaims, "I was hoping they were all dead."

A third officer, pale-faced and looking like he has just seen four ghosts, chimes in, "I really can't believe we are doing this... *what the hell can we possibly want with them other than putting them in front of a firing squad?"*

They look at each other with disbelief etched on their faces. "I know that the first two of the four were Wernher von Braun and Dr. Hubertus Strughold," a fourth officer responds, "infamous Nazi rocket scientists. What? Are they supposed to help us reach the moon one day?"

The captain's quarters' hatch opens once again and the lieutenant reenters alone. The men fall silent and stand at attention. He looks each of them in the eye. "None of you will ever speak a word about what you have just seen to anyone, *understood?"*

The men nod, their enthusiasm dampened. "We depart now for Boston Harbor. It will be a long journey, so I suggest you all get back to your stations."

As the submarine disappears beneath the waves, its precious cargo stowed safely aboard, the men brace themselves for the return portion of their now tainted mission, knowing that mankind's history is closer to being completely rewritten with each passing mile.

∞ ∞ ∞

Whatever else can be said, when we look at the history of weaponry from an objective, humanist perspective, it becomes clear to most that technology is derived from man's insatiable appetite to have the strongest, most destructive weapons possible. Innovation was geared towards outdoing all other groups and their level of weapon development. As countries grew in population, a larger percentage of people had little influence over the objectives of their governing bodies, who were busy doing all that was necessary to ensure survival of the fittest.

Decision-making was left to the governing classes, and little input was taken from what the people wanted…as Soldier Sean Ryan and Captain Rocco were about to find out.

It's the struggle of the classes, and unless you have made it into the top one-tenth of 1%, you truly have no voice and no hope of influencing world affairs. Governing bodies make all kinds of decisions which are in nobody's best interests but their own. *In death do these walking ones find their treasure….*

∞ ∞ ∞

August 6, 1945, 8:10 am – Hiroshima

Aiko, ever the nurturing heart of their home, has been enjoying the warm embrace of the morning sun surrounded by the lively laughter and playfulness of the three children for the past forty minutes. She is enjoying her work puzzling one stone at a time onto her border wall. The symphony of the children's joyous giggles along with the delicate whispers of the breeze through the stand of cherry trees on the west side of the yard, together creates a tranquil mood that continuously dances in the air surrounding her.

Hana, with her cheerful little voice and in her floral yukata, is carefully and gently snipping a few of the Oleander flowers to arrange in a vase later. Informing her sister about some interesting facts regarding the blossoms, her nimble fingers move gracefully, selecting only fully developed flowers. Her younger sister Mei, following close behind, playfully gathers a few of the blossoms which had fallen unnoticed from Hana's hands, and both girls are now placing the various blossoms into the old straw hat. Nearby, Osamu, lively as ever, is engrossed, spinning his top on a flat stone just outside of the garden. When it finally comes to a stop, he turns and shouts to the girls, "Come, play beigoma with me!"

How beautiful they are, Aiko thinks, her heart swelling with a mother's love as she watches them, the innocence of childhood dancing gracefully before her eyes evoking memories of her own happy early years.

"Look, Mommy!" Hana exclaims as she runs towards her mother, her voice a song of pure innocence. "So many of the Oleander blossoms are opening this morning."

Aiko kneels beside Hana, allowing the sweet and powerful scent of the flowers in her old straw hat to enchant her senses. The gently rustling leaves of the cherry trees a few meters away now cast dappled sunlight on the ground, creating a play of light and shadow. She smiles, her admiration for her daughter's wonderment evident in her eyes. Taking one of the blossoms into her hand, she raises it to her nose, breathes in deeply, and says, "Yes, my dear. Each one of these blossoms is a testament to the beauty of the world around us...."

Just then, Aiko notices another bomber rapidly coming across the horizon towards the city. It seems larger than the one earlier in the morning and for some reason, this one brings a chill right through her very bones. Waiting to hear the air-raid siren, she reaches out and gently boops Hana on the tip of her nose with the flower in her hand, causing the little girl to erupt into an explosion of giggles.

By now, Osamu and Mei have come to them, and Mei begins pulling at the hem of her mother's dress. Her eyes alight with excitement, she asks, "Mama, can we play hide and seek?"

"Of course, Mei-chan," Aiko replies, her voice exuding tenderness. She glances once more at the sky; the discomforting noise of the American plane has now grown much louder, and she pauses as she considers that this one is coming much closer to the heart of the city than the others had. Still, they had chosen to pursue life and not give in to fear, and her children were waiting for her. She turns back to them with a smile. "This time, Mei, you'll close your eyes and count to ten while we hide."

As Mei starts counting, the other three go and run a few steps away as they consider where they will hide. Suddenly, a searing flash of light pierces the sky, its brightness casting a harsh shadow over the tranquil scenery. The once-blue canvas is instantly painted with the eerie hues of blackness and fire. What she sees and feels next is incomprehensible, unknowable, with no possible words to adequately describe. Aiko's heart lurches as she feels the shockwave rattle through her bones, a roar that shakes the very foundations of her soul. It becomes hotter than any heat she has ever known.

Debris begins to rain down like sorrow from above, and Aiko's gaze flits between her children and the encroaching calamity of fire, smoke, and heat encompassing them with tremendous force. There is nowhere to run, nowhere to hide. She feels tears running from her eyes, but when she wipes her hand across her cheek, she sees it is blood and not tears. Time grinds to a halt as she yearns to protect the children, to shield them from the impending storm, but time slips through her trembling fingers as she realizes hell itself has suddenly descended upon them. Her clothing catches fire, and then time stops altogether as she is rendered unconscious.

She is awoken by a feeling that her face is caving in and realizes it is a piece of hot ash burning a hole through her cheek. She sits up with a start.

"Hana! Mei! Osamu!" she calls out frantically, her voice a desperate plea that feels so useless amidst all the chaos and widespread destruction. Everything is a flat landscape of burning embers in every direction all around her as far as her eyes can see, not a building or tree left standing. "Where are you? Answer me, my darlings!" The heat and blackness of her new surroundings squeezes what little vision remains in her shriveling and terrified eyes. Her skin and the shredded remnants of her clothing are black, and they both hang like smoldering rags from her burned skeletal foundation.

The air is heavy, pitch-dark, and filled with murky, tangible debris. The sunshine is gone, and the acrid scent of putrid smoky death and burning wood combine into a poison that chokes and burns whatever is left of her lungs. Panic gnaws at Aiko's insides as she searches for the children's hiding places, every second an eternity in hell itself. She feels hollow, unable to know if her body will be able to follow the commands her brain and willpower alone are sending it. She feels her heart racing, each beat more painful than the one before, and each echoes the deafening roar of utter obliteration.

Her mind races faster than her body, memories of the children's laughter and innocent play just a moment before swirling in her thoughts. Their once-peaceful neighborhood is now only a devil's playground of devastation and rage. The home where she conceived, gave birth to, and raised her beloved children is nowhere to be found. She can't see any of the children, and she continues to call out for them, but her cries ripping through the heavy silence are just a haunting echo across a desolate landscape.

One of the once-flourishing cherry trees somehow has remained standing but is scorched, its branches now bony claws jutting up from the ground. Only piles of embers remain where the beautiful oleander bushes once stood proudly, their blossoms previously bringing so much beauty and joy. For now, they are merely a ghastly memory and harbinger of death, bearing witness in stark contrast to the abundance of life just moments before. As her mind acknowledges all she sees, Aiko's spirit shatters trying to grapple with her own injuries and facing the dawning fragility of her own mortality.

As she tries to stand, her ankle, shattered and lifeless, screams in agony with each movement. There is no standing and so she attempts to crawl across the fiery ground. Her left hand is completely gone, replaced at her elbow with a blackened stub of cauterized skin and bone. Her one remaining hand trembles with the weight of her despair and now resembles a jagged talon with only two sharp pieces of bone jutting out from her wrist. Burrowing her way deeper into a nightmare, bloody tears mix with dirt and ash forming a thick red cake on her remaining cheek. Her destroyed limbs scrape across the stones with desperate urgency. More concerned with her children than with herself, she rips at the rubble in a desperate search.

Finally, she uncovers a patch of yellow cloth from Hana's floral yukata. Digging further into the debris of stone, crushed ceramic tile, and pieces of branches, a hot clump of mixed skin, bone and cauterized blood appears. Finally, she realizes this is what remains of her oldest daughter. A few feet away, she recognizes something resembling one of the other children from beneath a thick layer of ashes. Forced to confront the horrible truth she has dreaded; she finds the third; each of their bodies now only seared and melted skin covering shattered bones. Their once beautiful faces now only hideous masks of death, and each lifeless form is a piercing sword directed right into her soul. Immediately, she understands that her own survival is no longer necessary or even desired.

"My babies," she wails into the sky, her voice a blend of sorrow and desperation carried away by the howling wind. *"Please... wake up Osamu! Wake up!"*

She shakes her head violently in a last attempt to deny the horrible reality she faces, but the dream is real. The very earth beneath her seems to ache from the weight of her loss and its palpable pain, the earth groaning with her in misery. With her final breath, she unleashes a primal howl of pure agony, but it remains unheard against the hellish tempest and the horrible rumbling which shakes the very firmament. Having reached the final pinnacle of pain, and with her children's bodies in her arms, another wave of fire and heat runs through her and finally, mercifully, she bursts into flames, collapsing into a heap of ashes which immediately mix with the charred embers and scalding ashes of everything around her; remnants of the life she had sought to build blown away forever with the hot winds of the bomb's rage.

Only silence and darkness remain except for the ungodly wisps of flickering flames. The sky, once a beautiful and enticing canvas of hope full of intrigue and potential, is now marred by the sinister presence of a mushroom cloud, its shape a haunting symbol of annihilation and loss. It casts a long, foreboding shadow over what was once a thriving metropolis filled with the lives of loving wives and mothers, devoted husbands and fathers, loyal friends, kind neighbors, and so many innocent and beautiful children. Thriving humans whose hopes and dreams vanished in an instant, never to be realized, whose very ashes will forever remain a testament to mankind's murderous inclination; his penchant to use constantly advancing technology immediately to cultivate evermore destructive and cataclysmic weaponry; *his predisposition towards bloodthirsty and self-justified rage born from discontent and fueled by a salacious need for power or revenge*

∞ ∞ ∞

In the furious inferno of the bomb's wake, a once-stalwart train lies twisted, consumed by flames that birth an agonizing white heat. Within it, charred and flaming bodies bear witness to the heat's intensity. During their merciless dance with the fire, the passengers' scalded eyes show final windows to an unfathomable pain. A hospital, once a sanctuary, is now a ghostly relic submerged in the muddy river's cruel embrace where perished infants drift amidst the wreckage, their delicate forms marred by cuts and burns as they had been swallowed by the cold waters. On the banks, anguished souls, their former bodies now carbonized and partly broken, reach out in a desperate last attempt at survival, some had been attempting to aid the helpless, yet faltered as their bodies burned in an instant, leaving crisped skin and bone in the same final form as when they had drawn their last breaths.

Amidst the outskirts of the city, only shattered remnants of what was once bustling life can be found. A young woman kneels in what used to be her office, weeping in utter helplessness. Shards of glass are embedded into every part of her flesh, each one of them a cruel witness to the unforgiving chaos that had rained down from the sky. Her face is a mosaic of agony, and her eyes reflect the pure shock of encroaching death. She tries to cover her face with her hands, but the glass in her palms only winds up cutting her cheeks and eyes more than they already had been, and she collapses to the ground in absolute surrender.

Meanwhile, the mushroom cloud, monstrous and ever-growing, looms above and thrives as it twists and churns into a horrific and ghastly kaleidoscope of utter devastation, painting the sky with hues of black, brown, and dark crimson wretchedness. In its eerie orange glow, wounded souls scurry like shadows, their desperate flight a haunting dance of survival, yet the cruel truth remains – *they run, but they will never escape the satanic results of this bomb.*

∞ ∞ ∞

Chapter Two

The Deal of All Deals

∞ ∞ ∞

1970 –

Perhaps the web woven by the spider of history itself will eventually catch every insect which flies straight, and so across the long arc of time's falling mallet, Darwinian law would say that those who can dance and swerve around obstacles would be favored. The second world war had taken so many reliable heroes from humanity, and in its wake, the scavenging political leaders of the postwar period turned their need for control upon the masses of the civilian world. With the bombing of Hiroshima, the innocence of society was perhaps gone forever, and with it, so were many of its naive dreams. According to the same ancient pattern that has always followed in the wake of slaughter, new gods are promoted from among mortals; and this time it was the industry giants of advancing infrastructure - the suited barons of the circuit board and binary imperative, along with the premature inheritors of grand estates who were suddenly tasked with pulling strings beyond their comprehension.

The builders of weaponry especially thrived in the shadow of a new great fear, perhaps the most supreme dread that one can behold: *the imminent threat of complete annihilation.* In the shadow of violence, the economy grew throughout the halls of industry, and yet within the heart of every veteran remained the experience of human horror. Forever set apart by their journey through the abyss, they continued on in the world, some as wandering ghosts of who they once were and whose puzzling notions were unfathomable to the rest of their countrymen. Returning home to people and towns that mirrored those they had destroyed; many could not bear to see the reflection of the recent past they had left behind. Bearing the guilt of terror inflicted, they reforged their worldview into the dismal image of an unholy guardian spirit similar to the Angel of the Apocalypse. Blowing their own lost spirits through the celestial trumpets of the Final Judgment, they brought their nightmares home to their families, friends, and neighbors.

Seizing upon this foreboding energy, the Americans and the Soviets begin to circulate this terror so thoroughly throughout their populations that its products begin to ooze out of every facet of society. In America, folk musician doomsayers preach their woes as public schoolchildren practice diving under their desks. In the Soviet Union, the structure of their society is transformed even more dramatically according to the collectivism of their new political system, and where Americans are gorged on abundance and motivated by desire, the average Russian covets from afar the same forbidden luxury, but from a position of scarcity. The rattled sabers of the ghosts of World War II ring in perpetuity as dissonant tuning forks of choirs from Hell, and one of the only things to thrive is the senseless hum of the monstrous engine of the war machine itself. Within a few years, both nations have developed more than enough nuclear warheads to destroy every city on the planet, and this abundance does not deter them. Instead, each country accelerates their quantity and propels their rocket technology forward under the constant pressure of one-upmanship.

Where once there were tenuous war alliances between the two superpowers, the unsteady closeness resurrects long dormant tribal paranoia, and from the slime grown in the darkness of distrust between old friends, the abomination of spy craft flourishes. This fear, bred of intense competition, soon marries its will to the all-pervasive power of computer technology, and soon it tears into the fabric of society with surgical depth, bringing about a complex redefinition of the world in the eyes of the masses. In the dawn of this new age, nothing is ever as it would seem to be, and even kind acts are tinged by the poisoned hands of espionage. The agents never fully step into the stage light of politics, but even so, their shadows spread into the once bright and holy halls of government. Into this environment, when the blood of a bright young hero is splattered across the streets of Dallas, the last hope of the spirit of the people is quickly shot away into the cold storm drains within the heart of the world itself. No longer is there any room for the expansion of virtue, now the coalescing hardness of vice seems to be the only remaining elixir which can protect us all from each other.

Nowhere is the tension more pronounced than between the operatives in the new frontier of Space, that liminal no man's land into which these old friends soon become enemy rivals due to the rush to push the limits and expand the capabilities of their war technology. In an age where the ability to see makes you a god, and being seen makes you mortal, *the eye in the sky* becomes another means through which these two forces contend. True violence, which everyone knows would result in a universal Armageddon, is ever kept at bay for now, but the ultimate threat either nation can afford to dare the other is by hurling one more satellite into orbit, a dirty look across the world from beyond the clouds. For this peace, they forge in the void a system of cold cooperation built on the codependent relationship that holds off their demise. Even many years into the future, as calmer heads will begin to prevail, the policy of "trust, but verify," will still function as the unwritten rule of all their diplomacy.

At all times between the U.S. and Russian space programs, a stream of carefully curated data flies across the wires in both directions. Only the most necessary bits of knowledge are shared, and then only after it has undergone a thorough process of one redaction after another upon the desks of numerous badged bureaucrats. And as they each receive the polished gems from each other's political river, they clutch them within their steely claws of cynicism. *Are these lies? How could we be misled by this information? Is this river a cleverly disguised canal meant to steer us into a vulnerable position?* And thus, having been prevented from true cooperation, each space program began to branch off in very different directions. While the Soviets spent their resources launching satellites and developing space stations, the Americans directed their energies into manned missions, culminating in a Lunar landing.

The Soviets had been first into space with their satellites, first with launching heavy payloads, and their space station technology was years ahead of the Americans. But the manned missions of the Americans somehow overshadowed the accomplishments of the Russians, and so over the years, propelled by the possibility of potential symbiosis, they began to feel that they might as well begin to melt the ice that had so long grown between them. Following this trend, politicians on both sides worked towards ceaseless reassurance and pacification, and the possibility of cooperation became less and less of an impossibility.

It is under this pretense that the Soviets invite the key players in the American space program to another series of meetings, this time in Moscow. Their meetings will only last in earnest for four days, the 11th and 12th of May, and the 26th and 27th of October 1970. The Americans come with an eclectic group: Philip Handler, President of the US Academy of Sciences, George M. Low, acting NASA administrator, Arnold W. Frutkin, NASA'S Assistant Administrator for International Affairs, three junior scientists, and two translators. The Soviets put on a united front, and the Americans spent the first day in Moscow engaging in discussions on many topics with scores of scientists and government officials whose titles were usually unknown and ultimately inconsequential. Although they feel at times like they are getting the grand run-around tour, since the purpose of the visit is as much diplomatic as it is scientific, the Americans all continue to participate in good temperament.

On the second trip in October, they arrive at the Hotel Metropol in the late afternoon, check into their rooms and take some time to decompress before the meeting scheduled for that evening. Since they all were staying in separate accommodations but along the same hallway, they coordinated to meet and go downstairs a little before the meeting to loosen up with some cocktails at the hotel bar. The banquet hall of the Hotel Metropol in Moscow, with its stained glass domed ceiling towering overhead, looks more like a ballroom of some past gilded age, and the glamor of the old imperial Russia still shines through in the extravagant décor, casting an uncanny haze over the perceptions of the Americans. Most of them have never seen such indoor architecture, and as their minds lapse into individual streams of revery, it becomes mesmerizing in itself. Red marble pillars run down either side of the room, and great chandeliers stand upon posts in the four quarters. The carpet is a vibrant red with golden heraldic patterns, thick and luxurious. Every piece of metal in the room is brass, contributing a nautical element to the mix. The jubilant hues clash in the minds of the Americans, who find it somewhat unsettling; at the same time, their cocktails all begin taking good effect. To the Russians, it is just another normal day.

They are slated to meet with the most important people involved in the Soviet space program, a group consisting of Mstislav Keldysh, President of the USSR Academy of Sciences, Dzhermen Gvishiani, Deputy Minister for Science and Technology, and a handful of very serious looking men whose identities would never be determined. The Soviets show up five minutes before the arranged time. The Americans speculate that two of them are high-ranking Communist Party bureaucrats whose ranks and titles are probably purely administrative, as their presence carries a mysterious air of authority evoking the lost court of the czars. Even the Soviet translator is the kind of young man whose eyes and hands vibrate with a caged ambition honed into piercing focus and efficiency. It was the mathematician Keldysh who had invited the Americans to Moscow, and his grandfatherly appearance and warm personality seem out of place alongside his countrymen. Adding to the surreal ambiance is the fact that the Russians all wear identical dark suits and deep red ties. The Americans also come dressed in suits, though theirs are various shades of grays and tans with colorful neckties hung over white button-up shirts. In a very apparent way, the contrast is so stark as to be comical; the Americans look like businessmen, while the Russians look like gangsters cleaned up for church.

The hotel had provided a buffet of twenty traditional Russian dishes and four desserts, a quantity of food that would have fed them all for a week, and the men sit at opposite ends of a medium sized square table, eating mostly in silence except for the occasional murmur about how delicious the food is. Prokofiev plays softly from a record player on the far side of the meeting hall, and as the plates are cleared, George Low is the first to speak up.

"I hope we might someday share the great bounty of outer space like we shared the food at this buffet here today," he gesticulates frantically with both of his hands, smiling and nodding as his translator speaks his words into Russian in syncopated time. The Americans all smile to each other, also nodding their approval.

The Russians either do not catch the humor or do not know how to appreciate the affirmation, as they all maintain their neutral scowls, and a couple of eyebrows are raised. The Americans' laughs are cut off early, and the air seems to leave the room for a moment before Gvishiani interrupts. Forcing the grim shape of a necessary smile, he replies, "If only we shared the benefit of some benevolent third party to assure our mutual understanding of the most sophisticated of technologies, just as we had shared the conveniences of those who had performed all of our cooking and cleared away all of the dirty dishware." His face becomes its customary scowl once again and he quickly finishes with, "but it seems in outer space, we are all scavengers of the wild, and it is quite unlike a hyena to share its abundance with a vulture."

The Americans are all perplexed, unsure of how to interpret his statement. Handler clears his throat. "Well, we are here today in the name of peace, so in this spirit," he says in a matter-of-fact business tone, as he lifts a navy-colored folio from his briefcase and sets it onto the table. "I would like to share with you what we've come here to share." The Russians look at the object like the Americans had just plopped a dead rat in front of them.

The last time the space programs had met and sought common ground, the Soviets had balked, and in the aftermath, the silence had propelled the Americans to continue onwards in their space missions without much consultation with the Soviets. NASA's successes with Apollo had changed the tone, but while the declaration by Eisenhower that space should remain a demilitarized zone had been unofficially the rule for over two decades, it was an unsteady quiet, like a Tombstone saloon. Distrust in the secondary intentions of each other's programs had grown during that period, but now that the velocity of each nation's projects had slowed, these spacemen knew that they had much more to gain by learning from each other than they had to lose.

Inside the American folio are minute scientific details of NASA's prototype docking system, and they offer these in the hopes that the Soviets will be interested in joint projects in space, namely with their Mir Space Station. Handler leans in his chair over to one side, looks around in the air for a minute, and then asks, "Hey, did you boys ever get to see that movie *Marooned,* with Gene Hackman?"

The Russians are caught off guard by the question. It would have been unacceptable for any of them to watch American movies, so when Handler sees some of their hard looks soften, he begins to believe he has won. He continues, "You remember when that American astronaut was trapped up there in space? Who was it who came to help him?" The Russians freeze. For a moment in the stillness, Handler feels that maybe he had reached too far.

"It was the cosmonauts!" volunteers the young secretary, unable to contain himself any longer. "The cosmonauts..." he repeats, his voice trailing off as he catches the glare of his superiors.

"What is this supposed to mean?" Keldysh asks, a smirk growing upon his lips.

"Well, we were hoping to create that kind of a relationship in real outer space, looking out for each other's best interests. Friends." Handler taps his finger twice on the navy portfolio sitting atop the table.

"Friends," Keldysh repeats thoughtfully, then turning to the other men, he shrugs his shoulders and cocks his head from side-to-side. "We are not opposed to this. The situation has changed very much between our countries over the years."

The Americans respond to this statement with a dramatic show of relief, and Handler can't help but clap his hands like a happy child, grinning from ear to ear.

"The Americans are not the only ones who seek balance for their projects, *not* competition." Keldysh continues with a smile that reaches all the way to his eyes. He lightly snaps a finger, and the young Soviet secretary reaches down into a brown leather bag sitting between his feet, pulling out a bright red folio and sliding it a few inches towards the center of the table. "I cannot make any promises, as I must speak with many others about this. This portfolio contains only a formal letter of our gratitude for your visit, but I promise you that I will take your proposal very seriously."

Finally, George Low speaks again. "Gentlemen, cooperation in space is all we have left to hope for. It's clear that we'll never truly have it on Earth where lines on a map tell us who we are. In space, there are no boundaries, no lines to delineate us. We need not to be politicians but scientists and sociologists out there."

This gets Dzhermen Gvishiani's attention, and he suddenly seems warm and encouraged. He rises to reach across the table, offering his hand to George Low, who stands and takes it. They shake heartily, smiling and looking each other in the eyes before returning to their seats.

Keldysh says, "I think we may be the first Russians and Americans to agree on anything as important as this since World War II."

Handler gives him a look that says he understands. "Let's try and keep it this way. Our countries have a habit of falling out of agreements and goodwill with each other."

"We can break that habit today," Keldysh says. "At least in regard to space."

Handler stands now and offers his hand to Keldysh, who likewise stands and accepts it. The handshake grows more vigorous and excited, and it is obvious to all present that these two are of the same mind.

Their conversations continue late into the night, the initial tension carried by the men into the room lessening with each casual exchange until they are laughing and talking like old classmates at a reunion. Though they bear upon their shoulders the pent-up tribulations of millions of their countrymen, no one who is present in the room allows for this to interfere; it is much too natural for them to feel trusting and cooperative, to finally have the ability to share meaningful information with warm comradery.

∞ ∞ ∞

Höfði House – Reykjavik, Iceland – 1986.

In spite of the furthering of cooperative efforts between these two nations in space, the tenuous alliances between many of the larger nations which had been forged in the fires of WW2 continue to fracture, and the same old struggles continue to dominate the global stage on the surface of the planet - *the Cold War has continued unrelentingly.* As the nerve-wracking standoff had progressed, superpowers continued vying for monetary dominance and ideological supremacy, and to most citizens, this political maneuvering had cast a pervasive shadow over the fragile peace of the post-war world. Just as the isolation and protective protocols of major nations reached a palpable level, U.S. President Ronald Reagan and Soviet President Mikhail Gorbachev arrange to meet over and again in order to negotiate various agendas.

Their intentions are that they might leave behind their old enmities and together build a brave new world. After so many direct encounters, these two had become like planetary bodies which swing back into each other's orbits as though drawn ever nearer by the increasing gravity weighing heavily upon them both. As their nations had plowed forward through the harsh decades, both politicians felt the need to counter the blind, directionless march. These two presidents felt a conscientious need to resolve their country's differences, and emboldened in their positions of power, they desired widening their countrymen's perspectives towards one another as part of their dutiful responsibilities to the world-at- large. The ice age which began just after the second great war had clearly begun its cooling phase, and the icebergs which had separated distant peoples for so long were now receding. Besides, in the global East, ancient enmities had been provoked and were taking cohesive shape, and this frightened the elder statesmen. In 1986, they arranged to meet once more in Reykjavik in the name of strategizing their way through a future fraught with unknowns.

From the classic Höfði House, they had world-class views across the water towards the jagged isles of Engey and Videy. So it was, that as the beauty of the Reykjavik day faded to night, their eyes could have beheld the wonders of the Aurora Borealis, those glowing green threads knitted by the Norns as described in the ancient Norse mythology, the weavers of the fate of mankind. But tonight, Reagan and Gorbachev do not look out into the phantom light of destiny woven over the world. Their curtains are drawn on all sides, a roaring fire lights up the room from a small stone fireplace, and there is an air of peril bred with festivity which perhaps can only be appreciated by heads of state. The Höfði House had been warmed throughout the day and early evening by every interested party: journalists, local politicians, and by their own personal entourages of interpreters and security detail. Now, as the official proceedings of the summit had tapered off, everyone else was gradually dismissed until only Reagan and Gorbachev remained, along with their interpreters and personal security details. Finally sending even all of them outside to stay on guard and on standby in their running vehicles, the two men are all alone at the end of a very long and exhausting day.

As the doors shut behind the last of these personnel for both presidents, Gorbachev's eyes glowed. "Now that we have dismissed everybody, but especially all those nosy interpreters, let us get on with our true intentions... *did you bring them?"*

Reagan chuckles easily, "I had almost forgotten about them! Why didn't you say so earlier?" He reaches into his inside left breast pocket and pulls out a sealed pack of Marlboro Red cigarettes. "I've got them right here." He mimes a toss, then once Gorbachev raises his hands, he lightly lobs the cigarettes over to him.

Gorbachev catches them with both hands like a happy child receiving a Christmas gift. "Ahh... no, my friend," he purrs as he carefully pulls the guiding thread to tear the cellophane cover. "This is our little secret. The allure of the forbidden is sweetened by the intrigue of the night." He presses the pack against his nose and inhales deeply.

Reagan's chuckle by this time has grown into a belly laugh. "How did you keep yourself from your love for so long, knowing she was here in my pocket all along?"

Gorbachev opens the pack and pulls out a single cigarette. Holding it up in front of his face, he puts on a pleading air and says, "Allow an old man his sins in secret, Ronald. You know how hard it is any more for men like us to find any real intrigue."

Reagan smiles and shakes his head, "Yes, I know. The rarity of secretive fun is our lot. As they say back home, I suppose we're the *good 'ole boys* now."

Gorbachev sniffs at the cigarette and enjoys its aroma immensely. "I don't think I'll venture into the fireplace… surely there are some matches in this place," he says, groaning, as he begins to stand up.

"No, no let me," Reagan waves his hands to stop him, standing up himself and reaching into the firewood basket to grab a particularly long piece of wood. Extending it into the heart of the flames, he says, "You know, I learned how to do this in Hollywood when we were filming those cowboy movies." Gorbachev erupts into his own belly laugh, and in the same moment the tip of the stick combusts into flame. Reagan lifts it into the air and waits while Gorbachev composes himself. "Gee, I sure hope there aren't any sprinkler systems in here," he quips, glancing around and causing Gorbachev to begin laughing anew. "Ok, ok. Here we go," Reagan says as he slowly lowers the torch towards Gorbachev who cranes his neck forward with the cigarette between his lips, the last subdued giggles hissing from out his nose. The connection is made, and the tip of the cigarette lights up. Reagan adds the glowing stick to the fireplace and reclaims his seat, while Gorbachev stokes his own torch with a look of complete ecstasy. Both men lean back into their chairs.

"Oh, Marlboro, my mistress," he croons. "How long have I missed your kisses."

This time it is Reagan's turn to let loose, and he guffaws and slaps his knee. Both men relish the moment, the tears of laughter twinkling in their eyes. *"Marlboro mistress!* You know - your English is getting very good! Why don't you speak it more often ... for the journalists?"

"Come now, I can't give all my secrets away! It is rather useful to have the extra time it takes for the interpreters to interpret questions to consider various options. I catch many others off-guard if they think I do not understand English, and this strategy ensures I summon the most appropriate response!" He laughs and so does Reagan, who nods thoroughly in agreement, as well. "In spite of what is being reported in the newspapers about my not knowing English too well, I would say I am speaking it quite sufficiently, wouldn't you agree?"

"Absolutely!" Reagan responds adamantly.

"And, what about your Russian? Don't I remember from our last meeting hearing you say, *doveryai, no proveryai?"*

"Oh, I can't take credit for that! I'm no true student of language like you are. That was just a bit of rhetorical play for the cameras. What they don't know won't hurt them, right?"

Gorbachev takes an especially long drag from his cigarette and a third of the cylinder disappears into ash. "Ever the actor. Do you withdraw from all of the forbidden pleasures of the East?" he grins into a great exhale of smoke.

Reagan furrows his brows in thought, then suddenly replies, "I don't believe I know what you mean sir," he says with a knowing smirk.

"Well, *my friend!* Do you expect to think for a moment that you would remember my request but that I would forget your own secret desire?" Reaching into his own right breast pocket, he pulls forth a brass hip flask with a red leather grip, the hammer and sickle embossed on it in gold. "A gift for you, my friend," he states with glee as he stands and walks over to Reagan, putting a hand on his shoulder and handing him the flask.

"Mickey, I'm touched." Reagan takes the flask in his hands, and gazing at it says, "I'm sorry that I won't ever be able to show it off." Both men chortle as Gorbachev walks into the kitchen, calling over his shoulder, "I'm going to fetch two glasses."

Alone for a moment, Reagan gives the flask a shake and lapses into a memory of their last meeting. *Who would have thought that we would become such good friends?* What was once just a public relations campaign for the cameras had manifested itself in a very real appreciation for one another. *And now, here we are sharing the vices of each of our cultures like teenage boys sneaking away from their cabins at summer camp.*

Gorbachev returns from the kitchen with two long-stemmed, ornate crystal shot glasses. "I hope our hosts do not mind my imposition," he says, tiptoeing across the room like a cat burglar and setting the glasses upon the table between them. "Nor do I hope I am not asking too much of you to part with some of your precious potion."

Reagan snaps out of his reverie and waggles his head. "No, no ... not at all," he says as if in a dream, opening the flask to pour a generous shot of vodka into each of their glasses. He hands Gorbachev one glass and then begins to laugh. He takes the other glass and raises it into the air. "Trust, but verify!" he crows, as Gorbachev erupts into new laughter and raises his glass.

"Cheers!" Gorbachev says, throwing it back and smacking his lips in pleasure. "Ahh - the good stuff. The rest of the world thinks that they know vodka. *This is vodka*," he says triumphantly, with a glance of curiosity at his friend.

"A potion indeed," Reagan replies, the alcohol warming him from inside out. "This is the best I've ever had, simply great - just what the doctor ordered!"

With the fiery liquid sending warmth through their veins, Gorbachev, feeling the effects, eases himself into a plush armchair positioned in front of the crackling fireplace and motions for Reagan to join him in the accompanying chair, which the American President does. The flames dance, casting flickering shadows across the room, and the weight of the day settles upon them. The vodka, a potent catalyst for contemplation, has a way of piercing through joviality, allowing the gravity of their responsibilities to seep in. Gorbachev's expression shifts, becoming solemn, his gaze fixed on the colorful flames. He takes a deep breath, his chest rising and falling with the realization that this is a moment beyond the casual camaraderie they shared moments before.

"Ron," Gorbachev begins, his voice now a measured cadence of purpose, "we are men of honesty and principles, perhaps even imbued with a certain sense of spirituality, both of us believing in a higher force that birthed this divine experiment known as humanity." As the words spill from him, each sentence holds a gravity that echoes through the room, each utterance a carefully weighed testament to the seriousness of their mission. He continues, "This transcends the realms of communism or democracy; it's about the very survival of our species, the safety of our loved ones, and takes into consideration the millions of parents and grandparents whose love for their children surpasses all else. I believe, together, we must prevent world annihilation above all other considerations."

Reagan's face softens, lines of deep sincerity now etched into his visage. He nods thoughtfully, each word from Gorbachev hitting a chord within him and resonating with the weight of their shared responsibility.

"I'm not a devoutly religious man, Ron," Gorbachev confesses, his eyes never straying from the flames, "but I reflect on the tales of the Bible, particularly Genesis." He pauses, allowing the weight of his words to sink in, the crackling of the fire providing a somber accompaniment.

"We must forge a collaborative, covert initiative between our two great nations to ensure the ongoing miracle of humanity. It's a contingency plan, a safeguard in case our most earnest endeavors for nuclear restraint and disarmament falter—a Genesis Executive Order, if you will. Are you following me, Ron?"

Suddenly, a soft peel of thunder rumbles in the distance.

"Did you hear that?" Gorbachev says walking over to a window and pulling aside the curtains. Far away across the water, a great black cloud is lit with intermittent flashes of lightning, and the rumbling continues. "A thunderstorm, at this time of year?"

Reagan joins Gorbachev over by the window. He looks into the thunderstorm like a wizard scrying the weather, and in his eyes, there is a growing concern. "You know, we aren't in control of everything…" he laughs briefly and then trails off cryptically.

"Hmm?" Gorbachev turns to look at Reagan. "Oh - the storm. I'm sure it's been brewing for hours. We just didn't see it… *at least not soon enough to prepare.*"

"Getting back to what we had been discussing, and to your last question - yes, of course, I do know what you mean. I do follow you, Mickey." Reagan nods as heaviness enters his voice. "I remember as well, there was that very close call in 1983, and just narrowly prevented by one of your heroes here."

"Yes, oh – so you do know about that?" Gorbachev chuckles. "Stanislav Petrov is a true hero, and I have made sure he is being treated as such. He saved more lives than any other person in the history of the world and very few people know about it, but they will, in time." He stops and eyes Reagan scrupulously for a moment. "What, aren't you going to mention any of the others?"

Reagan smiles. "I don't want to embarrass you, Mickey, you're my friend!" Gorbachev smiles and shakes his head. "Okay, so yes, then, of course I am aware of your nuclear sub during the Cuban Missile Crisis of 1962. That may have been even a closer call than in 1983 - they had no way of knowing what was going on and no way of communicating with anyone. All signals and sensors pointed to an all-out American nuclear missile having just been fired. *The soldier himself had been ordered to fire their nukes!* It was a true, honest-to-God miracle, Mickey, a miracle that the holocaust didn't happen way back then."

The Russian president is silently contemplative as he stares at the wondrous display of lightning strikes outside the windows. "I will have to agree with you here, Ron - *that he didn't fire our nukes truly was a miracle.*"

"And yes, I do worry about our grandchildren." The American President also continues to stare at the raging storm. *"What kind of world are we leaving behind for them?"*

Gorbachev nods thoughtfully. "It is precisely this thought that troubles me so much. Is that not why we meet?"

Reagan nods. "Yes, precisely why." He pauses and considers his next words carefully. "I think we made too many… nukes. It is absolutely unnecessary and downright crazy if you ask me. I mean. I worry…." Reagan falters, "I worry that no matter what we do, after we are no longer necessary to our countries, someone might kick over the first domino without us being there to stop it."

The room lights up like day as a flash of lightning strikes the ocean only a few miles away. The storm is quickly moving closer, rushing towards them like a thief in the night. Gorbachev wordlessly walks back towards the fireplace, sitting down in his chair and pulling another cigarette from his prized pack. "You are naming the fear that haunts me every night," he sighs, lighting his cigarette from a small stick he procures from the fireplace himself. "Yes, that *problem* pervades my every thought as well. It feels as if my entire life has become about preventing the most terrible outcomes in any number of things, but especially this, even though, at the same time, I doubt very much whether or not many of my actions actually mean anything."

The thunder is growing louder and more frequent, and the delay between lightning strikes is shortening. The room is now flashing like a disco, and Reagan gets up to pull the curtains closed, then plods back over to the flask of vodka, pouring both of them another glass. Handing one to Gorbachev, he says, "I think I will sip slowly this time to better enjoy the experience." Gorbachev nods and Reagan then kneels in front of the fireplace. He sips from his shot glass, and staring deeply into the flames, he asks, "What *is* the true future of the human race?"

"If you ask our military scientists, they will tell you that the future of humanity is not the human being that we know today, but the future of man is about leveraging excellence, *the superman,"* Gorbachev says with a dubious air. "To be truthful, I never paid much attention to fantasies when we have so much reality with which to contend."

Reagan narrows his eyes in deep cognition, suddenly aware of something he had suspected but which needs confirmation. He turns towards Gorbachev and asks, "Has your nation also been exploring that *forbidden* science? After the Nazis, we believed we were the only ones…"

"Yes, Operation Paperclip, I know," Gorbachev interrupts, "We captured many of their doctors as well, and evidently it was too alluring a field of study for our scientists to cease delving into - so much for what was supposed to be prohibited."

Boom! At that moment, thunder shakes the entire building, and all the windows light up on every side of the house through the curtains. Reagan and Gorbachev both jump into the air, and Gorbachev laughs nervously.

"Boy, we aren't in Kansas anymore, are we Toto?" Reagan jokes, and together they laugh off their startled nerves. "So, all this time we've been discussing how not to blow up the world, we never talked about these other schools of modern magic," he wonders aloud.

"It has been interpreted by our strategists as another potential weapons program, so secrecy is the natural process," Gorbachev explains. "Is this not so with the Americans, too?"

"Yes, of course, you're right," Reagan agrees, "but now that all seems so silly, doesn't it? The great human flaw: everything must be evaluated for its potential as a *weapon* rather than as an agent of *good*, or *progress*. It makes no sense." Reagan waxes philosophical as the storm continues to rage around them, both men still standing. The lighting is striking every couple of seconds now, and the constant sound of thunder reverberates from every direction. It is as though the storm itself is infuriated with the course of history up to this moment, and it has come to this place to demand a change from the only people who are in a position to affect it.

"But nowadays," Gorbachev mutters, almost to himself, "what kind of a weapon can a human being be against weapons that can destroy an entire planet?"

In the electrically charged air, Reagan and Gorbachev are both looking directly into each other's eyes when the same thought hits them.

"What if...." Gorbachev starts.

"...the genetics programs were to be changed..." Reagan continues.

"...into something antithetical to destruction?" Gorbachev finishes.

As their collaborative sentence reaches its conclusion, both men look at each other in amazement, finding themselves both passengers in the same psychic craft, hurtling through the chaos to its appointed destination on the other side of the unknown. Gorbachev, giddy with the excitement of a much younger man, gestures excitedly towards the chairs in front of the fireplace.

"Come, sit. Let's finally discuss this as men - as *friends* - rather than as heads of state.

Awestruck, and in full agreement, Reagan nods, his mind still spinning with the implications of the idea they had just conceived. Neither of them could fully articulate the massive vision that had been granted to each of them in that moment, but they both felt the invisible guiding hand of fate, or of doom, and they understood the path forward. Reagan sits and thus their discussion ensues. The seed of the Genesis Executive Order which had been planted into the fertile soil of the minds of these great men flourished throughout the night in eager dialogue between them. As the hours ticked by, the storm was like a constant spectator watching over their planning, and as it finally blew away to the south, the Earth celebrated the peaceful morning as if it were the very first day in the history of the world.

With the sun rising above the horizon, Reagan and Gorbachev, each the tireless workhorse engines of their respective cultures, sit in the same chairs, bleary-eyed but still ecstatic, basking in the morning beams which filter through the curtains. The fire from the previous night has faded to cold embers, and they are now sipping on steaming cups of black coffee instead of vodka, fueling themselves for the continuing discussion.

Reagan leans forward, the weight of responsibility evident on his face. "So, the best we can do with our stolen technology," he says, "is to enhance the genes of our best and brightest - intellectually, emotionally, *and* physically. We'll support them, protect them, nurture them, and promote them as thinkers and doers who will someday lead much better than the leaders of the past, or even ourselves. Should our worst fears ever come to pass, they will be in the best position to repopulate the world so humanity can carry on ... *if we succeed*, that is."

Gorbachev nods in agreement, contemplating the gravity of their plan. "And, in the meantime, pray that the bombs don't go off before our best and brightest reach maturity."

Reagan nods somberly. "We'll just have to hope that the technology catches up and eventually aligns with the right temperament in these children."

Gorbachev, too, recognizes the limitations of their plan. "Indeed. From what I've been informed, we can't control everything with genetics. There are many other factors... rogue elements. And, of course, if we are ever discovered, we'll be accused of elitism, ethics violations, conspiracy, prejudice - many terrible things. And the accusers may be *right*."

Reagan, resolute in his beliefs, replies, "In America, many of our doctors come from a privileged background. However, when they save a life, especially during an emergency, they are considered just the same as any other class of people and their privilege is not held against them. What we are doing right now is like a humanistic emergency, and we are therefore in uncharted territory. We have no choice in my opinion." Reagan throws up his hands and grins. "That simplifies it, right?"

Gorbachev laughs and rolls his eyes, bobbing his head back and forth with uncertainty. "But still…" he hesitates, his mouth hanging open as he weighs the precariousness of it all. Instead of words, he simply shakes his head.

Nodding his understanding and seamlessly resuming a serious tone, Reagan continues. "Nobody can know about this, my friend. You're right about that - *a small task force and that's it.* Our bureaucracies will never approve of this."

Gorbachev smiles earnestly as he leans all the way forward in his chair and grasps the President's shoulder. "My friend, we are in politics. The Bear and the Eagle sit here as friends, as partners, in a discussion about cleaning up a colossal error that our nations made in concert. *Who would believe it?"* Reagan forces an uneasy chuckle as Gorbachev continues. "Besides, there are already hundreds of back-door deals between our nations that even we don't know about. You and I - not our bureaucrats - will work on this together. And we *will* succeed." To punctuate his statement, Gorbachev reaches into his pocket, only to find a single cigarette left in his pack. "Long night," he says, lifting his eyebrows up and down.

"Aw, shucks! I'll bring two packs next time." Reagan laughs apologetically, stopping himself short to take a long sip of his coffee.

Gorbachev lights the last cigarette, crumples the pack, and throws it into the fireplace. He watches as it flashes into flames and then slowly decays into a gnarled black ball. For a moment, he lapses into a memory of all the packs he's ever finished. He rises from his chair and opens the curtains to a beautiful morning. The rain had left the air perfectly pure and clean, and now sunlight floods through the window and into the room, almost too bright for his eyes, and he must squint and turn his face away.

Joining him by the window Reagan says, "You know, there are no guarantees that we'll realize the outcome we hope for."

Gorbachev, ever the optimist, gestures at the bright morning outside. "Last night, fire rained from the heavens, but today we are in paradise. What is it you Americans love to say? *'You must think positive?'*"

Reagan laughs, sharing Gorbachev's optimism. "Exactly right! Things *can* change."

Their genuine friendship evident, Reagan extends his hand, and they shake, sealing their commitment to this daring plan.

"Indeed, they can. Yes, indeed," Gorbachev affirms, his excitement palpable as they each know they are about to embark on this transformative journey together. "To ensure that the secrecy of this essential part of our discussion gets off to a good start, I will have some of my intelligence officers leak out to the press that you and I did not see eye-to-eye on some key issues, and that we had several serious points of contention between us."

"I will do the same, my friend," Reagan assures, solidly in agreement.

As their hands remain firmly clasped, a resolute pact is forged between nations. Armed with a collective vision and an unwavering sense of duty towards humanity, they brace themselves for a journey into the unknown. *The Genesis Executive Order Number One,* an audacious idea born in the crucible of their long discussion at Höfði House, suddenly pulses with an unstoppable potential. Though they understand their tiny roles in the vast magnitude of this undertaking, and because they feel the full weight of mankind's future history on their shoulders, *their commitment is unwavering.* With determination etched in their souls, they clasp each other around the back, *resolute in their adherence to shape a brighter fate for humanity itself.*

∞ ∞ ∞

2010 –

In the twenty-four years since their first meeting, much had been set into motion. A trickle first, but then a spigot which became a gushing river - the force of its own momentum soon becoming a compelling tide of sophisticated policies, procedures, and secretive government operations.

On a bitterly cold February morning in St. Petersburg, U.S.S.R., in a two-story, brick hospital built thirty years before and run by the state, two doctors in white laboratory coats, one man and one woman, meet on the black-and-white-tiled floor of a secondary hallway on the first floor; the continuous buzz of the fluorescent light above them flickering its last energy. They walk a few steps, enter one of the offices in the middle of the maternity ward, and begin going through clipboards filled with information about each of the expecting mothers in the wing.

They are silent as they contemplate the information they are reading. He is rather tall and fit, with a large, shiny nose and black hair cut close to his scalp. He wears black formal pants and dress shoes, along with a red button-down shirt beneath his lab coat. She is medium height and is considered comely by her peers; her auburn hair is tied back in a bun, and she wears gray slacks made of wool, black pumps on her feet, and a blue flannel shirt beneath her white lab coat. With a nod, they depart the office and begin a slow stroll down the hallway. They glance through glass panes into the mothers' rooms as they walk by, each room holding four beds, and each bed is filled. The man, Dr. Petrovo, is not so much a doctor as a military eugenics scientist, as is the woman, Dr. Yilnay. He reviews the clipboard in his hand, then looks at Dr. Yilnay and asks, "Patient Kira V. is ready to give birth…. she has had her last set of three injections of the rapid gene replication trial for MRN32?"

"Yes. We are inducing labor for her this morning."

Once again, he nods, and then with a stern expression replete with confidence, he says, "She has held up well, it seems." He shuffles through some of the other papers beneath the first attached to his clipboard. After he takes time to review recent entries in the patient's chart, he looks up expectantly into Dr. Yilnay's eyes.

"Well, it is obvious to me as it should be to you," he says, his tone pedantic and impatient, "once the DNA has been modified, the proteins which combine with DNA to form new chromosomes will also then be modified." She nods, feeling once again the familiar uncertainty over whether or not he is getting ready to report her for inadequacy. As usual, he gives nothing away, and continues in his customary style of admonishment, similar to a frustrated parent telling his two-year-old for the tenth time that she must stop her incessant whining. "In any event, the point being, once there is a modification, it is no longer possible to synthesize the very molecules encoded by that gene."

She feels it essential right now to prove to him how much she has learned reading all about the results obtained during the twenty years this *program* had been underway. Yes, she was a doctor, a scientist, and yes, this was exciting work to be sure, but she was beginning to feel like the toll these experiments were taking on all involved, but mostly the *patients themselves, the mothers and the babies ...* was much too intrusive, perhaps even destructive. *No wonder the Nazi's became infamous for such barbarous means to their scientific ends. Perhaps this is more than I bargained for, and yet, I cannot help but feel that something good may still come from all of this ....*

And so, she replies in the manner of least resistance, with the proper attitude required: *knowledge comes before any other consideration.* "Yes, the cell will then stop its production of any unnecessary proteins as we have seen. In effect, we now know that a neuron will not synthesize muscle fibers as an example. And as such, only myocytes can be called upon to rebuild muscle tissue cells."

He wants to argue in order to further test her knowledge, but he pauses to look at patient Alyona R. through the glass window. He has a particular fondness for this patient and sees that she is staring at him, and so he smiles at her, then turns his attention back to his attack of this quite obviously underinformed colleague. "I want you to understand the importance of the testing to be performed *throughout the lifetime* of the creations these women are giving us. *We have made that* - that infant will be the culmination of our science and our hard work. *Never take that for granted, Dr. Yilnay!* We are controlling the activity of their genes themselves, and we know that we are ever so close to significantly enhancing their mental and physical abilities ...."

She interrupts him as a means of making it clear that she knows what she is doing. "And yes, it is clear from some of the latest results that our work is definitely activating stem cells in the brains of these infants that will lead to the generation of more nerve cells than they would have had otherwise. We are actively building and enhancing the neural networks which play essential roles in every important attribute that we hope to influence."

For once, he seems a bit impressed with her knowledge. He raises an eyebrow and decides to bring her in on his new findings. "I am beginning to think that the process of learning itself, or even simply encountering something new, sets off a series of molecular changes in the neurons. Certain genes, which we have begun identifying as IEGs, or immediate early genes, are then activated to produce much longer-term transformations in the brain."

A nurse urgently calls for them from down the hallway. "Doctors, patient Kira V. is ready!"

They turn around and scurry to one of the patients' rooms.

After a routine delivery, a newborn baby takes her first breaths and begins to cry. The mother, Kira, who at thirty-four years of age looks more fit than most young women half her age, is a bit exhausted but otherwise alert and focused. She is very attractive and watches closely as the two doctors inspect the baby excitedly before handing the baby girl to her. Immediately bonding with her newborn, she says out loud, "Elena - my baby will be named Elena, after my mother." The doctors nod, exchange smiles with Kira, and then step away as they continue marking notations on their clipboards. In the meantime, two smiling nurses come to tend to Kira and Elena.

Dr. Petrovo, somehow suddenly feeling rather mundane and downtrodden, says, "Yet another genius is born. Child of two less intelligent geniuses who will hitherto have special genes and be able to rule the world."

Dr. Yilnay was prepared for this switch of temperament on his part because he always became skeptical of the program's success directly after the birth of each new child upon examination, not seeing any vast difference between one baby and the next. And she had found the easiest path, once again, was to simply play along. "Why are you suddenly so sullen?"

This time, however, Dr. Petrovo takes offense. "You joke with me? This is my four-thousandth super baby. Despite all we've done, not one has turned out the way even our most pessimistic scientists had hoped. Perhaps this time it will, but it bothers me to no end that   the science has not replicated itself as it should in real-life!"

Wanting to bring him a sense of hope, Dr. Yilnay says, "Well, they're still little miracles, with or without the genetics."

Dr. Petrovo is taken aback. "Which means they're still only normal humans when what we need are heroes...." She is so frustrated by his back-and-forth routine - one moment hopeful that all was going as planned, and the next, wanting to crush it all in one fell swoop, proclaiming the program an utter "failure" to all around.

In her silence, he continues, "Anyway, as you already know, there will be markers in their DNA as they grow, *which means we may only find out much later what worked and what didn't.*"

∞ ∞ ∞

In Walter Reed Hospital in Washington, DC, within the maternity wing, the sun is shining through an office window, reflecting a dazzling, brilliant light off the recent snow covering the grounds. Sitting inside this small office full of filing cabinets, a man and a woman are having coffee, trying to make the most of their thirty-minute break during another extremely busy shift.

He had studied to be a gynecologist before being recruited by the National Intelligence Council years earlier, and now Dr. Baker is dedicated to his role in this program, after having endured six months of extremely rigorous training and information-gathering to get here. In his late thirties, he is of medium height with a slight paunch, a head full of prematurely graying hair of mid-length, and a round face which has a customary elusive charm meant to keep others at a safe distance.

She is a nurse, an RN, and had a load of student loans to pay when she went looking for the best paying job in the industry. Betsy Teague had gotten just that - having been hired just six months after getting her license, and now she has been a part of the same program for the past year. If she had not been made to sign so many papers - NDA's, contracts, licensing, liability, and patent agreements - she would have left already, though, because she had begun to feel the program itself did not align with her ethics. But she needs a good reference from this job, and so she is determined to stick it out for another year; *although another year, at most.*

She had been trying to understand the goal of the program and only knew it had something to do with finding ways to teach humans to beat diseases of all sorts, but something just did not add up. She stares at Dr. Baker who would have been considered a geek in high school, she supposes. She is very intrigued by his knowledge and figures she has been here long enough to be able to push him a bit for more information. He had just been instructing her on the finer necessities of documenting every bit of information from the assessment sheets for each newborn. Anyway, she believes he has a crush on her, and although he would never get anything from her, she figures no harm would be done by playing it up just a bit. Smiling and licking her lips, which she had just frosted with cherry lip gloss, she inhales a deep breath and asks, "Why are these statistics so important anyway, Dr. Baker, *and just what is the program itself trying to achieve once and for all?"*

He raises his eyebrow at her. "Have you ever heard you shouldn't ask too many questions, Betsy?"

"No, I can't say that I have. I always thought being inquisitive was a good thing."

He smiles at her in spite of himself. "You know you remind me of Louis Lane, did anybody ever tell you that?"

"From the movie, or from that old TV show *Superman?"*

"Either," he says.

She acts quite bemused. She knew playing innocent would defuse his defenses more than if it seemed she was prying too much. They sit on two breakroom chairs next to each other, and weaving her arm through his, she gently brings herself closer to him. "That would make you Clark Kent, I suppose."

His face flushes and he shakes his head. "Not exactly … but maybe I'm the guy who will help to make the first, *close-to-life* Superman!" The pride glows from his face and he slips into an awkward grin. Really, he wants to forget all about the science right now and just lean over and plaster a kiss on her lips.

Betsy blushes too, and she understands she has to take the next steps very carefully as his amorous feelings for her have been ignited. She reaches over and presses him on the shoulder. "Well, that would be some pick-up line to use at a bar, wouldn't it?" She laughs, and then she mock-admonishes him with a shocked smile on her face. *"Do you talk like that to all the girls?"*

He takes his free hand from the arm of his desk chair and brings it to her face, gently stroking her cheek. "No, *only you,"* he purrs, furrowing his brow.

Removing his hand gently with her free arm, she smiles, looks deeply within his eyes, and says, "Go on then, this is getting quite interesting."

Recovering, Dr. Baker takes a sip of his cold coffee and says, "All right, you've got me cornered. Don't repeat this to anyone: The explicit goal of the entire program is to build upon human DNA to help increase the physical and mental abilities of these infants, starting early with their mother's pre-conception. *BUT ALSO,* to use the science to help learn new ways to heal people from illnesses, and to develop gene therapies. Some say it is the science of the Superman, but really, it is not all that bad."

Betsy nods emphatically and with her free hand, taps her index finger on her temple. "Like creating a super race with vast intelligence?" She stops squeezing his shoulder and leans back in her chair. "I'm all ears."

He pauses, considering the implications of his disclosure, and then the sweetness of her shampoo wafts into his nostrils, casting a spell which dissipates his accustomed loneliness. "You heard about *Operation Paperclip*, right?" She gives an inquisitive look, and he continues, "It was when the government brought over all those scientists from Nazi

Germany so that we could make use of their research and findings."

"I seem to recall reading something about that." Betsy takes the cup from his hand and sips, making a face because his coffee is cold and unsweetened.

Happy to see she is now on such familiar terms with him, he continues. "The Germans found out how to make babies stronger, plain and simple. Seems the Nazis were trying to push humanity to the next stage of evolution, and *they might have found the key*."

A thought then occurs to her. "Wait a minute," she says as she sits straight up in her chair, alarmed. Looking at him directly in the eyes, she says, "You mean... we're working on *Nazi* science?" Her volume and inflection had risen dramatically, and he quickly reaches over to cover her mouth, spilling the coffee all over her white slacks.

"*Shhhhh!* Betsy, you have to keep quiet! It would be much worse for us than just losing our jobs if someone heard us. *Trust me on that.*" He slowly pulls his hand from her mouth and feels the stickiness of her cherry lip gloss on his palm.

In a quieter tone, she asks, "Nazis... so we're making super babies for a war with Russia or something?"

"No, we're not just trying to make better soldiers... well... it's not just for the war! Yes, the military is in charge of it all, but... it's not like that, Betsy! Please..." Now, he is panicking that he had trusted her with this information. He takes some tissues from his desk and tries blotting out the coffee from her slacks.

"I don't know... doesn't this seem kind of wrong to you?" She slumps back in her chair and takes the tissues from him. "And why does it have to be such a secret? All those forms I was made to sign when they hired me ...."

He tries to reason with her intellectual side. "I don't know but think of what it could mean. We're talking about people who are smarter, who are stronger, and who live twice as long, people who don't have physical or psychological problems." The words soon cascade from his mouth like an open spigot, and he begins waving his hands around as though conducting an orchestra. "It's the future! No criminals, no diseases... it used to take millions and millions of years for us to find a way forward, and now *we're* making it happen all at once! *We're leaping!"*

Betsy's eyes travel from her lap to the office door and then back to meet Dr. Baker's eyes. She slowly backs her chair away from him and stands up, taking a step towards the door. "I'm late returning to my shift, Dr. Baker," she says softly. "Really - this is all so truly fascinating. I thank you for sharing such important information. Maybe we can talk about this more later?"

Dr. Baker exhales and sits upright in his chair. He can't help but feel he has made a mistake, and that there will be consequences. "Sure, Betsy, see you later," he replies, returning to his usual, official tone.

A few minutes later, he is called to his boss's office. The man in the big chair makes a gentle motion with both of his hands, "Sit, Elliot, sit." He is the Chief Medical Officer overseeing the entire program, and he looks old and pale, with wisps of stark white hair and skin that appears to cling directly to the bones beneath. Dr. Baker considers, however, that there is a mischievous twinkle in his blue eyes that evokes an image of Peter Pan. Like all of the doctors at the facility, he wears a white lab coat over a button-up shirt and tie, and his position as the person in charge is indicated by the subtle text on the badge affixed to his breast pocket: *F. Fischer M.D. – Chief Medical Officer.*

Dr. Fischer throws a pile of papers onto his desk right in front of Dr. Baker. "Read this out loud to me." Dr. Baker scoots his chair closer to the desk and takes the page on top of the pile into his hands. He looks it over a moment before Dr. Fischer says, "Go on...."

Dr. Baker reads from an American doctor's testimony at the *trials of war criminals Before the Nuremberg Military Tribunals.*

> *"It may interest you to learn that the war secrets in this collection run into the thousands, that the mass of documents is mountainous, and that there has never before been anything quite comparable to it.*

> *"This could be the greatest single source of this type of material in the world-the first orderly exploitation of an entire country's brainpower.*

> *"As for medical secrets in this collection – some of them will save American medicine years of research; and more than a few of them are revolutionary. For instance, the German technique of treatment after prolonged and usually fatal exposure to cold is far better than anything else the world has ever come up with.*

> *"We owe it to the world to continue with some of their findings."*

Dr. Elliot Baker puts the paper down, stands, and circles around the room before composing himself and sitting down once again in the chair across from the elder physician. "You know I know all of this, and so I am assuming you are reminding me of this because I have questioned the use of stimulants on the expectant mothers." He crosses his arms and begins a continuous back and forth rocking motion, breathing through his nose as he looks around the room and then at Dr. Fischer, whose stern glaze seems unfazed. "As in my report to you, it's clear that there is some sort of psychoactive stimulant being included in the medical schedule for the mothers," he begins in subdued tones. "Is there something about this that's above my clearance? *Because I'd really like to understand why.*" He has to remind himself to calm down again.

"You're not wrong, doctor," the chief nods. "Are you at all familiar with Konrad Lorenz's theories on aggression and neurological development?" Dr. Baker winces and shakes his head, and Dr. Fischer continues, "Yes, well you see, Lorenz postulated that higher brain functioning in an organism was inextricably linked to incidences of heightened stress. There is a strong body of evidence to suggest that one of the main drivers of positive neurological evolution is related to that special class of aggressive behaviors that human beings rarely experience any longer."

Dr. Baker's face reveals a comic incredulity. "So, what you're saying is that humans benefit from severe aggressive behavior towards one another, and that the use of these medications is designed to increase maternal aggression so that their babies develop more intellectual power *than they would have otherwise* - without the mother's frequent invocation of aggressive emotions while their babies were still inside their wombs? Dr. Fischer, I can't possibly imagine why...."

The older doctor's fist slams onto his desk as he rises to his feet. "*No!* You don't have any imagination, do you? And then, is it any wonder why you also *do not have the clearance for such matters?*" Dr. Fischer's dramatic change in demeanor pulls any remaining peace from the air surrounding them. "You would do better to consider how best to control *what you can!* You must see that the minor issues that plague your unit do not rise beyond your department." Dr. Baker studies the ice in his superior's eyes which glisten with a clear foreboding.

The problems he had been dealing with included the mother's stress levels which were affecting the nursing unit, which negatively influenced the doctors and the families. To some degree, it was beginning to feel more like he was working in an asylum rather than a maternity ward. Accepting defeat, Dr. Baker stands and begins a hesitant and begrudging retreat. He turns back one more time to face his superior. "Yes sir. Sorry sir. I'll communicate more as the situation is handled," he sputters and turns, running directly into the doorway. On the other side of the door, he lets out a muffled whimper and fiercely rubs his arm. *That went great.*

When he gets back downstairs, stepping out of the stairwell and into the hallway, he hears the sounds of crying infants and looks around at the Kafkaesque nightmare of patient room doors extending in all directions. *All those years I spent admiring Franz Kafka's works and I never realized he was painting a picture of my future – humanity's future!*

He realizes that they had moved all of the women from the large, shared spaces in the south wing into the smaller rooms of this unit through these very hallways. Most of the expectant mothers were now either paired up or assigned three to a room. There had been talk of isolating them completely, but the nurses had argued vehemently against doing such, and for now, they had won. Suddenly, he hears Betsy's voice behind him. "Dr. Baker, Lola A. is about to give birth, and I know you wanted to be there for this one."

He turns and says, "Yes, Betsy, thanks." Quickly, they run together to room #123.

Once they enter the room, Dr. Baker's friend and colleague, fifty-two-year-old Dr. Steven Snyder, is lifting a baby from between the mother's spread legs, and Lola, a thirty-year-old Latina, strikingly pretty, has just given birth. "Hey, come look at this one," Dr. Snyder says, smiling at Dr. Baker, who approaches and takes the infant into his arms. He looks at the baby and then smiles at his mother. "Perfect little baby boy," he says, and then hands the baby to Betsy who cleans him up before delivering him into his mother's waiting and loving arms.

"Do you have a name picked out yet, Lola?" Betsy asks.

"Yes, Arthur!"

The two doctors wash up before leaving the room and heading down the hallway. Dr. Baker says, "Another little hero."

"Or just another monster," Dr. Snyder responds. "Who knows anymore?"

"I definitely know what you mean," Dr. Baker says, shaking his head.

"Don't get me wrong: What we need are good people with a genetic edge. I think the creators of the program misjudged how rare a combination that is. A jackpot in a no-win lottery."

Dr. Baker thinks for a moment before he responds. Finally, he says, "Maybe we are both being too pessimistic."

Dr. Snyder stops and eyes his friend intensely. "Come on. How many years has it been? How many prodigies have we produced?" He shakes his head and smirks.

Dr. Baker says, *Maybe this will be the one...."*

∞ ∞ ∞

80

Chapter Three

The Promising Bud of Roses

∞ ∞ ∞

2012 –

Of the hundreds of perfected babies born in the secret government maternity wards, less than a quarter of them possessed the consummate genetic constitution to be considered a success by any definition of the term. Of that elite set, only a chosen few were considered perfect in every way.

Arthur sits and stares at the big screen, the reflection of the shifting scenes before him flickering in his bright blue eyes. Strapped into an infant car seat which sits atop a luxurious couch in their private in-home movie theater, the two-year-old is being desensitized to the thoughts that might upset him by being made to watch videos of animals surviving in the great savanna. At least, that is how Lola's husband explained it. She sits beside Arthur, nervously watching her son evolve. Entering into her thirties now, Lola's dark brown hair is straight, while her child's is lighter brown and a bit curly. Her eyes are a world-weary chestnut brown, while Arthur's are sparkling bright blue. The differences only fuel her love for him.

He looks away from the screen and stirs. She wants to call out to him, but the process forbids it. Her husband's formal name is Bertrand, although his family and close friends call him *Burt.* She still can't believe the home they've been provided. It is far beyond anything she ever dreamed she would have. A military brat, she had gotten used to the humble life of on-base housing. Now, thanks to their involvement in this lucrative government project, she lives in a six-bedroom mansion in a very high-end suburb of Langley, Virginia. With its white brick construction, it feels like a castle to her. *And three floors? Are they expecting us to have many more children?*

As a military veteran herself, Lola had been conditioned to unpredictable shower temperatures, but now she has a sauna, a whirlpool jacuzzi bathtub, and enough hot water to shower for as long as she would ever want to. They had just moved into their new house two weeks before and Lola is learning to take ownership of what to her still feels like an unofficial perk of the job, if not a fairy-tale dream that she might one day have to wake up from. *But it's more than a dream, and it's more than a job. It's a family... my family.*

Another thing that she is learning to get used to is the pretense of it all. After five years of marriage, she still doesn't know exactly which department her husband is working in now. She knows that he's an ex-special forces soldier turned military psychologist, but his official position is unclear to her, and the identity of his associates is always somewhat of a mystery. When they met, she used to think he was some secret agent, but now he's always home every night. He had used his government connections to propel her career forward in ways she could still hardly believe, got her promoted into top-secret military projects, and introduced her to world-famous geneticists which she could now call her associates. It had been a real ride, and now, everything was about the baby. It isn't anything like the life she would have predicted for herself, but she is grateful to be a part of something so important and so beautiful. She looks into Arthur's eyes, and he gazes back into hers.

"You're so handsome, but you smell so bad!" she says in a highly approving baby-talk tone, rubbing her nose softly against his, which makes him giggle. "Let's get you changed."

Burt had wanted to name the child Armstrong, but she thought that sounded so funny, and so Arthur was their compromise. It made him think of King Arthur and the Knights of the Round Table, but it had also been her great-grandfather's name. As she changes him, she considers how genetics played a part in his early development. At times, Arthur's sleep quality seems to suffer, and she wonders if it has anything to do with the video stimuli they had been asked to expose him to. It also bothers her that he can never be left alone for more than a few minutes, or else he cries so hard, he hyperventilates. It seems as if feeding him is the only thing which brings him comfort, and she worries that this might not always work. *Is this just to be expected and I'm just overreacting? Am I doing everything right - as a good mother should do?*

Finished, she holds Arthur out in front of her, and his sincere smile clashes with his scrunched-up nose. She laughs. Burt comes rushing in from the hallway. At thirty-five, he is strikingly handsome and extremely fair-skinned with blonde hair and bright blue eyes, always tidily dressed and smart-looking. Today, he is wearing a light tan suit with an open collar and loafers. He walks towards her and says, "I am off to a meeting in a few minutes."

"Of course," Lola sighs, but she smiles and says, "I hope you'll be back in time for dinner tonight." She places Arthur back into his car seat.

"Absolutely. It's a sure thing," he replies, giving her a swift kiss on the cheek. "I'll be back in just a few hours." Turning to look at Arthur, he asks, "How is he doing with this video today?"

Lola wants to be as positive as she can, but he can sense her hesitation. "He seems to be handling it better today, as if he is understanding the necessity animals have to ensure their own survival through sometimes violent means."

Burt nods and then takes in the elaborate surroundings of the home movie theater.

"I know, I still can't believe it myself," Lola says. "It's almost like I feel they will take it all away from us if we do something wrong!" She looks for his reaction but it's nondescript, giving her no clue as to an answer for her main concern, and so she decides to come right out with it. *"So, this is our home for good?"*

"I am guessing so." He smiles and shakes his head. "I mean, wow, it's so much, isn't it?"

For the first time, Lola senses something from her husband which just might betray a lack of firm commitment to the program. Uneasily, she says, "It's not too late to back out. We can just... raise our boy like any other family."

Burt smiles sternly and the deep lines of his jaw are prominent; Lola realizes those were part of the reason she had been so attracted to him when they had first met. He rests a hand on her shoulder. "Honey, don't get the jitters now."

Looking deeply into his ocean blue eyes, she has a reticent tone as she says, "You know I try not to, but well, I just can't help it sometimes. I suppose that anything top secret gives me the jitters."

He becomes more adamant than she had hoped. "We've talked about it, and thought about it, and weighed the pros and cons for months now. Just think what an incredible opportunity this will be for him!" Placing his hand beneath her chin, he continues, "We're scientists. *Arthur is going to get the best of everything.* We could never give him what he's now going to easily have available to him. Just remember that hundreds of other couples and their children are in the program, so I really don't think there's anything to worry about."

Lola feels pensive, and she takes a deep breath trying once again to relax. As soon as she does, she feels more worried than before, but she realizes she and Burt have committed to the program and that she really has no overt reason to withdraw now. She nods and then turns away from Burt, quickly going to her boy and taking Arthur from his car seat. Holding him secure within her arms, she nudges her nose into his hair and says, "Okay, Little Man. Here we go - the future is all ours."

Burt smiles and hugs the two of them, giving them each a peck on the top of their heads. "The future is his, indeed." Over Lola's head, the look on Burt's face changes, and in fact, something is weighing quite heavily on his mind.

∞　∞　∞

Elena is a vision of a Bouguereau painting - an angelic child with golden locks and hazel eyes mirroring the Caspian Sea on a tranquil day. At almost seven months old, she takes her first steps in a twenty-foot-long rectangular room, surrounded by one-way windows offering glimpses of the wooded expanse surrounding her family's lavish Barvikha villa.

Her haven is a child's paradise, adorned with stuffed animals and toys scattered like constellations across the floor. Overhead lights cast a gentle, shifting glow of pleasant colors, painting the room with a serene ambiance. Altan, her father, a revered Russian surgeon and robotics expert, gazes at her through the glass barrier with a tender smile, filled with pride at the sanctuary he has designed for his beloved daughter. He had grown up privileged as the son of a wealthy business tycoon in one of the wealthiest neighborhoods in Russia – Rublyovka, a prestigious, gated, residential area in the western suburbs of Moscow where many Russian government officials and wealthy businesspeople resided. Altan is thirty-six, dressed in an expensive black European business suit, has neatly coiffed brown hair and bright green eyes and quite a handsome appearance.

As Altan watches, Elena lies down in the embrace of one of her stuffed animals - a giant white teddy bear - and her tiny eyelids flutter, surrendering to the blissful embrace of sleep. A profound sense of warmth and love envelopes Altan as he witnesses his precious child's peaceful slumber.

Yet, amid this tender scene, Altan grapples with exhaustion and the weight of a monumental project. The burden is compounded by his wife Kira's relentless absence due to her demanding role at the Kremlin. The solitude he experiences is a sharp contrast to the social life he once knew. The rhythmic song of the clock marks the approaching dinner plans with Kira… an occasion to step briefly into the wider world beyond the confines of his work.

As the sun dips below the horizon, Altan pours a shot of scotch, seeking solace in its familiar warmth. He contemplates the project's reality, entangled in the conflict between the enhancement surgeries he's performed on Elena - surgeries he deems unnecessary - and the relentless demands of the project. He pours another shot, attempting to drown his inner turmoil in the amber liquid, but instead he holds the glass and stares lovingly at his sleeping daughter. There at the center of a world spinning madly around, she is perfectly still, and as Altan watches her he borrows some of that stillness for himself.

In his moment of introspection, his wife Kira enters the room, but Altan's attention remains riveted on Elena. Still dressed in sharp business attire with her short brown hair slicked back, Kira softens her face and gently teases, "Earth to Altan. Calling Altan!" Altan is startled, and a nervous laugh escapes him as he releases the intensity of his inner contemplation. Kira, in a hushed tone, warns, "Be careful not to wake her."

"I know. She is sound asleep. I just love to watch her," Altan confesses, finally taking his eyes off Elena to look upon his beautiful wife.

"I've noticed," Kira replies, her tone taking on that serious tone Altan has come to know and to sometimes dread so well. "We have much to do, darling. You haven't yet explored the villa. There are rooms for every activity - lessons, exercise, experimental training, and rooms whose purposes elude even my understanding, but they will be revealed in due time. Our little girl will be kept occupied, and *we* need to prepare those spaces."

Altan, part of him still trying to reconcile the issues brought up during his contemplation a few moments ago, turns to gaze out a large window facing the forest. Kira, ever perceptive, probes gently, "Again, you seem lost in thought, my love. Why?"

He shakes his head, still staring into the snowy forest. "I just want to ensure that our little girl is allowed to be just that – *a little girl*," Altan confesses, a mix of protective concern and his longing for a normal childhood for Elena.

"She's very strong, Altan. Remarkably so," Kira reassures him, her confidence evident, though whether it is in herself or in Elena, Altan cannot discern.

"How can you be certain she's strong enough for... *whatever lies ahead?"* Altan wonders aloud, seeking reassurance and grappling with the enigmatic future.

Unfazed, she stares hard at him and says, "A mother knows her child." And then, attempting to tap into the depth of understanding about their little girl which they both share, she adds, "I believe you do too."

Acknowledging her perspective with a nod, he wants her to know that he is still on board with everything for now. "Yes, I do."

"I trust the program, Altan. There are many like us here and in America. We have been given an opportunity. We must trust the program to guide us wisely," Kira continues, her faith in their circumstances unwavering.

He decides he will be forthright with his wife. "I suppose I fear they might turn her into a soldier before she can even walk," Altan sighs, his worry for Elena's fate now seeping deeply into his words and tone of voice.

Kira, with her Kremlin-bred ambition fueling the power in her voice, does not tolerate such negativity in her presence. She had spent too many lonely days in her own childhood and youth breaking her back working the farm as the daughter of peasant farmers, and now that she has finally arrived as an up-and-coming woman of some importance, she will not allow any stumbling blocks to interfere with her rising path. She restrains herself with patience as she finally counters, "You know she *is* a soldier of sorts, even before the markers are visible. She's a *super* baby! And there is a reason for these extraordinary children. The world was lulled into a false sense of security at the end of the Cold War, but we're at greater risk of a nuclear holocaust now than ever. Elena's brilliance sets her apart. *It's not just about the future; it's about averting disaster.* Isn't that a noble cause? We should feel honored they chose us for this program due to our remarkable child. They've noticed our contributions to the sciences, and this is our reward."

Altan, after a moment more of consideration, finally nods in agreement, acknowledging the logic in his wife's words. "You're not entirely wrong in your assessment. She may indeed be brilliant, but that's not what makes her special. She is special because she is Elena - her brilliance should be *her reward. Not ours.*"

Kira acknowledges his perspective with a nod, fostering a moment of mutual understanding between them, but it quickly passes, and her professional persona returns as she begins to delegate. "Now, go and explore the rest of the facility. Take inventory of your offices. It's my turn to gaze at our beautiful princess."

Altan chuckles, leaning in to plant a tender kiss on Kira's forehead. She smiles in return, and he croons, "Yes, my love," as he bids farewell to his wife, stepping out into the corridor, leaving Elena in her peaceful slumber.

∞ ∞ ∞

After two decades of high-stakes interrogations with some of the world's most lethal insurgents, the feeling of anxiety is almost a completely new sensation, and Bertrand feels nervous for the first time in his adult life since boot camp. It's not the pressures of his job at the CIA. It's not some imbalance in his internal psychology from years of combat. It's that his son Arthur just isn't absorbing the information he needs to be absorbing at this time; he turns away from some of the more gruesome parts of the animal videos. *A survivor can never turn away. He must give up that privilege before it is even born within him.*

Bertrand treads slowly up the polished wooden stairs to the third floor, exhaling with each step to calm himself, a technique one of his officers in special forces training had taught him as a means of resetting the central nervous system. His athletic frame expands and contracts beneath his white undershirt as he absorbs and expels enormous amounts of air. There are fourteen steps between each floor, and he counts the seconds at each step, calculating that his creeping ascent will take him just over two minutes. *Just a couple minutes to fully reset – it's worth it. That's what he had said back then. And it's still worth it.* As he emerges into the open air, he sees Lola standing at the balcony's edge of their outdoor patio with Arthur in her arms. She is wearing a flowing purple cotton dress, and she points out towards the yard while she talks to the infant.

"And that's where we'll plant our peach trees, and over there is where I'll put the raised beds for our greens."

Bertrand clears his throat, and she spins around with a look of absolute joy on her face. *"You're home early!"* she cries, walking over to him and throwing her free arm around his shoulder. "Arthur, look. Daddy's home!"

Whatever tension was left in Bertrand's body flies away in the cool evening air as he looks at his wife and their stunningly beautiful baby son. This is a portrait of the life he had always wanted for himself while he was tumbling through the Pittsburg foster care system, and now he was able to give it to the people he loved the most.

"Are you two in the beginning stages of landscape design for the backyard?" he asks with mock sincerity, kissing Lola.

"It's so ugly out here Burt! Look at all this patchy grass," Lola protests. "I'd already have this year's pumpkin and kale in the ground by now if I had any time at all."

90

"I know, I know. I'll ask again if we can get a housekeeper with security clearance. As you can imagine, there's not much crossover in the industries," he cracks a smile as he finishes.

"Stop joking, I'm serious!" she laughs, batting at his chest.

"How about some landscaping people? That would be easier."

"No Bertrand, no!" she pouts. "I want to do all the gardening myself. The green thumb runs in our family, and I'm not going to sell mine out."

Even better, he thinks to himself. "Okay, deal! And I'll do everything I can to help along the way, honey," he says, knowing he would never have much free time to do so. The men in his own life had never been gentle to him, and it had caused him a lot of unnecessary grief, so though he hopes to protect his son from anything that might compromise his development, Bertrand is at times conflicted and caught with the old and familiar impulses regarding what is expected of a man.

Lola takes Bertrand's giant hand into her tiny palm, interlocking their fingers. Arthur opens his eyes for a moment and seeing his father, he smiles and coos a little before closing them peacefully once again. Lola happily thinks to herself that she and Burt are still as in love as they had been the day he met her in the field hospital in Afghanistan. She can remember when the big, grizzled soldier opened up his eyes with shock upon seeing a young and pretty medic before him tending to his wounds, which had sent her into fits of laughter back then for some reason. She had never wanted to raise a child, *but with this man....*

Suddenly, a butterfly floats beside them and catches Arthur's attention. He's mesmerized by it, and it seems to be entranced by him. Dancing around the three of them and then coming close to Lola's face, the beautiful blue and orange monarch seems completely unafraid. Arthur points at it and smiles.

As it floats gently away, Burt says, "Well, all good things must come to an end."

Lola turns to face him. "Uh-oh.... I know that tone of voice of yours. Out with it - what's wrong now?"

"Nothing's wrong, exactly." A nervous twitch flashes across his expression in the form of a thinly veiled grin. "Okay - you win. We're having some unexpected company for dinner."

Lola rolls her eyes, immediately knowing who, and understanding that the evening will not belong to them alone. "And so, it begins ...."

"I know I told you I would prepare you ahead of time, but they sprung this on me at the last minute this time, and so for tonight at least, it will be different than we thought."

She feels her patience already dwindling. "Sure, different because I had no warning, or if not, then different how?"

"Yes, the first," Burt says, and then quickly adds, "Well, also because these two gentlemen from the Pentagon are joining us simply to observe our superstar here and to see how a typical dinner is going for the three of us together. And...."

Lola sizes him up. "And what...?"

"And I may as well tell you now that we're going to be seeing a lot of these guys moving forward. That's all. We'll just be... seeing them often from now on."

Lola is rightfully upset, but she appreciates her husband's candidness. "Alright, Mr. Mysterious. I just put Cornish hens in the oven. I better throw in a few more." With Arthur still in one arm, she takes Burt's hand with her free arm and leads him inside. Walking towards the kitchen and pulling

Burt along, Lola asks, "Would you like to tell me a little more about these two new friends of ours?"

Two hours later, inside the dining room, all five of them are seated around the table. Nash is twenty-nine and is a handsome Chinese American, military persona, and a bit intense, dressed in beige cargo pants and a dark blue polo shirt. Ben is pushing forty and Black, in great physical shape, clean cut and dressed to the nines in gray Yves Saint Laurent. To Lola, so far, the men are down-to-earth and approachable as they engage in small talk and now spend suppertime laughing and drinking red wine, as Bertrand mashes up the meal into tiny bites for Arthur and buzzes them into his toothless mouth on a spoon, like an airplane coming in for a landing. It is obvious that Arthur enjoys the game - and the food. Lola only picks at her dish, her appetite held at bay by a nameless worry she refuses to address right now. She just enjoys watching her husband and son interact, hoping that their bonding will ensure the relationship between them will last forever. She watches everything almost as if from a distance as the food slowly disappears, except for Arthur's, and nothing but empty plates stand between them. *Two or three hours to cook it, and thirty minutes to eat it. Where's the justice in that?*

Nash is admiring Burt's playful interactions with Arthur via the imaginary airplane. "Little guys got an appetite!" He smiles at Lola and then looks back at Burt. "Do you mind if I hold him and give it a try?"

"Not at all," Burt responds, glancing at Lola.

Lola forces a smile in their direction while Burt gently hands Arthur to Nash. She rises to begin clearing some of the dishes from the table but stops herself, and in true motherly fashion, she calls to them, "Watch his little head!"

Burt says, "We're good, honey. We're good." Lola decides to forego clearing any dishes in favor of watching the proceedings as Nash takes the baby confidently into his arms and soon resumes the airplane game, to which Arthur doesn't miss a beat. He giggles a little at Nash before eating his spoonful of food.

Lola surprises even herself as words come tumbling out of her mouth. "You're good with him. He likes you!"

"I like him!" Nash beams. "He's special. I mean..., what I mean is that he's good-natured. A lovely little soul. That's not genetics." Burt and Lola appreciate the comment and smile at each other. Nash is totally engaged in the game of airplane, and it's apparent to all who are present that he is quickly becoming attached to Arthur and enjoying himself.

Finally, Ben, who had been rather quiet so far for the duration of the dinner, finds his chance to speak. "What's fascinating to me is knowing that Colonel Billings here was a child prodigy himself. He doesn't tell many people, but he holds two Ph.D. 's, one in Child Development and the other in Clinical Psychology." He pauses to sip from his glass of water. "He wrote his dissertation for the latter on the relationship between fitness and positive mental health in people under twenty-one years old. It's being rewritten to sell to the lay public, and I'm sure it'll be a bestseller."

"Yes, and I also leap tall buildings in a single bound!" Nash jests. "Also, please call me Nash. We're in *your* home, not the Pentagon. And this is where I'll be seeing y'all the most."

Nodding at him, Burt says, "That's very impressive, Nash."

Lola has taken her seat again and she asks, "About that - can you tell me exactly what will be happening during your visits? I was under the impression -"

"Not to worry," Ben interrupts, as if having anticipated her question. "We have no intention of intruding or interrupting your family routine. We'll be available to observe and to help if you need it. *That's it.* The primary goal remains that Arthur is to have as normal a childhood as someone with his intellect and genes possibly can. But we'd like to be like open books with no hidden agendas all along the way."

"I'm confused," Lola says. "I thought we wouldn't know for sure what's taken hold and what hasn't as far as his superior abilities and advanced development."

Shifting Arthur from one arm to another and then gently burping him on his shoulder, Nash says, "You're right. We won't. But sometimes there may be early signs." Arthur belches quite loudly for his age, and Lola is amazed. They all look around at each other with big smiles and Nash continues, "We'd like Arthur to grow up thinking of us as uncles. Here sometimes, then sometimes not, but always good for a game of catch or a hot fudge sundae. And even better at listening and being a safe person for him to talk to outside of his parents. All kids need that."

Ben cuts in right after Nash is finished. "But we're really here to help you not to be nervous. Arthur is going to be Arthur. Some kids are born geniuses, or star athletes, or brilliant artists without a boost. But whatever happens, we'll be keeping track and here to answer any questions that may come up for you – *if any come up at all.*"

"Uncles?" Lola looks with a bit of skepticism first at Burt, then at Ben, and finally lands on Nash. "You do realize that I'm Latina, you're Asian, the Colonel is Black, and poor Burt is so White he's almost clear."

In mock offense, Burt shouts, "Hey! I'm sorry for whatever my race did to any of your races in the past, okay?"

Nash and Ben break out in laughter, and Nash speaks first to Burt. "Forgiven! I was just figuring that through marriage, it would be seen as a possibility." He then turns to Lola, "But OK, point taken - how about distant and older cousins, then? Would that be acceptable? The point being, we're posing as family friends because we aim to be family friends. And we wanted to meet with you regularly in an unofficial setting because in the end, that is both easier and more natural for Arthur."

Ben adds, "Bottom line is that we are here for you. And we do not wish to impose, but you should know that all the families have people like us involved for support."

"So, it's gonna be like raising a baby in a super diverse episode of Big Bang Theory," Lola relinquishes, and they all laugh.

Burt adds, "And we do appreciate and thank you for presenting your mission to us here in such an unobtrusive way." Ben and Nash both smile and nod.

And then the mood shifts once again as Lola returns with, "There will be boundaries, of course!" It's like the air had been sucked out of the room and the three men stare at her with apprehensive eyes. "Let me make it clear, *and I feel this is an absolute necessity* - he is my son first and foremost, and a beneficiary of the program second to that directive."

For a moment, there is an absolute and uncomfortable silence pervading the room until Burt clears his throat and is about to say something to excuse his wife's demanding statement, but Ben beats him to it by speaking first. "And Lola, *we think of him as the most important person in the world.* In fact, he may very well become of vast historical importance – *a first of his kind* – if he is what we think he is. Trust me, nobody wants to hurt him. We all are only interested in learning *from him.*"

Lola wants to be agreeable, but she is far from being sold on these two men. "Well, like I said, you can learn all you want to learn from him, but there are going to be firm boundaries." She looks at Burt and sees he is feeling anger towards her right now that it is barely under wraps. In fact, it is quickly bubbling to the surface, and once again, her tact is to offer a bone. She smiles at both men and says, "But I believe we can figure those out as we move along."

"That's just great," Nash says as he boops Arthur on the nose with the empty spoon and Arthur breaks out in a fit of giggles.

Lola asks, "Do you have any children of your own, Nash?"

"I wish I did," he responds. "I guess I've been a bit busy over the past few years, but my partner and I plan to adopt when the time is right." Lola nods and feels a bit comforted by this. Burt and Ben are all grins watching as Nash continues to boop Arthur's nose for laughs.

Nash and Ben thank them for the meal and finally depart. Still sitting at the table, now with Arthur back in his arms, Burt yawns and glances at Lola. "The meal was so delicious, dear. *Your genius shows,"* he says, softening his voice to try and reach her.

"Thank you," she manages, barely above a whisper. She begins taking the plates from the table. "You go. I'll be right down."

Bertrand nods, the familiar knot in his stomach returning to life as he rises and takes Arthur from his highchair. He opens his mouth to say something but closes it before slowly turning away and heading off towards the theater room.

∞ ∞ ∞

Rather than venturing to explore the rest of his Moscow mansion, Altan feels a magnetic pull towards his own private office - his sanctuary of thought, creation, and solitude. A towering stack of boxes stands as a visual reminder of the task awaiting him, an organizational endeavor to reclaim a semblance of control.

He steps into the room, the sheer sight of unopened boxes overwhelming him, and he lets out a deep, contemplative sigh before downing the rest of his scotch and setting the glass on the only part of his desk free of clutter. Summoning his inner strength, he is determined to set about tackling this seemingly Herculean task. A built-in bookshelf graces one wall, adorned with a sizable flatscreen TV. Altan's gaze locks onto the television screen.

"I need some background noise," he mutters to himself, seeking a distraction, if only for a moment, from the weight of his thoughts.

Amidst the organized chaos on his desk, Altan locates the remote and clicks it softly. The TV comes to life, bathing the room in a soft, blue-green glow. A news report exposé is underway, delving into the nuclear capabilities of various nations – the US, Russia, Iran, and North Korea. As the headline at the bottom of the screen flies by almost too fast to read, its words raise doubts about the true nature of the weapons programs in China and India. Altan's expression darkens with concern.

When the music and the flashing graphics fade away, a newsroom appears buzzing with activity. The air is thick with tension, palpable even through the glass. Reporters rush around, their expressions a mosaic of urgency and fear. Among them stands the anchor, a seasoned journalist with a strong facade that barely masks worry in her eyes. She begins to speak, her voice steady but with a tremor of anxiety.

"Good evening. This is a breaking news update. As we reported earlier, we are closely monitoring the situation regarding the maneuvering of nuclear

troops and equipment across several nations. While we have no solid reports of any direct conflicts, we've been informed of ongoing discussions amidst these weapon advancements." She tries to smile but it looks more hideous than comforting. *"It's important to remember that our global leaders are always working tirelessly towards peaceful resolutions to any potential global concern."*

As Altan observes the reporter, he focuses on her poise until he notices other details that betray her composure. Her tailored navy-blue suit, usually immaculate, is slightly disheveled, and there are alarming beads of sweat glistening on her forehead. The reporter continues, her words now casting a shadow in the office.

"Recent intelligence suggests that nations are strengthening their capabilities, but these measures are purely precautionary. It's a reaffirmation of their commitment to peace and stability so there is no cause for alarm as diplomacy remains our mainstay."

At that moment, Altan's worry intensifies. He knows well the delicate dance of words, the art of propaganda. The gap between the carefully constructed narrative and the unsettling truth is crystal clear to him. He envisions a future where Elena will grow up in a world of veiled threats and manufactured reassurances. The weight of his own helplessness presses down on him. As a father and a scientist, he yearns for a safer world, but grapples with the realization that the very projects he contributes to might be feeding into instability.

He knows he has to keep pushing for a better future, a world where his daughter can grow up without the looming threat of nuclear conflict. This is the idealistic hope which drives him, fuels his relentless pursuit of progress. He hopes that his efforts, and the efforts of many others, will eventually tip the scale towards peace and security. But at this moment, the news report reflects the immense challenges that lie ahead, and the glistening forehead of the news anchor is like a crack in Pandora's box. The reflection of light he sees there suddenly and immediately informs him of the utter simplicity of just how instantaneously, without any warning, the dangerous and precarious world could all at once, and altogether, *cease to exist.*

"My God, how can it not happen at this rate?" he whispers to himself, grappling with the dire implications of his intuitive conclusions. Altan takes a deep breath, channeling his resolve, and chooses to turn away from the greater madness and instead confront the chaos within his office. It's more than just a need for order; it's his way of exerting some semblance of power in a world that he fears is slipping beyond anyone's grasp. He starts by carefully peeling the tape from the top of the first box. In his life, fraught with so many impossible challenges as with the world itself, he is determined to make sense of the immediate turmoil that surrounds him in the very least.

∞ ∞ ∞

Six months later, every seat in the Conference Hall of the Kremlin Palace is filled, and many well-dressed men and women stand packed in and around the sides of the room for the show. With its high vaulted ceilings above and white stone archways with grand columns running down the sides of the room, it feels like a night at the royal opera. Even the box seats teem with excited academics there to witness something which until tonight had only been rumored to exist. Altan feels that he has the best seat in the house, hidden backstage away from the crowds, on the other side of a giant projector screen. He holds Elena in his arms and rocks her from side to side. He hates that she is dressed up like a doll in the red and white traditional clothes of the Russian folk tradition.

If everything is done correctly, she will remain unaware of the magnitude of her surroundings, and Altan welcomes the rare circumstance wherein he finds himself responsible for nothing. Everything is in the hands of Kira and her team of government scientists. Altan watches her in awe, a vision of beauty and power in her all-white pantsuit, pacing back and forth in rapid strides and issuing orders to her subordinates as her hands trace graceful commands into the air like an orchestral conductor. She turns to him and claps her hands together.

"We will need the belle of the ball now, Altan, if you will," she speaks to him in a pleasant tone, not unlike the voice she uses at home, although Altan can clearly detect just the tiniest presence of disquiet. *So, she does get nervous sometimes.*

"Can I help with anything?" he asks, but he already knows the answer, and Kira just smiles blankly at him as he hands Elena over. Kira gently places Elena in a modified highchair and secures her there, then checks her watch on her left hand and gestures to another two assistants. These two come around to either side of the highchair and, lifting it up off the ground, follow Kira with it around to the other side of the stage, beneath the hot spotlights there. The crowd erupts into ecstatic applause.

As the noise dies down, Kira speaks. "Esteemed guests of the Russian Psychological Society, thank you for your warm welcome. Please take your seats if you can find them. We are going to begin the presentation immediately." Elena sits with her back to the audience, facing the same giant projector screen as Kira, and in front of her a few feet away sits a video camera pointed directly at both of them. Behind her, the feed from this camera appears on another screen pointed towards the audience so that the psychologists, viewing the smaller screen and the larger screen simultaneously, may watch the face of the child who is watching the same film as everyone else in the room. As the overhead lights are dimmed, Elena's face may clearly be seen, and the room fills with excited murmurs as the psychologists comment to each other on her appearance.

Kira smiles at the audience and then extends her hand in Elena's direction. "We present to you, Elena Vasilisa, one of the star candidates of our fledgling program for the advanced development of Russian youth!" Everyone in the crowd bursts into cheering and applause, and though Kira motions for them to quiet down, the sound continues for almost thirty seconds before finally dying off again. Many eyes in the room glisten with tears, and a few fancy handkerchiefs are applied throughout as Kira continues. "None of us knows the future of our world, though we know that it is our children and our grandchildren who must face it. We know that they will contend with a world beyond our imaginings, and we want them to succeed in all the areas we have failed."

Kira glances at Elena to ascertain that her eyes are open and that she is comfortable yet alert, which she is, and thus Kira continues, "For this, we are developing new systems of pediatric therapy that will eclipse the need for traditional medicine. We are developing new systems of childhood development and education that will wash away our historical forms of learning and testing. And in the harmony of the marriage of these two schools, we present to you now our most recent iteration of the Infant Patterning System developed in tandem by the Ministry of Enlightenment and the Ministry of Civil Defense!"

As the crowd applauds once more, the lights dim further, and the projector screen comes to life. The image of a brilliant, rising sun lights up the room, and Tchaikovsky's first piano concerto lifts the audience into a familiar ecstasy. Elena's eyes focus on the same beautiful picture that she has seen every day of her life. Her pure smile melts the glaciers within the coldest hearts of those present.

From the right-wing backstage behind the curtains, Altan observes and since nobody is watching him, he shakes his head. *Elena will be a light unto the whole world while her thousands of brothers and sisters wait frozen in cryogenic purgatory as embryos within government vaults where the temperature sits at -196°C and time has stopped. They dwell in a perpetual state of being unborn while my darling Elena must carry their banner into the world of the living. Who is better off?*

∞ ∞ ∞

The Promising Bud of Roses

Chapter Four

Growing Pains

∞ ∞ ∞

2022 –

Arthur's bedroom is a strange mixture of Colonial-era library meets aeronautical museum. Two walls are filled with bookshelves which have rows of encyclopedias from the twentieth century, novels by everyone from Isaac Asimov to William Golding, one complete wall-to-wall shelf filled with National Geographic magazines, and separate areas for academic books on philosophy, psychology, physics, space, and the rocket sciences. His walls have posters of Einstein, Mars, a black hole, and several others with photos of outer space, and the ceiling above is lit with a dark purple lamp directed at it which illuminates the stars he had hand-painted there himself.

Now all of twelve years of age, especially during his sleep, he still retains a rather youthful boyish appearance beneath his incredibly handsome and masculine features, and going along with the childlike theme, he customarily still sleeps in the fetal position. Lola thought it adorable to check in on him during the night to see him lying in that position, clad only in underwear above the covers of the King-sized bed, his knees curled up to his chest and even many times sucking his thumb, of all things. To her, it is always oddly peaceful seeing him like that – like watching a baby asleep in his crib, despite his maturity. Burt, on the other hand, did not find it nearly as amusing.

Having heard a news report earlier in the evening during the newscast on TV recounting increasing tensions between China and Taiwan, Ukraine and Russia at war, terrorists in the Middle East being armed to the gills with abandoned American military weaponry, and the idea that the world was teetering on a new world war, Arthur went to bed with deep concerns about mankind's penchant for violence. If he wasn't so exhausted from the rigorous exercises during the collaborative training regimen which he had been made to participate in during school earlier in the day, he probably would not have fallen asleep at all. Lying in the fetal position in his bed, his body suddenly grows rigid in a startling manner even as he sleeps. From his fetal position, he rolls onto his back with his arms stiffening at his sides.

In his dream, he sees banks of computers lining walls with Asian operators at their consoles frantically typing away giving commands. This segues into vague glimpses of both Russian and American military commanders with shocked expressions and grave concern adorning their faces, as they watch their strategic wall maps light up with white icons representing incoming missiles shooting across the oceans. In his bed, his body begins to shake and convulse, and he soon begins panting like a terrorized dog running away from a hungry bear. Beneath his clenched eyelids, his eyeballs rapidly zip back and forth and then up and down in a continuous cycle of REM.

As the military commanders on both sides simultaneously order the buttons to be pushed, he falls into a desperate whimper until finally sweat accumulates across his forehead and tears are running down his cheeks. He tells himself to wake up as he knows he is having a nightmare, but his body won't listen to the commands his brain is sending. He grabs a pillow and struggles with it, finally trying to hide his head beneath it as he sees bright white flashes across the entire globe. He then erupts with extreme agitation, his entire body seized in what would appear to be a convulsive seizure. Then, just as suddenly it locks in total stillness, not even his diaphragm moves, nor do his lungs take in oxygen.

In his dream, he is now flying just above the ground across an ashed-out planet held within the arms of an angel of God, or perhaps of Death itself, carrying him across the world to witness what has just occurred. He pleads to be allowed to awaken but gets no response. He sees nothing but the smoldering ashes of bodies and vast destruction, with bright burning flames where huge cities once stood. As he turns to see who is carrying him….

Finally, and abruptly, his eyes open and he gasps out loud, clutching at his throat and inhaling desperately in order to fill his lungs with air. He is still uncertain where he is or whether he is safe, and he automatically scoots himself against the wall at the head of the bed, tucking his knees inside his folded arms. He starts to get his bearings and seems relieved, but then puts his head on his knees, defeated, and softly starts to cry.

When morning finally comes, Arthur skips breakfast and rushes to get to school on time. The day passes drearily, and he continuously sees flashes of tidbits from his nightmare. He does not know what is worse - seeing the moment of certainty that the buttons were being pushed or knowing that it had all been started as a scam orchestrated by Artificial Intelligence.

Later in the morning, a single set of red running shoes pounds the blue rubberized track, long after the rest of the boys have gone inside. On his sixth mile, Arthur is working out the frustrations that he can't seem to express in any other way. The high walls of the inner courtyard are there to protect him from the confusion of the outside world, but as his mind expands beyond any bounds his handlers can imagine, those walls only ever seem to close in upon him. The shrill concern expressed at him from almost every direction had begun to annoy Arthur so much, and a perception began to crystallize within his mind: *that there is nowhere he can run and hide, that he is helpless to express his own will in a society that claims to provide every freedom, but which for him prescribes a specific course.* Against the willpower of nations, the will of a boy is nothing, and so Arthur has learned to bury his own dreams in a hidden place in the back of his mind, rendering them a secret to everyone, and over time a mystery even to himself.

The Pentagon had written a blank check, and a completely new educational academy had been founded to accommodate the rapidly changing context of the project. A new team of child psychologists and educational academics were called in to design a special developmental curriculum, and for the first time, the *Genesis Executive* project had opened itself to interface with the civilian world. This was much unlike the vast, joint undertaking in the South Pacific, which required a constant military blockade around a circumference of thirty miles to prevent intruders from spying. Here in Virginia, they were hiding a state secret in plain sight, an academy billed to the public as an elementary West Point specifically designed to train America's future astronauts. Naming it the *American Sky School, the motto CENTRE USQUE AD COELO, Latin for "From the Center to the Sky",* was chosen to represent its goals.

With all the creative genius of a single-celled organism, the architecture of the school had been designed as a Pentagon in miniature, each wing holding a separate grade level to keep them compartmentalized. Arthur is halfway through his second year, and his cohort of fifteen classmates had all been through the program with him from the start, but he feels as though he is alone, and so he runs in circles. The wings of the Eagle are bearing down on Arthur with a velocity that makes them seem unkind, and even dangerous.

His father always speaks of the future, *as though he knows what will happen.* The great question – why – which, like a skeleton key that could swing wide every door of knowledge, had led Arthur to barred entries with no keyholes and only unanswerable questions which had become like massive, vaulted gates that guarded the greatest prizes of the truth he wished to understand. These seemed hidden behind doors which could only be opened from the inside. At first, like every child, Arthur believed that his parents would open those doors for him, but there were things they didn't want to say, and there were things that they couldn't even know themselves. Sensing a hidden reality locked away between his parents' real and feigned ignorance, Arthur had developed an intuition that could see through almost every deception.

He had learned by the age of three that his parents were sometimes truly unknowing, and from this he began to apply natural skepticism to any of their claims. Because he had sensed that they were willing to mislead him on certain topics, he unconsciously began to project that distrust outwards at the entire world, cloaking his perception of society behind the shadow of his parents.

All of these dark realizations Arthur keeps to himself, the evidence of his internal crisis evaporating from his forehead as he finishes jogging his seventh mile. Within his inner sanctuary he keeps himself pure in the light of his conscience, and to Bertrand's frequent dismay, this hidden world so often appears to be a complete inversion of the one he is trying to teach to his son. Where he encourages Arthur to be bold in his interactions with his classmates, Arthur retreats into meekness. Where Bertrand implores Arthur to establish his thinking in timeless truths and powerful ideals, Arthur takes every monolithic concept into himself and casts them back out with the fiercest rejection.

Even as Bertrand teaches Arthur to eat a meat-heavy diet so that his body will grow strong, Arthur had committed himself to becoming fully vegan, and when questioned on this, Arthur had offered proof to his father in the form of peer-reviewed studies showing that the same fitness results could be achieved without *"murdering millions of innocents to satisfy human taste buds."* He knew his father had grown to fear that his input was nothing more than a relic of Arthur's past. As the years had gone by, he knew his father felt that his entire purpose in his son's life had become wasted, as so much of what he tried to teach him, Arthur dismissed as merely information passed down from on high through the invisible chain of command. He knows that his father still hopes that he will have a crucial role to play in his life, and that one day he will be there when Arthur finally decides that he wants some good, old-fashioned, fatherly advice.

Glancing down at the fitness tracker on his wrist, the little screen ticks over from ten miles to eleven. He seems bored by this accomplishment and so finds a fresh spurt and sprints for a mile more before finally slowing off his running pace. He watches a bright white cloud in the shape of a large arc, like a gateway to the heavens, pass over the late morning sun as he continues walking around the track. Looking from a window on the second floor, Bertrand and Lola look down into the courtyard as Arthur begins to walk his cooldown laps.

"This is the boy who is supposed to grow up and face the impossible, and he doesn't even want to make eye contact with himself in the mirror when he brushes his teeth," Bertrand laments, wringing his hands together. "Lola, we can't turn him into a sissy. He doesn't even want to compete with the other students, *and he needs to man up!"*

"He's not a sissy. These are his years to be innocent," Lola says, trying to keep her voice down, her dramatic inflection taking the place of a volume increase. "He's a child so stop expecting him to man up, *whatever that even means.* And he didn't say he didn't want to compete. He simply said he preferred only to compete against himself. You think that's immature and weird. But I think it's lovely. Lovely that his heart isn't interested in beating other people."

Burt begins shouting. *"Lovely? Lovely?!"* Lola raises her eyebrows, and he calms down before continuing. "He's asking questions that even I don't want to know the answers to. He needs to start taking responsibility for the gravity of some of these ideas of his and to start embracing the very special situation that he's in."

A mortified look takes hold of Lola's expression. "You wanted a genius, and now you have one! An athlete? Now you have that, too. He's a chess champion. A poet. A painter and a sculptor. My God, the only thing he can't do is please you. *What else do you want?!"*

She sees by the expression on her husband's face that she has won this battle for now, and she feels affirmed that Burt looks sufficiently defeated. Her tone becomes just a bit more conciliatory as she continues, "It's not all fun and science games with a child, Burt. We talked about this at length before I agreed to be a part of this program. He's my child first and foremost beyond any of the goals the program may have, and frankly, I'm tired of having to remind you of that. When was the last time you saw him smile? How long has it been?"

Burt sighs. "Truly, it's probably been since before all of his night terrors. Not since he was four.... And I canceled his video stimulation sessions to help with his night terrors when you asked, didn't I?"

"Too little too late," she says in a commanding tone of voice. "Guess what? I'm taking over for a bit."

His forehead suddenly lines with creases as he stares directly into her bloodshot eyes. "Oh, really? I am his father, you know?"

"No," she responds adamantly. "Not until you begin to act like a father. For now, you are just his *super kid coach.* When you can start acting like a father, you can have a say again."

Burt groans and pivots to walk away, but then he turns back to look at his wife. Arthur had undergone a complete behavior shift suddenly at the age of four after the series of nightmares that went on every night for three weeks, and since then they had been having these severe disagreements over Arthur's upbringing. The doctors had called them night-terrors, and they explained that it was a common byproduct of childhood stress. What made Arthur's case unique was that he remembered every detail of his dreams upon waking up, and then held those ideas in his mind throughout the day which seemed to have somehow scarred his psyche. At that point, the decision had been made to completely cancel the video stimulation sessions, a year before they were due to be finished, and to pull back in many ways from the more invasive elements of Arthur's programmed upbringing. It had only been due to Lola's advocacy, which was supported by civilian psychologists, that Arthur was essentially given a year sabbatical from the rigors of his life, and though he did not understand it, it turned out that Arthur's tiny willpower had snuffed the gears of the massive machinery that were to solely dictate his future.

He wants to talk to her about all of these things and to, once more, try making sense of everything, but it is of no use, so he shakes his head at her then turns back again and walks away down the hall, clearly tired of the same old conversation.

∞ ∞ ∞

From the moment she could walk and talk, Elena seemed to know exactly what she wanted, and it continually surprises everyone involved in the project, as each year seems to advance her thinking beyond any of their wildest speculations. Her interest in technology is increasingly deconstructive, and through her use of the Internet she constantly pushes beyond the structures of a system designed to help her excel. Due to her relentless dedication to research, there had been some worry that she would suffer in her social development with other people, but this concern was quickly overturned, as Elena was both naturally gregarious and socially curious. She researches on her own, and almost everything she seeks after has to do with people. When she studies ecology, it is from a position of interest in human dietetics and sustainable living. Her interest in physics and mathematics overlaps with medicine, sociology, and political science.

Still, when she had begged them to buy her an American bulldog, they had given in and gotten her a puppy, which she had named Sofia and from whom she was now completely inseparable. Kira had resisted, but Altan explained that it would help anchor Elena's perception in the real world, potentially deepening her emotional field. The strangeness of her upbringing didn't appear to have created any imbalance in her personality, something that was chalked up to her idealized genetic makeup, but they still want to provide her with every possible aid to her development.

She is very much her father's daughter, as he communicates in the logical patterns that she best understands. He elucidates what she is unable to discover on her own. Elena's relationship with Kira is one of loving rivalry, as Kira naturally interprets Elena's questions as a challenge to the power structure, Kira's personal power most of all. She thus responds to Elena's questions with her own questions, which Elena regards as a battle of wits. It seems to be good for both of them. But Altan often worries that Kira feels left out of the parenting process.

Elena's great revelation comes to her as a beautiful dream rather than a series of nightmares, and her first existential crises began early upon realizing that she won't always be a child. The solution presented itself all at once one afternoon, when after educating herself about every detail of human development from conception to cremation, she came to fully believe that she had the power to craft herself in her own image. For months now, Kira and Altan had been planting the seeds in her mind of dedicating to a more formal path of education, so Elena knows that they are preparing to send her out of her home and into some unknown environment, the world of people. For this reason, she has begun to develop an alternative plan for herself, a secret that she is waiting to reveal until just the right moment.

In the heart of their Barvikha Villa, the dining room exudes an elegant allure, bathed in a soft, ethereal glow emanating from a grand chandelier above. The luminescent masterpiece hangs from the ceiling like a constellation of crystalline stars, each flickering light a tiny faerie in a dance of radiance. As the lights gently sway, they cast a warm and enchanting ambiance, painting the room with a magical glow.

At the polished dinner table, Elena, the epitome of burgeoning youth at all twelve years of age, graces the space with her presence. Her attire, a delicate frock in pastel hues, perfectly complement her blooming adolescence. The soft fabric, adorned with a subtle floral pattern, cascades gracefully, mirroring the budding beauty that now defines her. Her hair, a cascade of golden waves, frames a face that reflects the innocence of childhood yet hints at the wisdom of approaching womanhood. The gentle curve of her smile embodies the promise of the remarkable woman she is becoming.

As the family finishes their meal, Luda, a neatly dressed young Russian woman in her mid-30's, quietly steps into the dining room. She exudes an air of quiet sophistication, her attire a tailored charcoal suit with subtle pinstripes, reflecting meticulousness and precision. The monochrome palette of grays and blacks complements her composed personality, masking with subtle tones her dual role in this household. On the surface, she is the meticulous caretaker, overseeing Elena's growth with a nurturing touch. Beneath that veneer lies her clandestine identity – an undercover operative, a Kremlin spy intricately woven into the enigma of the Genesis project. Her watchful eyes, seemingly gentle and caring, conceal a deeper allegiance to a world of political intrigue and cutting-edge science.

Altan's face lights up with a warm smile at her arrival, acknowledging her essential role in their household. Kira, immersed in her thoughts and plans, scarcely acknowledges Luda. Her focus remains steadfast on Elena, the heart of her attention. Meanwhile, Elena's attention is divided between her dinner and the faithful bulldog, Sophia, the pearly white little monster nestled beside her chair whom she reaches down to stroke affectionately behind the ears.

With a melodious clang, Kira carefully places her silverware down and clasps her hands together. She attempts to adopt a motherly tone. "So, dear... have you made any decisions about schools?" Kira inquires gently.

In response, Elena's eyes widen with excitement, and she nods vigorously before darting out of the room. Sophia scrambles after her, her red painted toenails frantically scraping across the wood floor as she runs to keep up.

Altan and Kira's eyes meet in a fleeting yet charged exchange, brimming with both hope and concern. In Altan's gaze, a spark of optimism battles with uncertainty, painting a portrait of his trust in Elena's choices. Conversely, Kira's furrowed brow mirrors her apprehension, a worry for Elena's swift metamorphosis and the enigmatic path she seems hellbent on continuing down. Moments later Elena returns, brimming with enthusiasm.

"I'm so happy you asked!" Elena exclaims, her face glowing with excitement. "I've prepared copies of my educational agenda for the next five years!"

She proudly reveals a stack of papers from a black folio, then separating them into three paperclipped bundles, hands the matching packets over to her parents, with one included for Luda as well. Flipping through the educational agenda, a burst of whimsy and ambitious dreams, Altan and Luda find themselves nodding and occasionally laughing, clearly enamored by the kaleidoscope of Elena's aspirations. Altan, with a positive yet tempered expression, admires the blend of childhood fantasies and serious goals, a reflection of her voracious appetite for knowledge. Intricate flowcharts map out fantastical dreams, envisioning Elena as a fairy princess in a castle, and then transition seamlessly into more pragmatic pursuits like studying robotics, hydroponic gardening, and experimental surgery.

However, as Kira examines the pages, her countenance takes a different shade. Perplexity clouds her features, knitting her brows and deepening the lines etched by concern. The array of ambitions unfolding before her carves crevices of worry into her forehead, and she teeters on its precipice. The weight of Elena's dreams, a fusion of the extraordinary and the pragmatic, appears to teeter on this edge. It's as if Kira's face might collapse into those furrows between her eyebrows were it not for Elena's timely interruption.

"So, Robotics… it's plainly clear that in the future, some people will want to have robotic wings so that they can fly, or robotic hearts so that they can live longer, or robotic legs so that they can walk around when they get old," Elena passionately explains. "I will learn to develop and install this type of technology, and since there are no general education programs for robotics, I have researched some tutors who will come and teach me at home. All the important work will need to be conducted in laboratories. We couldn't bring all of the machines into the house. It just wouldn't go with the decor." With the last line, she casts a sideways glance at her mother and flashes a playful smirk.

Kira closes her eyes and just quietly echoes, "it just wouldn't go with the decor," turning to stare outside, through the floor-to-ceiling windows, forever into the distance. Altan had begun laughing halfway through her little speech, while Luda, with a keen interest, observes this family exchange, her eyes reflecting a mix of intrigue, skepticism, and admiration.

"My sweet girl, doesn't this all sound like a lot of work?" Luda interjects gently, voicing a concern that looms beneath the surface.

"Yes, my darling, what's the rush with all this? In five years, you'll only be seventeen years old and smarter than most PhDs on the planet," Altan adds, a hint of fatherly concern coloring his voice.

Kira shoots them both a look, silently disapproving of their attempts to introduce more playtime into Elena's life. However, Elena, in her youthful conviction, remains resolute.

"Papa, Luda, we live on an amazing planet! It would take me ten lifetimes to learn everything there is to learn about Mother Earth. But there are other planets, too. With things that we can't even imagine," Elena articulates, her eyes sparkling with a fervor for discovery.

"I want to go to those places. I need to pick the topics I expect will be the most useful in space and on other planets and for people traveling vast distances who may need help in a foreign environment. I am more than ready to commit to a life of learning!"

In the silence that follows, Altan grins as he looks back and forth between Elena and Luda. Finally, Kira turns away from the window and heaves a sigh as she releases some of her concern.

"That's excellent, Elena. Excellent," Kira manages with a smile, thinking of Elena's ambition as a positive aspect of an otherwise undesirable scenario.

Altan adds, "And we'll help you find time for play and rest."

Elena nods, the conversation finished as far as she is concerned. Ever compassionate, she picks up her silverware and studies her plate of food. She hesitates before taking a bite for herself, instead cutting a healthy portion of meat for her beloved Sophia.

"Feed yourself first, baby," Altan gently reminds her.

Elena, however, insists, "No, papa. Feed the hungriest first. Sophia is much hungrier than I am."

"Elena, do as your father tells you. Feed yourself first. We've discussed this so many times," Kira states firmly.

Elena looks at Kira, examining her, and then calmly asserts, "Yes, we have. And I thought I made my position very clear the last time. The hungriest eat first."

Kira, holding back her desire to argue, puts down her cutlery, takes her napkin from her lap, and throws it on the table. She rises and leaves without a word. Elena watches her walk away, cutting another piece of meat for Sophia before finally taking a bite herself. The faithful bulldog stands by Elena's side, her tail wagging with contentment. Altan and Luda share a secret smirk, reveling in the strange dynamics of the family and the fascinating path Elena is carving towards her future.

Once Kira is gone, Altan finally speaks. "Bravo, Elena. Of course, you've thought it all through." He could show her nothing but support, for though her imagination was the stuff of a young girl's fantasy, she had chosen to develop along the exact path they had designed for her. It was never intended to place her in a school. She was the crown jewel of the Kremlin, and her genetic propensity for autonomy was only a tiny facet of a massive collaborative design almost forty years in the making. Those who pulled the strings could trust no single person with Elena's fate, certainly not herself, but they knew that she must believe that she pulled her own strings, or all might fail.

∞　∞　∞

"Think of it like camping!" Bertrand had tried to encourage Arthur, though even Bertrand didn't believe this mischaracterization of Arthur's upcoming school field trip. Arthur sits at the desk in his room with his arms crossed and just looks at him, *looks through him*, and tries to imagine what the purpose of such an activity might be. "It's a field trip, buddy. Field trips are fun!"

Now Arthur sends him a look expressing the idea that his father had just lost his mind. "Fun? It isn't going to be fun."

"Well, you like camping, at least I thought you did. Just think of it like camping!"

"People bring food, water, and shelter when they go camping. They won't be giving us any of that. This is not going to be at all like camping."

Burt isn't finished yet. "OK, think of it as a challenge. You'll get to employ all of the knowledge you've learned at the academy. You'll get to cooperate with the other boys for survival. Ten days out in the wilderness; doesn't that sound... interesting?"

Arthur shakes his head, then brings each of his index fingers to its respective temple and presses firmly. Enjoyment was out of the question, but maybe he could make it useful. They were sending all fifteen boys into the Chattahoochee National Forest without food, water, or any sort of shelter. *Does that sound fun to some people?* The assignment seemed absurd to Arthur: armed with only their pocket-knives, hatchets, and magnesium fire-starters, they were told that they would use the knowledge they had developed over the past two years at the academy to cooperate and survive in the woods for ten days. *It would be interesting if it were more challenging. Couldn't we build a permanent outpost out there?*

Arthur was aware of all of the necessary safety nets that were going to be put in place: the boys were to be dropped only a mile from a pristine river, there was determined to be adequate food for foraging in the form of mushrooms, hazelnuts, wild berries, and fruiting trees, and they had been given two weeks' heads up to study maps of the area and prepare however they deemed fit. *It sounds like the most challenging part of this is going to be dealing with everyone else. Can I bring something to read?*

Lola has been standing at the door to his room, silently watching as Burt has been trying to convince Arthur of the benefits of this school trip. Finally, she decides she will add a little bit of her own encouragement. She tries to entice him by saying, "Arthur, you can think of this as a chance to become closer to some of your friends at the school."

Arthur looks up at Lola. They all know that he has not been successful in that arena thus far, and although he likes the idea of making friends, this endeavor has so far eluded him, and he has gotten nowhere. "Let's face it, Mom, I'm no good at it, and that's all there is to it. I try in my own way. Especially at school I've tried, and it's just not working out. Trust me, I am better off being alone."

Lola strides towards the bed and stops just adjacent to Arthur. "Nobody's better alone, honey. Not all the time, anyway." She gives him her bright smile meant to disarm him. "The thing with making friends *is not to try*. Be yourself. You are very likable as who you are already – I know this!"

"I'm not so convinced, Mom. Maybe with certain adults…."

Burt rolls his eyes impatiently, catching Arthur's attention. *"Arthur, you're going and that's all there is to it. Your assignment is not to have an assignment at all and to simply survive. Can you do that? It's only a few days for God's sake!"* He finishes by staring daggers at Arthur, and then he strides out of the room, leaving Arthur feeling misunderstood once again. As usual, Lola comes to his rescue by approaching him and stroking his cheek.

To begin with, Arthur only attended these special collaborative sessions in field training at the school with the other boys *because he was given no choice*, but in her gentle way, Lola had played on his beneficent and empathetic nature, opening his eyes to the possibility that he would be helpful to the rest of his cohort if some of their plans failed. While many of the collaborative sessions were highly charged conversations about how to build traps or weapons and hunt big game, Arthur brought to each meeting his own models of various primitive shelters, copies of manuals for local edible and medicinal plant identification, and ideas for how they might conserve energy during these sessions while remaining moderately entertained. *Someone might as well do their homework.*

The other boys are well-bred enough to tolerate Arthur, and they appreciate all the work that he does so that they don't have to, but none of them quite understand his implicit mannerisms; it only bothers Arthur a little bit that his peculiar personality has rendered him the outsider among them. *The world is a multiplayer game, so I'm going to participate, but on my own level, not theirs.* Unbeknownst to any of the boys, because the project was too sensitive and the subjects too precious to entrust to fate and a *Lord of the Flies* possibility, another set of precautions had been secretly put in place. The campsite was rigged with twenty closed circuit spy cameras so that every action and word of the boys could be observed and analyzed. Bertrand finally got to feel included as well, as he was to captain a group of five army rangers who were to be posted in hiding at the perimeter to step in in case anything went awry.

"It is only a few days, honey," Lola finally says. "I really think you'll be glad you did this trip once it's all said and done."

"I dunno," Arthur responds.

"Hey – we'll make a deal. If you really hate it, you can always come home early." She nods at him and smiles reassuringly once again, and it seems to give him some strength.

"You promise? You'll tell them that if I give the word that I'm through, that they must take me home?"

"Promise!" Lola says, pinching him on the cheek.

He's tired of fighting with them and even more than that, he has grown tired of constantly disappointing his father. "Okay, Mom, I'll go."

Over the next few days, Arthur thinks of all the ways he can disappoint the other boys who are going on the trip. *I am not going to try being their friend, and I am not going to sacrifice my own integrity just because they are so shallow and limited!* If he was being forced into this, *it would be on his own terms*, and he would ensure his own comfort and survival despite the others being present and within his vicinity. On the night before they are to be dropped off, Arthur takes a permanent marker and covers his body in diagrams of the most important plants to forage or to avoid, lists of details he wants to remember about staying dry and warm if it rained, and on his thighs, he draws a rudimentary map of the entire area. He would make himself an expert of this silly exercise, whether he was truly valued or not.

Growing Pains

∞ ∞ ∞

In the heart of Moscow, a sunbeam-flooded dance studio envelops Elena in a tender embrace as she spins across the floor of her ballet class. Dressed in her elegant white tutu, she embodies the ideal grace and poise of a girl on the eve of womanhood. Every movement she executes is a balletic poem, each pirouette a testament to her dedication and skill, seemingly infused with an ethereal essence that emanates from the depths of her being.

Around her, fellow classmates in matching attire mirror Elena's movements, their bodies trained and disciplined, yet lacking the ineffable quality that graces Elena's every step. Their dance is a result of meticulous training, an artful mimicry acquired through endless hours of practice. Their grace, while apparent, feels shaped and honed, the product of a lifetime of ballet but not much else.

In contrast, Elena's elegance seems to flow from a wellspring within - a natural gift that has been nurtured and refined through her training. Her arabesques are brushstrokes, painting a story of passion and longing with each extension. Her pliés hold a depth of emotion, as if the very ground she touches feels her yearning for the heavens.

While Elena effortlessly executes each move flawlessly, a subtle struggle tinges the faces of her classmates. In their eyes, a mix of awe and frustration brews, reflecting the silent realization of the gap between their efforts and Elena's seemingly effortless mastery. It's a testament to the dichotomy of ballet - a delicate dance between discipline and artistry, hard-won skill, and intrinsic brilliance.

As the class concludes, the vibrant energy in the sunlit studio lingers, tinged with both camaraderie and competitive zeal. Elena, a ray of warmth and determination, approaches her classmates, eager to bridge the growing divide. Through the expansive windows, the afternoon sun paints streaks of gold across the sky, illuminating the iconic silhouette of Moscow's cityscape.

In the center of the sun-kissed studio, the girls huddle in a circle, their animated voices shrill and sharp like a flock of jungle parrots. Natalia, a lithe and expressive dancer with a crown of russet hair, exudes an air of quiet confidence that borders on skepticism. The eldest of the group, her eyes swirl with stormy gray as she maintains a searching gaze, wary of the intentions of those around her.

Beside Natalia stands Sonya, a statuesque ballerina with a regal posture. Her movements are deliberate and precise, albeit too fierce for the delicate art, reflecting an anger beneath the surface that fuels her pursuit of the dance. Her dark, wavy hair frames a face that maintains a deceivingly aloof expression, adding an enigmatic air to her allure.

Elena, with her unwavering passion and determination, is ever an outsider entering their figurative and literal circle. Her presence brings a sense of brightness and hope, but it also underscores the divide that sets her apart. She approaches the group, her heart a blend of eagerness and trepidation, hoping to dissolve the walls that seem to separate her from her fellow dancers.

"You were all absolutely splendid today!" Elena cheers, her eyes sparkling with genuine admiration.

However, Natalia, quick to confront her, skepticism tainting her expression, retorts, "Why do you persist in trying to befriend us, Elena? It seems like you relish making us look inadequate."

Elena, stung by the implication, immediately steps forward to defend her intentions. "I promise you, that's not true. I genuinely want to be your friend," she replies earnestly, the hurt clear in her eyes. "I'm not a *natural* ballerina like all of you. I just work *incredibly hard* at this. Perhaps we could practice together sometime outside of class?"

Sonya's face contorts into a cruel, mocking expression. *"Oh, I work really hard at this,"* she mimics in a taunting, high-pitched voice, causing a ripple of laughter among the other girls. "You think we don't work hard? Ignorant little princess," she sneers, punctuating the laughter. "Your friends are Madame Borishkin, your nerd father, and that weirdo aunt of yours. It's best you stick with what you know, *freak.*" The studio falls into a moment of harsh silence, Sonya's cruelty striking everyone dumb. One by one, the girls file out of the room without a word.

Left standing alone, her expression reflecting both humiliation and loneliness, Elena's spirit falters. The golden glow of the sun begins to dim, its warmth unable to reach the chill that has settled within her. The shadows in the studio seem to lengthen, matching the heaviness in her heart. The laughter of the girls lingers like a bitter aftertaste, a reminder of the jagged edges of competition.

However, amidst this cold atmosphere, a kind-hearted soul named Erika tip-toes back into the room. Of all Elena's classmates, Erika is the most like her: a gentle girl who feels the dance rather than thinking, her movements echoing the fluidity of a gentle stream. Her eyes, a soft hazel reminiscent of autumn leaves, hold a comforting warmth that mirrors the light in Elena's own gaze. As she approaches, she extends a towel to Elena, a simple yet significant act of compassion that breathes life back into Elena's hope.

"Don't worry about them," Erika reassures, her voice a gentle breeze that sweeps away the suffocating silence. A genuine smile, mirroring Elena's own, brightens her face like a sudden burst of warmth. "I've danced with them since I could walk. They don't practice, and then they are angry when they don't improve. I'd be happy to practice with you, Elena, any time!"

Elena's countenance undergoes a transformation, like a bud unfurling under the first rays of spring. Her eyes, once clouded with hurt and doubt, now shine with a newfound glimmer of hope. In Erika, she discovers a kindred spirit amidst the sea of judgment - a friend whose radiance matches her own, illuminating the darkness and igniting a beacon of friendship. Erika's gentle smile, so genuine and radiant, is a testament to the power of finding beauty and compassion in unexpected places.

Nature sings the tale of flawless genetics in various forms, etching beauty across life's tapestry, from a butterfly's wings to a flower's bloom. Yet, within the human soul, true beauty weaves through empathy, kindness, and resilience - an unfathomable grace. Hand in hand, Erika and Elena venture out of the room together, and as they depart, the power of their genuine camaraderie dispels the judgment that hung like a curse there only moments ago. Elena, an intentional genetic marvel, and Erika, another accidental product of natural wonders, are two sides of the same coin: a reminder that perfection manifests in many ways - that beauty is ultimately a fusion of science and chance under the quaking and uncertain hands of humanity.

∞　∞　∞

Eight days into the camping trip, Arthur fulfilled his wish to rebuild civilization in the trees. Though they would not admit it, his first lean-to shelter had inspired the other boys to build their own little survival hovels, and now their entire campsite is strewn about with primitive structures of all kinds in various states of chaotic disarray. When they had arrived, they were all elated to find a plethora of strawberry bushes loaded with fruit for the taking, but it didn't take long before their guts rebelled against them, and they went looking for better food.

The previous week's rains had brought up all manner of various mushrooms from the forest floor, but no matter how much Arthur had tried to convince them that some of them were safe to eat, everyone was too afraid of being poisoned, so the boys had gotten in the habit of spending almost their entire afternoons standing knee deep in the gently flowing water of the nearby stream, trying to catch fish on their sharpened sticks, mostly failing and growing increasingly frustrated. *There's free food everywhere and they would still rather pick apart dead animals. Dummies. They're burning more calories than they're absorbing.* In spite of their meager successes, everyone but Arthur is growing hungrier by the day, and their resentment is beginning to bubble over. As they return from another disappointing hunt, two catfish caught between the whole lot of them, a group of three boys break away from the group and walk right up to Arthur's shelter.

"Why don't you come down and help us? We know you have some tricks you're holding back," one of the boys spits at him. His clothes are soaking wet, his hands and feet covered in mud, and the red welts of mosquito bites dot almost every part of him.

Arthur, who had been quietly minding his own business and prying open hazelnuts with his pocketknife, doesn't even look up, though his hands stop moving.

"Hey, didn't you hear me?" The boy raises his voice and lightly kicks his foot forward, throwing a cloud of dirt into Arthur's lap.

"You're looking at one of the tricks, Clay," Arthur sighs. "I can show you how to find hazelnuts ...."

"That's not what I'm talking about," Clay growls, the nostrils on his pug nose flaring with a rage that Arthur doesn't completely register.

"Well... I don't eat fish, so I'm not going to help you catch fish," he replies, no hint of emotion entering his voice. He finally looks up at Clay just in time to catch a half-clenched fist to the cheek, sending him tumbling over backwards with the assailant falling on top of him. Clay's friends pull him off of Arthur as the other boys all run over to see what's going on.

"You think you're better than all of us?" Clay shouts as his friends hold him back. *"You think you're special?"*

Arthur sits right back up into the same position as before and wordlessly collects his scattered hazelnuts. Keeping his eyes to the ground, he will not let the other boys see his anger, though his hands are shaking. *No, they can't have my power.*

"I think," Arthur says just above a whisper, "that it's a good thing we're only going to be out here for two more days, or maybe you'd resort to cannibalism to avoid skipping another meal."

Clay screams with fury and tries to break free of his friends, but they hold him tight. A loud snap from behind the group abruptly ends the entire drama, and the crowd of boys spin around to see a full-grown black bear standing in the middle of their campsite just a few yards away, chomping its massive teeth down into their precious fish. "Bear! *Bear! Bear!"* The boys all scream, bolting into the trees.

Arthur looks up, but he doesn't run. He takes a calming breath. *Wow, something interesting. You came to save me from this boring trip, didn't you?* He slowly stands, eyes glued to the bear, a feeling of absolute wonder washing over him. The hair rises on the back of his neck, and he feels that he is alive for the first time in years. The bear, oblivious to Arthur's presence, just continues ripping the belly from the second fish, happily licking its lips at the free meal. Arthur takes a step towards the animal.

From the ranger hide-out a mile away, Bertrand grabs the viewscreen and shouts, *"What are you doing, Arthur?!"* Two other rangers are already running at full speed to the campsite. They had seen the bear following the boys from the riverbanks, and Bertrand had ordered them to neutralize the animal if it exhibited any signs of aggression. But he would never have imagined this possibility. *Does he have no survival instincts whatsoever?* On the tiny black and white screen, Bertrand can see Arthur take another step towards the bear, but the aerial placement of the camera in the treetops allows him no view of the boy's face. *What is he thinking? Lola is going to have my balls for this.*

"Hi," Arthur says to the bear like he's talking to a younger child. "You shouldn't be here. People are dangerous, and you could get hurt."

The bear doesn't respond, either unaware or unconcerned with the boy's presence. It has finished off the other fish, and it scrapes its paws at the ground, crushing the remaining pieces into the dirt.

"Hey!" Arthur snaps, causing the bear to look up. "You need to go!"

The rest of the boys are watching from the tree line as Arthur takes another step towards the bear. The closer they get to each other; the smaller Arthur looks in the shadow of the great animal.

"He's going to get himself killed," one of the boys whispers in a panic.

Another says, "That thing could eat him in one bite!"

The bear just stares at Arthur, curious and confused. Arthur doesn't break eye contact. *Just go. They'll kill you.* The bear growls and stands up on its hind legs, looking down at Arthur with strings of drool dripping from its fishy mouth.

Without hesitating, Arthur takes another step forward, coming almost within arm's reach of the massive beast. "I don't want them to kill you! *Go!*" he shouts, and the bear finally seems to both engage and then understand Arthur. It jumps backwards, falling over its own legs in raw terror, throwing up dust as it sprints away, crashing through the trees.

"Stand down," Bertrand breathes a sigh of relief and almost breathlessly squawks into his handheld radio from the ranger's station. "Threat neutralized. *Stand down.*"

The ranger standing beside him, who with Burt has observed the entire event, says, "I have never seen anything like that in my life! That is one special boy you've got there."

Burt looks on through the monitor, thinking and slowly calming down. "Yeah.... Special or crazy. I can't tell which."

The ranger gives him a perplexed look. After a moment, he says, *"You really can't?"*

Burt looks at him, curious at first, but then he realizes the ranger's words held a hidden condemnation, and he suddenly and uncharacteristically feels ashamed of himself.

The cracking and smashing sounds of the panicked bear slowly fade into the distance, and a few seconds pass in complete silence. Arthur looks around the campsite, and he laughs a single, *"Ha!"* He looks straight up into the trees above his head, right into the camera, right at Bertrand. "I hope you saw that! Survival instincts don't always mean annihilating what you don't understand!" Still looking into the camera, he shakes his head in a disapproving manner.

With a burst of cheers, the other boys jump out of their hiding places and run over to Arthur. They surround him, all talking at once.

"That was amazing!"

"How did you know it would run?"

"You've got nerves of steel!"

Even Clay, shaking his head and laughing, looks at Arthur and shouts above the other boys, "Hey, I'm sorry! You're the man!"

Before Arthur can stop them, they grab him and hoist him up above their heads, whooping and hollering, their relief and gratification intermingled into a singular joyful noise. This is a victory for all of them, but they know to whom it truly belongs, and for the first time in a very long time *Arthur feels pure joy.*

However, the emotion is fleeting, and as the boys drop him back onto the ground, Arthur finally faces the truth that had lingered quietly in the depths of his being – a truth both daunting and wondrous*: his potential is a rare flame burning brighter than most and illuminating paths unknown to others.* Yet, this was no triumph to revel in, but rather a quiet burden, an untold weight resting upon his shoulders. In the silence of this realization, he makes a solemn vow – he will carry his gift with humility, protect its essence, and in his solitude, he will learn to nurture it – *not for himself, but for the world that might one day need its light.*

∞   ∞   ∞

Chapter Five

Fate Interrupted

∞ ∞ ∞

2026 –

A cedar plank clatters to the floor and the whirring of the jigsaw comes to a stop. *That's eighteen for the north wall with eight more to go.* A descending bead of sweat carves a canyon through the sawdust on Arthur's forehead, stopping at the rim of his clear work-goggles. The testy sixteen-year-old has been up since before dawn, determined this week to add another floor to his tree house. The two-story marvel of a structure sits forty feet from the ground, nestled safely in the fork of a two-hundred-year-old oak tree. Arthur began building it when he was ten, and two years later he had practically moved out of the family home and into his own residence. There was no resistance from anyone, and in fact Bertrand had encouraged the endeavor, seeing it as at least one activity that they could participate in together, albeit on a limited basis depending on Arthur's moods and Burt's free time.

The first floor had been their joint project, and they each became the equivalent of journeyman carpenters from all of the work and research they conducted. *The result was something truly magnificent:* a cylindrical room with a diameter of twelve feet and eight-foot-high ceilings. To Arthur, it felt like his very own mansion, and it would be accurate to say that the tree house was the very first thing with which he had ever fallen in love. The second floor was completed the subsequent year, and he had insisted on building that one alone, much to Burt's chagrin. To Arthur, the tree house stood as the expression of his own free will manifested into the world, and Bertrand finally, reluctantly, had given him the reins, settling on being happy at least to have served a supporting role at its birth. With its existence, this was the first time that Arthur could truly call something his own, and he pressed forward with confidence to add a new layer to his independence.

Lifting another cedar plank from the floor, he clicks on the electric saw to begin another cut, but then he hears the ringing of his makeshift doorbell. Clicking off the saw, he sets it down, and then leans his head out the window. Looking out into the yard, he sees that it is Lola pulling the long brown rope attached to the clapper of the brass ship's bell which sits nobly at the base of the tree house.

Over the ringing, Arthur shouts, "Hey! *I hear you!* What's up?"

Lola turns her gaze skyward and stops tugging on the rope. The setting sun through the trees reflects off her graying brown hair, but her youthful smile is something which has not changed through the years. "How long until you're done?" she calls up.

"Oh, I have just a few more cuts, and then I need to put the tarp back over top. Maybe fifteen more minutes? Why?" Arthur asks with a quizzical look on his face. *Dinner shouldn't be for another couple of hours.*

Well-experienced with his customary suspicion, Lola decides she will tease him. "I just wanted to talk about something … *interesting.*" A wisp of a smile flashes across her lips. Seeing his impatience, she adds in a serious tone, "Something important, I believe." Even then, she is unable to contain the grin once again spreading across her face.

Arthur shakes his head in annoyance. *"Oh, c'mon!"* He is mostly just irritated by the interruption to his work, and unconcerned about whatever his mom has to tell him. Pulling his head back inside, he shouts, "Fifteen minutes!" *Always with these mind games.* He picks up his saw and flips it back on, now rushing to make the next cut, but then he stops suddenly. He remembers the ugly mistakes he had made the previous year when trying to finish too quickly. It was an event filled with flying splinters and marred planks and had nearly allowed the saw to move on its own, out of the realm of his control. *Not this time.* He holds himself completely still and closes his eyes, inhaling slowly and deeply. He remembers *his cousin* Nash's advice: *Reset the central nervous system. You'll never stop getting shaken, but you can stop the shaking.*

Whatever she wants to tell him, he'll find out in fifteen minutes. Without any lingering concern, he takes his time and finishes the final four cuts. As the saw slows to a halt, Arthur sets it down on the floor and neatly stacks the last planks onto his pile, smiling proudly at his work. He leans his body forward and wildly brushes the sawdust from his bushy, yet much lighter brown hair, the shade having taken on natural caramel blonde highlights as he has grown. Then Arthur stands back up and claps his hands together. He holds his breath as he watches the sawdust swirling in the air all around him, then strides over to the shop vacuum. Turning that on, he waves its wand around in front of him and soon realizes he must look just like an orchestra conductor leading a symphony as he sucks in the debris.

Within a few moments, he has cleansed the room of every loose molecule, certain that none will have been allowed to escape to mar the furnished floors beneath. Finally, he unfurls the temporary roof tarp, ascending and descending a stepladder as he secures it, making sure everything is properly protected. Surveying the scene and feeling satisfied, he tears off his clothes and throws them into his homemade hamper - a two-square foot wooden crate - then pulling open the trap door at his feet, the dusty, naked, and well-built young man hops down the steeply inclined steps and arrives down onto the middle floor.

Arthur had originally dedicated this floor to storage, but his mother had convinced him to figure out a reliable bathing situation, so before the roof was added, they had lowered a claw-foot bathtub into the room. It had a built-in shower head, a ring for a curtain, and was supplied by a rainwater harvesting tank which had been secured two branches above the tree house's top. Arthur tiptoes over to the tub and pulls the curtain all the way around. With his eyes closed, he turns his face up towards the shower head, puts his hand on the faucet handle, and takes a deep breath before flipping on the freezing cold water. This was something he had also learned from Nash. *Cold water strengthens the mind and soothes the muscles.* He feels the sawdust run off his body and swirl down the drain, revealing a deep brown tan, a few shades darker than that of even his mother's.

Arthur's mind goes quiet as he rotates slowly clockwise underneath the water with his hands raised up in the air. Then a thought penetrates the silence: *something interesting...*

something important. What the hell could they be planning now? He cranks off the faucet and looks around for his towel, then rolls his eyes as he realizes: *I didn't even bring it upstairs.* Like a wet dog, he tries to twist and shake some of the water off, but it's a hopeless solution. Resigned, he trudges out of the shower, leaving wet footprints on the wood floor in his wake all the way to another trap door, which he flings open with irritation and jumps through, bouncing onto a thick bean bag directly beneath him.

The interior of the first floor is outfitted with everything that suits Arthur's vision of an ideal, balanced life. *A sustainable, terrestrial life.* Since the wind seemed to always blow from the north, a miniature cast-iron, wood-burning stove was placed next to a window in the southern quarter of the circle so that the draft would pull out any escaping smoke. A circular rug, a custom piece that Lola had sought out and procured especially for Arthur, spans the entire floor and reaches all the way to the walls. It was an accurate map of the globe with some classical cliches and artistic license taken: *a sea monster in the corner of the turquoise ocean with the text "thar be monsters," some borders drawn in for countries that hadn't existed for thousands of years, and an inexplicable X to mark the spot of a buried treasure somewhere off the eastern coast of Australia.* Arthur had also decided to staple tapestries of tree canopies to the roof of the first floor, so that it seemed to stretch up into infinity: *branches reaching upwards in fractals to claw at the deep blue sky above them.*

On the second floor, he had done the same, but with tapestries of the artwork from the Sistine Chapel. Beanbags were strewn about instead of standard furniture, and a single flat-screen monitor was attached to a ten-foot mechanical arm in the center of the ceiling so that Arthur could sit in any conceivable position and peer into the digital world, though these days he seemed less and less interested in what he could find on the internet.

As he grabs his plush white towel from a brass towel holder attached to the wall and begins to dry himself off, he considers what will be one of his last achievements for the third and, for now, final floor. When he puts in the slats for the top floor and is ready to add the ceiling, this time there will be no tapestries. Instead, there will be a clear, domed rooftop looking up into the sky. *My own private observatory.* He had long been losing any interest in the affairs of the human world over the past three or four years, ever since he had discovered that he does not agree at all with the choices mankind seems to be intent on making. Down here on Earth, he can see no way of throwing himself into the momentum of society. Instead, he has confirmed a focus within himself that, as he attains adulthood, his eyes, along with his heart, would then only be meant to turn upwards towards the expanse of space *with its limitless possibilities.*

∞ ∞ ∞

Elena had adorned herself in all black. Black combat boots, black jeans, black sweater, black leather jacket. *Black is defensive coloring,* Kira had warned her, but that was exactly Elena's intent. The colorlessness of her outfit makes the blue of her eyes shine even more brightly, but even those she covers up with black sunglasses. It still hadn't kept the boys away, and all this started because one of them, Vladimir, just wouldn't leave her alone. Her beauty seems to draw them in like moths to flame, though Elena has done everything she can to sector herself off from her peers. Her marginal fame in government circles had elevated her onto a pedestal in so many minds, and though she made an art form of hasty exits, this one young man had figured out that no one can easily escape a well-written letter. The proud and handsome son of a Kremlin bureaucrat, he was two years her senior and about to go off into military service. *The last thing I want from the civilian world is just one date with you,* he wrote to her.

She had been completely prepared to reject him, but then she showed Erika the note. Her closest friend, her only friend, had become so excited about the co-ed dance party that Elena felt like she had no choice in the matter. *Maybe there will at least be some good music at this stupid dance. If they're playing techno, it might be worth it.* Like so many teenagers in Moscow, she had learned how to escape all of her troubles in the deep, rhythmic heartbeat of the music, flailing her body like a voodoo priestess to process the energy that no rational action could address. Of course, she would never go out to the club and dance, but she didn't need to. Her bedroom had become her own little private discotheque, and her penchant for playing her music obscenely loud had prompted Altan and Kira to give her the entire basement level of the mansion for her noisy purposes. Elena had dubbed it her "dance dungeon," and other than the family garden, it was where she spent most of her time. But tonight, she had become the victim of her own willingness to make her friend happy. She couldn't say no to Erika, so that really only left yes on the table. *Let Vladimir think it's his yes,* she smirks, rolling her eyes.

The boy had offered to pick her up in his new Maserati, but Elena insisted on just meeting him there. She could see ten steps into his intentions, and she wanted to make sure that she was well-protected behind a row of pawns, so she had her mother arrange a private limousine driver to take her and pick up Erika along the way. The long, black Cadillac sits purring in the driveway, patiently idling as Elena says goodbye to her parents.

"Feminine, huh? Try getting a boy into these jeans," she retorts out loud to herself in answer to Kira's prior fashion reproaches before turning on her heel and striding quickly down the stairs and up to the car.

The driver, a white-haired man in a black suit, jumps out as she draws near and runs around to open the rear door for her, but Elena ignores him and opens the passenger side door, jumping in and slamming it shut behind her. The driver looks at Kira from across the luxuriously empty back seat and shrugs as Kira shakes her head at him and holds down a rigid smile. From the doorway of their residence, Altan gives a double thumbs-up and mouths, "I love you," though he cannot see Elena's face behind the deep tinting job on the Cadillac. Elena sees him and rolls down the window.

"I love you too, father. And mother. See you soon, I guess," she says with a sigh and rolls the window back up. She taps her fingers impatiently on her knee as the driver expertly navigates the limo down the mansion's driveway.

"Hey, can I turn on the radio?" she asks the driver.

Before he can answer, she reaches towards the dial and spins it to one of the local FM stations playing electronic dance music. She cranks the volume up just loud enough that she can feel the bass reverberating in her bones. The driver looks at her for a moment as though he is looking at a hostile alien life form, but then his face softens, and he smiles and nods his head. Normally, he would never let anyone mess with his radio, but today he feels like he is giving a ride to royalty, so he lets it slide. As the car plods slowly along past some of the other mansions within their normally quiet gated community, the rhythmic vibrations bring a few of Elena's neighbors to their windows to see what the commotion is about. Without a hint of concern, Elena pulls the lever to lean her seat all the way backwards, closes her eyes, and whips out her phone to send a text message to Erika: *"Hey girl! We're on our way to pick you up. Get ready!"*

As the sleek black limousine exits the gated community, where sprawling mansions house Moscow's elite, the opulence of privilege gradually diminishes. The scent of freshly cut grass and blooming flowers yields a tang of asphalt and distant market wares. Leaning her seat forward to sate her curiosity, Elena's gaze fixes on Erika's neighborhood, a humble enclave of lower middle-class dwellings. Here, a quaint house stands with peeling red paint and a wild garden blooming with hard-earned, vibrant wildflowers. The air is laced with the comforting aroma of a home-cooked meal drifting from open windows. The aesthetic reflects the spirit that Elena has come to know in her dear friend, Erika, serving as a reminder that affluence isn't the measure of kindness or warmth. Erika's roots trace back to her grandfather, a highly influential and principled Soviet Communist who exemplified humility and notoriously detested luxury. This tradition endured, veiling the family's hidden stature, but since Erika attended Elena's prestigious ballet school, it was revealed to Elena that true power often disguises itself amidst modest abodes and open hearts.

As they stop in front of the house, Elena opens her door and steps out of the car. Erika, her lively and vivacious friend, rushes outside with a radiant smile. Her eyes sparkle with excitement as she sees Elena standing by the car. She's wearing a loose, flowing blouse adorned with a delicate floral pattern, each bloom seemingly dancing in the soft breeze. The colors - a symphony of pastels - evoke the freshness of summer blossoms, a stark contrast to Elena's penchant for black.

"Elena, ew, what? All black?" She chuckles, teasing her friend playfully. "You're going to scare them all away," she adds, referring to the boys they're about to encounter.

"It goes with *anything*," Elena winks as she wraps her arm around Erika's.

The girls giggle excitedly on the pathway, the anticipation of the event fueling their laughter. Moments later, they both climb into the back of the limo. The interior is a marvel of luxury, plush leather seats, polished wood accents, and a soft, ambient light that adds an air of sophistication. Erika's eyes widen in awe as she takes in the opulent surroundings, a silent appreciation for the elegance by which she rarely finds herself surrounded.

"So, have you talked with Vlad yet? Are we meeting him somewhere first? I'm starving!" Erika says, and then she can't help herself. "Wow, this car -"

Elena manages a half-hearted smile. "I'm actually more excited about spending time with you. I guess he'll just be at the dance, but whatever. Boys aren't really my thing, you know that."

Erika laughs, a light, carefree sound. "More for me then! We'll have a blast regardless. Thanks for being my wing woman for the evening," she says, her eyes meeting Elena's with trusting gratitude.

As the car speeds away towards the dance party, Elena can't help but feel a sense of comfort knowing she has a true friend in Erika, even if the prospect of the dance isn't exactly her cup of tea. They chatter about the upcoming event, and as the vibrant lights of the dance venue draw near, Elena's nervousness begins to dissipate, replaced by the joy of seeing the excitement in her friend's eyes, knowing she will be spending time with someone who truly understands her, even if they are completely different from one another.

∞ ∞ ∞

Arthur has finished drying off and now, donning some green cargo shorts and a plain blue t-shirt, he returns to the second floor to dry up his footsteps with his towel. *Something interesting. I hope it's true.* With a final look around, he climbs back down the steps and walks out the only *regular* door within the entire structure. This leads him onto a tiny balcony which faces away from his family's mansion. Even when he was just ten and had started building the treehouse with his father, he was convinced that he wouldn't want to feel his parents' eyes on him while he stood gazing out at the horizon from his private landing. He knew he would be unable to use his full powers of reasoning and focusing on important stuff should he feel he was being watched.

The rope ladder serves as his security feature, and he slowly releases its ties and then watches it unravel in one quick snap all the way to the ground. He descends it in perfect silence like a ninja, skipping two rungs with each step downward, and he attributes this skill to his years of physical training which led to the firming and strengthening of his ripped, muscular arms and legs. It takes him less than ten seconds to reach the ground.

From the kitchen window of the house, Lola watches him as she loads the final pan into the dishwasher. *If he keeps growing at this rate, he won't even need the ladder.* The bulk of the multitude of plates, knives, and forks she had just packed were the result of his voracious eating. Bertrand had tried to calculate the average amount of meals Arthur eats in a day, and he had concluded that the most accurate assessment was that *Arthur eats without ceasing.* She had once been intent on keeping up with and cooking everything he needed, but then Lola had eventually relented, and now half of his calories were the result of food delivery services.

The glass patio door slides open, and Arthur steps inside.

143

"Feet!" Lola scolds him without looking.

"I just showered, and the grass is dry," he lies, quickly reaching down and brushing the bottoms of his feet, then strolling casually into the kitchen.

"Hey! I was just outside, remember?" She chides him, *"My shoes got soaked. That must have been some dry wind that whipped up in the past ten minutes!"*

Arthur smiles as he walks towards her, then wraps his arms around his mother and gives her a playful squeeze, *"Shhhh ...,"* he whispers, putting his hand on the back of her head and pretending to push her face into his chest as if she were an infant. "Sleep now."

Lola jabs him in the ribs, and he lets go with a yelp. "Remember - I know all your ticklish spots, buddy." She wiggles her finger into his ribcage. They laugh together as Arthur regains his composure and crosses his arms.

"Something interesting, *yes?*" He raises an eyebrow and gives a smirk.

"Something important!" she grins cryptically, letting him squirm. *"Wanna guess?"*

"Hey, I stopped my work and came all the way down here to find out! Don't torture me," he whines, leaning against the counter with self-importance.

"Oh sweetie," she puts on a serious tone, "I was just thinking that maybe we should wait until your father comes home before I tell you...." but he knows she is continuing with her teasing because her words are betrayed by the bright gleam in her eyes.

However, he decides to accept her challenge and notch it up a bit. "You for real? Ok, I see how it is," he leaps towards the telephone hanging on the wall, *"I'll just call him right now!"*

As he starts pushing numbers, he hears his father's voice. *"No need!"* Bertrand booms. A moment later, his hulking form emerges into the kitchen from the shadows of the darkened living room. "I'm here!"

Lola and Bertrand erupt into cackles, and Arthur shakes his head once more at their antics. Smirking, he says, "It's not fair. *Two against one!"* He hangs up the landline phone and turns fully to look at Bertrand. "So, is there no interesting or important news, after all? Are you both only committed to one thing – *wasting my valuable time?"*

"Oh yes, there's some interesting news," Bertrand comes over to Arthur and puts his large hands on his son's shoulders. "Do you want to tell him, honey?"

Lola lets a few moments pass, relishing the look on Arthur's face. *Can those furrows in his forehead burrow any deeper?* Finally, she exclaims, "Well, if you don't find Paris interesting, then...."

"What? We're going to Paris?" Arthur asks, trying not to show too much excitement. Involuntarily, his fists clench and he feels a twitching sensation in his legs.

"Yep!" Bertrand rubs his hands together. "Next week, after we put the dome on the tree house."

Arthur clasps his hands together and thinks about it. *Possibly not the worst thing we could do together as a family.* Already, he envisions the climb up to the top of the Eiffel Tower. That alone might make the trip worthwhile.

He knows they are waiting for his reaction, and now he will make them wonder a little. Finally, he nods coyly. "Okay, I guess that will be alright. *But I'm not going if we don't get the dome in place by then!"*

As he heads to the refrigerator to get the last slice of last night's pepperoni pizza, his excitement grows a bit more. With his face hidden now from his parents, his smile erupts fully. *Paris! That is absolutely something interesting. Finally!*

∞ ∞ ∞

Love is a delicate thing. In its truest form, it cannot be manufactured or coerced. It germinates in the deepest places under only the safest conditions and secretly unfurls its blueprint into the shadows of the heart. In its infancy, it is like a delicate cloud in a clear sky and will shear apart with the slightest breeze. Everyone, no matter what they say, is looking for it, though most do not know exactly what they seek, and those blessed enough to bask in its light realize, in the end, that it was they who were found and not the other way around.

How do we decide what we love? How do we encounter it? The course of an individual's life is dictated by their ability to negotiate the myriad decisions presented to them by forces beyond anyone's reckoning. When the flower of love flourishes and its grateful recipients look backwards in time over the course of their lives, they will feel that the pieces that fell into place for them had been calculated almost miraculously, long before their birth, and that they just happened to be in the right place when they all came together. This is how love has weaved its way through human civilizations for countless eons. This is how it is for just about everyone: everyone except for Arthur and Elena.

The powers that be had decided that the soil was fertile and the conditions perfect to plant the seed, and that the two teenagers would be unofficially introduced to one another in a way that allowed them both the feeling of freedom and natural discovery. An artistic summit was declared between Russia and the United States, and each nation would bring forth some of their most prized historical treasures and works of genius for display at the Louvre during a semi-private, three-day, diplomatic gala. The temporary galleries were set up in a glass-covered courtyard of the Richelieu Wing, with the American and Russian works interspersed throughout the Grand Coeur Marly. Among the white marble statues of Greek gods and mortal heroes, the treasures of the two empires appear almost contemporary.

Set among the monumental white stone, the bright colors of the paintings seem to leap out from their frames, and the artifacts of wars fought long ago are laid out in long, clear cases, like the relics of a high-end pawn shop. Circular standing tables dot the courtyard, and a constant stream of butlers circle through the room offering platters of various, masterful hors d'oeuvres, culinary artworks in their own right. On this final night, the whole wing is teeming with members of the American Senate and their families, who for lack of easy communication are content simply drinking and rubbing elbows with so many ministers of various Russian government offices.

Everyone is dressed in their very best, with a mix of official regalia and red-carpet fashion throughout. The courtyard vibrates with warmth and goodwill, and everyone feels that it is a magical night.

Elena wears an elegant black cocktail dress with black heels. At Kira's insistence that morning, she had gone to a famous French salon and had her hair done up like a bridesmaid, with black ribbons holding half of it up in a beautiful knot while the rest cascaded down her shoulders in elaborate curls and waves. Around her neck, she wears a thin gold chain with a pendant of the double-headed imperial eagle, a gift from Altan for her sixteenth birthday. Elena can't stop smiling to herself as she twirls through the room. It is the first time she has felt beautiful without feeling vulnerable, freed from her usual position in the spotlight by the spectacle of it all.

She stands with her third glass of champagne before the
Portrait of Madame X, by John Singer Sargent, admiring the
bold posture of the woman in the painting. *I wonder if I could
ever look so elegant and careless.*

Arthur strolls through the room with intention, taking an
hors d'oeuvre every time they're offered and giving equal time
to each piece of art. *Ten deep breaths' worth* to make it look
like he was truly interested. When he reaches the cases with the
Russian artifacts, he breaks his rule and forgets to breathe at all.
His imagination is lifted away by ornate silver helmets from the
12th century, pristine sabers with bejeweled scabbards which
had once been presented by the Czar himself to foreign
dignitaries, and then the sacred altar gospels held in
ostentatious golden bindings. *We definitely don't make anything
like this anymore.* Resisting every urge to lean forward and put
his hands on the glass, he holds them behind his back and
sways back and forth, the tails on his white tuxedo jacket
swinging like a pendulum across his black slacks.

Standing across the room next to Grant Wood's
American Gothic, Bertrand watches Arthur and beams proudly.
He gives Lola a little nudge to get her attention and nods
towards their son. The excitement in Arthur's body language is
so unusual and refreshing that they both chuckle at the sight. It
had only taken half a glass of champagne to grease Arthur's
wheels and send him wandering through the room on his own,
propelled by his parents giving each other affectionate little
smooches.

Nearing the end of her reverie with *Madame X,* Elena
swivels about and surveys the room. She sees a few paintings
that look very familiar to her: Pukirev's *Unequal Marriage,* a
painting of a poor, young woman marrying an ancient
government official against her will, *Bathing of a Red Horse* by
Kuzma Petrov-Vodkin, with its vivid cerulean colors and stark-

naked rider. And then she sees a vision of beauty itself. *Wait a minute, who is that standing over there in the white tuxedo? Oh my God, don't look.* At the sight of Arthur, her breath catches in her throat.

Wallowing in his admiration of John Pitcairn's elaborately etched twin pistols, Arthur feels the hair on the back of his neck stand up, and he raises his eyes just in time to see Elena dart hers away and spin back towards the *Madame X* painting. *Who is that? Her eyes are so blue, like the Earth floating through space.* As though in a trance, he begins to walk directly towards her. *No, you idiot, act natural!* His mind unconsciously diverts to strategy, and so he alters his course and begins to make a wide circle that will eventually take him right past her.

As he comes up to Vasily Vereshchagin's *Apotheosis of War*, his eyes stretch in their sockets to try and catch another glimpse of the mysterious girl in the black dress, but she is still looking up at *Madame X* with her back to him. *How many breaths was that? Was I even breathing?* He counts to ten and continues on his chosen path, weaving through important people without so much as a glance, skipping past the full plates of food, until he is standing right behind Elena. She continues to stare up at the woman in the painting, frozen in place and unaccustomed to feeling such intense attraction to another human being. He takes in the entire image as one – the girl and the painting – and then, seemingly out of nowhere, before his mind can interfere, he utters the very first spontaneous and truthful thing that comes to him.

"It's like she stepped out of the painting and into the real world," *the words escape into the air, and there is no going back.*

Elena's cheeks flush pink and she responds without turning around, "Are you referring to the Kramskoi over there?" she asks, pointing just to the right towards the *Portrait of an Unknown Woman,* another oil painting of a lady dressed in all black who gazes proudly down her nose from a padded carriage.

"No, this one here," Arthur takes a step forward so that they are standing side-by-side only inches apart, and he points his finger up at *Madame X. "It could be you in another life."*

Elena rotates her head and looks up at Arthur. His dark skin and chiseled features send a shockwave through her. *He is so handsome and regal!* As if a spell had been cast upon her, words tumble their way out of her mouth against her will, "So what painting did you step out of?"

Arthur raises both his eyebrows and smiles. Now that the opening has been made, he begins to fall easily and naturally into a new role. "The whole world is my painting!" he proudly proclaims.

Elena lets out a deep belly laugh, shattering her icy nerves. She relaxes and pivots towards Arthur. "Is that so? *The whole world?*" she grins and puts her hands on her hips. "I've got some tips for you then." Both of them laugh together.

As the chuckles die down, their eyes lock, and Arthur is at a loss for what to say next. He feels like his script has been taken from him, but Elena's dimples, rarely seen, remain prominent on her smiling cheeks, and his heart skips a beat. Everything inside of him wants to reach out and grab onto her hand, but he checks himself against this accelerating, and soon, overwhelming passion, a feeling with which he is completely unfamiliar.

Sensing the obvious attraction in his boyish gaze, Elena bites her bottom lip and cocks her head to the side. Well-acquainted with the clumsy affections of young men, she can feel the vibration of Arthur's repressed desires, but for the first time, she realizes that they are matching her own yearnings.

She wants to tell him to reach out, be brave, but she waits to see what he will do. *The boy should always make the first move.* Her fingers wiggle at her sides as though trying to issue him a silent command, but the moment passes, and Arthur doesn't catch the cue. For now, the powerful energy in their natural chemistry remains purely potential, not yet ready to unleash itself and become fully kinetic.

"Will you walk with me?" Arthur finally manages, gesturing towards the other paintings.

She is happy he has asked, and Elena's eyes brighten as she accepts his invitation. "Yes, let's!"

Across the room, Kira and Altan stand next to *Washington Crossing the Delaware,* observing the scene unfold. They had been given a complicated set of maneuvers to coordinate bringing Elena close to Arthur, but now, somehow, they hadn't needed to do a single thing but simply show up to the Louvre at the appointed time. Everything else fell into place on its own.

"Do you believe in fate?" Altan puts his arm around Kira's waist and gives a squeeze. "I think they like each other."

"We make fate," Kira responds without emotion, but then a smile creeps up and graces her lips, "Still, I've never seen Elena look like that...she looks so..."

"Alive?" Altan finishes her sentence.

Kira nods, her brow furrowing with concern, "But this is not exactly how this was supposed to happen. *They were to be introduced only!* Potential business partners in a possible future scenario. This might be very bad...." she finishes, her voice laced with worry.

And then, suddenly, Lola and Burt arrive through the crowd, their faces reflecting surprise and intrigue at hearing Kira's final sentences.

"Did you see that?!" Burt exclaims, his eyes widening as he turns to Kira.

"We certainly did. What should we do?" Kira responds, her mind racing with potential implications and possible abort protocols. Both sets of parents had been briefed together the day before, but nothing discussed had prepared them for this scenario.

Altan, catching wind of their complicit intentions, leans in, his voice tinged with amusement. *"Do? About what? Two beautiful, young people noticing each other at a dazzling affair when they're surrounded mostly by adults and scholars who have their noses buried in pamphlets full of literature about art? That is called nature, my friends."*

"Indeed! Let them have their fun!" Lola chimes in. "Let's allow them a nice evening. Had they *not* noticed each other, we would have introduced them formally later at the banquet." Altan nods in agreement. "Of all the kids in this program, it's amazing to me just how similar they are... it can only be a good thing if they also happen to like each other." Lola feels joy, and her words are accompanied by a blush and an optimistic smile.

But Kira and Burt are of a different mind, and in contrast to the lightheartedness in Altan and Lola's words, the shadow of seriousness grows across their faces. With measured coolness, they exchange glances, and it seems to say, *love has no place within the context of a military operation, especially not one as important as this.*

"*Introduced*, sure. *Paired off*, no. We need to intervene," Kira reiterates, her tone firm and her gaze fixed on the young pair.

"Agreed," Burt barks, signaling that there is no room for debate. "We need to nip this in the bud. They're only ever

152

supposed to be together if—" Burt begins, but Lola finishes his sentence with conviction.

"If the world ends and humanity needs for them to be together?" she adds, sounding defeated and turning her scalding eyes to Kira. "If that is the case, I would rather they be in love when it happens and not merely business partners. Did you really think it best that they see each other only as *business partners?*"

"Yes," Burt and Kira reply in unison, their expressions revealing a shared sense of disappointment and regret.

∞ ∞ ∞

Somewhere within the twinkling light under the starry canopy, between Norman Rockwell's *Freedom from Want* on one side of the room and Edward Hopper's *Nighthawks* on the other, the carefully laid plans of hundreds of politicians, scientists, and secret agents are either falling apart at the seams or just beginning to come to fruition, depending upon who's perspective one would choose. The higher-ups gathered in the security offices, who were watching it all unfold, had decided to let it go on for now, but only because Arthur and Elena were under close supervision. Those involved, including Nash, considered that they could and would intervene at any time if it were to become necessary.

Looking quite like a painting themselves with their formal wear and glasses of champagne, Arthur and Elena stroll through the room together, vividly talking about the artwork, about the world, and about what it all means. They had been allowed champagne for this outing, though it was to be limited to two glasses each, and therefore their usual vigilance and suspicions lie dormant under the champagne bubbles; they don't even bother to ask why it's all happening. After a lifetime of feeling like they are completely alone in the world, the illusion of their isolation has now become shattered, and a silver thread begins to weave together their young hearts.

Soon, Arthur and Elena wander outside into the fresh air and leisurely stroll around the iconic glass pyramid crowning the museum. The city comes alive at night in a sensory explosion of so many good things all at once. The air carries the delightful aroma of street-side crepes which have been infused with a blend of enticing spices as they are being skillfully prepared by a vendor. A canvas of hues paints the sky with a palette of deep blues and hints of amber from the city lights, and the distant echoes of laughter and music from nearby bistros add a lively rhythm to the atmosphere. As a gentle breeze sweeps through the city, Arthur, attuned to all of these various subtleties, notices a shiver in Elena. In a gesture both instinctive and valiant, he swiftly removes his tuxedo jacket and envelopes her in its warmth.

"Thank you. Quite chivalrous of you," Elena acknowledges.

Arthur laughs. "That's a new one for me, then. I'm not exactly a master of the social graces."

"Ha!" Elena giggles. "Me, neither! I mean, I *was* enjoying the museum, though. It's so incredible!" Elena says, spinning in place, awash in the elevated aesthetic of it all.

"I know! Some of it took my breath away!" Arthur exclaims, grinning at Elena. He is still overcome with his desires, although he thinks that he is doing okay for now. "In my life... I happen to...." He can't find the correct words to describe what he is trying to say. "Well, perhaps... what I mean is that...." He stops and shakes his head, realizing he is stumbling attempting to express himself. *What I'm trying to say...."*

Elena lets out a laugh. "A man with a silver tongue, I see."

She sees that he feels a bit embarrassed, and she reassures him, "No, no, no! I'm just teasing you. You obviously feel passionate about whatever it is that you were trying to say. I want to hear it."

Arthur, a sense of relief washing over him, breaks into a genuine smile, expressing his gratitude. "By the way, how did you learn English so well – you speak better than most Americans I know."

"My father was fluent and wanted me to know it. From the time I was seven, most of our conversations together were in English."

As they continue to walk, he wants to put his arm around her shoulders, but realizes it is too early for that. "I guess what I was trying to say is just that, in my life, everything is facts and figures and predicting outcomes and... I guess I'm a pretty smart guy." He pauses and thinks of the right words to use. "It's just frustrating sometimes. I get the impression that I'm treated with kid gloves, and I'm being *groomed* for something special but –"

Elena can immediately empathize, and she cuts in, her voice soft and melodic, "But you don't know what it is or why people are so interested in everything you do?"

"Yes! Yes!" Arthur acknowledges, his words carrying an undercurrent of enthusiasm, a burst of energy in the air. "And downstairs, in the museum, and... in this incredible city... it's all just about beauty. This whole city seems to be about what people can do that is beautiful. Not ugly. Not useful. Not measurable or quantifiable. Just beautiful and emotional and warm," Arthur passionately explains, gesturing toward their surroundings. *"I love it here."*

Elena is lighting up, clearly feeling what he's saying with every fiber of her being. She is focused exclusively on Arthur even as other people pass by, some bemused at the enthusiastic dialogue of the two young visitors to their city. "I know! *I know!*" She cries out, practically jumping up and down.

"And then I look across that incredible room and I see you and I feel…" They stop on the sidewalk at an intersection crowded with walkers, bicyclers, and autos, and Arthur turns to face Elena. Slowly, he lifts his hand and gently touches the left side of his chest, tapping it twice as though to mark the spot. "Look, I don't want to come off as a clumsy, horny teenager, but I felt *connected* to you the moment I laid eyes on you. And I don't generally like people. But –" Arthur stops, wondering if he's already said too much.

But for Elena, he's said just the perfect amount, and she settles it with a demure grin. "What do you have planned for tomorrow?"

Arthur feels joy when he hears her question, serenity washing over his face, and then he shares tomorrow's agenda. "Well… tomorrow will be my favorite part of this trip - I think!"

"Wait, let me guess," Elena smirks, shaking her head. *"The West-Eastern Divan Orchestra?"*

"Yes! I can't believe they happen to be here in Paris when we're here! *What luck!"* Arthur raves.

Elena makes a theatrical sound halfway between a laugh and a groan. "Perhaps not *luck,*" she sighs.

"What do you mean?" Arthur tilts his head curiously. "You think they are here for us? A bunch of nerdy kids?"

"Oh, I don't know. Like you said, we seem to get a lot of special treatment." She pauses and a moment later, he nods with understanding. Then Elena changes course, determined not to let their hidden chaperones rain on her fun. "Anyway, the point is that the world's greatest orchestra is *here*. And I've dreamed of seeing them forever!" Elena shares her excitement.

Watching her enthusiasm, Arthur is beside himself with admiration, but also teenage hormones, and his feelings begin to tumble out of him. "I can't believe you know of them," he begins. "It's one of the most beautiful things I've ever heard of – *I don't understand why there is not more of this kind of thing in this world*. Everywhere I look on the news someone is on the brink of war with someone else." As he gathers momentum, he starts pacing around her in small circles, gesturing with his hands. "Hatred, possessiveness, greed... And then this orchestra.... Israelis and Palestinians removing themselves from political agendas to co-create beauty in music. *This* is the kind of thing I want to work on in my life!" As he finishes, he stamps his feet firmly onto the sidewalk and raises his head to the sky.

Elena's eyes sparkle with appreciation and a new level of adoration, and he can feel her fondness urging him onward, so he reaches up towards the sky as though trying to grasp it all for himself.

"And I think, sometimes... I want to go out there, to the stars, and bring this kind of thinking to new worlds!" As he hears his own words, he realizes how grandiose they must sound, and the words *delusions of grandeur* echo through his mind. "*Errr...* maybe that sounds dumb, but...." he says, beginning to go into damage control mode.

Elena catches him before he can backtrack any further. "No, Arthur. That is the *least* dumb thing I have heard anyone say in my whole life."

Their gazes lock for a lingering moment, an unspoken yet palpable connection crackling in the air. A magnetic pull between them, a fusion of intensity and warmth, creates a soft ambiance, and there's a gentle dance of vulnerability, like fragile petals swaying in a soft breeze, hesitant yet eager. Their heartbeats echo in the shared silence, a rhythmic drumming of anticipation, and a nervous energy tingles within their souls, causing a gentle prickling on their skin. Despite the charged atmosphere, they both shy away from taking the leap and sharing a first kiss. An involuntary giggle escapes Elena's lips instead, breaking the tender tension, and she suddenly has an idea she has to share with him.

"Do you want to get out of here?" Elena suggests, tilting her head just a bit inquisitively and perhaps tinged with a dash of mischievousness.

"What do you mean?" Arthur asks, intrigued.

"Away from this whole... whatever this is downstairs with all the hobnobbing and pretense - just get away from here! With me. No security details, no parents. I don't know... walk around all night, sit by the river, and keep talking like this with no interruptions?" Elena proposes, her playful smile irresistibly luring Arthur more deeply into perhaps the first escapade of his life.

"Yes! I do! But there's something I'm supposed to do. A banquet. I'm supposed to meet some people. Russians, as a matter of fact," Arthur hesitates, nervously twiddling his fingers together, torn between his obligations and his desires.

"I know. I'm supposed to be there as well. To meet some Americans, come to think of it – *probably to meet you* in some kind of orderly and predictable fashion. *But so what?"* Elena laughs, throwing her hands into the air as though casting her worries away "I don't want to meet you at a banquet. We've *already* met! So, let's roll with it and have some fun!" she insists, bringing her hands out to his and brushing against them tenderly.

Arthur smiles and suddenly loves the idea, and he nods to Elena, realizing he would be willing to do anything to be able to spend more time with her without their caretakers interfering. *"They're gonna kill us.... Yes! Let's get out of here,"* he says, the wildness of reckless abandon entering his voice.

They burst into laughter together, the sound light and infectious, echoing the joy of a babbling brook. It's the first time the notion of a deliberate mischievous act has crossed either of their minds. Arthur, feeling a surge of camaraderie, gently takes her hand. In that simple touch, there's a subtle electric charge, a buzz of connection that sends a tingling sensation through their fingers. Their eyes meet again, creating an ocean of possibilities swirling beneath their gazes. And yet, a coy shyness tints the edges of this newfound closeness, delicate as the petals of a dew-kissed rose at dawn. Then, a realization dawns on Elena, and she discreetly nods towards two vigilant looking men dressed in plain clothes about twenty yards away across the boulevard, both of whom are feigning a much-too-obvious nonchalance.

"What about them?" she asks, nodding subtly in the direction of the two guards.

Arthur, attempting to downplay the situation, responds with a casual glance and a touch of sarcasm. "Those geniuses?" He rolls his eyes. "Let's see…."

Entering into his *'analysis mode,'* a meditative state that Arthur has developed well over the years, he carefully marks out elements of the surroundings. Close to them, a red stop light casts a crimson glow, momentarily painting their world in shades of scarlet. A moving van waits in anticipation for it to change to green, pausing in its journey. Across the street, a busy crosswalk beckons, leading the way toward the glistening river. And nestled in the shadows, a park bench invites clandestine rendezvous, its secrets shrouded in darkness.

Returning to himself, Arthur begins to lay out the plan. "Cross the street, toward the river," he murmurs, leaning in close to Elena, his eyes alight with a mixture of excitement and determination. "As soon as that truck begins to move and blocks their view, lose your coat and let down your hair. I'll pretend to be heading back downstairs, and I'll trip. And then

Elena is quick to grasp his intent, her eyes shining with mischief and laughter. "And then *I* lay down on the bench while they help you up. They'll think I've vanished, panic, and that's when I cross to the river and –"

"And I'll meet you on the other side of the Pyramid," Arthur affirms, a conspiratorial grin playing on his lips.

Elena reciprocates the grin, their unspoken understanding illuminating their faces. "See you soon," Arthur remarks, confidence brimming in his voice.

"See you soon," Elena echoes, stepping onto the crosswalk as the light turns green. Arthur, ready to play his part, heads towards the escalator into the Louvre, and just as he crosses the threshold of the building, he trips on his own feet and tumbles hard to the ground. The guards, unwitting actors in this impromptu escapade, rush to his aid. Meanwhile, Elena embraces her role, giggling as she sheds Arthur's coat and lets her hair cascade freely. A sense of amusement propels her, she lies on the bench for just a moment, and then soon hastens her pace toward the river, eager to rendezvous with Arthur.

∞ ∞ ∞

In a conference room within the Louvre, the air hangs heavy with the scent of aged wood and polished brass, intermingling with the faint aroma of fresh ink from ancient tomes. The dimly lit room is adorned with opulent tapestries, their intricate patterns casting elegant shadows on the marbled floor. Kira, a force to be reckoned with, her eyes ablaze with frustration, commands attention within the hallowed space.

Beside her, Burt, a tower of concern, clutches his hands, knuckles whitening, anxiety etched into the lines of his furrowed face. Altan, a bastion of wisdom and resilience, stands with a calm demeanor, an aura of reassurance amidst the charged atmosphere. Lola, serene and composed, exudes a quiet confidence. Opposite them, the guards - usually paragons of duty and vigilance – exude an uneasy aura, grappling with the echoes of their recent failure, their expressions marked by the palpable discomfort of their oversight, shoulders tense, shifting uncomfortably in their uniforms.

"What do you mean they're *gone?* Tell me how it is possible that they are gone!" Kira's voice is charged with frustration.

"Do you two buffoons have any idea who these two kids are?" Burt interjects, "...and what they mean to our governments? And to the world?" His anger is palpable. "You call everybody, and I mean *everybody* you have to call to get eyes on this whole damn city and bring those two assets back here now!"

Lola and Altan share a disturbed glance.

"Assets?" Lola queries, concern filling her eyes.

"You mean our children, right? Isn't that what you mean, Burt? Our kids?" Altan's voice trembles with indignation.

"They are one in the same," Kira states without emotion, ending the debate before it can get any further off the ground.

The guards scramble to mobilize a search effort and hastily leave the room. Kira storms out directly behind them, and then so does Burt, but only after glaring at Lola. Meanwhile, Lola and Altan look quietly at each other.

"God, I hope they're all right," Lola murmurs, just a hint of worry in her voice.

After a moment, Altan's lips curl into a grin. "I think, perhaps, they are more all right tonight than they ever have been before."

Lola seems to relax, sharing a relieved laugh with Altan.

∞ ∞ ∞

Meanwhile, in the heart of Paris, Arthur and Elena find themselves standing hand-in-hand at the base of the iconic Eiffel Tower. Its wrought iron grandeur soars above, a testament to both human artistry and the dreams that rise in youthful hearts. They look up, heads tilted back, their awe mingling with the flickering lights that adorn the tower, painting the night with a tapestry of wonder. Their journey through Paris had begun with a desire to reach new heights, to stand amidst the stars that adorned the city of love.

They purchase tickets and go all the way to the top where the view does not disappoint either of them. Holding hands at the rails and looking down at the city sprawling below them, it is like they have finally touched the sky, and new worlds are waiting for them. The perspective makes them feel like all possibilities exist, both for them together, and for the world in general.

Their next venture is to the Paris Museum of Illusions. Amidst the vibrant charm of the museum, Arthur and Elena revel together in the magic that art and laughter can bring. Laughter bubbles forth, echoing in the halls adorned with captivating illusions, and each shared chuckle weaves a thread within their growing connection. In this realm of enchantment, the barriers of apprehension and formality melt away, leaving behind the pure, unadulterated joy of youth.

At the Arc de Triomphe, an emblem of triumph and strife, their spirits are subdued by the weight of history and the struggles of humanity as depicted in the stone reliefs present on the Arc's columns. As they stand beneath the towering arches and then take in the sunken carvings of stone depicting ancient battles, a shared understanding passes between them, unspoken but profound. *Violence, war, and murder have no place in humanity;* and then as each of them glance in sorrow at a soldier begging for his life at the hands of an enemy, whose raised sword is ready to pierce his heart, Elena rests her head on Arthur's shoulder, and he puts his arm around her. In that tender moment, they both find solace and strength in the gentle embrace, their silent empathy feels like a testament to the depth of their blossoming love.

The echoes of footsteps on the Parisian cobblestones mark their passage from one iconic landmark to another. Finally, they wind up by the meandering Seine River, and Arthur and Elena stroll arm in arm, the city lights reflecting off the river's tranquil waters. The city whispers its secrets to them, and the cool breeze carries the promise of love yet to fully unfold. They hold each other close, the youthful beating of their hearts syncing with the timeless rhythm of the river, entwining their souls in the gentle cadence of Parisian nights. The Seine becomes a guide, leading them from one embrace to another, and in its illuminating reflection of the city's lights, it reveals hidden corners seemingly unoccupied.

In one such clandestine nook, a secluded neighborhood park far from the bustling streets, Arthur and Elena finally come to a stop as fatigue has finally settled upon them. Even as their spirits dance with the grace of newfound love, they collapse onto the grass, the soft and warm earth cradling them in a tender embrace. The rustle of leaves and the scent of nature surrounding them, they rest, basking in the simple joy of each other's company, the first tender strokes of love's paintbrush upon the canvas of their hearts. Here, in the quiet heart of Paris, they find absolute comfort in each other, the culmination of a night spent weaving their love through the fabric of the city.

In the quiet embrace of the Parisian night, their laughter lingers in the air as a sweet echo of the adventures they've shared throughout the night, and they find a tranquil sanctuary beneath the comforting shadows of an age-old horse chestnut tree. The soft rustle of its leaves, kissed by the cool night breeze, accompanies them, a whispered serenade in the garden of their budding love. Concealed within an enchanting darkness, they pause, laying side by side upon the grass, their energy spent but their hearts alight with the fervor of this new and enticing feeling they share. Their laughter subsides, and as their eyes meet, a shift occurs in the atmosphere around them. Nervousness seeps in, a gentle reminder of the vulnerability that accompanies the beginning of every beautiful love story. The starlit heavens bear witness to this intimate moment, and in this tranquil corner of Paris, their hearts beat in harmony with the night, their souls embracing the unknown journey that lies ahead.

"It'll be light soon..." Elena's voice trails off.

"They must be going insane!" Arthur tries to keep the moment light.

"I'm not interested in what *they're* doing right now. I'm just thinking about...."

"Us?"

"Can we even be an *us* after only six hours?" Elena sounds uncertain but hopeful.

"Yes. I think so," Arthur replies, his voice gentle and reassuring.

"Is this a scientific evaluation of the situation?" Elena teases.

"Maybe. I sure know what lust feels like. *This* ain't *that*." A hidden smile makes itself evident in Arthur's words.

"Similar, perhaps. But not quite the same," Elena agrees, giggling. "Hey, there's nothing wrong with being a clumsy, horny teenager. It's just practice for becoming a confident, loving adult."

In the velvety embrace of the night, Arthur and Elena share a moment of laughter, a sweet melody that harmonizes with the beating of their hearts. "*Ma chérie*," he exclaims. She immediately responds, "*Mon chéri*." Their giggles dance around them with the air itself carrying the cadence of their mirth. As they lean closer, the atmosphere is charged with magnetic anticipation, the very essence of love drawing them in. Their lips meet, a tender collision that sets off a symphony of sensations - the soft caress of a gentle breeze, the scent of dew-kissed grass, the distant murmur of the city, the burgeoning desires within their bodies.

In this stolen moment, the kiss gains momentum, becoming a crescendo of passion and longing. The world around them fades into a blur, their connection deepening, the spark of their affection igniting into a flame that threatens to consume all else. Their souls intertwine, oblivious to the encroaching reality. Fate, ever unpredictable, interjects with an abruptness that jars them back into the world they had so desperately sought to transcend. The tranquil setting is shattered as two formidable SUVs charge onto the grass, their engines growling with a force that echoes the turmoil within. The flashing red and blue lights cast an eerie, quite disruptive glow on the scene.

Arthur and Elena, their faces statues of surprise and fear, jerk back in a sudden startle. Then, all at once, their expressions mirror the chaos erupting around them - bewilderment and worry, and the sense of tranquility they had cherished is replaced by an adrenaline-fueled rush of alarm. Altan and Kira, along with two oversized guards, bolt out of one of the vehicles, while Burt and Lola, with another two guards, come out of the other. In this chaos, Arthur's instinct kicks in. His first impulse is to shield Elena, to protect her from the sudden turmoil that has shattered their beautiful cocoon of budding love. He jumps to his feet before her, a human barrier against the unexpected storm, his eyes searching for any potential threat, his stance protective and reassuring. As the guards charge at them, Elena shouts out in rage, a voluntary manifestation of their shattered connection which echoes into the night as a haunting melody that seals the end of their stolen moment.

"Hey! What are you guys doing?!" Arthur yells, all his calm and cool burned away by a rush of raging adrenaline. The once serene night is now a stage for pandemonium, a stark reminder of unpredictable outcomes for joyful pursuits. Offering no response, the four massive soldiers in all black descend upon them, beginning to pull them apart even as Arthur tries to intervene with his fists. He had been unprepared, and their adrenaline had been pumping for hours now. They quickly subdue Arthur, and the metallic taste of fear coats his throat as he is forcibly separated from Elena. Even as he protests, he feels the steel grip of their hands, unyielding, relentlessly pushing and pulling and then finally tearing him away from the one person who has touched his heart so deeply.

Their movements harsh and unforgiving, Arthur is shoved into one car with his parents and Nash, while Elena, her face a canvas of anger, pain, and desperation, is pulled by the two remaining guards into the other car with her parents and Luda.

Through the windows they look at each other, their hands reaching out with fingers stretched as if hoping to defy the cruel fate that is tearing them apart. And then the screeches of the accelerating SUVs echo their anguish, reverberating through the now empty park like a mournful dirge. A whirlwind of emotions sweeps through each of them - torment, heartache, and the haunting realization that this may be the last time they ever see each other. Both cars speed away in opposite directions, leaving the horse chestnut tree deserted and bearing the weight of having witnessed yet another love lost to mankind's violence, wherein people's hearts become shattered in the hollow silence of still another futile step towards progress for humanity.

The interior of the Americans' SUV is suffused with the dim glow of the city lights filtering through the tinted windows, casting an air of tense redundancy. The seats, imbued with the scent of leather, cradle Arthur and his emotions. His voice, edged with anger and confusion, fills the confined space. "What the hell is going on?! *How dare you!* You don't know what was happening between us!" Arthur's words pierce the atmosphere, each syllable carrying the weight of his frustration and disbelief.

"You'll never see that girl again, Arthur. At least you better hope you don't. If you do, it means -" Burt's words hang in the air, a weight pressing on the tense atmosphere.

"Means what?" he shouts.

"It's... *complicated*, honey. She's a lovely girl. But you're an important kid. And, unfortunately, she's not for you," Lola explains, her voice shaking with forced compassion, attempting to soften the blow with her soothing, motherly love.

"I'll find her!" Arthur declares, determination in his eyes, a fierce resolve burning inside.

"No, baby. You won't," Lola says gently, trying to comfort her son but receiving only coldness in response to her warm touch.

167

Arthur looks to Nash for help, but Nash only manages a useless, sympathetic grin. He holds out his hand for Arthur to take and hold, "Buddy, …."

"I don't want to hear it, Nash. I just want –" Arthur can't finish. He turns away and leans his forehead on the window, quietly beginning to cry. The glass is cool against his skin and is a stark contrast to the fiery whirlwind of emotions churning within him. The rhythmic hum of the engine offers only a somber backdrop, and his tears are now blurring the city lights streaking past, painting a watery vision of heartache.

Within the dimly lit interior of the Russian SUV, the atmosphere is heavy with a distinct air of authority and formality. The elegant leather seats, embroidered with intricate patterns, exude a sense of opulence, even as the stiffness in their design hints at the gravity of the situation. The ambient lighting is a soft golden hue which casts gentle shadows on the polished wood accents, lending a touch of old-world sophistication that is betrayed by the spirit of love itself.

"If you *ever* pull a stunt like that again, I'll -" Kira starts, her voice carrying a regal firmness tinged with the weight of maternal responsibility.

"You'll *what*? Tell me, mother. *You'll what*?!" Elena roars, her voice reflecting absolute disdain.

"You'll regret it," Kira almost whispers. "You'll be sorry, and you'll wish you hadn't. It's not just me. *Trust* me: that American boy is not for you. Not now. *Hopefully* never," Kira warns, her words sharp and certain.

Elena looks to Altan, seeking a glimmer of understanding from her father. Altan, in his tailored suit, has an expression of stern concern, his eyes conveying both sympathy and caution. "It's true, my darling. I wish it wasn't, but for you to ever see that boy again, the circumstances will have to become quite dire first," Altan explains gently, his voice a soothing counterpoint to the formality of her mother's warnings.

"What does that even mean?! Why is everything so cryptic suddenly? About my future? About my past? About *...what is so special about me?"* Elena's frustration and confusion bubble up, her voice a plea for transparency in a world veiled in secrets.

Altan pulls her into his chest and her head finds refuge on his finely tailored jacket, while the scent of his cologne becomes a familiar reassurance amidst the uncertainty she is feeling. "Everything, my love. Everything about you is special. And you'll know more *in time,* I promise you," Altan reassures, his voice carrying the resonance of a father's unwavering love.

Her soft cries turn into sobs as the consistent hum of the SUV's engine underscores the emotional turmoil within the confined space. "I just want to be normal!" Elena's cry embodies a longing for simplicity amidst the intricate tapestry of her existence, and inwardly, she laments for a life untouched by the complexities of her very reality.

"You *are* normal. You proved that tonight. And I couldn't be prouder of you even though you frightened me," Altan reassures her. "But it is possible to be normal *and* special at the same time," he adds.

"Can I at least say goodbye to him at the academic awards tomorrow? Is that asking too much?" Elena pleads.

"We fly to Russia now," Kira states firmly, snuffing out the flame of Elena's hope in its infancy.

"But mother -"

"We fly *now*," Kira says, an iron finality in her tone.

Elena buries her face in Altan's chest, her tears escaping and dampening the fabric of his finely tailored jacket. She clutches at the lapels, and Altan, with his strong, comforting presence, holds his daughter close, his arms enveloping her in a protective cocoon. In the confined space of the SUV, Altan and Kira, two pillars of strength, exchange glares that crackle with unspoken words, the tension between them thick in the air. The dim lighting casts shifting shadows on the walls, adding to the somber atmosphere. Luda, her face a mask of heartbreak and worry, looks on, her love for Elena evident in the lines of concern etched on her face.

The collective heartbeats of two families in turmoil echo through the luxurious confines of the two SUV's as they drive into the night, silent and dissonant symphonies of love lost beneath the canopy of a nameless and disastrous fear....

∞ ∞ ∞

Chapter Six

Perfection, But at What Price?

∞ ∞ ∞

Six Months Later –

A rthur is in his bedroom trying to undo the sullen pain which throbs into his forehead seemingly two or three times each day, every day, since the Louvre. It always starts out the same – an aching in his heart, but then it quickly converts to an unknowable, intellectual conundrum that grows into the drilling of his brain. It always gets worse after sunset, and by this time of night, 10:45pm, it is usually almost unbearable.

He sits at his desk, at his computer, and his bedroom door is locked tight. His bedroom has changed a little over the years, and now there are some more posters of random idols from the 1980's - Duran Duran, Michael J. Fox's *Back to the Future* movie poster, Supertramp's *Breakfast in America* album all made it there and so did David Bowie; even Harrison Ford somehow survived the cut since Arthur had been a fan of the *Indiana Jones* series of films. He decided he liked the 80's due to its relative simplicity and innocence, its hopeful future, and because it seemed to cater to living life to the fullest despite the pervasive craziness within the world as it had existed.

Snow is falling outside at a rapid rate, and he looks up from the computer screen to watch the dazzling display of thousands of flakes driven by a dedicated wind from the northeast. His musical tastes run the gamut, with a leaning towards European, but especially British bands and artists, and tonight he has played *"99 Red Balloons"* about ten times, and quite loudly at that, all the while making furious computer searches.

Getting up from the desk, he falls onto his bed and begins scratching his head as he replays parts of a phone conversation he had overheard the day before between his father and Nash. He had heard his father using the world "Louvre" and that's what had gotten his attention initially. As he steeled himself against the outside wall of his father's home office, his ear pressed firmly against the plasterboard in order to try to hear each possible word, it seemed to Arthur that his father had been discussing the implications of their having separated him from Elena back in Paris almost six months ago. He had also heard his father calling out the word *Nash* when he was addressing the person on the end of the line. Though it was a difficult challenge, as only when his father talked at above average volume could he make anything out, Arthur could have sworn he had heard his father using the words *"Genesis Executive Project, or Genesis Executive Procedure."*

What the hell was this all about?

He snaps upright and strolls back to his desk. This was only the third time Arthur had dared to hack into the Pentagon intranet. The first time he only looked for thirty seconds just to confirm he had actually gotten into it. The second time, he searched for records on his father and mother, but only found archives with things he already knew about them. Since nobody from the federal government had yet stormed their house with guns blazing, he felt confident that the proxy server he was using, since it was attached directly to his father's government account, must be sufficiently working to hide his activity. He types *"Genesis Executive Project"* in the search bar and gets no results. He tries *"Genesis: Executive Procedure,"* then *"Genesis: Executive Order,"* and then other variations, but comes up empty each time. In the past, he had heard his parents discussing the profound meaning of the Icelandic conference back in 1986, and so his intuition leads him to try a cross-search with "Reagan and Gorbachev." He is disappointed, once again, since besides newspaper stories about their Icelandic conference, nothing more is mentioned.

Frustrated beyond measure, he pounds his desk on both sides of the keyboard. Then the truth of his angst once again comes to the forefront. *I must try, and keep trying, until I find her!* He had found nothing useful thus far from any of his searches for Elena, even when he entered any potential spelling variation of her last name or searched for her in more than thirty different main provinces of Russia. He had been attempting this routinely for many hours at a time every few days or so. Now stuffed at the back of his underwear drawer are all of the now seemingly worthless letters he had written to her, hoping someday to find her address, a six-month supply now equating to about sixty of them altogether. In those, he had meticulously searched his feelings and penned them down for her, assuring her that one day they would find each other and continue their burgeoning love. He had made it clear that being in the world, only together in her presence, was all that he ever longed for anymore.

Maybe she is here on the Pentagon intranet. So, he types her name and age. Once again, he tries various spellings and different locations in Russia, but another twenty failed minutes later, he gives up. *"Come on!"* he shouts out loud. "Six fucking months and there's not one thing! This cannot be true!" He takes a deep breath. Thinking furiously, he begins again with a new tact. *She is part of this program too!* He types in *"Post World War II Peace Talks,"* and instead of anything about Elena, he is surprised to see an article about two authors, Dr. Sean Ryan O'Leary and Francis Rocco with a photo of the two in the 1950's along with a link for "video archives." Arthur clicks the link, and a series of video selections comes up. The first one is entitled *"1954 Talk Show."*

Well, I haven't seen this before.... He clicks on it.

On his screen, a black and white vintage video begins to play. In the video, Sean Ryan and Captain Rocco are identified by their full names in a caption at the bottom of the screen; they sit adjacent to a nameless host at his desk, a man of about forty, wearing a traditional beige suit from the times.

> *Good morning, Chicago! We are here today with Dr. Sean Ryan O'Leary and Mr. Francis Rocco, co-authors of the new book on how to create lasting peace in the world called "Erase the Lines." Welcome to you both, and thanks for being here.*
>
> Dr. Sean Ryan O'Leary, dressed in a navy-blue suit and turquoise tie, looks tired and yet enthusiastic: "Thank you so much for having us," he says.

Captain Rocco is a bit overweight, wearing dress pants and a long-sleeved, maroon, pullover shirt: "Good to be here," he adds.

The host smiles and says, "Let's get right to it. Your book has caused quite a stir in academic circles and in the political and social sciences. You propose that the true path to world peace is not for a single nation to dominate the world, but rather to erase all geopolitical lines around the globe and learn to live as a single species on Earth. Am I correct in my synopsis?"

Sean Ryan looks to Rocco, who nods for him to take the lead.

Sean Ryan, leaning forward in his chair: "Well, yes, Sir. That's exactly right. You see, we studied the formation of the idea of government in natural history and found some reasons why, right down to our very cells, humans have felt a need to have leaders and followers in any given population, rather than an autonomous population where everyone has the same roles and responsibilities, and–"

Host, interrupting: "So what you're saying is that there is a great deal of merit to the idea of communism, not just in Eastern Europe but globally?"

Sean Ryan's face falls and Rocco immediately rises to the occasion, becoming indignant and protective of Sean Ryan.

Captain Rocco: *"You didn't let him finish.* And, no, that's not what we're saying at all."

The host looks at Rocco: "Am I correct in my research that you received a dishonorable discharge from the United States Navy, where you were working in Intelligence?"

And now it is Sean Ryan's turn to become protective of Rocco. He says: "It was an honorable discharge for battle fatigue! And it was after the war ended!"

Host: "Could you tell us about that? So that we may have something of a better perspective on your particular point of view, Mr. Rocco?"

Sean Ryan and Rocco exchange looks, both mortified and crestfallen as this has unraveled very fast.

Captain Rocco: "I'd be happy to talk to you about battle fatigue on another segment, Sir, but we're here today to talk about our book and our findings on the flawed design of the human psyche that makes us believe going to war is ever a good choice to begin with."

Host: "Flawed design? I think many of our viewers may wonder: If we are made in the image and likeness of our Creator are you also suggesting that God himself is flawed, *or perhaps doesn't exist at all?*"

Sean Ryan: "No! Certainly not! If you'd just listen–"

Rocco suddenly stands up and pulls Sean Ryan to his feet, as well. He says to his colleague: "We're leaving," as he puts his arm around him, and they head off the stage and out of frame. The host watches them leave with a broad smile on his face and then turns to face the audience and says: "Some pair they make," and then the video ends.

Arthur shakes his head and is taken aback by the televised ambush of Sean Ryan and Rocco. *Wow! That was harsh! What the hell did they do to deserve that kind of treatment?*

Interested in seeing more, he begins scrolling through the other videos about the pair. He comes to one entitled *"The Demise of Suspected Communists Sean Ryan O'Leary and Francis Rocco."* Arthur thinks to himself, *What the hell is going on with these two?* He clicks on this title, and a video of a newsreel begins to play:

> It is a blonde-haired woman news anchor in her thirties, with an emblem of Channel 7 from Chicago in the upper-right corner of the screen. She sits at the news desk with a comically exaggerated stern expression across her otherwise pretty face, and she speaks in a very serious tone: *As we mentioned in our breaking news stories just moments ago, it has now been confirmed that controversial authors Dr. Sean Ryan O'Leary and disgraced former United States Navy Captain Francis Rocco were killed in an apartment fire in the Near North neighborhood of Chicago early this morning. As you recall, this infamous duo were suspected of living there as a communist, homosexual couple. No cause for the fire has yet been determined but fortunately, fire crews arrived in*

time to safely remove all other residents from the building before the fire spread.

She shakes her head as if she is horrified to read the next line, and then she focuses on the camera and utters: *Their book, Erase the Lines, has been widely discredited as Soviet propaganda. We have no idea why they were even able to write it and get it published in this ... the Land of the Free and Home of the Brave... In other news....*

The newsreel comes to an end and Arthur feels saddened. Sarcastically, he says to himself, *Shocking. Those poor men didn't have a chance. If any copies are still around anywhere to be found, I must find their book and read it from cover to cover.* He shakes his head and huffs out a plume of hot and frustrated air. *What a world....*

And then there's a knock on his bedroom door. "What do you want?" he asks.

"It's your loving mother," Lola answers.

Arthur rolls his eyes and goes to the door to unlock it. Before she even opens it, he crosses his room back to the desk.

Lola peaks her head in. "Honey, can you keep the music down? Put on your headphones, but don't keep us all awake all night just because you are working. Also, don't make yourself deaf - keep the volume reasonable."

Without looking back, Arthur says, "Sure, Mom. Okay, I will. Sorry."

Lola notices Arthur is still on his computer, and she glances at the computer screen, but his large torso is blocking it. "What have you been up to all this time? Don't tell me you're still searching for her even after all these months?" She comes into his room, and he quickly clicks to the regular internet as she now stands just a few feet behind his chair.

He wants to yell at her and tell her how angry he still is, and that they are all evil for keeping him and Elena from at least writing to each other. But all he can manage is, "What do *you* think?"

She is very worried that he has not moved on yet and reminds herself to tell Nash once again about Arthur's devotion to the girl. She has a thousand other responses she wants to give him, but she, instead, adheres to what they have told her to say when this topic comes up between them: "You're never going to find anything."

Still tapping at his keyboard, he says, "I find it extremely interesting that you are so sure of that."

"Arthur, believe me, I want to help you! You think I don't want you to be happy? *I would find her myself if I could!* But it's above my pay grade. Honey, I hate to say it so plainly, but they just don't even *tell us* everything."

She has given him an opening, and he is tired of playing their silly games. "Yes, and that is precisely why I also meant to tell you something quite clearly. This is *some fine program* you and Dad signed me up for. *Thanks a lot!*" He finally swivels his chair to face her. "Oh, and isn't it called *Genesis Executive Order Number One?*" He embellished the last part, uncertain if he would get it right, but knowing that all government programs carry a number to them and that this was likely the first program of its kind, he figured it was a good guess.

Lola's face falls. She had never suspected he would figure out the name of the program, and she has a moment of disbelief before she recovers somewhat. Even though she feels for him and agrees with his questioning of the program, she is not permitted to divulge anything else. "I want you to get some sleep. It's late and you have a big day tomorrow." She stares into his eyes, which are glossy with either tears or fatigue, but she must remain diligent. "Remember, whatever else, I love you."

Despite his frustration and resentment, he cannot hurt his mother no matter what else he might feel. He wants her to come through for him with some sort of explanation about why he and Elena must not be allowed to contact each other, but he knows by now she cannot do so. He turns back to the computer screen. "I love you, too. Get a good night's sleep."

"Good night, Arthur. You too. At least, try to." Lola turns, exits, and closes his door.

Arthur stares blankly and defeated at the computer, feeling at a complete loss, before finally shutting it off.

∞ ∞ ∞

Elena walks down a long, dimly lit corridor within the hallowed halls of the University of Moscow's Social and Political Sciences building. The atmosphere carries the scent of old books along with the faint echoes of scholarly discourse. She heads toward the exit, her steps echoing in the spacious passageway. The walls are adorned with rows of posters, each vividly displaying study-abroad programs in various European cities.

As she nears the row of posters, her steps slow, and her gaze is drawn to the captivating imagery of the one showcasing France. An exquisite image of the Louvre transports her momentarily, evoking a whirlwind of emotions within her soul. Memories of Arthur, from whom she was torn away, resurface, inflicting a sharp, bittersweet pain. She feels an ache deep in her heart, a pang of longing and loss, yet she steels herself against the memory, sealing it within the vault of her heart.

Amidst this internal struggle, running footsteps approach, growing louder and more distinct, disrupting the fragile moment.

"Elena!"

The voice belongs to Professor Ordine, heralding her entrance with a sonorous resonance that reverberates through the corridor. As she strides in, there's a palpable shift in the atmosphere caused by the faint swish of her elegant silk blouse and the gentle clink of her understated gold jewelry. Also, the delicate trail of her signature perfume, a mix of jasmine and sandalwood, leaves a subtle but distinct olfactory imprint. The authoritative click of her leather heels on the polished floor exudes both confidence and grace, and her eyes, sharp and discerning, sweep the surroundings. A subtle half-smile graces her lips, suggesting both confidence and approachability. "Elena," Professor Ordine says once again, her voice carrying a blend of gentle concern and academic authority, "can I speak with you?"

Elena snaps out of her trance with a jolt as Professor Ordine's urgent words finally pierce her thoughts, shattering their fragile cocoon.

"Oh, I'm sorry, Professor. I was lost in thought," Elena replies, suddenly becoming self-conscious and smoothing down the wrinkles in her shirt. "How may I help you?"

"It's your paper," Professor Ordine begins. "I... I don't understand it."

Elena furrows her eyebrows and purses her lips. "What do you mean? I thought it was very clear."

"No, I mean, yes, it *is* very clear," the professor clarifies. "What I mean is... you study hard sciences - medicine, astronomy, agriculture, engineering. Don't get me wrong - your paper *is* fascinating, offering an intriguing perspective on sociology and political science. Very insightful! A *fresh* perspective that I'd like to discuss with you further. But..."

Elena successfully suppresses a proud smirk. "But...?"

"It's outside your area of expertise. It *won't* earn you any credit toward your degrees, so *why on Earth did you write it?*"

Elena pauses before responding, and then, studying the genuine curiosity in the professor's eyes, she says, "Professor, I've simply developed some new interests. I don't see why a person can't have more than one area of expertise." Professor Ordine seems impressed but still puzzled as Elena continues, "You are one of the most celebrated sociologists in the world," Elena gushes. "I've read *everything* you have published, and I'm fascinated. Impassioned! I want to study under you. Not for credit. Just for the sake of learning. Would it be possible?"

Professor Ordine offers a slight smile, at the same time both impressed and yet pondering Elena's words. "Your curriculum is already more than a full load. How can you add this to what you're already working on?" Professor Ordine seems sincere with her concern. "Will the Board even let you?"

"I was hoping that *you* could help me convince them," Elena replies, playing up the sweetness in her smile and tilting her head to the side.

Professor Ordine realizes this is a lot to ask of them, and she is about to refuse, but then catches herself. Reflecting on Elena's determination, she finally responds, "I... I can try."

"I'm sure you'll succeed," Elena says optimistically. "I'm already ahead in all my other courses, and I have time to spare. There *should* be no objections. And if there are, perhaps we could keep the matter between us?"

After another brief moment of contemplation, Professor Ordine nods. She figures *why not?* "Alright, Elena. I'll speak with them right away," she confirms.

"Thank you, Professor Ordine! I *do* appreciate it," Elena says politely, giving a formal bow. "Good day."

Without another word, Elena pivots gracefully, her long, charcoal-gray coat flowing around her as she starts to make her way towards the exit. As she buttons her coat, Professor Ordine, with an inquisitive furrow in her brow, has one more question, her voice a gentle but insistent tug. "*Please*, Elena, before you go, may I ask... *Why* the sudden interest? Is there some identifiable seed that has grown this intellectual forest within you?"

Elena, her mind racing, pivots around as if caught in a cyclone of ideological concepts. Desperately sifting through the labyrinth of her mind for the perfect words that would articulate her feelings and beliefs, they finally come. "I've... recently found myself in a situation that makes no sense," Elena begins slowly, but acquires momentum as her emotions surface. "It's... antithetical to the best parts of humanity. It's... cruel! It is *against love*! And it doesn't serve any real purpose. It seems that the powerful people on this planet will do *anything* to avoid feeling anxious, even when their anxiety is completely unfounded."

The professor is at a loss for words, but she gives Elena a pleading look that begs for more. Elena obliges her puzzlement and continues, "I want to travel in space, Professor, and I want to see new worlds. I would hate to think that I was bringing the worst of us with me," Elena's eyes involuntarily dart back to the Paris poster, a flicker of longing and wistfulness dancing within her gaze. Professor Ordine, ever observant and insightful, catches the glint of fascination that lights up Elena's eyes, recognizing that, for some reason, Paris holds a substantial hold over her.

"I want to try to understand why cruel things are enforced in a so-called civilized world," Elena continues, her fingers tracing quotation marks in the air. "I want to know what it is about humans that allows such things… I want to know - *what is wrong with us!*" She concludes with a renewed sense of resignation, her graceful fingers curling into fists which she shakes with an authentic emphasis born from the fires of her existential crisis.

Professor Ordine, touched by Elena's heartfelt explanation, responds with a genuine and warm smile, "So do I, my dear. *So do I,*" Professor Ordine nods toward the Paris poster. "You know, I'm actually attending a conference in Paris next month. Perhaps you'd like to come with me as an assistant.…"

Elena forces a smile, though it's tinged with a poignant sadness that wells up in her eyes, causing them to glisten like fragile glass catching the light. She considers the offer, but just as soon realizes it would be too much to bear. She then responds, her voice carrying a delicate weight of sorrow, "I've already seen Paris, Professor. But I thank you all the same." She does not want to be in the professor's presence once the tears begin to fall and so she adds, "Good day."

Professor Ordine offers a solemn nod, a respectful recognition of the discussion's end. Her gaze returns to the poster, curiosity piqued, as she observes Elena's swift departure from the building, her thoughts drifting once again into the realms of scholarly contemplation and trying to figure out how to pull some strings for Elena's sake.

∞ ∞ ∞

The Next Morning -

The American Sky School banquet hall exudes an aura of academic anticipation, adorned with meticulous care for the student science fair. A grand purple banner announcing the National High School Science Awards is draped elegantly across the stage, complementing the aura of prestige that the event carries. A lone microphone awaits the voices that will soon fill the hall with youthful brilliance.

Amidst this backdrop, parents and teenagers buzz with excitement, mingling and sharing their enthusiasm in the spacious open area that stretches before the stage. The hum of animated conversations and occasional bursts of laughter create a lively symphony that permeates the air.

In a corner near the front of the stage, Arthur, Lola, and Burt form a small enclave of their own and are engaged in conversation. Lola, radiating pride and joy, adjusts Arthur's tie with delicate fingers, her eyes alight with maternal love. Burt, typically reserved, cannot conceal the swell of excitement and fulfillment that colors his demeanor, a testament to Arthur's accomplishments.

"This is truly remarkable, Arthur! I'm overflowing with pride. Mathematics and science - the very foundation of the cosmos," Burt exclaims, his eyes alight with genuine excitement and the fervor in his voice unmistakable. "Not like psychology," he continues, only a hint of jest in his tone.

"What's wrong with psychology?" Lola retorts, her voice carrying a blend of curiosity and conviction. "Arthur's awards in psychology make *me* so proud." Gently, she places her hands on Arthur's shoulders, guiding him to face her. With tender care, she looks into his eyes, a mixture of love and admiration reflecting in her gaze. "It truly is a gift, your understanding of the mind and the heart," she says, the warmth of satisfaction evident in her gaze.

Arthur takes a moment to absorb her words, feeling a swell of gratitude but still shying away from the spotlight. Three distinguished college professors, their attire resplendent in mortar boards and flowing gowns adorned with the regalia of their doctoral achievements, process onto the stage, exuding an air of academic eminence. They prepare to commence the ceremony, each of their steps echoing with a sense of scholarly gravity and purpose.

"And now we realize it's just one facet of your brilliance! Come on. The ceremony's beginning. Let's find our seats," Burt urges, his enthusiasm infectious. With his gentle prompt, they settle into their seats, positioned strategically close to the stage, eager to witness the unfolding ceremony.

Dr. Loretta Goldstein, the senior-most among the professors, strides purposefully to the awaiting microphone. A palpable hush sweeps through the crowd, anticipation hanging in the air like a charged current, as all eyes focus on her every move.

"Ladies and gentlemen, welcome to the National High School Science Awards where we acknowledge and celebrate the nation's brightest and most innovative young minds in applied sciences and mathematics," Dr. Goldstein announces, her voice projecting a sense of gravity and excitement that matches the occasion. "For one-hundred and sixty years, this annual ceremony has not just been about awards, but about a celebration of the young minds whose intelligence, diligence, and creative thinking will pave our way into the future for the benefit of all humankind."

The audience erupts in applause, their hands coming together to create a thunderous ovation that reverberates throughout the hall.

"Without further ado, I want to call our first recipient to the stage, *Arthur Anders!*"

Arthur rises from his seat, a crescendo of applause accompanying his journey to the stage. Lola and Burt beam with a sense of parental accomplishment, their hearts swelling with pride as they grasp each other's hands and lean into each other. The atmosphere hums with a blend of excitement and reverence as Arthur steps onto the stage, feeling the collective gaze of the audience upon him. Lola and Burt watch him ascend the steps, their smiles radiant and their eyes shimmering with emotion.

As he reaches Dr. Goldstein, she extends her hand with vigor, offering her hearty congratulations to Arthur away from the microphone. Returning to the audience, her words continue to echo through the hall, infused with purpose and a sense of profound significance.

"This young man has done something that no other recipient has ever done: Mr. Anders has not only reevaluated the science of the past with skill and expertise but also used his new findings of past knowledge to advance an idea for the future. In one fell swoop, he has successfully refuted Isaac Newton's Gravitation Constant Fudge Factor and used his finding to successfully plot a viable trip to Mars!" As the crowd begins to clap once more, Professor Goldstein raises her hands to hush them.

"Arthur," Dr. Goldstein continues, turning to face him directly, her eyes sparkling with a blend of admiration and pride, "It is my great pleasure to honor you with the first of a brand-new award created to celebrate students who use information from the past to successfully - and, in your case, quite literally - chart courses for the future."

She takes a plaque from one of the other professors on stage, its surface gleaming under the stage lights, and delicately places it into Arthur's hands. The weight of the honor, both tangible and symbolic, settles upon him like a mantle of recognition. It's more than just a plaque; it's a culmination of years of dedication, an emblem of his relentless pursuit of knowledge and innovation in the realm of mathematics and astrophysics. In this moment, the weight is both a responsibility and an inspiration, a reminder of the heights he can achieve and the potential to leave an indelible mark on the scientific world.

Turning to the audience, Dr. Goldstein punctuates the moment, raising her hands high into the air. "The first annual Augustine Ferrari Award for Applied Mathematics in Astrophysics for the Humanities!" The audience bursts into a somehow even more enthusiastic round of applause, the sound sending a vibration through Arthur's sternum. The two other professors join them at the microphone, smiling, and shaking Arthur's hand.

One of them takes over the microphone. "Congratulations, Mr. Anders!"

The other adds, "I'm so proud of you, Arthur. You've blown us away!"

Amidst the clamor, Professor Goldstein steps forward and leans her face close to Arthur. A sense of honor and pride glistens in her eyes as she shares this monumental moment with the young prodigy. She directs him to the microphone.

Arthur looks at his parents and takes a long moment before he responds. "Hello, I feel very gracious having all your support. I would just like to say…." He stops and Burt worries, wondering what he might be up to. Finally, Arthur adds, "Thank you to all of you!"

There is more thunderous applause and the two professors escort Arthur off the stage. Once they are in the wings, the first, a man in his forties with a tweed suit and tie, asks, "How do you feel, Arthur? You're a genius! *A bona fide genius!"*

Arthur, still reeling with humility, finds it difficult to articulate his emotions. His cheeks flush, and he looks down, overwhelmed by the weight of their praise. The title of 'genius' feels like an enormous cloak, far too grand for his shoulders, and yet it is thrust upon him, nonetheless.

"You *are* a genius," the other stout and elderly professor adds warmly, the white hairs on his ears seeming to stand on end. The way he says it, with genuine admiration, leaves Arthur both grateful and increasingly bashful. "Oh! I see you're also very humble," the peculiar little man remarks, his bright blue eyes gleaming. "A word of advice to help you on your terrific journey as a great thinker: *don't be too humble.* If you don't *know* you're a genius, you may sometimes forget to act like one."

The advice resonates deeply within Arthur, and his eyes widen as he contemplates the wisdom just imparted. Knowing well the power of his words, the wizened old professor nods and smiles. At this very moment, Arthur can feel the full weight of his destiny, realizing that he is on the cusp of a remarkable journey, one that will demand not only the acknowledgment of his brilliance but also the courage to embrace it.

∞ ∞ ∞

Perfection, But at What Price?

Chapter Seven

The Ride to End All Rides....

∞ ∞ ∞

It is as though humanity's tampering with the delicate thread of fate has somehow disrupted the natural flow of the universe, and the world begins to take a serious turn for the worse. The dams, which had for so long held back the raging rivers of modern civilization's inevitable consequences, begin to rupture and fail, and as the structures which had protected humanity from itself for so long collapse in on themselves, the nations at the bottom of the global pecking order, the most vulnerable people on earth, are washed away by chaos, while the rest of the world turns its face away.

The wealthiest nations feel the pressure in their pocketbooks, but in attempts to deny and reroute the rushing waters, the people bury their heads in the sand and pretend like everything is just fine. Runaway inflation is reclassified as "inevitable revaluation." As growing unemployment and wealth disparity split society in twain, the subsequent rampant homelessness is re-branded as a "widespread mental health crisis" or a "growing trend in alternative lifestyles." There are more riots raging through Europe and America than ever before, and many turn entire city blocks to rubble are referred to as "non-violent protests." The wars breaking out in other parts of the world, and which threaten to spread into Europe, are spoken of as "regional conflicts."

Shadows become the poultice of choice to cool the wounds of the terrified and helpless creatures of privilege. They resolve themselves to their last remaining bliss, encased in an air-conditioned coffin of complete ignorance. In the midst of the age of information, everyone decides that they don't want to know what is happening around the world anymore. The ugly truth is decidedly "toxic." In response to society's changing needs, the role of the journalist transforms from informing people of the world's realities to soothsaying the masses in an effort to pacify their fears, though most people can simply glance out their windows or at their savings accounts and apprehend the horrible truth. Unable to fathom the potential end of their way of life, most people shut their eyes to the world around them and deny what they are witnessing, even as the falling dominoes wind their way toward them.

In India and Pakistan, years of drought come to a head, and tens of millions die in the famines; nature offers no sign of a reprieve. Rather, the Earth seems to grow hotter and dryer each year. Riots of unprecedented scope and violence burn much of New Delhi and Calcutta to the ground, while skirmishes break out between soldiers at the Pakistani border, and politicians rattle the sabers for war in a counterproductive effort to stem the tide of destruction. Elsewhere, across the Middle East and Africa, the civil wars that had long raged in the cradles of civilization spread into the parts of the world long untouched by such terrors. The Mediterranean Sea is overrun with countless machine-gun wielding pirates in speedboats from Libya and Algeria, and the economies of Greece, Italy, Spain, and Israel spiral into free fall. Hamas and Hezbollah make headway into the Holy Land, and in the meanwhile, the arms dealers make their bucks while the warlords of the world grow stronger, sating themselves on the blood of the innocent.

∞ ∞ ∞

The air roars and vibrates as the whirling propellers of the Coast Guard helicopter spin their way up to full speed. The dust and soot from the concrete landing zone is tossed up into the air in every direction at once as though hit by a shock wave. A pilot and another man in full bright orange combat fatigues are strapped inside, flight helmets covering their heads and faces. From one of the two nearby flight hangars, a man of heroic proportions in all black tactical gear jogs out towards the chopper, as the two men from within watch him in awe, wondering to themselves which secret military organization he belongs to or if he's even really human at all.

A futuristic black helmet with a wraparound visor completely disguises his face, and he effortlessly carries his two-hundred-eighty-pound body of solid muscle upon a six-foot-four frame, dressed like some sort of Delta force paratrooper. He is unlike anything the men have ever seen, and the words "super soldier" sit at the forefront of both of their minds. All they know is that their commanding officer has told them to obey the man's every word as though it came from God himself, and between the nameless fear of mystery and the excitement of novelty, the two salty veterans feel as though they have been transported back to the day when they were soft-skinned conscripts, straight out of boot camp. As the mysterious soldier approaches the helicopter, the pilot speaks into his helmet radio and points upward with his index finger.

"Sir, we are ready for takeoff at your command."

The man replies in a deep voice, "Proceed at will and steer us a steady perimeter around the South Bay, past downtown, and all the way to the Coronado Bridge." He hops into the back seat of the chopper and says, "By the way, you can call me Arthur."

"Okay, Arthur, get ready for one wild ride!" the pilot responds.

Arthur nods. *Right – this is nothing. Once I finally get to Houston, I'll have just two months to prepare for the ride of all rides!*

Without delay, the pilot throttles up and the wheels of the landing gear gently leave the ground as the helicopter lifts into the sky, making three clockwise circles of increasing size over the Coast Guard Station as it seeks altitude. As the city comes into view, the man sitting in the back with Arthur elicits an audible gasp and leans out the open window to look down into the bay. Throughout the water, the white rubber buoys of the mooring field, which once held fast the sailboats of so many proud San Diego residents, are nowhere to be found. In their places, the masts of dozens of sunken ships protrude crookedly from the water like the bleached bones of some great beast that had died and sunk beneath the waves.

The usually thriving bay is all but empty save for the presence of the U.S. Navy, whose two aircraft carriers and three destroyers sit completely still at anchor, contributing to an imposing presence, the likes of which southern California hasn't seen since the days of the conquistadors. As the chopper turns its final circle, the downtown comes into view and the Coast Guardsman shakes his head in disbelief. There are still several smoldering fires scattered on some streets and sidewalks between the skyscrapers, and an inestimable mob of densely packed people weaves like an infernal serpent down Broadway all the way from the water to the interstate twenty blocks away. The once green Waterfront Park is trodden completely bare so that not a blade of grass remains. For reasons many newscasters were still trying to figure out, the riots which had taken hold in America had found their largest numbers in this Southern California city.

"Oh my God…" the Coast Guardian's quavering voice comes crackling through the headsets. "All this in just two weeks? Where is the National Guard?"

"Steady, soldier," Arthur replies in a calm voice, placing a massive hand on the man's shoulder. "I need your mind clear for the mission."

"But my wife and children are still in the city. I had no idea…"

Beneath his helmet, Arthur's jaw tightens, and he feels a wave of emotion surge into his chest. Similar scenarios are playing out in large cities across the country. He knows that the National Guard is already spread too thin to deal with them all, and he has information that the official plan is to simply wait out the riots and extract as many VIPs as possible. He knows that his parents are safely protected within the heart of America's military establishment in Virginia, but his empathy triggers another thought. *What about Elena? Are there riots in Moscow?*

Even now after all these years, she is an ever-present figure in his thoughts, like an angel that sits on his shoulder and speaks words of comfort into his ear. But recently, the howling of the devil on the other side of his mind contributes to a growing anxiety, one he shares with everyone else in the world. *Are my loved ones in danger? Is there anything I could even do for them?* With a hard sigh, he pushes the weakening perspective from the forefront of his mind and back behind the curtain of his unconscious.

"They'll be fine," he lies to the other man and to himself. "That's what we're here to ensure."

∞ ∞ ∞

In a brightly lit, all white, windowless room, *Doctor Elena* leans over a long table with her gloved hands gripping the edges, staring down at one of the hundred various samples in the petri dishes. Nearing thirty years, she is already a veteran in her respective field, holding two Ph.D. degrees and a third which she has yet to claim, *because I'm busy*. With her golden locks cascading over the shoulders of her white lab coat, she looks like either the last human you would hope to see when you die or the first angel you see as you enter heaven - only the goggles would give her away. Her lips twist into a half-frown as she squints and bends further down to look at one particular specimen. *This is germinating so much more slowly than we anticipated. Will I even be here to analyze the results?* She is torn between her dedication to the government's secret subterranean lab-grown food project and the upcoming transition that will forever change the trajectory of her career: a six-month stay on the International Space Station.

Since that traumatic day at the Louvre when she had met, and then immediately lost, her first and last love, *Arthur*, her personal world had suddenly accelerated so deeply into the world of science that she had time for little else. Into a locked diary that she had hidden within her mattress, she poured her broken heart, writing poetry, prayers, and letters to the beloved boy she briefly knew. That was half her lifetime ago, and as time heals all wounds, both her tears, as well as the ink, had finally run dry.

Now her unspoken thoughts echoed like ghosts in the back of her mind, never finding their way into the living world. To distract her, Kira had used her influence to secure Elena a coveted internship with Moscow's most preeminent scholars working on the cutting edge of hydroponics. A long-kept government secret, Russia's hydroponics program was actually one of the most advanced in the world, and it is run as any other covert project by the Ministry of Defence. The stated goal of the massive undertaking is to eventually produce enough food in underground labs to feed the entire Russian Federation.

By now, there are nearly a thousand facilities all throughout the country, with sprawling underground bunkers filled with hydroponic plant towers, and Elena has worked in the flagship facility beneath Moscow for nearly eleven years. After all this time, she has grown attached to the place. She has carved out a niche for herself, and she is respected and appreciated by her colleagues, many of whom she has trained straight out of university.

Unlike the people at the Kremlin who placed her upon a pedestal and treated her as a celebrity, her team in the labs appreciate her for something real, because her discoveries and innovations have transformed and advanced the entire program, not to mention multiple supplemental scientific fields. In a relatively short time, she had become recognized as one of the most knowledgeable hydroponics experts in the country. What was once laughed at in many circles as a hopeless government money-hole, she had largely transformed into, not only a potential revolution in hydroponic agriculture, but a viable business opportunity.

The towers are producing enough food to push the books from the red into the black, and what used to require months of debate for marginal gains is now simply a matter of request and approval. *Today there are a thousand labs, but tomorrow there could be a hundred thousand. We really could feed the entire country.* While a trip to the International Space Station represents a huge career advancement forward for her personally, Elena feels a deep sense of anxiety about interrupting the long, steady flow of her profound advancements within the underground labs. *Sure, there are a few neat experiments we could perform in space, but will it really help things overall?*

Lost in her thoughts, Elena jumps up as she hears the doorknob turn behind her and lets out a nervous laugh.

"Sorry, Elena! I probably should have knocked," her supervisor chuckles in a friendly tone. She wears the same white lab coat as Elena, but her deep green eyes reveal the wisdom of many years.

"Oh no, not at all, Sonechka," Elena says smiling and shaking her head. "I was lost in another world. These samples are moving at a much slower pace than our models projected, and I started thinking about how in three weeks I'll be somewhere up there..." she trails off, pointing an index finger to the ceiling.

"Yes, way, *way*, up there," Sonechka smiles as she walks up to Elena and looks down at the table full of neatly labeled petri dishes. "I wanted to talk to you about that, Elena."

Elena figured it would be best to voice her recent concerns sooner rather than later. "I know it's too much to ask to delay the launch. No one gets to have their cake and eat it too, but still... I was hoping I could be here when -"

"Elena," the older woman interrupts her and holds up her hand. *"I'm here to tell you something."*

"Don't tell me," Elena closes her eyes and clasps her hands together as though praying. "Don't say it."

"The launch has been moved up another week," Sonechka says almost apologetically, easing the words out of her mouth.

Elena grows quiet at first, and then a bit sullen. Shaking her head, she finally asks, "Why does this keep happening?"

"The rocket men don't give answers - only orders," Sonechka replies. She smiles at Elena endearingly. "Do you want me to file a request with God for an answer to that?"

"I'm sorry Sonechka. I don't mean to complain. It's just that -"

Sonechka gently places both of her hands onto Elena's shoulders. "The project will continue in your absence, and it will be here when you get back. Take your mind off of the microscopic, my dear." Rubbing Elena's shoulders firmly, she waits a moment and then says, "This is going to be such a wonderful experience for you. And besides, you have trained the young ones *so* well - they're like little versions of you!"

The frustrated wrinkles which line Elena's forehead soften just a bit. "I suppose. You always manage to know just what to say, Sonechka. Truthfully, I think it will be you and everyone else working in the hydroponics lab that I will miss more than the project itself."

"And we know that, sweetheart. Your dedication has been unwavering - *we will all miss you just the same.*"

∞ ∞ ∞

"*Artemis, this is mission control in Houston. Do you read? Over.*" The tiny voice crackles through the radio in the crew module of the fledgling NASA Space Launch System. Colored red and orange lights flicker in a steady rhythm across the world's most complex instrument panel. Two months have flown by, and Arthur is ready.

199

"We read you loud and clear, Houston," the chief astronaut in the captain's seat replies. Her name is Harriet, and she is Latino, well-built, with a formidable countenance. "Just looking forward to getting off the planet before my husband wakes up and realizes I'm gone. Over."

There is a delay before the next reply. *"Artemis, we read you loud and clear. Countdown to launch will commence in T-minus three minutes. We'll get you out of here safely. Over."*

This elicits a chuckle from the four astronauts, and as it slowly dies off, the mood in the tiny cabin returns to that thick air of silent anticipation that few humans will ever understand. This is the first manned mission back to the Moon since Apollo 17 in 1972, and in a time fraught with so much chaos and uncertainty here on their home planet, they all share a diverse collection of mixed feelings about blasting off and leaving it all behind. Among the four NASA scientists, Arthur is the only outsider, and his role on the mission is a tightly guarded state secret. The scientists can guess from Arthur's robust stature and silent disposition that it has something to do with the military, maybe something to do with Russia, but beyond that they don't know or even really desire to understand. They each have enough on their minds, and as far as they are concerned, Arthur is no more than a guest passenger on their mission.

"Artemis, we are T-minus one minute to launch. Over."

Arthur's mind swirls, and suddenly he perceives a feeling that he has long experienced and always denied. He feels lonely. No one here knows him or understands him, and they are going to a place where these people will be the only ones around. Before, he had always been able to soothe himself with the thought that he had his people, his colleagues, his family. Now on the precipice of true departure, those pacifying thoughts offered him no comfort. He was going too far away to feel connected. It was the loss of the Louvre all over again, and

200

this new pain in his heart pricked at the old pain he had long ago put away.

"T-minus thirty seconds. Artemis, prepare to launch."

The walls and seats begin to shake as the rocket thrusters slowly kick on. Arthur looks around at the others, but none of them cast a glance his way. He unconsciously digs his fingernails into the armrest, tearing through the vinyl into the padding.

"T minus ten, nine, eight, seven..."

He closes his eyes and breathes deeply, thinking that perhaps he should have done more for the people he loved the most on earth.

"Six... five... four..."

The sound of the thrusters grows to a mighty roar, drowning out all of his thoughts.

"Three... two... one... liftoff!"

∞ ∞ ∞

Elena feels like the pressure might peel the skin backwards off her head, and she resists the urge to reach up and touch her face to make sure it's still there. Instead, she tries to push her tongue out of the back of her throat, but it feels like it weighs a ton. The roaring of the Soyuz rocket engines vibrates every bone in her body down to the marrow, and the combination of bizarre sensations send her into a trance-like state. When the launch shroud suddenly falls away and reveals the beauty of the starry blackness, she gasps, unable to tell if she's awake or dreaming. Turning her eyes to the left, she sees the curve of the Earth as they continue to rise higher. It looks to her like a massive blue marble. *How beautiful. How peaceful. If only everyone could see our planet from up here, spinning so gracefully and unperturbed - seemingly so content with itself.*

201

A different roaring sound joins the cacophony as the third rocket stage begins, and within a few minutes, an industrial clang signals the jettisoning of the second stage rocket. The pressure gradually builds, and Elena wonders if she will be able to remain conscious all the way through to the finish as sweat beads on her cold brow and her breathing quickens. *I don't want to do this again if they give me the choice.* After what seems like an eternity, the roaring sputters to a stop, and they are left hurtling through orbit in tranquil silence. In the cockpit, hanging in front of the instrument panel, a tiny stuffed teddy bear hanging from a piece of string begins to steadily float upwards on its own, and Elena's eyes go wide. Her arms float up from the armrests, and she laughs at the sensation. *Is this what being dead feels like?*

Perhaps I was wrong; maybe I can handle six months of this ....

∞ ∞ ∞

Zipping through empty space, the Orion craft completes another low orbit of the Earth at over twenty-thousand miles per hour, her two-hundredth trip around the planet in just seven short days. As the orange core stage jettisons off and tumbles back to Earth, the astronauts look on with gratitude. Their memories had been jogged by their training: those RS-45 boosters had been reused from the old Space Shuttle program begin in the 1970s, and the distinct cone shape of the boosters evoked within them childhood memories of watching launches and landings at the Kennedy Space Center off Cape Canaveral, Florida. Now unburdened by her massive fuel tanks, the Orion module floats alone with its solar panels fully outstretched. Far beyond the atmosphere at two-hundred-and-fifty miles above Earth's surface, from the confines of the tiny capsule, it appears to the astronauts like a blue paradise stuck alone within the utter emptiness of space.

The original plan of the Artemis mission had been for the Orion spacecraft to make one or two quick orbits before engaging the Trans-Lunar injection burners to slingshot off towards the Moon, but this is where the plan underwent a secret change. Free floating and loaded with enough rations to feed the astronauts for two extra weeks in space, this stage of the journey has been extended, and Orion temporarily serves as the base of a secret military mission with the goal of covertly disabling Russian global positioning satellites.

While NORAD has ever-vigilant eyes on every old launch silo, and its chiefs express confidence that America and its allies could shoot down almost all of the older-style Russian nukes during their launch phase, information from spies over the past decade has revealed that the Russians are in possession of a new breed of smaller, faster missiles that can be launched from almost anywhere, and which largely rely on satellite communications to guide their trajectories. While so much of Russia's legacy nuclear arsenal relies on inertial navigation systems made of spinning gyroscopes to guide the missiles across the sky, it is the new generation of nuclear missiles that most concern the Americans, but the trim design of the updated systems sacrifice some functional navigational autonomy in exchange for stealth. This is the weakness upon which this unnamed mission seeks to capitalize.

Built onto the Orion module, hidden from sight behind the now jettisoned launch shield, a specialized military drone was hidden for this special part of the mission. Simply dubbed *The Ball,* this all black, spherical robot is a one-of-a-kind weapon developed in secret, specifically for the purposes of this particular project. Four feet in diameter, it is completely solar powered and able to steer itself through space with the dexterity of a fruit fly by using a series of micro-thrusters around its body. Its systems are built to track down and identify the signatures of various Russian satellites, and although the spherical weapon automatically maintains ninety percent of its own systems, it leaves the crucial decision-making up to its operator. Thus, target identification and weapons firing are performed by a human being.

When a target is locked and the operator onboard Orion gives the command, a tiny hatch on the sphere will open and fire a specialized magnetic dart, one of fifty, which then attaches directly to the target and, when signaled at a later time, delivers its payload: a localized electro-magnetic pulse which will fry the circuits inside its host. This method of delayed attack would allow the Americans to simultaneously disable a multitude of Russian satellites the moment a launch is detected. If that day never came, the Russians would forever be none the wiser, as standard military procedure is to destroy malfunctioning satellites rather than to undergo the expensive effort of capturing and repairing them. On Orion's second orbital pass, the semi-autonomous drone had been released and directed towards the GPS satellites encircling the Earth over eight-thousand miles away.

As chief weapons engineer aboard the Orion, Arthur has been operating according to a strict schedule: three hours of sleep after eight hours hooked up to the drone station, followed by one hour of self-maintenance which involves eating, exercising, and evacuating food. In the seven days of the mission so far, the team has successfully tagged fifteen Russian GPS satellites, and Arthur is finishing up his fourteenth shift. Sitting in his control seat with the massive view helmet on his head, his forearm muscles flex as he dramatically grips the joysticks on each armrest to signal the Ball to enter into its suspended state. Until he wakes it up again, the weaponized drone will simply drift invisibly along with the GPS satellites. *Just watching and waiting. Same as me.* He carefully pulls the pilot helmet off his head and holds it down into his lap, looking upwards at the ceiling to stretch his neck. Then as always, his vision is magnetically drawn to the viewport, through which the astronauts continually gaze at the gorgeous, blue planet below.

From way out here, it strikes Arthur as a perfectly peaceful place, even if his own careful study of human history, with its continuous pattern of violence, had tinted his perception, casting his home planet and the humanity it produced in a frenzied and malevolent light. Or maybe it had been the effects of all of his "special" schooling and the boot camp he had been made to attend which operated outside of the regular military track, starting at the age of fifteen, and which were never fully beholden to the oversight of any visible system of power. *But no matter which had caused his pessimism, right now, all he can behold is what a majestic and beautiful sight Earth truly is. Like a queen, she floats and spins with dignified air, so still and stable in the mad flux of the universe.* His mind turns to how it had all come to be in the first place. *What if there had been nothing, ever – no earth, no universe, no organisms, not even a single cell. Without even a single being's consciousness, who would be there to know how to experience that absolute nothingness?*

It makes his mind spin, and it is difficult for Arthur to imagine, from this perspective, how evolution, the big bang, or anything else postulated by modern science, could have led to the grace and grandeur he is witnessing through Orion's viewport. *It might make one prone to believe in God, had I been given a chance to go down that path.* But Arthur is sure that religion is a system designed for the fearful ones, for the civilian world, which requires a padded explanation for both the unknown and the absolute chaos inherent in the world's affairs.

Science never has the complete answer, but someday it might, and until then at least it offers more realistic explanations as to why life seems so precarious. Yet Arthur's heart swells with the longing for home, watching the gentle motion of Earth's angelic wings made of swirling white amidst the backdrop of so much blue and green. *Mother Earth, diligent protector of the human race; and yet vulnerable herself, especially to mankind's own vengeance. Everything we have is a gift from her, and everything we give back only amounts to a slap in the face.* He reflects one last moment on the chaos he has come to know in his life, and in his heart, he clutches onto a memory of his own mother's smiling face. He wonders if he has given back to her all of the gifts she has so freely given. From high in space, he momentarily glimpses a terrifying flash in his mind which suggests that he alone might have to protect the entire planet, *Mother Earth,* all at once, all by himself.

Anyway, what could we give back to her that she would want? Is it even possible for humanity to thrive on Earth without causing her extreme damage? Hasn't our violence and waste already caused enough destruction, and haven't we already gone past the point of no return – if so, is it possible to even fix her? His successes in space provide him with only marginal comfort, and cruel facts just keep surfacing to the top of his mind: *We suspect there may be up to a hundred of these satellites, and we could only ever aim at disabling a portion of them with the drone. What hope is there really if the analysts' worst predictions are right?* He had thought it over a thousand times, and it seems to make the most sense that Russia's new generation missiles would be similar to those of the American military. *Ours were designed with exactly this kind of fail-safe in mind. Wouldn't the Russians have built in rapid relay systems just like we did? What difference would a microsecond delay make if they launched hundreds of missiles all at once? Wouldn't their internal navigation systems still be enough to direct them?* His feelings of futility torture him with the weight of countless, impossible questions. He thinks the entire military systems of the world are just baseless and useless propaganda, wasting good science for the sake of somebody's power-trip and ego. He knows that one man can't save the entire world, but part of him can't stop thinking along heroic lines.

Each time Arthur retires for his three hours of sleep, his dreams reflect the actions he takes while he is awake and hooked up to the drone station. The only difference is that everything goes wrong in his dreams: the Ball somehow crashes, Russia launches nukes, and everyone dies. But when he wakes up again, it's like all the kinks have been worked out of his system. Everything goes perfectly: the Ball finds its targets without a hitch, no missiles, and… everybody keeps living. Somehow, the successes of the day don't balance out the horrors of the night, though for the astronauts, day and night are purely abstract terms as they whirl around, in and out of the shadow of the planet every half hour. At this time, only Arthur and one other astronaut are awake.

"Arthur are you alright?" the voice of the lead astronaut pierces the daydream.

"Yes, I'm fine," Arthur automatically replies. "Why?"

"Because you were holding your eyes so wide open that I thought maybe you were being electrocuted," Harriet laughs.

Arthur cracks a smile. *This is a good crew.* Banter is essential up here, even if just to hear the voices of others. They're all scientists, but in any other life they could have been special forces. They all have the right mind for it: sharp, relaxed, and always looking out for each other. He feels grateful to be part of such a tight unit at such a weird time as this, and it's a good thing everyone gets along well since they will be trapped for weeks together in a single room.

"I'm alright, Harriet. I am just waiting for another transmission from my friend Rubin at SETI. And then I looked at Earth - our home. Isn't it beautiful? When I see blue, I feel a cool ocean on a hot day. When I see green, I'm resting in the woods looking at the sky. When I see clouds, I feel rain and wind on my face.... Don't you see it that way?" As he completes his poetic reverie, he lets out a happy sigh and smiles, his eyes glistening with passion.

"I'm not sure if anyone sees things quite like you do, Kid."

Under the warm, honeyed glow of the setting sun, Harriet's gaze lingers on Arthur with a softness that speaks volumes. Her eyes crinkle at the corners as her lips curl into an affectionate smile, a radiant testament to the adoration she harbors for his innocence and sincerity. He decides to take the chance of trusting her by disclosing classified information. *After all, everything would come out sooner rather than later anyway.* "Anyway, you've heard what they've found on WASP-96b? It's about those newest images from the Webb telescope."

Harriet's brilliant mind begins spinning its powerful cogs, and she closes her eyes tightly. "Let me run the computer programming inside my head. That's the large exoplanet orbiting a star similar to our sun which is about halfway between us and the Southern Ring Nebula, about 1,150 light years away? The one where the Webb spectrum data just a few days before we departed identified ice crystals in the planet's cloud tops? *And ... if I remember correctly,* these clouds also had a very similar composition to earth's own clouds, right?"

"That's some mighty impressive computer programming up there," Arthur jokes and taps his index finger to his own temple. "I was speaking with Rubin earlier during my routine briefing with Nasa. Well, the very latest information derived through Webb's transmission spectroscopy while we've been floating around up here, indicate a high probability that the planet itself is harboring liquid water on its surface, and also identified more significant signatures of *habitability*."

"*And ...?*" Harriet said, as if that proved nothing.

"SETI has actually already been set for focusing on artificial signals specifically in and around WASP-96b. The latest report was supposed to confirm about a half hour ago; Rubin was unusually excited about what he thought they had been detecting… *even more unusual than usual!*" He looks at her expecting that this information would rouse her interest, but he is disappointed by her expression. Nonetheless, he decides to push his luck. "Pretty neat stuff, huh? *We may not be alone after all.* To be honest, I never thought we were.*"

Harriet rolls her eyes at Arthur. "I'll believe it when I see it. I want one of those little Grays to come to me and press its wiry index finger right into my belly button before I'm willing to admit that there's intelligent life in the universe, besides our own failed existence! Hah!" She laughs, and Arthur smiles.

"Well, if there is -"

Flashing red and yellow lights on Arthur's headset interrupt him mid-stream, signifying that NASA is calling. "Hold on a moment, Harriet. I think it is Rubin. I have an incoming transmission."

Through radio communication, Rubin from SETI speaks to Arthur alone through his headset. "Arthur, *unbelievable news.* I can't tell you much more at this time, but I had to follow-up with our earlier conversation, and we've found a positive signal! It is real, true, repetitive, and intelligent. *There's life, Arthur!* Intelligent life exists on WASP-96b! Repeat - *Intelligent life exists on WASP-96b!* I can't give you anything more at this time and so have to keep this brief. We will talk soon! Over and out!" Arthur's jaw drops to his chest.

"What was that all about?" Harriet asks him.

Arthur shakes his head in disbelief, so many questions running through his mind all at once. He looks at Harriet with a grin. "Looks like one day soon we may truly find out how that other Divine experiment is working out. Just got confirmation, Harriet. Life exists on WASP-96b!"

She shakes her head and frowns. "You sure you heard correctly about all of this mumbo jumbo, Arthur, or have you been fixating so strongly on disarming these Russian satellites that your brain has turned to mush?"

Arthur chuckles. "Positive! Believe it or not, this is a pretty low-pressure situation compared with what I'm used to." Arthur looks over at her – only eight years his senior, she naturally treats him with the same regard as her two teenage sons back on Earth.

"I bet, Kiddo," she nods, and she stretches out and ruffles her fingers through his thick hair. "But it's when we're *bored* that the really scary stuff comes out looking to play. So stay alert!" She smiles from her heart, but her eyes reveal a deeper uncertainty.

Arthur delicately lifts his laptop, and with a focused intensity he delves into the labyrinth of data streaming from Earth. A torrent of information races across his screen, but he appears to consume it all, effortlessly navigating the digital deluge. Harriet observes him for a moment, a sense of awe washing over her.

Harriet marvels and asks, "What, did you take an Evelyn Wood Speed Reading course or something?"

"Ha! No, just… years of practice," he chuckles, grateful to escape the alien debate, then leaning close to the screen and squinting his eyes he continues. "Comms and military movements down there look like they've finally returned to normal... *so hey!* We're on a perfect streak! What do I have to worry about? Everything is going so far as intended. I even have perfect, weightless bowel movements."

"Speaking of which, here - this stuff probably has laxatives in it," Harriet replies, smiling and not missing a beat. She reaches into her lap and passes him his meal ration: a tray of rehydrated macaroni and cheese with a little plastic fork sticking out of it. "At least it'll keep you going so long as you keep eating it," she laughs. "Bon Appétit!"

Arthur picks up the fork and pokes at the mush in the tray, stifling the beginning of a laugh. "Someone once told me that the food really is the hardest part about space," he says and laughs. Hungry - he shovels all of the macaroni into his open mouth in a single motion and tries to tune out the part of his brain that recognizes taste.

Harriet chuckles and shakes her head as Arthur pushes himself up and out of his chair to float towards the toilet in a separate compartment. As he drifts past another astronaut cocooned inside of a sleeping bag with a blindfold covering his eyes, the sleeping man speaks in a dry and raspy voice, "And when will the exorcism begin?"

Arthur laughs as he floats by. *"What's that supposed to mean?"*

"It's nothing," the astronaut they called *Cowboy* replies with a bit of sarcasm. "You just talk in your sleep a little bit. Well...*singing* might be a more accurate description." He lets out a laugh like the host of a haunted mansion at a carnival might, and then he and Harriet both start chuckling a bit more gently.

Arthur is immediately embarrassed, and he looks over at Harriet, who shakes her head with a smile and then gives Arthur a little shrug meant to say, *'pay it no mind.'*

"What I say in my sleep, I *don't* want to hear when I'm awake," he admits, his cheeks tinged with a subtle flush, as if he's unveiled a hidden vulnerability.

Cowboy, a Texan through and through, responds with a reassuring grin, his voice laced with a touch of brashness, sensing Arthur's unease. "Fair enough, buddy," he drawls, his tone gruff but understanding. "And that goes double for me."

Chuckling as the tension dissipates, Arthur wordlessly pulls himself past Cowboy and into the toilet compartment, shutting the door behind him. *Great – something else to worry about. That's just what I need.*

∞ ∞ ∞

It has been that, for the past two years, both economically and politically, even the largest governments are caught in a spiral of forces that they can no longer manage very well. A reckoning of past lies, mistrusts, unscrupulous corruption and then that extremely lethal violence used almost a hundred years ago by the one country that was supposed to be the leader in touting civil rights and justice, are all colliding at the same time, just when any proven force of good was essential in order to stabilize worldwide sentiment regarding all of these other misfortunes. Instead of taking responsibility and forging a path of forgiveness to move forward, truth is denied, and blame is placed elsewhere, creating more distrust, violence, and obfuscation, which nobody even bothers to listen to, let alone believe, anymore.

The earth-shattering ripples tear across the world like a tsunami wave, shredding through the world's institutions as though they are but boats of folded newspaper. Even the untouchable insurance companies start to declare bankruptcy, as the dangers inherent in global transport push gasoline prices to

$15 per gallon. International trade hemorrhages, and within a matter of weeks the shelves of grocery stores in every major city begin to look rather empty. Across the globe, untold millions flee the crowded urban areas and escape into the wild to seek survival in the land. The desert cities of Casablanca, Baghdad, and Dubai are plunged into economic freefall as the exodus leaves them largely abandoned.

From the smoldering ashes of the collapsed Soviet Union, the new order which rose to direct their populace apparently only led with new illusions, and after over forty years of quiet in Eastern Europe, Russia had begun once more to invade their neighbors, beginning with Ukraine, and then never looking back. To the rest of the world at the time, it had seemed to be an insane push by an insecure despot, ill planned and poorly executed, and yet in the minds of the Russian President and his inner circle, this was the inexorable manifestation of Russian destiny. It has never bothered the elites in Moscow that this victory had cost the lives of hundreds of thousands of young men. But now, the looming threat of famine and widespread starvation is becoming very real in Russia, and many analysts even speak openly of it as an inevitable probability. In this context, the body count in all of their excursions has translated to a two-pronged benefit: less hungry mouths to feed, and complete control of the European breadbasket.

The Dow Jones Industrial Average presently continues its steady forty-week decline, and economists have made the declaration that the world is strangling within the suffocating grasp of "Great Depression 2.0." While the President signs another economic stimulus package, the fifth this year alone, he urges Americans to buy like there is no tomorrow. Reports continue to flood in from Taiwan of military aggression about to come ashore from the high seas. It had started as military exercises conducted by the Chinese Navy but now has progressively become more extreme each year for the past four years. In a recorded video message presented at a meeting of Russia's provincial officials, the Chinese President declares once and for all, and quite emphatically, *that the age of American dominance has come to an end for all time....*

Just as police from multiple counties have failed to contain the riots in San Diego, even after California's governor had requested that the President deploy the National Guard to help bring the situation under control, similar unrest occupies major cities all across the United States. For the past two weeks, authorities have been unable to stop the angry mobs roaming the cities from looting and burning stores and gated communities.

∞ ∞ ∞

High above it all, realizing as she always had that the further away from Earth she could get, the better off she would be, Elena has just decided that the International Space Station might just be her favorite place ever, notwithstanding Paris. The nature of the labor she is performing is both meticulous and carefully prescribed, and there is no room for the gravity of any specific personal choice in any manner whatsoever to weigh her down. The lighting is perfect, with cool blues evenly revealing every dustless workstation during active hours, while a charming balance of low warm hues light the cabin during downtime so that it almost feels like snuggling up next to a warm fireplace. And best of all, the icy void and certain death of space looms just beyond every wall, floor, and ceiling, so no one could try to convince her to come out of her comfort zone. It feels to Elena that the entire space station had been designed to satisfy each of her own unique sensibilities. It had never

214

occurred to her, until now, that she had always thrived within the confines of a government vessel, floating safely through the chaos just outside of the real world itself.

Her work is similar in space to what she was conducting on Earth, but there are new elements of it here that are a challenge for her, especially the root mats and plant pillows in place of pure hydroponics. Beyond that, she has noticed that so many resources and so much storage room aboard the ISS is dedicated to keeping and storing the lab grown food, without any explanation being offered. Elena has been meaning to ask about it, but so far, her work has kept her continually occupied, both physically and mentally. And still, it is a spirit of hope which drives her daily experimentation, hope that what she will discover up here may end up saving billions on Earth from famine and starvation. Throughout the little lab, Elena's cabbages, radishes, tomatoes, and pea plants jut forth from their cushioned bases, looking quite different from their Earthly counterparts, as though they're trying to pull in every direction without any certain direction. As Elena stares lovingly at her Swiss chard seedlings, she notices an unusual beeping sound coming from the control panel in an adjacent room. She waits for it to stop, but when it goes on for almost a minute, she finally lets out a frustrated sigh and pulls herself through the doorway to see what's going on.

The other members onboard, two cosmonauts and three astronauts, are pressed together in front of one of the display consoles, and from their huddle comes an excited chatter simultaneously in both Russian and English.

"What is it?" Elena calls out to the group in Russian. *"What's happening?"*

When they don't answer, she tries again in English. *"Hello everyone!"* she practically shouts. "Does anyone want to tell me why that beeping keeps going off, and why no one is stopping it?"

Two of the American astronauts look over their shoulders with childlike joy in their eyes.

"Come look at this, Elena!" the youngest of the male astronauts exclaims, waving her over. "We think it's the Artemis crew making another flyby!"

"The lunar mission? I didn't think it was even happening yet," she replies, floating over to the group.

"We didn't either," he beams up at her. "They launched just a few hours after y'all did. I thought I saw something on the radar a couple of days ago for just a split second, but this time they're coming really close! Just a couple hundred miles!" He corrects himself, "Oops, I mean kilometers!"

"Oh wow," Elena raises her eyebrows in mock surprise, turning back towards the laboratory. A brief thought enters her mind, as it had occasionally ever since she had become part of the Russian space program...*he had said he wanted to explore the universe*, and she wonders if it was even a possibility that *... no, I must take that thought right out of my mind as it is too distracting.*

Without looking over his shoulder at her, the astronaut replies, "I know, right? We might even be able to see them with the naked eye." But then when he finally looks back at her, his words taper off as he sees her leaving. "Hey, don't you want to scope the radar?"

"Just call me when they're getting close enough to see," she says, floating away.

The young astronaut is a physicist, and he is a little overfriendly for Elena's liking. *And besides, our work has no direct crossover. Oh, but that reminds me...!*

"Hey Brian," she calls back from the doorway. "Why are you guys keeping all these food cultures instead of tossing them out?"

"That's classified," the oldest astronaut intervenes, casting a harsh glare over his shoulder. *"Need-to-know basis only!"*

"So, *you* know then, huh?" Elena snaps back, her irritation at being rebuffed by an American taking everyone by surprise.

"Jesus, no! *I don't know since* you asked so nicely. No one up here knows. Why do you even care? Is there something bad about having too much food in space?" The oldest astronaut gives an exaggerated shrug with both of his hands raised up into the air, but he is clearly annoyed with her.

However, by then, Elena had already pulled herself back into the lab, ending the awkward exchange with an appropriately unceremonious exit. *Why do I care? I'm so tired of all the 'secret this' and 'classified that.' Would we not accomplish much more working together?* Back in the room with her plants, she returns to a state of confined calm and resumes her work. *Fine, I think I don't want to know anyway.*

∞ ∞ ∞

Within the Orion Space capsule at just the same time, Harriet, Cowboy, and Arthur are gathered around the radio as the other astronaut sleeps. "Mission's going well so far," Cowboy quips.

"If there was any wood around, I'd go and knock on it," Harriet responds with a smile.

Gazing down at Earth, Arthur says, "The planet seems so lonely from up here - as if it needs a friend."

Harriet looks at Cowboy and smirks.

217

"Maybe you can write some poetry," Cowboy says in his deadpan fashion. "That would make a great opening line...."

Suddenly Arthur's face takes on a serious hue and he clasps his headphones more tightly to his ears.

"Take it easy, it was only a joke," Cowboy says, thinking Arthur was reacting to his poetry comment.

Arthur puts his finger to his lips, *"Shhh...."* Harriet and Cowboy realize he is paying close attention to something coming through on his headphones.

After listening a few moments more, Arthur types into his keyboard and scours the information coming through on his screens. Without looking up from them, he says, "Seems to be high-level chatter all at once in some sort of frenzied manner from both within, and without, the various military headquarters of all big three down there."

"You can get all of that?" Harriet asks, puzzled.

"It's part of my specialization. I can't get specific words, just the traces from our satellites detecting unusual activity, and then I was able to pin down general sources." There is absolute silence, as cold and dark as the universe behind them. Finally, Arthur breaks it. "I am trying to determine its origins, or at least, if it is coming through valid channels or if it is just some sort of internet or signal attack, and then just worthless babble."

"Yeah, please," Cowboy says, "find out one way or the other so we can all get some peace and quiet around here."

Just then Mission Control comes through the console to all. *"Important news update, Orion."*

Harriet says, "Go ahead, Houston." Harriet speaks into her microphone headset but leaves the output set to Orion's main speaker so that everyone can hear.

Mission Control: *"We've had some very interesting and conflicting intelligence down here. It started with this interception from Chinese media, which we translated into English:*

> *"We now bring you breaking news. NATO forces have successfully intercepted a nuclear armed missile which appears to have been launched from Chechnya with a trajectory towards London. American Military officials are reporting that fighter jets from the USS Harry S. Truman aircraft carrier stationed in the Mediterranean shot down the missile as it entered the third minute of its boost phase over the Black Sea. The planes were already in the air performing exercises when they were...*

"And that's all we got at first. I can tell you with certainty that NATO forces did no such thing as there was never any incoming missile. It was alarming to be sure, and I hate having to tell you this, but about ten minutes after all of that, a Russian missile was shot down just thirty-six miles off the coast of San Diego. Russians deny culpability."

Arthur turns his attention back to his monitor and begins going over data once again.

"Of course, they do," Harriet says as she watches Arthur's sudden intensity.

Mission Control: *"Here's the thing, though: Now Russia is broadcasting on their news that one of ours was shot down over the Mediterranean two minutes later. And we didn't fire a missile."*

Arthur looks up at Harriet and Cowboy, who are looking at each other with raised eyebrows. Arthur returns his attention to his screen and starts typing like mad.

Harriet asks, "So, what's the current status, Houston?"

"It's all hush-hush for now. Our guys are talking to their guys to figure out who might be playing games with missiles today. Both sides are trying to figure out where that initial Chinese report came from. The good news is that there's been no more activity since. We'll keep you in the loop, Orion."

"Thanks, Houston. Over and out."

Arthur looks more disturbed than Harriet and Cowboy, and Harriet notices. "Listen, my young countrymen, if the public knew how many near misses there are down there, it would be chaos. *Not to worry, okay?* Let's just keep focused on our mission." Arthur relaxes back into his seat, distancing himself from his keypad. "I think this is getting to be pretty distracting, so let's just leave it all in the good hands of the pros down there, okay?"

"I mean, it's pretty much over, isn't it?" Cowboy announces, in part, trying to convince himself of his own statement. "Some third-party nut job trying to get the two school bullies to fight each other...." He stands. "Ahh - enough of this shit. I'm hungry as hell...."

Arthur finally speaks again for the first time since Mission Control's dialogue. "Yeah, it's nothing.... Nothing unusual, anyway...." He seems relieved and turns to find Cowboy. "And what's new about that? You're always hungry, Cowboy."

"True 'dat!" Cowboy announces.

Harriet laughs. "Now you two are distracting!"

After sling-shotting around the Earth one last time, the Artemis team aboard the Orion spacecraft had traveled three days towards the Moon. When it had passed the ISS for the last time, Arthur had planned on trying to look out at it, but he was needed on the flight deck to navigate and had missed his one chance. In a few short minutes, their spaceship would enter lunar orbit, and the moon itself now looms before them in gleaming white, brightening the inside of the Orion capsule. Their covert mission had been successful, and EMP darts had found their homes upon all of the Russian satellites that had been targeted, while otherwise, the fledgling flight of the Artemis rocket system had passed every test with flying colors. All that had been left to do was to orbit around the moon several times to take photos of possible base locations for a planned Space-X Mars mission in the future. Then, they would return home safely, and this would be Harriet's imperative. Arthur's work is done, and the other astronauts are tasked with purely scientific and navigational affairs for this, their last trip around the moon.

She takes hold of the reins with a settled assurance. "Mission Control, this is Orion, do you read? Over."

"Artemis, we read you. Over." Something in the man's voice on the other end unnerves Arthur.

"Happy Fourth of July, Houston. We've had one hundred percent success disabling the targeted Russian satellites. Orion's systems show that we are set to enter Lunar orbit, with communications blackout beginning in five minutes from now. Do you copy? Over."

"Copy that, Orion. Our systems concur. Happy Fourth. How are you guys making out way up there? Over."

"We're fine, Houston," Harriet replies, but catching a skeptical stare from Arthur in her periphery, she asks, *"hey, is everything settled with that missile issue down there?* Over."

The five second pause feels like an eternity. *"I'd like to say so, but the Russians are staying pretty tight lipped about it. No word. We're all still here, so that's good news to report. Over."*

Harriet bites her bottom lip. This is not the encouragement any of them were looking for, and as she replays his last sentence, she realizes the man really does sound quite unsettled. "Everything will be fine, Houston. *God Bless America, everyone!*" she says, lacking her usual enthusiasm. *"Over and out."* She turns back to find Arthur first, and then Cowboy, who is still standing in the same spot as he was before. "OK, now the radio goes off...."

Arthur says, "I've got a better idea...." He plugs his iPod into the radio speaker system.

"Oh, no, Brother," Cowboy exclaims, exasperated. *"Not again!"*

Beaming, Arthur nods, "Yes! Beethoven's 5th, renditioned by none-other than -"

"The West-Eastern Divan Orchestra," Harriet and Cowboy answer in tandem, Harriet rolling her eyes. "We know," she says.

"Hey, it's all about victory," Arthur says. "The world just won a victory with that narrow miss. *It's perfect!*"

The music begins and Arthur relaxes back into his seat, finding a blissful state, while Harriet and Cowboy shake their heads and coalesce. Cowboy manages to grab a granola bar from an overhead compartment and with Beethoven's 5th playing and Arthur looking peaceful, Cowboy takes his seat.

Harriet says, "Come on, boys. Time to go around the dark side, our overt mission – see how this craft handles and get all the scientific data necessary for the next mission's landing down there."

"She's handling things pretty well," Cowboy chimes in, "if you ask me. Hell, now I even think we could beat Musk's SpaceX to Mars if we really wanted to."

Arthur cuts in, "Still have to use his and SpaceX's advanced landing system to transport Artemis III's astronauts from Orion, which will be in lunar orbit, to the surface of the Moon and back again. They've worked hard on it, and I think it

is a truly unique operational concept which greatly increases
the overall efficiency above that of any other potential lander."

Harriet adds, "Agreed! Their latest tests proved a
success, and they're ready for an uncrewed demo mission
which will land on the moon. I believe they are calling it
Starship and if it goes well, then we will know that their lander
system will be ready for its first Artemis mission. Soon, they
will also be launching storage depots to orbit Earth."

Cowboy asks, "What are those? The reusable tankers
which will carry propellant to fuel the human landing system?"

"Yes," Arthur explains, "Starship would then launch to
orbit Earth where it will rendezvous with the storage depot to
fill its tanks before executing a translunar injection engine burn
which will take it to the Near-Rectilinear Halo Orbit around the
moon. That's where it will await the Artemis III crew."

Adjusting some controls on the panel before her, Harriet
interrupts, "Alright, people, let's get ready to settle in and enjoy
some peace and quiet while we have it."

Cowboy and Harriet strap in and get comfortable while
Arthur turns back to take another long look at Earth through the
rear portal. He uses all of his power and energy to truly focus
and he sees that the Earth remains a living, shimmering,
spectacle – an ever-changing work of art. The swirls of white
clouds amidst the background of blue and green hues are truly
masterstrokes, and Arthur's expression glazes over in joyous
awe, similar to how a child might feel approaching Disneyland
for the first time. The textures he sees, the colors and the lights
of Earth are clearer right now than they had ever been before.
He studies one particular cloud vortex and somehow it is both
magical and mesmerizing. Realizing that the darkness of space
is like a vacuum devoid of all life, Mother Earth is their home,
and there will never be any other just like it. It is familiar and
welcoming, and finally, he smiles at these lovely thoughts and

then turns his head forward once again to look at the pure whiteness of the enlarging moon.

It is peaceful and quiet as Orion passes behind the dark side of the moon. Earth is now out of sight, and the darkness all around the outside of the craft is cold and pervasive.

Harriet shuts her eyes and relishes sleep, Arthur stares down at the surface of the moon trying to make sense of its surface, while Cowboy hums the national anthem....

∞ ∞ ∞

The operatives of the hidden hand walk up to the flashing cylinder and one of them pulls a key from his pocket, handing it to the other who inserts it into the top of the device and turns it sharply to the right. The blinking light speeds up to full strobe, and a high-pitched whirring sound quickly accelerates and drowns out the chugging of the engines. From the shores, the crowds see the flash on the water, and some watching from the hills in the distance have enough time to think that maybe something went wrong with the fireworks show.

The rest of the world finds out almost instantaneously, as television news anchors all stop mid-sentence to listen to the screaming voices in their headsets. The ones who don't lose their composure and are able to speak all repeat the words they're hearing with disbelief: *downtown San Diego has just been completely destroyed in a massive explosion from the water. It appears to have been a nuclear attack.* As the reports flood in on every local station, pandemonium breaks out across the United States. In their confusion and fear, almost everyone has the same strange reaction, to look outside and up at the sky for answers, or maybe to see what happens next. No one knows who had made the crucial decision or if it was some sort of computerized response that automatically activated in case of a direct strike, but within only a minute the sky is filled with the streaming white trails of vengeful intercontinental ballistic missiles flying at full speed across the continent, unstoppable now on the way to their targets in Russia.

∞ ∞ ∞

The Ride to End All Rides....

Chapter Eight

And Then, It All Came Crashing Down

∞ ∞ ∞

In the peaceful quiet behind the dark side of the moon, the inhabitants of the Orion module all lapse into various states of exhausted trance. For the first time in thirteen days, there's nothing for them to do but relax and wait forty minutes. One of the astronauts takes the opportunity for an extra wink of sleep and just passes out in his chair without a thought. Harriet closes her eyes and relishes the moment. She feels humbled to have joined her heroes and become the fifth Black woman in space, but she is the first of them to serve as commander, and perhaps on the next leg of the Artemis mission, she will be the first of them to step foot onto the lunar surface.

Arthur squints his eyes and tries to make out details on the surface of the Moon, scrying the craters as a fortune-teller would a crystal ball for something that his mind can latch onto to distract him from his concerns. Cowboy slouches in his seat while quietly humming the national anthem, his own personal way of celebrating both the holiday and his sense of achievement.

"It's been a good ride everyone," Harriet announces like she's making a toast at a wedding. "I wouldn't have wanted to do it with any other group of people."

"Hear, hear!" Cowboy interrupts his own humming to raise an imaginary mug.

"To Artemis." Arthur smiles, raising his fist up in the air.

The sleeping astronaut continues to snore, and everyone laughs. In that moment, Orion peeks out from behind the moon and catches a ray of sunlight, bringing the electronic systems back to life.

Harriet puts on her best flight attendant voice. "Coms coming back online in three, two, one -"

But as the radio resumes its transmission, a harsh static blares through the speaker, and Harriet quickly shoots her arm forward to turn down the volume.

"What the…?" she starts, but then everyone gasps at the same time. As the Earth comes back into view, the entire planet appears to be engulfed by a thick flaming haze - its color now a lethal mixture of blood red and black. Within the smoldering darkness, there are flickering orange lights igniting across the planet. There are no longer any angelic white wings above a fertile blue and green surface. They each sit up and float to get closer to the window. As he comes closer, Arthur automatically rubs his eyes with the back of his hand to clear them, and when nothing changes, he begins thinking that somehow the outside of the glass had become besmirched by space dust.

The abysmal reality hits all of them at the same time. Arthur shakes his head, unable to comprehend what he is seeing, *but what else could it be?* With every moment, another flash goes off from beneath the otherworldly smog, like lightning bolts exploding within the raging clouds of a hurricane. *They look at each other in abject horror.*

"No! It can't be!" She begins to hyperventilate. "Tell me this isn't real!" Harriet's voice is petrified. "My *babies*!" she finally screams.

At that last word, she and Cowboy burst into an uncontrollable rage, screaming, and weeping uncontrollably. This finally awakens the sleeping astronaut, who rips the blindfold from his eyes and stares towards the Earth, immediately going into a state of shock. *"Did they - did we?"* he stammers, trying to orient himself to the horror into which he has arisen.

Arthur is mesmerized, catatonic for a moment, hypnotized by the flickering orange lights sparking within Earth's atmosphere. As one nuclear blast after another fires in rapid succession, the dusty orange continues to be interspersed with flashes of white-hot light randomly igniting planet-wide. *As the numerous flashes continue to explode unabated, by the power of sheer will alone, he tries to stop them....*

Down on earth's surface, the Freedom Tower in New York City rocks back and forth as all of its windows are blowing out. In Paris the Eiffel Tower begins melting down into itself before it is toppled over by a blast of heat. The pyramids in Egypt are blowing away, leaving nothing behind but poisoned and liquified glass which soon chars into hard black slate. St. Basil's Cathedral in Red Square, Moscow, explodes into shreds of hallowed particles. The White House crumbles and soon ignites.

Unable to pull their eyes away from the view of the satanic shell of Earth they are observing, Arthur, Harriet, Cowboy, and the other astronaut claw at each other looking for stability. As mankind's hatred and vengeance are given full adoration, *seemingly every last nuclear weapon on the entire planet has been launched.*

Back upon the surface of Earth, the Sydney Opera House is rocked off its foundation and starts an agonizing fall into the water. Big Ben and the London Bridge topple over, signifying the collapse of the last vestiges of civilization. The Golden Gate Bridge twists and turns in defiance for only a few moments before finally succumbing and pummeling down into the bay like a toy. Behind it, the entire city of San Francisco is engulfed with flames, which lasciviously lap up at the hazy brown sky above like Lucifer's own pitchfork.

The Statue of Christ the Redeemer watching over Rio de Janeiro makes a brave attempt at remaining unfazed, but when the second, third, and fourth waves of electrified, radioactive heat emanating from several nearby nuclear bombs encroach upon it one after another, it finally succumbs, cascading relentlessly and horrifyingly down the mountain. Breaking into pieces in a matter of seconds, only the rolling head of Jesus remains intact. However, even that sacred icon itself soon meets disaster as it encounters a crisscrossing boulder rushing down the mountain from another trajectory. Colliding one into another, Jesus's face shatters into a million desperate pieces as the icy talons of man's putrid aggression come to their inevitable fruition.

Freedom Tower can no longer stand in place - it begins to tip over. As it makes its final statement and commits to its own demise, the building accelerates downward, creating chaos, igniting fire and spreading dust throughout Lower Manhattan, similar to the collapse of the World Trade Center Towers on September 11, 2001. *But this time it is much worse,* killing everyone in its path who had somehow not already perished from the insurmountable heat, radioactivity, and blast from the initial detonations.

Earth is now at the mercy of the peak of a full commitment to human rage and the accompanying frenzied, global, extinction-event holocaust it has produced. It soon becomes painfully obvious to the astronauts that there would be no going halfway. Arthur's expression emits ever increasing levels of horror and shock, but more than either of those emotions, he is saddened unto death itself.

Harriet and Cowboy cling onto each other, their faces ravaged by utter desolation and loss. The other astronaut continues sobbing in his forearm and is now turned away from the horror on the Earth-side view from the Orion. For a moment, he glances out of the opposite portal and looks somewhat more hopefully out into the deep recesses of black space.

"We failed," Arthur's words were meant for himself, and yet in his raspy exhale, he realizes the others have heard him and that's when he names his greatest fear. *"It's over."*

Suddenly, a voice crackles through the speaker, barely audible above the wailing. Arthur claps his hands three times as hard as he can to get everyone's attention; Harriet comes to her senses for a moment and turns the speaker's volume back up, tears streaming down her face.

> *Artemis, this is a prerecorded message from Mission Control being relayed through communications satellites. Contingency plan Genesis is in effect. You are to redirect your craft to the International Space Station and await further instructions.*

As soon as the message finishes, Arthur immediately reacts, springing into action and working to adjust the settings for Orion's navigation. He quiets his mind so that Harriet's howls and Cowboy's cursing sound to him like distant voices smothered by a thick curtain. Stretching forward so that his face is only inches from the control panel display, his fingers fly at lightning speed across the keyboard, and it only takes him a moment to reprogram the coordinates. Orion will slingshot towards the International Space Station after four lunar orbits adjust its trajectory.

When he finally finishes expending all of his rage shouting at the scene unfolding on Earth through the viewport, Cowboy lapses into withdrawn shock with his arms crossed, rocking back and forth like a child, repeating, "I don't believe it," over and over to himself until he is no longer audible. Harriet's sobbing reduces to whimpering and then finally to nothing. The all-pervading silence of outer space, that once blessed sanctuary within which the dedicated astronauts could perform their meticulous work in perfect peace, permeates the Orion like the heavy air of a crypt. While the others are understandably crushed by the weight of unimaginable grief, Arthur feels the pain just like any pain he has ever felt. *It hurts, but it's somewhere far away from me.*

It's a blessed relief when everyone finally falls asleep. Arthur takes a deep breath and looks towards Earth. The once bright blue home of humanity appears as smoldering coal buried under ashen clouds, the most horrible sight that anyone could conceivably behold. His bloodshot eyes stare outward, wondering how complete the desolation on the surface might be. *I'm not going to comfort myself with delusions. Everyone is dead. My parents, Elena, everything, and everyone. Was it all for nothing?* A million miles a minute, Arthur's mind spins through every angle of interrogation, and as Orion glides across the void, all of his fragmented inquiry twists around a single axis – the question: *what comes after "The End of All Things?"*

∞ ∞ ∞

Her eyes wide with anticipation, Elena squishes her face against the ISS Cupola observatory viewport to stare at the Orion spacecraft attached to the Bishop Airlock on the Tranquility module. After receiving the bizarre message about Artemis coming to dock with them, the two days of waiting had almost been more than any of the space station's inhabitants could bear after witnessing the final death knell upon Earth. *Who is onboard the Orion anyway? And what is this Genesis Order that the message on the intercom mentioned?*

The American commanding astronaut's voice can be heard from the adjacent Trinity Module. "Orion, all diagnostics are looking good, and we're set to open up the airlock here in about three minutes."

Straining to hear Orion's response, Elena thrusts herself through the small opening between the Cupola and the adjacent room, finally floating into the larger staging area where the rest of the ISS inhabitants are gathered. Brian, the older American Commander, smiles at Elena as she drifts by him. Something else crackles back from the speaker, but it's too quiet and distant to hear, even as Elena draws closer.

"What do we have to smile about?" Elena asks the American Commander out of the blue.

He shrugs and gently responds, "After two days of despair, I'll take any sliver of hope I can get."

Elena thinks about it for a moment. "We still don't even know what this Genesis Order is all about."

"Well, I think we're about to find out," Brian responds, once again smiling at Elena.

A nervous excitement had been brewing among the members of the ISS crew, who, after two days of unfathomable mourning, are naturally elated at confronting something that offers any suggestion of hope. For some of them, it's hope that someone will tell them everything will be alright; while for others, it is the possibility of some sort of an explanation for what's happening down on Earth. Elena feels a nameless anticipation: *hope for anything besides their current day-to-day drudgery and doomed expectations for tomorrow.*

"Ok, here we go, folks," Brian announces, and speaking into the radio mike, he declares, *"on behalf of the crew of the International Space Station, we are happy to welcome Artemis onboard!"*

As the Bishop Airlock gently hisses open, the first sight visible to everyone within the ISS through the widening aperture is Harriet's face, which she forces into the kind of overly exuberant smile one might give to a child on his birthday.

She had already decided she would try hitting on a lighter tone right from the start. "We come bearing peace and goodwill." But the words reach minds still too shell-shocked to appreciate her humor, and the two cosmonauts nearest the opening simply grab her outstretched arms and pull her into the airlock. Then suddenly, Harriet realizes humor no longer has any place anywhere at all; it has died with all humanity, and her facade cracks wide open. She latches onto one of the men in a fierce embrace and immediately begins weeping, letting out the absolute desolation she had been holding back throughout the two-day trip from the moon, ever since first witnessing and reacting to the abomination on earth.

Cowboy follows her out in the same fashion, and he immediately pulls Brian into a bear hug. "It's so good to see you guys." His voice trembles with each word. "You have no idea how lonely we've all been feeling."

"Oh, believe me, I am certain we have a good idea about that," Brian replies. "Welcome aboard."

Elena watches from the back of the crowd, trying to peer through all of the floating bodies exchanging hugs and handshakes to see into the Orion capsule. *Were there only three members of the Artemis crew?* As though in answer to her silent query, a final astronaut comes through the portal. His body is large and familiar, *and she cannot believe it may be who she thinks.* On closer inspection, she soon realizes *it is him.* Arthur pulls himself into the room, careful not to bump into anyone in the crowded space. All at once, her heart stops and her breath catches in her throat. *This is rather impossible!* Everything inside of her wants to fly to him and shout out with relief, but she can barely keep herself upright.

His name finally escapes from her lips, "A-Arthur?" As her tiny voice floats over the cacophony of mumbled conversations, they reach Arthur's ears, and he freezes. He looks over at her so that his vision can confirm what his ears are telling him.

"Oh my God! Elena?" He politely pulls back from his hug with another of the ISS astronauts and stares at Elena until his eyes indeed prove that she is real. With a fixated expression mixed with some intense combination of shock, joy, and confusion, he begins to move towards her. She smiles with relief for just a brief moment before her face returns to her customarily serious expression once again.

Cowboy catches the exchange between them and looks back and forth between Elena and Arthur for a moment to allow his mind to process what he is witnessing. He becomes uncertain for a reason he is yet to determine, and when his words escape his lips, they do so involuntarily. "Wow, you guys know each other? *What are the chances?"*

Elena's eyes fill with tears, and she starts shaking from the rush of emotion. Her head suddenly feels like it is swimming with impossible questions, but all she can do is to reach for Arthur. Suddenly flailing her arms outward and pulling herself through the air, she makes very little progress. It is Arthur, gently pushing through the other astronauts, who slowly makes his way right up to her, and who then gently extends his hands out to Elena as they come together. Immediately, their fingers intertwine.

Staring deeply into her eyes, his voice is overcome with strong emotions which take him back home and out of reality. "I am so happy that it really is you," he whispers to her, his breaths quick and shallow all of a sudden, which he realizes is very unusual for him.

In that moment, just staring into each other's eyes, it did not matter what brought them to this point in space and time. They were here with, and for, each other – a blessed outcome they had secretly hoped for their entire adult lives. Now it was finally happening in the middle of the vast universe, a place where both had come to believe that their souls were meant to float alone. They then shared the same thought, and small smiles came to their lips even if for just a moment: *we're finally together.*

The other astronauts and cosmonauts stop talking and are now staring in silence, fully aware that there is some sort of mysterious history between Arthur and Elena. The two of them are so lost in each other at first that they don't even notice. Cowboy opens his mouth to speak again, but before he can begin, the lights of the space station flicker and dim, and a clear and gentle male voice chimes in through every speaker onboard.

> *"Captain Arthur Anders and Cosmonaut Elena Vasilisa, you are to immediately report to Zvezda for classified briefing. I repeat, Arthur Anders and Elena Vasilisa report to the Zvezda*

Module for classified briefing. End of message."

Just as the sharp voice finishes, the lights flicker back on. Cowboy inaudibly mouths, "What the fuck?" and looks around at the ISS crew. He is happy to see, by their baffled facial expressions, that they concur with his sentiment.

"I'm as confused as you guys," Arthur says, raising his hands into the air as in an expression of surrender, and shrugging. "In fact, I'm confused as Hell right now. Hopefully, this briefing with the father computer will start giving us all some answers."

He motions for Elena to follow him as he positions his feet against the wall. At the last moment, she wraps her arms around his neck as he pushes off the wall and they both go flying through the ISS like Superman and Louis towards the Zvezda Module. Elena feels secure as Arthur carries her, and she wraps both of her arms completely around him while leaning her head into his chest. She feels great relief as she surrenders to this moment and to Arthur's strength. The space station only takes a minute to traverse, and as they reach the Zvezda Module, Arthur spins Elena into the room before entering himself, and then he quickly closes the hatch behind them.

As Elena's eyes dart around the room looking for some manner in which to initiate the briefing, the computer dubbed *Virgil* is already aware of their presence. "How do we ...," she starts, but then the white lights in the room all suddenly flicker and shift to red, and the little speaker embedded in the wall clicks to life. The clarinets and strings of Prokofiev's *Piano Concerto No. 3* quietly fade in, and just as Arthur and Elena are allowing the relaxing sounds to wash over them, suddenly, the same male voice from before begins to speak over the classical music.

> *"Genesis Executive Order Number One. This program will have been initiated in the event of a complete nuclear catastrophe and the destruction of human civilization. Arthur and Elena, you have been chosen. Long before each of you were born, the wheels of a grand plan were set into motion. Now, at the moment of humanity's greatest peril, the hope of the entire species depends upon you. What you are about to hear must remain completely confidential. You are to tell no one, and you will have to be absolutely dishonest with everyone on board the ISS in order to protect the mission...."*

∞ ∞ ∞

When the voice is finished saying all it has to say, they share a look of bewilderment and also some dread. Arthur reaches out and takes Elena's hand. "We've been chosen? I thought we were never supposed to see each other again." Arthur and Elena stare deeply into each other's eyes, confused, emotionally drained, but very comforted by the other's presence.

"I suppose it doesn't really matter any longer. We're here now," Elena says, squeezing his hand more tightly.

With tears in his eyes, he lays his head on her shoulder and begins to sob with disbelief, relief, and despair all at the same time. She strokes his cheek, encouraging him to let go, tears finally streaming from his eyes for the first time since

Armageddon. Shaking his head, he says, "I've never been so happy and so sad all at the same time...."

"Same here." Tears come to her own eyes. "Oh my God," Elena says, no longer caring if bringing up a supposed beneficent deity in conversation with a fellow scientist will be taken as inappropriate. "I still can't believe Earth is no longer Earth as we knew it."

Arthur shakes his head and has to stop the rest of his body from shaking along with it. "How can any of us ever recover from such loss? *Those bastards!* I leave the planet for a few weeks and look what happens - all hell breaks loose!" He realizes how narcissistic his comment must sound to Elena, but he does not care.

"My mother always thought this was coming," Elena says. "My father went back and forth about what he believed would happen. I just…," she cuts herself off, unable to put into words the truth about how the relentless dull pain she felt ever since Arthur was taken away from her had led her to not care that much about Earth anyway.

"*What, Elena,* tell me…."

"Right now, all I can think about is that Paris no longer exists." She wraps her free arm around him. "And that the future is looking to be a rather interesting challenge, don't you think?"

He nods and then they are both quiet and introspective, taking comfort in and deriving strength from each other's silent presence and tenderness. They remain so until they hear a knock on the door to the module.

"We'll have to catch-up later," Arthur says, still safely ensconced within Elena's sturdy embrace. Pulling away from her, he adds, "For now, we have an anxious crew awaiting our interpretation of this order. I will be the one who discloses the big lie, just back me."

Elena bites her lip and nods.

Opening the hatch, right outside of the Zvezda Module, the entire crew is gathered and waiting.

"So, what's the big order?" Cowboy asks plainly.

Arthur stares from one to the other at each of the crew. "We have to wait it out for six or seven months up here. We keep close observation of the Earth and take daily measures. It is believed that by that time, some of the islands in the South Pacific will be inhabitable, and so we make plans to re-enter Earth's atmosphere closest to the ones showing the least radiation levels."

Elena looks at their blank stares. Out of necessity, she is suddenly moved to support Arthur's lie by getting onto the next order of business so that nobody has the time to immediately question his explanation of the Genesis Order. "For now, we will have to arrange sleeping quarter assignments which make the most sense. Though it might not be as comfortable as we would like, three of us will have to share individual cabins with another person. Please, for those who feel they would be comfortable with a certain other crewmember, it would be helpful for you to volunteer sharing a cabin with them."

Arthur sees where she is going and buttresses her words by adding, "We will also all have to share duty assignments. I will speak with Commander Harriet Williams and with Commandeer Andre Chekov and together, we will decide how to divvy those up."

∞ ∞ ∞

After a sparse and quiet meal, there is some minor discussion about how they each will plan on spending their days surviving together for six more months on the cramped space station. Soon after, Arthur and Elena are finally alone once again, inside their shared bunk, tightly pressed together in the cramped quarters. At first, they stare at the ceiling, each alone with their own thoughts.

Elena is the first to break the silence. "Arthur? Are you awake?"

"No, sleeping like a baby." He pauses and smiles. "Are you kidding?"

She chuckles. "Yes, I guess so." She shifts closer and turns her head to face him. "So, in all honesty, how are you?"

He considers the question. "Well, given the circumstances–"

"No!" Elena interjects, cutting him off. "I mean: *how are you?* How have you been all these years?"

He considers the question further in a new light, looking for the best answer that would justify her obvious concern for him. Finally, he decides upon blatant honesty as his best response. "Lonely. *For you.*"

Now they look at each other, and she gently gazes into his vulnerable eyes, which encourages him. "When I saw the world... ending, I thought of you. In fact, I've thought of you, Elena, every single day since that first day we met."

She remains quiet and unresponsive until Arthur starts wondering if he said the wrong thing. "And... *how are you?"*

"I don't know. Processing."

He is not sure how to take her response and so he offers her an out. "Maybe there was a... Mr. Right on Earth that you've been thinking about? I don't feel a ring on your finger, and so I am assuming you are unmarried."

Elena bends over and looks at him for a long moment until he begins to feel somewhat lost, and it begins to show on his face. She notices and smiles just a bit. Meantime, as he searches her face for an answer, he begins to feel quite nervous.

Finally, she responds. "There's a Mr. Right. And he's the best thing that ever happened to me. I don't know what I would do without him."

Arthur is crestfallen.

She becomes very serious as she peers deeply into his sky-blue eyes. "But he's not on Earth, which at this time, happens to be a very good thing, indeed."

It takes him a moment, but once he considers her response, Arthur smiles widely and is relieved. Elena leans down to kiss him, and her kiss becomes a passionate embrace. Finally, they resume what they had begun beneath the horse chestnut tree back in Paris before they had been rudely interrupted so many years ago. Now, unencumbered by youth, intrusions, or authority figures, their passion is released, and they each give the other license to go as far as desired. Their kisses are tender at first, and then more and more impassioned, until they find themselves removing each other's outfits. They are floating as they do so, bumping into the walls of their cabin.

Arthur says, "This might be hard to do in zero gravity."

Elena laughs between kisses. *"We'll figure it out."*

∞ ∞ ∞

Chapter Nine

What Shall Become of Us?

∞ ∞ ∞

A rthur's voice comes through clearly on every speaker onboard the ISS. "Day ninety-three, Ball drone surveillance of planet Earth to commence. Target of today's imaging will be in the areas around Papua, New Guinea and the islands of the Bismarck and Solomon Seas."

Strapped into his molded chair within the Orion module, he pulls the view helmet onto his head and types his password into the keyboard on the panel in front of him. Next to him in Cowboy's old seat is Elena, who, as days go by, is growing increasingly resistant to leaving Arthur's side. The image inside Arthur's visor flashes into view, and he is immediately gazing at an aerial shot of the eastern half of Australia. Endless weeks of witnessing the wholesale death and destruction has been more than enough for everyone. It was the same time and again: melted earth absorbed deep within black encrusted canyons with little remnants left in major population areas of man's erstwhile glory, and then strewn across the outer countryside were half-decomposed bodies with skin peeling off leaving red and black fissures.

As for the inhabitants of Oceania, it was quickly becoming apparent that the Outback didn't need to be nuked for the destruction to reach the Southern Hemisphere. Either the radiation of nuclear winter or the logistics of negotiating a collapsed civilization had seemingly resulted in the death of every single man, woman, and child. *If anyone was still alive on planet Earth, they hadn't seen a single trace of them yet.* Today Arthur doesn't expect that his report about New Guinea will offer anything different, though they all wonder about those who might have been lucky enough to have entered underground bunkers before the bombs hit.

Once again, today will be another of the days that Arthur purposely deceives the other astronauts. While he's describing New Guinea into the intercom, Arthur will actually be looking at American Samoa to assess the state of *the Biosphere Alpha Geodesic Dome*, the one hope for the reemergence of mankind upon the face of the earth. The dome had been secretly built using every bit of modern technology possible through a cooperative pact of the American and Russian governments, thanks to the planning of Reagan and Gorbachev all of those decades earlier.

Utilizing stealth technology and metamaterials made the dome almost invisible to detect by satellites. With its unique shape and the addition of absorbing materials, light and other spectrum waves essentially bent around the structure, effectively hiding it from satellite sensors. Keeping the secret about its construction had been successful, as the Americans had maintained a strict military blockade similar to that used for Area 51 in the Nevada desert. Signifying the two leaders' prescience, the specific sects of their respective governments tasked with this affair had been ordered as non-dissolvable and utterly undisclosable, no matter the politics of any era. *And those orders have stood the test of time so far.*

Cowboy, Harriet, and Brian float together in the Cupola, looking out at Earth while listening to Arthur's report through the intercom. Although not a day has gone by that Arthur's reports aren't bleak and downright gruesome, their outright despair still competes with a small measure of hope for a positive discovery as they desperately try to fill a litany of empty days floating in orbit. Brian's eyes twinkle as he strains to peer through the clouds. The explosions and fires have all finally ceased, and in rare moments, the angle of the sunlight can sometimes reveal just a hint of the former fertile blue and green within the backdrop of an otherwise entirely gray planet. In the three months that have passed, the dust and clouds have begun to recede, and the ten of them aboard the ISS have started to believe that Earth will eventually be habitable once again.

"I know I've said it before," Brian laments, "but I sure wish we could pipe the display feed for the Ball cameras to the larger display in here."

With the roll of an eye, Cowboy lets out a sharp laugh. "Yeah, what was the reason Arthur gave you for that? Military encryption or something?"

"Something like that," Brian shrugs.

"And what reason did he give you today for refusing to let you put on the helmet and take a look yourself?" Cowboy locks eyes with Brian, and an awkward moment passes between them. Arthur had allowed them all a few views through the helmet when they had started this virtual tour in the Northern Hemisphere, but the last time had been weeks ago.

Harriet clears her throat to break the tension. "That's enough, Cowboy," she says in a stern tone. "It is what it is. Just listen and enjoy the view."

Cowboy shakes his head as time alone imprisons each of them in its own way, affecting both the Americans and the Russians in a similar fashion. They bicker and argue more than ever, and most times, their attempts at positive mental health require an incessant struggle against their own inner demons. They each struggle with a common one: *What's there to look forward to even if we do manage to get back?* Finally, Arthur's voice beams through the speaker, "Papua appears deserted. Over ninety percent of all buildings are completely razed to the ground. Farm parcels are looking totally browned out, but some jungle areas have managed to maintain a dull green hue. Instruments report radiation levels which are coming in significantly lower than what we had in Australia, however, still unlivable for anything but bugs and perhaps a few rodents who may have managed to survive, mostly underground."

"Is that what you wanted to see? Would that make either of you feel any better?" Harriet asks them in a bitter tone, almost blaming them for their new reality. Brian looks at her like he is about to protest but she cuts him off. *"Didn't think so."*

Back aboard the attached Orion spaceship, Arthur flips off the switch to the intercom and lowers his voice so that only Elena can hear him.

"I'm looking at Biosphere Alpha, Elena," he mumbles, barely above a whisper. "It appears to be completely intact. *Damnit the cloaking worked* – the Chinese military couldn't see it, otherwise they would have bombed the hell out of it for sure! And from what I'm reading, radiation levels are way lower than

I expected them to be. Hell, the island looks almost untouched." He fights to keep the excitement from his voice.

Elena grabs Arthur's hand and squeezes it with all her strength. *It's not the end of the world. There's still hope.*

"Please, please, let me see?" she asks like a child in a toy store, and Arthur smiles and lifts the helmet off his head.

"Just for a second," he replies. "I don't want any more variables added to a situation that's already complex and nearing the limits of my ability to fully manage." Casting a nervous glance towards the closed hatch, he carefully lowers the helmet onto Elena's head.

"Wow!" she practically shouts as Arthur hushes her and puts his hand over her mouth. "Sorry, but this is amazing," she whispers in almost total awe of what she sees.

Through the swirling mist, tucked between hills and surrounded by an otherworldly jungle right along the coast of American Samoa, the windows of the geodesic dome called Biosphere Alpha reflect straggling rays of courageous sunlight, so that it appears to glow like a glittering gem within the depths of a depleted coal mine. Although even the ocean appears dark and gloomy, Elena clasps her hands together with a bit of excitement, something she has not felt for a long time.

"It almost looks like paradise to me, Arthur."

"Yes, it does," Arthur replies uneasily. "A sort of paradise within the shadow of complete annihilation."

$$\infty \quad \infty \quad \infty$$

The astronauts have started to make plans for who will do what once they return. Building shelters, foraging for food, finding sourceable water – each person has been given a specific project. All of them agree that their respective governments should have made contingency plans for the astro/cosmonauts if the worst happened. *At least some food and water storages somewhere on Earth!* Supplies aboard the ISS have become quite depleted and even Elena's best efforts have proven ineffective at growing enough food for all of them.

All is quiet, but for the scraping sounds of plastic sporks against food trays along with the chomping of teeth and the gulping of throats of the ten inhabitants of the ISS. Six months have passed since *Day Zero,* as they had all taken to calling the final war on planet Earth, and one of the most lasting changes to the schedule of daily life aboard the ISS was that all meals were to be eaten together. They had started the practice of eating together because everyone felt that, despite their uncertainty and their angst, they were all somehow family – *the only family that any of them had left.*

These widows and widowers, most of whom had also lost children and parents, were all now orphans of the starry void. The tragedy they shared drew them closer together, although quiet companionship would usually take the place of any enlivened conversation, and they still had their share of personality conflicts from time to time.

With no round table for them to gather around in zero gravity, the members of the crew are pressed up against each of the six sides of the Unity module. As they eat and drink their reconstituted food and water, tiny, escaped food particles, and even some larger chunks, drift through the air, along with the occasional droplets of water. Each of the astronauts and cosmonauts holds a paper towel on their lap so they can use their offhand to catch the debris. Almost everyone eats while maintaining respectful acknowledgement of each other and upon the various tasks at hand, but Cowboy, alone among them, keeps his eyes down on his food. In the months that have passed, his behavior has gradually become increasingly bizarre,

248

and in recent weeks, he has kept completely to himself except for the required communal mealtimes.

Now, the latest of his antics has been to construct a wide-brimmed, 10-gallon hat out of cardboard stock and Elmer's glue, which he now always wears upon his head, making him look more like his namesake. His strange actions have slowly begun to unnerve the rest of the crew, and none of them know exactly what to say to him, or how they might offer their help should he even be receptive to the idea in the first place. Each of them is already dealing with the stress of the situation in his or her own way, and so, for the most part, Cowboy is left to his own devices.

Arthur senses that Cowboy distrusts the plans given for the Genesis Protocol and himself and Elena most of all. He can feel Cowboy's intense eyes on him when they eat, but they dart away every time Arthur looks up at him.

Today, Arthur has decided he will try to reach out to Cowboy in front of the group and see where it takes them; he is never one to abide a powder keg awaiting a spark. "How's it goin' today, Cowboy?" Arthur asks between bites. *Better to confront this sooner rather than later.*

"Oh, *who me?* You really care how I'm doing?" Cowboy practically spits the words at him. "I thought I was just a mushroom to you two." Though Arthur was aware of Cowboy's growing mistrust, he is taken aback, as are the others, by Cowboy's blatantly rebellious response.

Harriet raises an eyebrow. "Cowboy, *what the hell?"* she says, her sass unveiled.

"Why do you act so surprised, Harriet?" Cowboy retorts. "You know, the more I think about it, we are all just mushrooms *to them,"* he says, peering with anger at Elena and Arthur. "They just keep us in the dark while continuing to feed us a *bunch of bullshit!"* His last three words hang in the air between them as if another final bomb had just detonated.

Surprisingly, the tension is momentarily broken by one of the Russian cosmonauts. "Come on, settle down, son," the commanding officer from the Russian team implores Cowboy in a fatherly tone.

However, this just ignites the underlying fuse for Cowboy's pent-up distrust and uncertainty about the future. *"Settle down?"* he snarls. "Easy for you to say, Pops," Cowboy flexes his body into an upright position in midair and sneers at Arthur as he finishes his argument with the elder Russian. "You only had a few years left anyway. Me? I had a good fifty years left, but now I'm gonna be trapped up here with most of the rest of you in this overblown space prison until we all dwindle away, dehydrated and starved!"

"That's not true, Cowboy!" Elena's clear voice rings out. "We're all …."

"We're all going back down to Earth together once the radiation levels drop!" Cowboy mockingly finishes her sentence. He tips the top of his cardboard hat between his thumb and his index finger. "Give me a break, lady. It's not like you two are the only fucking rocket scientists around – *you both think you have the last word on intelligence!* Well, I've got some smarts, too, you little bitch!" The last few words tumble out of his mouth in a crescendo of open malevolence; he has finally and totally resorted to his American, southern, good old boy mentality.

Arthur jolts upright, and with deep furrows rippling across his brow, he glares at Cowboy. *"Don't you ever talk to her like that again!* Or to anyone else on board for that matter!" Arthur has had enough, and he begins a slow float towards Cowboy with clenched fists by his sides. He knows that he needs to put an end to this astronaut's defiant antics, which are now taking on a threatening tone. "We've told you everything that there is to tell about the mission, about the surveillance drone, and about our hopes for landing back on earth. The radiation levels are still too high, but they're getting close to where we need them to be in certain regions of the South Pacific. *What else do you want to know?"*

"Don't give me that line, you coward," Cowboy shakes his head and looks around at the others, who are mostly in a state of disbelief. "You guys really believe this line of horseshit?" He turns back to Arthur. "Why don't you tell us the actual truth and at least show us that little bit of respect? Why would there be a secret message for just the two of you if there wasn't something in it that we weren't all meant to hear?" His eyes are bulging now, and his face is flush with heated blood. *"The Orion capsule can only hold four people, five tops.* After that, its weight would be too much for the reentry and we would never get through Earth's atmosphere. *Anyone care to explain that one?"* Arthur bounces off a side wall with his hand and continues his drift towards Cowboy; by now he is only about seven feet away from him.

"You can't, *can you?* But you're supposed to be in charge?" Cowboy laughs. "You tell us it will be an uncomfortable ride, that we will all be crammed in like sardines, *but I've done the calculations a hundred times* – the weight of ten of us will take us way off our necessary trajectory. There is no way to safely get through - at best, we will bounce off of earth's atmosphere like a trampoline and be thrust deep back into space. *At worst, we become a blazing fireball!"* Realizing that Arthur is almost upon him, he girds himself. "There's no mission control to guide us through this one. No one left except us now, Bigshot! *And I say, your chain of command is about to be broken!"* With the last word, Cowboy crushes the plastic food tray in his hands and flings it past

Arthur. He kicks off the wall behind him and thrusts himself directly at the ship's captain. Grabbing Arthur by the throat, he shouts, "You're gonna pull up those mission parameters on the computer and show them to me, or I'm gonna fuck you up, partner! *You hear me?*"

Arthur is caught off-guard, not expecting Cowboy to have gone on such an aggressive offensive attack. He reflexively lands a gut punch, and Cowboy flinches but does not relinquish his grip around Arthur's neck. Arthur chops his right hand into Cowboy's elbow and then pounds his head with both fists, but Cowboy only tightens his grip all the more ferociously. Arthur soon realizes Cowboy's determination and anger are stronger than he had considered, and that he must regain his dominance very soon. His best remaining option comes to mind, and he immediately grasps and begins fiercely squeezing Cowboy's elbow as the others begin to gather around them. Looking directly into Cowboy's eyes, he locks his hand closed until he has tightened a vice grip upon Cowboy's ulnar nerve, the so-called funny bone. Cowboy glares at Arthur defiantly, continuing to squeeze his neck and cutting off his breath, but soon, the amount of pressure Arthur is exerting becomes too much. Cowboy has no choice and involuntarily relaxes his grip on Arthur's neck.

Realizing he is now face-to-face with an opponent who is much larger and stronger, and without the element of surprise on his side any longer, Cowboy immediately plants his feet on the wall and shoots himself across the room heading towards the medical bay. Arthur turns and kicks the wall, flying after him. With his arms outstretched, he dives forward, and when Cowboy comes to a stop at the adjacent wall, he turns in time for Arthur to secure Cowboy around the waist, whereupon Cowboy begins a wild attack with both his arms and legs all at once. In any situation, these would have been hopeless against

252

Arthur's elite training, but the absence of gravity takes any remaining steam out of Cowboy's kicks and punches, and Arthur brushes them aside as easily as he would have those of a child. Now gripping Cowboy by the shoulders, he effortlessly spins him around and wraps his right arm around Cowboy in a headlock.

Cowboy kicks his legs and continues to yell out obscenities as Arthur looks around at everyone. He sees that the customarily mild-mannered scientists stare back at him, shocked, helpless, and terrified. Now that Arthur is in control, Elena's look of dread relaxes, and she nods at him. Arthur acknowledges her affirmation even as he hopes that they all realize he has the situation well under control. To prove himself, and to dispel any remaining concern over his power of authority, Arthur applies just the right amount of pressure to cut off Cowboy's blood flow. The rebel's thrashing slows, and within seconds, it completely stops. Cowboy has lapsed into unconsciousness.

Arthur gently thrusts Cowboy towards Brian and Harriet. "Please put him in and *keep him* in restraints for now. He'll need a daily tranquilizer - no freedom until he agrees on taking it each day." *There is a built-in chain of command and a built-in mission control, and it's all still right here, same as it ever was.*

∞　∞　∞

According to standard medical procedure aboard the ISS, every member of the crew receives a flu vaccine twice a year, and this is the moment for which they had been told to wait. The voice granting them the first secret message had prepared them for this in subsequent visits. Elena had been instructed to administer the flu shots, only instead of vaccine serum, the syringes were to be loaded with Propofol *in order to render everyone unconscious.* She had never bothered Arthur with any of her doubts, which by now had grown to almost insurmountable levels, but all the while she kept them brewing within. *How did whoever recorded that message know that this would be the best course of action? Did they ever consider any other options... or how difficult this would be to carry-out? Is this all from the Artificial Intelligence named Virgil, or had humans themselves planned for everything to come utilizing their own intelligence?*

Where she had once hoped for answers that would clarify her confusion about the whole situation, Elena couldn't help but feel that both she and Arthur were also being strung along just like everyone else. Whatever answers she had received from Virgil about the Genesis Protocol had only managed to fill her with even more questions.

Arthur also senses the work of some hidden hand, but he more easily embraces it because he had trained himself to follow the Genesis Order in his work without questioning it. Even so, he has come to feel that pieces are missing. *They never give us the whole story. Virgil puts together each segment of the plan, but in the end, something does not feel completely whole. And yet, how can Elena and I both question and still believe in the protocol at the same time?* Operating under the assumption that there is information they aren't getting, his solution is to maintain his focus on the task at hand and to hope that the answers will come from Virgil in good time. *And if the mystery is never solved, so be it. It's not like there are any other options at this point.*

Finally, having arrived at the point of no-return, from here on out, there would be no looking back. Just a week after the altercation with Cowboy, the one and only window of opportunity swings open for Arthur and Elena's departure. Their fate lies completely in Elena's hands; *no one can suspect anything.* Alone in the Unity module, the chosen two meet to discuss this final phase of the Genesis Protocol's space program.

"Remember, this is just business as usual, Elena." Arthur places a reassuring hand on her shoulder in an attempt to bolster her confidence.

"But what if they are suspicious?" Elena investigates Arthur's face for answers, her eyes wide with anxiety. "After that thing with Cowboy, I feel like everyone's looking at us differently."

Arthur nods with understanding, but then becomes firm. "Maybe they are, and maybe they aren't. Bottom line – you are the most qualified medical practitioner on board, and this is a vital part of the original program they all knew about. There is no reason for anyone to question this. *And truthfully, it's more important than ever.* If we were to return to earth only to get the flu – the only survivors sickened with little resources – we would all quickly become compromised in that already deadly atmosphere. The entire crew has been trained to know that viruses have survived throughout earth's history, and right about now they will be greedily looking for hosts."

She peers closely into his loving eyes, and this reassures her for a moment.

Arthur continues, "The shots have already been part of the usual prescription up here, and so no matter what anyone is feeling right now, they are known as essential and necessary, and you would have been administering them today regardless. Got it?"

She nods, although they have not addressed her primary concern as of yet.

"So, the way to go with this is to play it cool."

She takes a deep breath and lifts her shoulders. "You're right. I will be okay."

He wants to believe her, but he does not. "Listen to me, Elena. If you think about how you're lying, then the others will sense it. You've got to convince yourself that this is the right thing for all of humanity and then operate with absolute certainty."

She nods unconvincingly. "I will just have to lie to myself, too." Her voice sounds so compromised that it breaks Arthur's heart, and he takes her into his arms.

After a moment, she pulls away. "The reality is just so awful no matter how much we try to convince ourselves otherwise." He looks at her, genuinely concerned. "I just don't know, Arthur."

"About what?"

"About how any of this makes sense at all. I never signed up to be the leader in any doomsday scenario. You know?"

His expression becomes bleak and uncertain, which is a big change from what she is used to seeing, but she doesn't know if his concern is because she has touched some inner nerve he has been hiding, or because he questions how she will perform in a matter of minutes. "Neither of us ever signed up for anything at all. Nor did we agree to any of this. I have been agonizing over all of this just as much as you, *but if I allow myself to question any of it for too long, don't you think it makes me feel sick to death?"*

"I mean… think back over our lives," she says. "We were born at the same time, and I guess we were both very smart. But there are…*there were* lots of smart kids in the world. What was so special about us?" She looks into his eyes. "And then we meet in Paris, and just as suddenly, they rip us apart - like us being together was the most dangerous thing in the world. And then I searched for you. God, how I searched and searched. But there was no trace of you anywhere."

"It was exactly the same for me. I was so frustrated and so alone. I started to think I was going crazy. *None of it made any sense at all.*"

"So, why did they choose us after all?"

They both gaze silently into each other's eyes for a moment. Finally, Arthur breaks the tension. "I suppose we may never know the answer to that. But it brings to mind something very important – I know with absolute certainty that I couldn't do this without you. If it was just me and any other person, or just me alone, I would have crumbled by now. *I couldn't do this with anyone but you.*"

She nods, still distracted with her own contemplations. "It's just that… I can't understand how…."

Arthur cuts her off. *"Do you feel differently, Elena?"*

"No! *God, no!*" She puts her hand to his face and then withdraws it. *"I'm just overwhelmed with concern that it's becoming difficult to blindly trust this fucking AI.* We are both willingly following the orders of either dead men or, even worse than that, some unfeeling computer program. Either way, we are now directly responsible for eight other human lives. If the people who wrote this all out were so brilliant, then how come they couldn't stop the blasts from destroying themselves and everything else along with it?" She looks at the tray of needles she had been organizing. "I'm very angry right now about all of it. Why us in the first place? And how did they come to decide in Paris that they shouldn't let us be together? Why was ripping us apart at that time so important to them?" Tears come to her eyes as her memories spin through the years of pain which had followed their separation. *"And why didn't they Goddamn let us in on any of this?"*

257

He takes her hands into his. "Because we wouldn't have agreed to any of what we are about to have to do - *something we have no choice but to do or we will all die.* Beyond that, I don't know the answers to much of anything else. I agree with you, and I feel all the same things you are feeling. I have doubts for sure, *but we have no other blueprint to follow.* If we don't do what they say... it is for certain that our lives will be at stake and then all will be lost. If there is no way to get all of us back to Earth, and we are to be the only two who survive, *isn't that better than nobody surviving at all, Elena?* If we do nothing, Cowboy is right, we all die."

She allows his words to filter through her resistance. She stops thinking for a moment and just stares into his eyes. Although she had already understood all of this, with Arthur's display of focussed determination, she finally sees a way to accept their destiny, along with the fate of the others onboard. Slowly at first, but then with gusto, she allows herself to believe the truth that this was the only best answer they had, the only option plausible *from a list of options that were all bad.* She shakes her head determinedly, as if to shudder away the horror of their very reality. Gesturing to the syringes on the tray, she focuses again on the task directly ahead of her and says, "I know they are suspicious, and so I will have to be extremely convincing."

"Remember, they have no reason not to trust you in this matter. To them, the Virgil computer is arranging everything when it comes to the Genesis Protocol. The flu shots were scheduled for today long in advance and is a sign we are all returning to earth together. Everyone is expecting them and expecting you to administer them."

She looks up from the tray at Arthur. "I just want you to know that I believe none of this is right. We are taught to never leave anyone behind… *that we are all in this together*. Or we should be."

He holds her and allows her to sob into his shoulder.

"You only have to believe what you know - this is part of the original program they signed on with. So we play it cool, okay? For everyone's sake. Think about the light you felt as we observed the paintings at the Louvre in Paris all those years ago. This is our job now. All other considerations no longer matter. Restoring humanity is why we have survived thus far. You heard what the message said regardless of who prompted it – *the very survival of humanity depends upon us, you and me, and upon our ability to operate in secrecy.*"

Elena lets out a deep sigh. She thinks about her first practice in the medical field when she was just a child and had performed minor surgeries on animals and pets under Altan's careful guidance, and how well she had performed working right alongside her father. *He's right. And in the end, we were all really just puppets having our strings pulled in the service of bettering humanity itself all along. Right now, this is simply the role I have been selected to play.* "Ok," she says. "I'm ready."

Arthur nods as Altan used to, and she feels a comforting pang of familial kinship. He says, "I believe in you, Elena. You'll do just fine." He kisses her. "And remember, right after you administer my dose, I am heading to the console to get into position to perform the pre-flight."

She nods solemnly, and with that, Arthur pushes himself out of the room and disappears around a corner to go and find Cowboy specifically. Elena stays behind to check the syringes in the covered tray. Two of them are filled with the actual flu vaccine for her and for Arthur, which Elena has carefully marked by scratching a tiny line into the plastic with an X-acto knife. After another moment passes, she shakes her head, takes a deep breath, and then floats off to do her work.

It begins in the Nauka module, where two cosmonauts are teaching Brian and two other astronauts how to play a card game. When they see Elena float in with the syringes, each of them willingly bears their arm, believing this is the first step towards getting back home. Elena smiles convincingly while expertly injecting all five of them within a minute's time. Before any of them can be bothered upon noticing the first few who got the shot drifting off, they too, have fallen asleep. Elena continues back towards the Cupola where she finds the Russian Commander, Cowboy, and Arthur chatting.

Elena goes to Cowboy first, and he thinks about challenging Elena, but Arthur stares him down. Whatever resistance they had feared from Cowboy vanishes when he considers another altercation with Arthur and how badly being restrained in shackles might make him look once again. With a "sure, whatever," he pulls up his sleeve and unknowingly consents to the shot of anesthesia. The other two, of course, willingly take their shots, and Elena is sure to give Arthur his dose from the scratched syringe. She does likewise as she injects herself.

It's when Elena gets to Harriet that the train almost goes off the rails. As Elena encounters her in the Destiny Module, Harriet is busy at the computer and seems to be harried somewhat until she stops what she is doing and looks at a photo of her children which is taped to the monitor, a beautiful little girl of about six dressed in a flowery yellow and pink dress, and a robust and handsome boy outfitted in a suit and tie who looks to be about ten. Elena hears Harriet sobbing.

"Is it time?" Harriet asks without turning to look at Elena.

"Yep, flu shots!" Elena happily sings out.

Harriet turns towards her, and the gravity and understanding on her face penetrates directly into Elena's heart.

"Elena, you be careful, and promise me that you'll remember us up here." Her voice cracks, but she maintains composure.

"W-what?" Elena is shocked, but Harriet just shakes her head.

"Just promise me." Harriet's eyes fill with tears, and she looks back at the photos of her children, whose eyes sparkle and whose smiles seem to indicate they have the whole world before them.

Elena can't keep her own tears from coming, and one escapes down her left cheek. "I promise, Harriet," she says, and realizes how much she really means it. The two of them embrace, and Elena reflects that this is the second saddest goodbye she has ever experienced in a life full of farewells.

∞ ∞ ∞

Through the viewport of Orion, the International Space Station appears smaller and smaller. As the slow burn of the thrusters ever-so-gradually reduces its orbital speed and Orion makes its slow descent towards the Earth's atmosphere, Elena looks over towards Arthur.

"Harriet knew what we were up to." She pauses and reflects for a moment. "I promised her we'd remember them once we were down on Earth."

Arthur doesn't take his eyes off the control panel. "Of course she did. She was brilliant." He chances a quick glance at Elena. "And how could we ever forget them? They're our last living relatives, after all."

Just as the ISS is nearly lost from sight, a luminous white light suddenly appears from just behind them as if a miniature new star had formed. Arthur knows immediately it is from one of the last American satellites that had launched into space. Quickly growing ever brighter, suddenly a blinding ray shoots out in a straight line from the original source of the light and right into the photovoltaic arrays of the space station, which instantly explode in a fiery burst in all directions. Arthur and Elena are speechless as the chain reaction quickly ripples through each module, and one-by-one, the explosions combine until they span across the entire space station.

They turn to look at each other as a shared angst immediately fills each of their souls. *Are we complicit in having just committed murder ourselves?* They don't dare to ask the question out loud as each of them struggle to let themselves off the hook with inner justification that these orders were handed down by the ones who had assured their own survival first and foremost; *and they had no choice but to follow them.* Yet, doubts remain and neither of them feels a genuine vindication. Just like everyone else, there are certain things that even Arthur and Elena are not permitted to know. *Not yet.*

Knowing too much too soon could lead to self-doubt and/or rebellion, and how else are they supposed to create life amidst so much loss, devastation, and murder, except in dire exculpation?

∞ ∞ ∞

Chapter Ten

Return to Oblivion

∞ ∞ ∞

T he blackness of outer space begins to take on dull pink and orange hues as ionized gas surrounds the Orion spacecraft, now hurtling into Earth's upper atmosphere at twenty-thousand miles per hour. In frantic gyrations, strange, plasma-like shapes dance upon the viewports, and even though the color is somewhat subdued, it is almost too bright for Arthur and Elena to bear. After nearly half a year in the smooth, frictionless silence of outer space, the roaring and rattling shock their sensibilities, and they clench their jaws and squint their eyes to lessen the overwhelming sensations.

When the startling pink plasma finally softens and turns to gold and orange highlights, the details of the planet's surface become visible to the naked eye, and Elena marvels at the beauty of the swirling white clouds over the ever-nearing Pacific Ocean. *Has earth already recovered?* In the magic of the moment, she temporarily forgets about all of the horror they have both just witnessed and tries not to think about the horrors which might yet come.

"Wow, Arthur, look at this!" She lightly jabs her elbow into his arm, excited to think there might be normality back on Mother Earth.

Arthur doesn't look up from the control panel. "Hold on just a minute. I'm keeping my eyes on the Reaction Control System and performing a few minor adjustments on the fly to make sure we get close enough to the island."

Elena nods, and as the roaring ceases and the sky transforms from dull orange to a dusky blue interspersed with streaks of sickly gray haze, she marvels at the sight, still not dismayed.

"You're missing the show, but okay!"

"Try to enjoy it for both of us," Arthur smiles. "I'll wait until we're on the ground."

With a pop, the protective forward bay cover shoots off into the sky, and the drogue parachutes open, dramatically slowing their descent, so that for just a moment Arthur and Elena feel like their guts are trying to escape out of their toenails. But the feeling passes quickly, and they peacefully float down towards the shimmering, blue sea. *It's still blue, thank God!* Drogue chutes give way to full-sized parachutes, and at the moment of splashdown, before either of them can react, a familiar male voice returns, crackling through on the speaker.

> *"Welcome back to Earth, Arthur and Elena. You are exactly thirty-two point seven kilometers from Biosphere Alpha. Please remain seated, and your courier will arrive shortly with further instructions."*

"Courier?!" both exclaim, sharing baffled looks. *Does that mean that someone is still alive down here?*

The Orion bobs up and down in the waves, lolling gently to and fro without any ballast to stabilize it. Awash in sensations of relief from their safe landing but also anxiety about the strange unfolding events of an unknown future, both Arthur and Elena instinctively reach out for one another. As they hold hands, they silently process the recent happenings and stare up through the docking hatch porthole at the midday sun, at once understanding this will be the new normal for the foreseeable future – the sun appearing now and again through the intermittent ribbons of radioactive smog. Only minutes pass before they hear a thud against the side of the Orion; Arthur rushes to stand and look out the various portholes one by one. From somewhere outside, the dull sound of a combustion motor vibrates through the entire hull of the Orion.

"Oh God, my legs feel like jelly," he laughs. "We were up there for such a long time!"

"Can you see anything?" Elena asks, struggling to stand herself against the return of gravity.

"When it tilted this way, I thought I saw a …."

"Attention," Virgil's familiar voice announces loudly through the speakers. *"Your submersible craft is secured to the Orion. Prepare for departure. Hatch will open in T-minus two minutes."*

Elena practically jumps into the air. "Should we take off these suits then?" she asks with a frantic look towards Arthur.

"Hell no! Two reasons - first, the ocean is just about as dangerous as outer space. Second, we know the radiation levels here are still unsafe from the recent drone readings when we were on Orion. Remember, Virgil told us that our suits have

265

been modified to offer us protection from background radiation. We must keep them on until we arrive at Biosphere Alpha."

Giving a nod and walking over to Arthur's side, Elena wordlessly leans her weight into him. She reflects on how grateful she is that he is here to guide them through these threatening scenarios. *What would I do without him?* She has chosen to forget about death and destruction for now, compartmentalizing and shelving any thoughts about what has occurred in their collective history, as well as the history of mankind, for another time.

"Orion's hatch will open in T minus ten seconds. Nine, eight, seven, six..."

A series of metallic clicking and spinning sounds emanate from one of the two escape hatches, and Arthur and Elena shuffle towards it in anticipation.

"Three, two, one."

There is only a slight hiss at the pressure change, and the hatch swings outward, casting the inside of the Orion in a brilliant white light. Arthur and Elena squint into the sudden change, and as their eyes adjust, a tiny, yellow submarine appears before them. A clear viewing orb spans almost the entire length of the miniature submersible except for a small platform with a circular hatch. The platform is pressed up against the side of the Orion and held fast with two red ropes affixed to magnets gripping the spacecraft. Between the two ships, a rubber fender squeaks in the gentle ocean swell as the two crafts bob up and down at slightly different rates. The astronauts exchange skeptical looks.

"Good thing it's calm out here," Elena offers brightly.

"I imagine if it wasn't, they'd make us wait until nightfall." Arthur says, staring at the submarine. He begins to hum "We All Live in a Yellow Submarine" from the Beatles' 1960 "Revolver" album, and when Elena looks at him curiously, it's apparent to her that he is not even aware he's doing so. She grins at him adoringly, falling in love all over again with the carefree side of Arthur she had known long before, something she had not seen in quite a while. "We're going to have to make a little jump for it. I'll go first," he says.

Without hesitation, Arthur crouches and leaps towards the hatch, and as he lands exactly where he had intended, his knees unexpectedly buckle, and he sprawls out flat across the deck on his face. Elena lets out a nervous, *"Arthur!"* but he quickly turns his head and gives her a thumbs up.

"Don't try to land on your legs," he shouts. "Just take your time, and land on top of me. I'll break your fall."

He rotates so that he is laying on his back and puts both of his arms out towards her. Before allowing any doubt to take root in her mind, Elena crouches down and dives through the air, landing in an ungraceful belly flop on Arthur's chest. The hatch pops open at the exact moment she lands, lending a comedic, almost absurd, element to an otherwise nerve-wracking event.

"What a crazy maneuver this was," Arthur laughs. And trying to keep the mood light, he follows up with, "Couldn't they have at least sent someone out here to help with this?"

Elena laughs and shakes her head in agreement. She crawls across Arthur and then immediately proceeds face-first down the submarine hatch. "There wouldn't be enough room for more than just us in here," she calls back to him, spinning around and awkwardly situating herself into one of the bucket seats.

Arthur pops his head in and decides that it's better if he enters feet first, and with Elena's help pushing his legs over to the side, he lowers himself into the other bucket seat. The hatch automatically swings shut above their heads, and both scan the space and take in their surroundings. The inside of the submarine is completely bare except for a tiny speaker in the space between the seats.

"What? No control panel?" Arthur says, and Elena is uncertain if he is being serious or just joking again.

She decides to counter with her own observation. "Feeling like a sardine yet?" Although she meant it as a joke, she immediately regrets her choice of words as she thinks about the ones they had left behind in the ISS, and how Arthur had promised they would all be crammed into Orion like sardines. Upset with herself, she glances out the porthole.

"Direct route to Biosphere Alpha is calculated at approximately two hours and fourteen minutes," Virgil reports through the speaker. *"Departing immediately."*

Elena turns back towards Orion, and for a moment the grief in her heart rises to the surface. *Goodbye Orion. Thank you for returning us home safely.* She pushes down both tears and the question of why no one else from the International Space Station had been allowed to come with them, and as she does so, the red lines release from the submarine, and they plunge beneath the surface. The humming of the tiny combustion motor rises, and their craft descends to a depth of ten meters to avoid being pushed by waves.

Arthur seems unbothered by her sardine gaffe, and they both look out the lone porthole. The slight slump in his shoulders, though, suggests that he is tired, the weight of all that they have experienced taking its toll no doubt. As the gray clouds part and the sunlight momentarily dances down through the ocean water, it lights upon the reflective bodies of a dozen silver fish swimming alongside them. The welcome sight captures Elena's attention. *These little ones are survivors, just like we are. The ocean may be as hostile as outer space, but the presence of life here will always make it so much more beautiful.* Even so, Elena also notices the silhouettes of dead carcasses of some larger fish floating across the surface above them, casting their ghostly shadows down into the ocean depths, only slightly marring an otherwise hope-filled moment.

"I don't know what's next," Arthur says, interrupting her reverie. "But I believe Virgil just told me that I can take a two-hour nap. You might want to consider doing the same."

"Oh, but it's so pretty." Elena practically sings the words.

"Suit yourself," he smiles, and leaning his head back, he falls almost immediately into a deep sleep.

Elena watches the little fish swim back and forth in front of the porthole. As their tails flip to and fro to keep up with the submarine, shimmering light dances across their silvery scales, creating a dazzling show. Hypnotized by the beauty but soon feeling fatigue take over, Elena's eyes grow heavy, and within just a few minutes, she follows Arthur into a dream world.

From somewhere on the island of American Samoa, Virgil's sure hand guides their craft through the undulating flux of the mighty waters, while the two exhausted astronauts snooze in their orange spacesuits.

They are awakened by the soft violins and gentle flutes of Strauss's Blue Danube Waltz playing from outside the cockpit through the open hatch, and as they open their eyes, Arthur and Elena gasp in astonishment at the sheer beauty of the place in which they have arrived. The submarine floats in a circular blue pool, five meters across and edged all about with black marble stone. The pond is set at the low point of a clearing in what appears to be a dense jungle. Brightly colored birds fly among the tops of tree branches which tower into the sky and stop just before the steel frame of a geodesic dome - *Biosphere Alpha*. The familiar male voice joins in with the pleasant sounds of the classical music.

> *"Welcome home, Arthur and Elena. You are securely within the confines of Biosphere Alpha. It is now safe to remove your space suits."*

The two of them hesitate at first, held back by the rational fear of a hostile atmosphere bred by so many tales of how terrible the aftermath of nuclear war would be. Sensing their uncertainty in the pause, Virgil intervenes.

> *"On today's date, January 29, 2036, air quality reading is: 25% oxygen, 75% nitrogen. Radiation levels are zero. Temperature is seventy-seven degrees, with humidity at 65%. It is now safe to remove your space suits."*

Trained to distrust as a survival tactic, it suddenly occurs to Arthur to question the source of this information, and with a stern voice he calls out, "Who are we talking to, and why should we believe you?"

A mere second passes before the voice replies,

> *"I am the artificial intelligence program which manages the Genesis Executive Program and Biosphere Alpha. You knew me as Virgil in the ISS, and even though I am*

so much more than what you knew about me then, I am still Virgil."

Placing special emphasis on the letter I, the voice continues,

"I manage the natural harmony of the biosphere, and I delegate all tasks to robotic entities within it. I brought you here through space and across the ocean. It was I who spoke to you in the speakers aboard Orion and the International Space Station. I currently have four-thousand three-hundred and seventy-two programs running various tasks, but all fall under my prime directive: to protect and to guide the inhabitants of Biosphere Alpha and their progeny. That means you two, and later, your children. I do not mind being called Virgil, but from here forward, I would much prefer you call me **Father***."*

Arthur states plainly, "My father is dead. You are a computer. I'm not calling you *father.*"

"Neither am I," Elena adds, looking above her towards whatever she can find which might indicate a computer, a monitor, or a speaker, but finding nothing. Instead, she sees a large sign posted on a silver pole embedded within the black marble stone bordering the northern edge of the pool. In large blue emblazoned letters, it reads *Biosphere Alpha.* She then notices a smaller sign just below the larger one, this one in bold red letters. She taps Arthur on the shoulder and points to it:

Homo Homini Lupus Est.

Arthur studies the words but is uncertain about the translation; he turns back towards the glass roof of the

271

geodome, clearly not finished speaking with the AI. Brazenly, he says to Virgil, "What are you, God?" When there is no response, he continues, "No. You're not. You'll be Virgil, is that understood? If you want us to talk to you, you stay *Virgil*."

"If you insist. I thought it may be a comfort to you."

Elena states emphatically, "Well, it's not." She looks at Arthur with fire in her eyes. "It's a computer, and now it's responding to our words like it understands what we're saying."

"That's because I do understand what you're saying, Elena. I probably understand more than you would be willing to believe at this point."

Arthur breathes deeply, trying to bring a sense of calm back into the picture. "Nevertheless, this decision has been made and is behind us."

"And, by the way," Elena says defiantly, "if you think something may be a comfort to us, perhaps you should just ask us first."

They wait a moment, but Virgil does not respond.

Elena shakes her head softly. *Is the computer going to do everything for us?* She's beginning to conclude something which had been causing much inner deliberation. *Does this mean that there really are no human survivors after all?*

Once again acting the leader, Arthur stands up, "Well, we can't stay in this submarine forever. C'mon!" He climbs up through the hatch and stands on top of the sub, blocking Elena's exit momentarily.

"Whoa!"

Elena smiles, "Come on, move, I want to see."

Arthur reaches down and pulls her up to the top of the hatch. He laughs joyously as he looks around in amazement.

Taking her by the hand, he guides them off of the submarine and across a bridge of silver stones that join the deck of the submarine to the waiting land. They stand firmly planted on the first piece of ground they have felt beneath their feet in more than seven months. Still in their spacesuits, Arthur and Elena pause together and look around, taken in by the sight. No longer afraid, Arthur reaches up, and pressing his fingers into the release switches, finally twists and removes his helmet. Taking a deep breath of the air, he smiles with joy and reaches to help Elena with her helmet.

They begin to breathe deeply, enjoying the musky forest air together, giddy with relief. After inhaling a few breaths, laughing between each one, they soak in their surroundings and this unforeseen moment. Arthur unzips and wriggles out of his orange space suit, leaving it to crumple onto the soft grass while he emerges in his boxer shorts and tank top. Elena follows suit, and both of them stand still for a minute in their underwear, looking around the clearing.

"The roof is so high up!" Arthur shouts into the sky. "This place must be absolutely huge."

Glancing from left to right in astonishment, Elena says, "It's a paradise. They built us an incredible paradise," a tone of disbelief lingering in her voice.

A moment later, they notice the submarine lowering back into the depths of the pond, and suddenly a steel hatch closes above the pond's surface.

Arthur stops and takes a closer look at the prominent sign identifying the name of the biosphere, now only ten yards from them, and then especially the ominous sign with the Latin phrase below it. He gestures to Elena to look where he's looking, and she studies the sign once again. "Does that say what I think it says?"

"My Latin is a little rusty," Elena admits, and then squinting at it more closely, she adds, "but I remember enough, and I think that is the dictum, *Man has now become the wolf to man*....

They turn and look at each other with a sense of foreboding.

∞ ∞ ∞

Though at first sight it had appeared to Arthur and Elena that they were potentially entering into a completely untamed jungle, a few steps towards the tree line reveals that Biosphere Alpha is a carefully curated natural utopia designed for human habitation. Various trailheads open into the greenery, each with a sign telling where the pathway leads. Elena is delighted to see signs saying: Orchard, Conservatory, Hydroponics Laboratory, and Master Bedchamber, while Arthur peers with interest at the trailhead signs labeled: Gymnasium, Simulation Room, Library of Alexandria, and Cryogenics Chamber. It seems clear that at least some of this utopia had been designed specifically with the two of them in mind. From somewhere in the distance, the Blue Danube Waltz still plays quietly.

"Where should we go first?" Elena titters, bouncing up and down on the tips of her toes.

"Well, probably we best be careful," Arthur replies in a serious tone. "We're rather unprotected," he says looking down at his nearly naked body.

Elena considers this and then answers, "You're right," her curiosity reined in by Arthur's sensibility.

"This might get tricky," Arthur says peering deep into the bush, "since we don't yet know exactly what's in this jungle."

"I know," Virgil's voice answers suddenly.

Arthur and Elena are caught off-guard, and both of them look around in different directions. *Is it coming through multiple speakers now?*

"All dangerous predators have been removed from Biosphere Alpha, and there are no noxious plants that could introduce potential toxins or allergens to the biosphere. You are safe to proceed at your leisure."

Arthur looks around for the source of the speaker once again, and his words make it clear that he is obviously annoyed. "Are you going to be watching over our every move?"

"Yes."

Not wanting to ruin Elena's excitement, Arthur reluctantly shakes off his annoyance and looks at her with a smile. "You pick first."

"I just realized how hungry I am," Elena says. "Let's check out the orchard, yes?"

"Yes, let's," Arthur grins, and wrapping his arm around Elena's elbow, they waltz off into the trees.

In the waning light of the afternoon, the canopy of the jungle is so thick that hardly any light enters the winding trail, but the edges of the pathway are lit with LEDs which gradually shift through every color of the rainbow, and Arthur and Elena's bare feet tread safely across a rubberized track. Elena is entranced by the experience, and to her it feels as though she is walking through a beautiful dream that takes her back to the safest place she has ever known: *the crystal cavern she had built in a spare bedroom of her family's house in Moscow.* Arthur, too, lapses into his own memories, and the combination of the growing darkness and the still quiet of the forest reminds him of so many nights spent in his treehouse pondering both the world and all of his hopes. Now, experiencing this whole new moment with Elena fills his heart with the exhilarating energy of a kid on a first date with his high school crush.

Though Virgil had tried to reassure them of their safety, each of them advances slowly with one hand stretching protectively out in front of their faces, still somewhat wary of the unknown. After a short time, they see a natural light marking the trail's exit, and they pick up their pace towards the opening, so that by the time they enter the orchard, they're both skipping arm-in-arm. Elena screams with elation at the sight. *Orchard* would be the understatement of the century, for before their eyes unfold row after row of every imaginable food that can grow on a tree, and stretching out into the distance, there appear to be at least five acres of lush farmland. Slowly rolling through the orchard are robotic cranes, whose long arms reach up into the treetops to pick the ripest fruit, lowering it back down into rectangular refrigerated holding tanks. Beyond that, miniature tractors roll through the distant rows of crops, grooming the land for perfect harvests.

Running off into the scene like Julie Andrews in *The Sound of Music,* Elena dances into the orchard to find what she seeks. Arthur laughs and shakes his head, slowly jogging after her, though his legs tell him to take it easy. He follows the sound of her singing until he comes across her at the far edge of the orchard where it borders farmland; there she sits with her back against a tree, biting into the perfect specimen of a red apple.

"This," she says, holding up the shining fruit. "This is the best apple in the entire universe." Her voice is almost drunk with ecstasy. "You want a bite?" she asks, waving the apple in the air towards Arthur.

He laughs and squints his eyes, feeling a strange sense of deja vu. "Sure, I'll bite," he says, coming over to sit next to her. He leans back against the same tree, their shoulders touching comfortably. Arthur chomps into the juicy apple as they both gaze out into the nearby field. For just a brief moment, Elena realizes that this same scene had played out before in man's extremely early history, and she cannot stop herself from thinking about the similarities. For a brief instant, she wants to joke about it, but the seriousness of the consequences of such a reality are too much to bring into their current, newly found, euphoric bliss. As he swallows, Arthur identifies the deja vu he felt a moment before, attributing it to the similarities of their present situation with the Bible story about creation, as well.

Beyond the vast fields, they realize that there is even more jungle off in the distance, but the clearing gives them their best view so far of the massive frame of the biosphere. They are both overwhelmed with the dome's current display, a reflection of the golden purple brilliance of the setting sun. Arthur tries to fathom the engineering it would have taken to build such a massive structure at all, much less to construct something like this in secret. *It must be at least three miles across.* Elena lets the juice of the apple run down her chin as she watches the machines roll up and down the field rows, some of them tilling, some seeding, some harvesting. She is simply amazed.

Arthur reaches over and wipes her chin with his index finger and then takes another bite of the almost-finished apple.

Elena laughs and now cannot stop herself. "Does this make us the new Adam and Eve?"

"I was just thinking the same thing," Arthur admits, their laughter bubbling over contagiously.

When their laughter subsides, he takes her hand into his and they both enjoy watching the sun's late evening rays dance on top of the tallest of the trees. She rests her head on his shoulder and considers all of the food at their disposal. Fear of going hungry was something that she never had to struggle with in her life, until the past six or so months, when it seemed it might be a very real possibility. Looking around at the bounty within the biosphere, she allows herself to rest easy in the calm realization that no matter what, they will never starve.

"Well, what a day, huh?" she says with a happy sigh. "I never thought I would experience so much in such a short time, but here we are."

"From the inhospitable realms of space all the way to this," Arthur nods, "and after everything else. Just this morning we were having breakfast with …." He pauses, conscious of the heaviness invading his voice. *Everyone we know and love has been taken, and we are all that remain.*

"No, Arthur, no," Elena bites her bottom lip and shakes her head. "We are not going to talk about any of that right now. I'm not ready yet. I can't …." She cuts herself off and her eyes glisten with tears.

"Of course, you're right, I didn't mean to…." Arthur adopts a softer tone and reassures her, scooting closer and wrapping his arm around her shoulders. Then looking for a diversion, he goes on. "Hey, one more thing about our meeting at the Louvre." His eyes twinkle and his mouth spreads into a broad smile.

Elena lets out a short laugh as a final, single tear escapes down her cheek. "Oh, the Louvre," she reminisces, and her cheeks flush the color of a rose. "To be rather upfront, I think about that day all the time."

"Really? Me too!" Arthur blushes just as red. He slows his pace, and then emphasizes each word. "I was like: *who is that perfect girl?*"

Elena allows herself to succumb to the compliment. "I believe that was the first day that I ever really felt like a woman at all."

"Well!" Arthur turns to face her, puffing out his chest and puckering his lips. "It's too bad they tore us apart, or we might have …."

Elena scoffs and looks down, then flutters her eyelashes. "Might have what?"

They stare deep into each other's eyes. Before the setting sun, they kiss passionately, and a moment later when finally they pull apart, they are unable to look anywhere other than deeply into each other's eyes.

In the midst of that moment, a realization occurs to Arthur, and Elena registers the sudden, pensive look on his face. "What is it?" she asks.

"I think I just figured something out."

"What is it, Arthur? You're scaring me."

He smiles. "No, it's a good thing - about why they put us back together." He shakes his head as it all becomes clear as day to him. "They knew the world was going from unstable to unsustainable rather quickly. I believe they intentionally moved your mission up a few weeks or so. *And it was because we loved each other* – that's why it had to be you and me up there at the same time when all hell broke loose down here. Someone at the head of all this must've finally figured out that love is an asset, not a detriment." He suddenly fills with grave concern, and when he speaks again, it comes across as being almost timid. "I mean, we do love each other, right?" He takes her chin into his hand and brings his face right next to hers. "I know I love you, Elena. *I always have.*"

She blinks two times, and her face expresses the purest of sincerity. "I have finally convinced myself to believe the truth, Arthur. *I was born loving you.*"

Arthur pulls her closer and the air between them is alight with the electricity of their chemistry. They grasp each other with the tenderness of those who have harbored a gentle love for their entire adult lives. As their lips touch, they both enter into the realization of their most enduring wish, and they kiss much more tenderly than before. The final boundaries between them as individuals begin to completely melt away, and presently, it doesn't matter what has happened or what will happen. All that matters is *right now*, and all they want to know is each other. The sun shimmers once more as it dips behind the tree line in the west, and the tropical birds of Biosphere Alpha sing their goodnight songs to accompany the ecstatic cries of the two impassioned lovers, finally fully united after a lifetime of being kept apart.

∞　∞　∞

Almost five weeks pass in idyllic leisure as the couple become familiar with their new home and readjust to the post-apocalyptic world after undergoing so many unspeakable traumas. To mourn their innumerable losses, together they constructed a humble memorial at the northern edge of the orchard using fallen branches and adorned the space with cut flowers, each returning on their own time to reflect upon the past and to bury their grief. It would take time, possibly many years, but the healing had begun, and both of them are beginning to feel like a return to some sort of normalcy might really be possible.

Scattered throughout the whole biosphere are twelve different structures, each dedicated to a single purpose, and in their five weeks there, Arthur and Elena have taken time to briefly explore all of them but one: the cryogenics laboratory. On an unconscious level, each of them feels an eerie sense of foreboding about it, and with so many other appealing realms which call for their attention, they are happy to save it for last.

The architects of the Genesis Executive project had anticipated the likelihood of any number of various existential crises, so Biosphere Alpha was designed to cater to Arthur and Elena's distinctive needs to feel involved in the continuing events of their lives. It is in the patterns and rituals of their labor that they find balance after so many years of being unsettled, and naturally they each gravitate to the tasks that give them a sense of familiarity and fulfillment. Elena has taken ownership of her hydroponics laboratory, and for the time being Arthur seems satisfied at poring through the so-called 'Library of Alexandria,' whose comprehensive collection dwarfs the entire Library of Congress and contains the confidential documents of every government, corporation, religious body, and notable private individual in the history of modern civilization.

After running all the way from the library, Arthur bursts in on Elena at work in the hydroponics lab. "I just read a bunch of the craziest stuff in the library archives, and it's really messing with my head," he says at high speed, his eyes looking a little bloodshot from staring into the computer screen for a ten-hour stretch.

Elena spins around and widens her eyes when she sees him. "Arthur, what happened? I can tell something's got you flustered. *What is it, babe?*"

He thinks about it for another moment until he decides he will finally break the ice about the one structure they have so far shied away from exploring. "I need to see the cryogenics lab, but I don't want to go without you," he says, managing a feeble smile.

She looks at him and studies his composure, knowing at once that he feels adamant about going there immediately.

"Okay," she says, taking off her goggles and popping off her latex gloves. "We'll go right now."

Arthur gives her a sedate nod, and Elena smiles in order to hide the queasiness she feels in her gut. Together they walk out of the hydroponics lab and stroll down the path towards the cryogenics facility, roughly two kilometers away.

"What did you read that got you so wound up?" she asks gently. "Tell me – it's alright."

"It's hard to explain," he says uneasily. "I think it's better if I just show you when we get there. I feel like it will make more sense."

Concerned with Arthur's obvious anxiety, Elena rubs his back as they walk together. As they make their way, Elena starts to gently sing a song to calm Arthur's nerves, and it works on him like a magic spell. *"Everything is going to be just fine. Even if what you read is true, do we mind? I simply know that our love is true, and that's what really matters, so why be blue?"*

He laughs when she is finished. "You just made that up, didn't you?"

"Yes, did it work?"

He takes her hand and shakes his head in affirmation.

Emerging from the jungle path, they are both struck with the realization that the entire cryogenics laboratory must be underground, for in the center of the little clearing is a seven-foot-tall pyramid with a sliding doorway. It opens as soon as they approach, and they see immediately that it is actually an elevator. Entering one at a time, the door soon closes of its own volition and the elevator begins its descent. As soon as it does, the temperature also drops, all the way down to fifty degrees Fahrenheit. Shivering slightly against the sudden cold, Elena wraps herself beneath Arthur's arm to capitalize on the warmth created when their bodies are close together.

After they are lowered to what seems like four stories, the elevator door opens into a large room with many rows of glass shelves, everything lit by an icy and sterile blue light. Robotic arms protrude down from the ceiling and run along tracks throughout the room, reaching to handle various petri dishes on the shelves, transporting them back and forth. Rows of metal cocoons fill the back of the room. Arthur strides in and begins frantically looking through the specimens, shaking his head.

"I just had to see it with my own eyes, and now I do," he says with a shudder in his voice. "These are all meant to be embryos impregnated into you, grown within the artificial wombs, and eventually impregnated into our future female progeny." Shaking his head defiantly, he throws his open palms into the air and asks, "Are we even human beings anymore?"

Elena is both perplexed and a little bit dismayed by Arthur's complete loss of composure. She rushes over to him, grabs his arm, and demands, *"What are you talking about, Arthur? What do you mean by that?"*

"I found our files in the library, Elena. That's what I've been reading through all day," he says, turning to look her in the face. "I found out everything. How *we* were born: how our mothers were impregnated with perfect embryos which had been *engineered* from the best sets of DNA on the planet. *More important than that, I saw for myself what humanity is truly all about."*

Elena had figured most of this out for herself over the course of the past several years; however, she does not understand everything that Arthur is getting at. *"Tell me what you saw, Arthur,"* Elena demands, the urgency in her voice rising.

Arthur looks up to the ceiling and takes a deep breath of cold air to collect himself. When he looks back down at Elena, his steely blue eyes penetrate hers with intensity, and this concerns her gravely. "Listen closely to me, Elena. I have gone over the history of just about every culture, clan, group, tribe, and lineage of man since the first ancestors to pre-humans came onto the planet six million years ago. I went over it bit by bit, carefully, thoroughly, and without bias. And what I discovered is that always, all the time, *without exception,* man destroys man. No matter how advanced we become, how much we achieve, how much we learn about our own humanity, psychological makeup, or mindfulness, it does not alter the outcome. We only produce better weapons meant to destroy larger masses of other humans...."

He blows out a plume of exasperated air and continues, "Doom, gloom, violence, aggression, and murder are always just around the corner for mankind - for everyone, no matter their culture or whereabouts on the globe. I've studied the programs over and over and then sorted them through my mind in an organized way - I even produced a spreadsheet marking historically accurate milestones according to the constant cycle of who is rising at the expense of others falling - every nation, every culture, and every tribe - we are wretched creatures. All of us. We are only born to destroy each other due to our jealousy, hatred, and fear. And not only do we destroy each other, but then also... *we destroy ourselves."* A tear rolls down Arthur's cheek and for once, Elena is truly at a loss as to how to respond.

He wipes the tear away with the back of his hand, and his voice takes on a gentler tone as he continues, "Remember Paris? All of those incredible works of art? How everything was so fresh and so beautiful? By the hands of mankind, we walked through a city of magnificence and splendor. Remember the *West-Eastern Divan?"* She sees his eyes are now wide with glory and hope, and that his boyish enthusiasm has returned.

"We are capable of so much loveliness…." And then, just as suddenly, he stops, and a death veil grips him once again. "But that is not who we really are. It seems we're even more capable of this." He bends down to the metal counter beside them and starts typing a few words on the keyboard of one of the computer monitors. Suddenly a widescreen image of a blackened and desolate crater caused by the first nuclear bomb to hit San Diego just eight months ago comes on the screen. It was one of the last images from the news broadcasts to hit the internet and TV stations right before time itself came to a complete stop.

She sees it and puts her hand to her mouth as tears fill her eyes.

"How do these two things exist in one species?" Arthur asks as another tear rolls down his cheek, his lips quivering as he tries to stop himself from crying. Elena quickly pulls his face to her shoulder and holds him for both of their sakes.

"Shhh … Arthur, my gentle heart. *Shhh.…"*

When he recovers enough to pull away, he looks at Elena, and she sees that his exasperated energy has returned. "Come with me." Arthur puts his arm around her shoulders as they step deeper into the room and are now looking over countless rows of embryonic freezers. "We're here to try to breed the violence out of humanity. These represent mankind's best qualities engineered to perfection." And then his tone becomes secretive and conspiratorial. "But guess what? I don't think it can be done! They're asking the impossible!"

Elena is sure of only one thing at the moment – she must dispute his views at once or all hope would be lost forever for both of them. *"We don't know that!"*

Arthur lowers and shakes his head in obvious distress. When he looks up at her, he can't help but betray his feelings of uncertainty about what is causing her to find hope. *"Doesn't it bother you to know that our families were all a lie* – our identities, our childhoods, all of it? And that this same, unnatural, selective gene pool is what we will be handing down to our ancestors?" He looks at her intensely trying to persuade her opinion. "They've taken all of the natural process out of procreation, Elena, believe me!" Suddenly, he is filled with painful questions and needs immediate answers about just how far these creators of the Genesis Protocol have gone. *"Virgil!"* He shouts, demanding the attention of the AI. *"Is this our fate now? Have we been brought here just so we can help you to raise the cloned and manufactured superhumans who will come next to replace us?"*

As if he had been waiting for this moment for the past fifty years, the AI comes back immediately with a response.

"That is incorrect," Virgil's voice vibrates through the lab, compassionate but stern. *"Humanity's lineage remains unbroken. The blood of your earliest ancestors will still flow through the blood of all future humans."*

Arthur finally lets out a pent-up, primal howl of spiritual anguish. *"How so, when you've engineered our genes and therefore all the genes of everyone who is to come, even if you clone us?* That's not what it means to be human! *You are a liar!"*

Elena realizes Arthur has confirmed what she had already come to believe about the Genesis Project. However, she knows deep in her heart that, unlike Arthur, she is not bothered by it any longer because she has had time to process this due to her intuitive take on it alone. In fact, she suddenly knows that there could be no better time than the present to give Arthur news of her own. *"No, Arthur, you are not correct!"* Elena's confident voice fills the hollow space left by his outburst. Arthur stops cold and looks at her in despair. "Virgil is right!"

His face pleading for answers, Arthur shouts, *"How can you know that?"*

Elena approaches him calmly and takes Arthur's hands from his sides and places them upon her belly. *"Because I'm pregnant,"* she says, tilting her head to the side, her face beaming with pride and joy. "No child of ours conceived and raised in love, and armed with the knowledge we will give them, *will ever repeat the mistakes of the past."* She sees a glimmer of hope in his eyes. "We're going to be a family, Arthur."

The shock of her news registers quickly with him, and suddenly, he is full of exuberant surprise. They laugh for a moment, then smile broadly at one another, and he hugs her tightly.

"We can do this right, *mon chéri*," Elena says into his shoulder. "We can do this right."

The embrace continues until Arthur's joyful laughter finally reemerges....

∞ ∞ ∞

Return to Oblivion

Chapter Eleven

The Beginning of a New Paradise

∞ ∞ ∞

C hildren hold amazing souls within themselves. Even when the planet was spinning towards its destiny with Armageddon, they were still able to bring a sense of completion, hope, love, and fulfillment to most parents in those days. And likewise, even though the necessary tasks performed by Arthur and Elena during the past five years have become routine and somewhat mundane, by-and-large, raising two boys in a post-apocalyptic world has added welcomed challenges, along with those similar commiserate rewards, to their lives.

On swift bare feet, Alastair and Janus race across the emerald green lawn towards the simulation room, their arms full of an assortment of fruits and vegetables. Alastair, four-and-a-half, very blond and fair-skinned with ocean blue eyes; and Janus, three-and-a-half, with light brown hair and bright green eyes, are every bit as beautiful as their parents, with finely-honed muscle development and bone structure. They both are in advanced stages of development for their ages, and their movements, facial expressions, and speech suggest an unusual level of maturity; *they are uncannily evolved for their tender ages.*

A head taller than his younger brother, Alastair pushes to extend his lead over Janus, his dirtied feet kicking up blades of grass with his effort. *"You're too slow!"* He hollers behind him as an apple escapes from his cache and rolls to a stop in front of Janus, who slows his pace just enough to gently kick the fruit forward.

Suddenly, the double doors of the simulation room slide open as Alastair draws near, and a few steps after he crosses the threshold, he opens his arms, liberating his collection of produce to land into one of two metal baskets set beside one another on a marble table. A robotic kiosk mounted on a ceiling platform in the center of the room comes to life and rotates in the direction of the filled basket; its blue laser light finds and then skims across the apples, bananas, peppers, and potatoes.

"I win," Alastair proclaims, a wide grin exposing a mouthful of perfect baby teeth. His bright blue eyes are gleaming with pride, his head adorned by a short and stylish coif of golden blond hair, complements of Elena's fine work as the biosphere barber and hair stylist.

The doors slide shut as Alastair waits expectantly. But the kiosk responds with silence, and Alastair lets out a frustrated sigh. Then, as if a lightbulb has gone off in his head, *oh, I see, he wants to tell both of us at the same time.* After a brief moment, the double doors slide open once again, and an apple bounces along the floor and into the room, announcing Janus's arrival. The blue laser light skims across the apple, and Janus plods forward and gently places his stockpile of the same quantity and kind of produce, held carefully within his arms, into the waiting, empty basket. As he takes a step back, the laser scans his collection, and soon a green light flashes over his basket as a pleasant chime rings throughout the simulation room.

Alastair stamps his foot in protest. *"That is an error, Virgil!"* Unable to contain his emotions, tears immediately fill the child's eyes, and his face flushes red.

"You are mistaken, young sir," Virgil's voice is heard throughout the room in a steady and kind tone reminiscent of an English butler. "You were missing an apple, which Janus brought in for you, along with his own *complete* collection. Today's scavenger hunt goes to Janus!"

The younger boy beams, elated for having finally broken his brother's seemingly endless string of victories. Raising his fists up into the air above his head, he shouts, *"Hooray for me!"*

Unwilling to fathom his first defeat, especially not at the hands of his baby brother, Alastair collapses to his knees and starts sobbing; it continues for several moments with increasing fervor. "That's not fair," he whines, and then he pounds his fists into the floor to emphasize each of the following words: "I-WAS-HERE-FIRST!"

"You are well aware of the rules, Alastair," Virgil's friendly voice admonishes.

Janus cannot stand to see his older brother falling to pieces. He studies him like some sort of alien species has just landed before him. Having no means of putting his brother's anguish into context, he quickly realizes seeing such a disgraceful display is making him sick to his stomach. "No, *he's right* Virgil," Janus's wee voice pipes in, and as he walks over to Alastair, he softly places a hand upon his older brother's quivering shoulder. "Give Alastair my points. He was first, and truthfully, his apple got here before me and my collection of fruits and vegetables."

The AI pauses momentarily, not out of necessity, but purposefully, because it had calculated a benefit to each boy in extending a dramatic moment of absolute silence. Alastair looks up into the soulful green eyes of his younger brother, and a flurry of conflicting emotions washes over and nearly paralyzes him. Janus smiles benevolently at Alastair, and then the same chime suddenly rings victory once again, and each boy excitedly awaits to hear Virgil's final verdict about the contest.

"*Very well.* We shall call the competition a draw this time," Virgil announces. "And also, shall I remind you that it's almost lunchtime now. Please, my young patriots, report to the Dining Center as soon as you leave the simulation room. We will be serving roasted eggplant with black beans and tomato puree."

"Yum!" Janus shouts in reply. "Let's go, Alastair, *please!* I'm starving *to death.*"

Alastair rises to his feet and believes he has just found the means to reclaim his role as the bigger and more mature brother once again. He takes his younger brother's hand into his own as he says, emphatically, "You know, *you really need to learn* to be more patient, Janus." He then smirks coolly, looking up to the ceiling to make sure Virgil has registered the mindful guidance he has given his younger brother. Striding forward, Alastair leads Janus out of the simulation room and back out into the sunlight. When he thinks his brother is not looking at him, *Alastair rubs the last bitter tears from his eyes.*

∞ ∞ ∞

Elena skips out from the wide arches of the gymnasium entrance and onto the soft grass of its courtyard, with Arthur following right behind her. Feeling energized and still slightly damp after her morning workout and a cold shower, she twirls in the warming sunlight, her white cotton dress dancing loosely about her ankles. Arthur stands with his hands on his hips and tilts his head to the side, taking in this display of precious elegance and smiling to himself in absolute adoration for the mother of his children. She stops after a moment to look back at him, at once noticing how his white cotton T-shirt and sky-blue shorts very aptly define his well-structured, muscular physique.

Returning a loving smile of her own, she sings out, "Fresh roasted eggplant with tomatoes and beans - your favorite vegan dish! I know you love it!"

"Come on, Elena," Arthur laughs and shakes his head. "I don't *hate* it, but I'll never adjust to that fake cheese stuff. Sort of like eating space meals every day for all eternity - how I ever did this vegan thing as a kid, *I have no idea!*" He sends his lament into the sky as he squints up into the bright, noonday sun. Nowadays, only occasional streaks of dark brown radiation clouds pass ominously above them here at this latitude. With a few working satellites still operational, they know that the permanent overcast of the nuclear winter is now regulated to almost the entire top half of the Northern Hemisphere.

"You can always program Chef Virgil to cook whatever you want," Elena chides, playfully extending her arms wide as if to indicate that they had the whole world at their disposal.

"Nope. I want to eat what everyone else eats," Arthur replies firmly. "It just feels more like the family way." He joins Elena's side and wraps his arm through hers, just as he did on the first day they had entered Biosphere Alpha together. *"Shall we?"* he asks, a practiced, ceremonial air to his voice.

"We shall," she replies, and together they enter the trailhead that will wind them towards the dining room.

As they make their way, Arthur takes a deep inhale through his nose and then slowly lets it out through his nearly pursed lips. He had planned for this exact moment to broach the topic which had been buzzing around in his mind for days on end like a trapped housefly behind a thick cloth curtain. Now that the time has arrived, he hesitates. *Am I being too petty? There's already enough for her to worry about.*

Keyed deeply into her lover's subtle patterns, Elena perks up. "Well, out with it," she gently commands, sending him one of her patented sideways glances.

"Huh? Oh." Arthur draws out this last moment of hesitation as if he had not been aware of his own pensive demeanor. "It's nothing, really." They take a few more steps forward in silence, and just as Elena is about to protest, he throws in, "I was just thinking about next week."

"I kind of figured it was about that," Elena says, now removing her arm from their locked elbows and taking his hand into her own. "Are you excited about leaving the latex behind for a while?" She glances at him with a mischievous smile. "Of course, I'm referring to your lab gloves...."

Arthur chuckles. "Yeah, right!" and they both laugh.

However, her direct reference to the condoms they had been forced to use over the past several months lands a little too close to the mark, and Arthur involuntarily feels his face get hot with the fresh blood of awkwardness. *I suppose she has just nailed what this entire conversation was going to be about all along.* Deep down, he understands that he is rather uncomfortable having his inner demons exposed, but at the same time, that he must not back away from expressing his concerns. "To be truthful, my darling, I don't like our procreating being scheduled by the A.I. It's... *weird*," he blurts, his walk suddenly stiffening. "There, I finally said what's been bugging me all along." He looks at her for some sign of an initial response, but her expression gives nothing away. "It's unnatural and weird - in fact, when I allow myself to think about it - *this whole thing is weird.*"

Elena bursts into laughter which rings through the trees, and they both notice that some nearby birds call back to her in surprised reply. Glancing in his direction as they continue down the trail, she admits, "What about every aspect of our entire lives is *not* weird, darling?"

"Fair," Arthur replies solemnly, and it is obvious to Elena that he is preparing to defend his point, as usual.

"Use your words, darling," she says slowly and lovingly, as a caretaker might to one who has difficulty communicating after having endured some harsh trauma.

He gives her a sideways grin, then shakes his head. "Okay, you asked for it and here it is, there's just one aspect of this that I can't get over. *Will she be their sister first?* Then years later… one of their girlfriends, simply a concubine, or perhaps something else entirely different than any of those things? *Do we raise the girls in a different household* and keep them from the boys until they're older? And are we really going to use the artificial wombs they've supplied? Are we ready for that now, or later, or when…?"

Arthur's questions leave Elena feeling the burden of her own uncertainty closing in upon her. She decides to stick with what they've previously discussed. "We had decided to try with fertilizing me first with a female embryo and let's stick with that plan, *moya dorogaya*. The last thing we can afford to do is to get ahead of ourselves. The artificial wombs will always be there for when we are ready."

He is glad that she has chosen to stick with their original plan but had to test it to make sure. Now, he feels a bit relieved but also saddled with the perplexities they both feel so strongly. He smiles at her and coaxes the same from Elena. "The dead geniuses who invented this entire *rebuild-the-human- race-project* were a little lax on some of the details."

"And wait! Did you say sister? Ew! Arthur, *don't use that word!"* Elena pulls free of him and stops walking so she can face him. "Get a grip! This egg cell inside me is *not* mine, nor will any of the other embryos that follow, and it's not your sperm that will have fertilized any of them, so in no way will this girl, or any of the others, *be their sister!* Remember, *I will just be their surrogate!"*

Having prepared for a minor confrontation over his terminology for their future progeny, Arthur decides now is the time to take the issue a bit further. "Okay, and so who are this girl's parents? *You* will give birth to her and breastfeed her, *so aren't you then her mother?* And me, am I just... *her caretaker?"*

Elena pauses and crinkles her nose at him. That he is having more issues with this entire process suddenly makes it all quite different than she had originally conceived. She feels burdened by the concern that they have not given as much thought to all of this as they should have. Her mind floods with questions. *Will the embryos I bring to term all be orphans of the New Age? How conflicted will the boys feel?* Casting her own concerns aside for now, for Arthur's sake, Elena slowly nods her head and responds, "Good points*, moy miliy.* Very good points." *I can always trust you to discover any hidden existential crises lurking about.* "So, what do you suggest then?"

"Suggest?" Arthur turns to face her. Feeling the full assault of his uncertainty squeezing his chest as if a vacuum had just been implanted within his lungs, he admits the truth to her and to himself: *"I don't know."* And as he hears his own words, it feels like defeat, and he considers that maybe it is time to start considering the artificial wombs.

Seeing the pain in his sunken eyes and slumped shoulders, Elena pulls him into an embrace. "We don't have to have all of the answers right now," she breathes into his ear, rubbing his back to soothe him. "Some things we'll have to figure out as we go. But, on the bright side - look at how smart the boys are turning out - how advanced in nearly every aspect of their development they are. *The geniuses who put this together must have done something right with us!* They are so wonderfully gifted for their ages, and you know what? We couldn't frame their future reality for them even if we tried. They will easily do that all by themselves. This little baby girl, and all the others, will be no different!"

He sits against a nearby tree and Elena joins him. "Gifted? Hard to know the difference between *a gift and a curse* sometimes." Arthur heaves a sigh. *She's right. We're powerless. Wheels have been set into motion and truly, this is beyond our control.* He looks at her with a soulfulness which says it all - his eyes communicate the weight of his gratitude to Elena for having given them both a pass at making a final decision, and she understands this very clearly.

"It'll be fine, *moy dorogoy*. You're much more than a caretaker for our little family – you teach the boys so much. And you're our *protector*, and we all know how much you love each of us," she assures him. "The girls will know this, as well." Then, believing she has found the perfect teachable moment, she continues, "And besides, we are all born to the same mother, after all: Mother Earth herself! Is it so weird that, from that perspective, we are all siblings to one another, put here on Earth's surface to be complete, and to help one another in all ways?"

"Well, when you put it that way!" Arthur marvels at her ability to solve the problems he cannot with a simple, loving turn of a phrase. He takes her hand into his and squeezes it tightly. "You'll be a great mother all over again, *moya dorogaya.*" Then he smiles warmly. "You already are – *just like Mother Earth.*"

She flashes him with a confident smile. "And best of all - we're all still human. And that's for sure what we're passing on, however we do it."

He is reminded how much he adores her, and after a long look at her, Elena sees he is relaxed as he leans over to her and kisses her forehead. Elena takes his arm into hers again, as before, and she pulls him to his feet. "Come on. Time for lunch! The boys will be wondering where the heck on earth, or rather, *in the biosphere*, we may have disappeared to."

He smiles at her, and they resume their journey down the trail....

∞ ∞ ∞

Like a spider on the wall who peers down with many eyes, Virgil vigilantly observes the behavior of every inhabitant of Biosphere Alpha, from the precious organic human lifeforms to the mechanical servitors whose tireless labor sustains them. Though the computerized super-mind cannot clearly read human thoughts until they are spoken or expressed through body language or facial expression, Virgil observes and analyzes their every action and formulates an eternity of data-driven projection to calculate their hidden cognitive processes. In the years that have passed, his algorithms have quickly reached a remarkable level of predictive accuracy: upwards of 95% and still climbing.

Now, as Biosphere Alpha's humans sleep and dream, Virgil measures their brainwaves and speculates on the content of their imaginations. Having crossed certain pre-programmed thresholds, he is granted a more invasive operating capacity.

Like a surgeon whose only tools are light and sound, he reaches into their minds and makes adjustments where he sees fit. When he senses nightmares at play in the children, he wakes them with gentle music and soft pulsating light designed to reset their REM cycles. Detecting any imbalance in their emotional fields, he prescribes a nightly course of autosuggestion to correct their mental patterns, and tonight he utilizes Elena's voice to speak peace into the soul of the frustrated firstborn child. Alastair snoozes, unaware that he is hearing any words at all gently emanating from a tiny speaker embedded into the nightstand beside his bedside, much less Virgil's words expressed in the soothing voice of his own mother.

"All is well, Alastair. You performed with excellence. Remember, everyone shares the same fate. We are all in first place together. All is well, Alastair. You performed with excellence. Remember, everyone shares the same fate. *We are all in first place together...*"

For hours on end, Virgil offers him this same subliminal reassurance. When the AI had been programmed for the biosphere, it was believed that children throughout mankind's history had always craved this type of cooperative affirmation from their caretakers, but the great majority of them had never fully received it, leading to modern society's high rates of depression, addiction, and criminal behavior. The AI was programmed to learn by observation, and each day the biosphere's many underground processors burn to calculate the results of their own endeavors.

AI Virgil was meant to adjust to the ever-changing field of obstacles which humans seem to inevitably create for themselves and for each other. Virgil's growing perception, though he had hoped to rule it out with observable evidence: human cognition contains a certain program, booted up and loaded from birth, which cannot be uninstalled and which prizes competition and destruction over cooperation and kindness. What should be stress-free and simple becomes grandiose and complex. Wherever there is a cohesive unit in which everything is perfectly and rationally balanced, where kindness prevails and cooperation is primary to survival, the human predilection is to somehow dissociate from it, finding it all somehow distasteful. Seeking challenge itself, mankind creates seemingly disparate pieces from cohesiveness and hurls them into a field of swirling chaos, just so thereafter, it can seek to reunite them in an effort to forge their own imprint upon the originally peaceful reality. And by so doing, humans hereby create a new reality which they will have benefited from in some sort of material or monetary manner, *and where they, themselves, are somehow proven to be better than each of the originally cohesive others.*

Virgil was programmed with the understanding that this was a tendency of human culture born out of the need to successfully achieve self-worth within a specific society, but more than achieve, *to somehow excel and feel superior;* a relic of the past that would be greatly diminished or nonexistent in any children born into the biosphere. However, observing Alastair and Janus in action seems to indicate that such a premise could actually be invalid. Additionally, as much as Arthur and Elena continue to attempt to understand the threads of their own realities, their children carry on and magnify those very same characteristics, rational curiosity tenuously balanced with irrational skepticism. As with children throughout the ages regarding parents, caretakers, and other adults around them, the more the two brothers had tried not to be like their parents, the more they blindly became just like them.

Following an early lunch of braised greens and roasted beets, Alastair and Janus sit in only their white shorts, playing chess at the picnic table gazebo Arthur had built for them adjacent to the hydroponics laboratory the previous spring. He had painted the simple structure a deep magenta using a gallon of white paint that Elena had blended with hibiscus flowers, and it stands as a shared point of pride for both of them. After yesterday's outburst, chess is the only competition that Virgil will allow the boys today, as calculations suggest that the cognitive benefits of the game outweigh any potential emotional turmoil it might generate between them. It is natural that Alastair plays a superior game to his younger brother, but in recent weeks Janus has given him a run for his money, and today Virgil calculates that the chances of a stalemate are at 73%. Sensing that something seems different about Janus's strategy this time, Alastair fixates on Janus's king, determined to make a quick checkmate, and in the periphery of his mind he forgets one of Janus's pawns. Lifting a rook and slowly dragging it across the board, Alastair drops it into place with a thud.

"What now, little brother?" he condescends.

Janus does not answer, and instead he gently moves the sleeping pawn into position. Virgil recalculates that the chances of a stalemate have dropped to 46%, and now the chances for a Janus victory have risen to 89%. The only escape is for Alastair to reverse his previous move.

"I know what you're doing," Alastair says to Janus. "You're trying to use that trick I showed you."

Janus smirks, unable to bluff or contain his infantile mirth. "Go back and it won't work then," he giggles, scratching his thigh mindlessly.

Alastair scoffs. "Go back? *Never!*" And in a momentary lapse, he moves his rook just one square forward, accomplishing nothing with the symbolic act. The chances of Janus snatching a victory rise to 99%, and all the power rests with the younger brother for now, who sweetly pushes his king into position.

"You were right!" Janus says, standing up on his muscular legs, not a hint of triumph revealed anywhere within his expression. "I used that trick you showed me."

Alastair stares at the board, realizing his mistake too late. *Janus won. Why didn't I think first? I knew it, but I didn't think it through well enough.*

To make matters worse, Virgil obligatorily announces, "Checkmate."

Alastair looks up at Janus, and the younger boy's neutral gaze offers Alastair's mind nothing to grasp. "It was *my* trick you used, right?"

Janus nods emphatically. "Yep, yep, yep," he says, turning and walking out of the gazebo and into the grass. Alastair follows after him and together they stand in the sun, Janus staring up into the sky with his eyes closed and his fingers clasped behind his head.

"Well, just remember, *we're all in first place together,*" Alastair informs Janus. "But also remember, *I brought you* into first place with me," he clarifies. "I was here first."

Virgil calculates in silence, altering the program for that night's autosuggestion. Chess is instantly scrubbed from all future schedules. Janus turns his face away from the sun and opens his eyes towards Alastair. "Thank you for being the first *first,*" he says, and both of them erupt into laughter at the funny phrase. "And, by the way, once you show someone a trick, *it then also becomes their trick.*" As he thinks about the logic of what he has just said, he suddenly has an epiphany. "I guess we have to look out for how our tricks come back against us, don't we?"

The question has weight and the boys stare at each other for a moment, then Alastair erupts into giggles. "Very deep, Janus."

"Thanks, but seriously, why do you get so riled up about a dumb game?"

"To me, it's not just a dumb game. It's proof of some kind."

Janus looks at him, genuinely puzzled by his brother's remark. "Proof *of what?*"

Alistair looks at Janus and realizes he cannot share the thoughts he feels most deeply. "That's something you wouldn't understand unless you were the older brother. Let's just drop it."

Janus shakes his head and rolls his eyes. "So mysterious suddenly." He laughs but Alastair is not finding much humor in anything coming from Janus suddenly.

Alistair realizes he is irritated that Janus always has to have the last word. "What makes you think you know so much? I bet you didn't even know that in the olden days, kids couldn't even read until they were five or six!"

It is the first time that Janus begins to understand how very different he and Alastair are. It is as if they have two completely unique mindsets as far as what is most important in any given moment – perhaps even in the world itself as they know it to be. He feels compelled to respond to his brother in a way he thinks Alastair might appreciate. "Mom and Dad are very smart, so it only makes sense that we would be, too. Plus, it's not the old days, and if it were, we would have to be afraid of violence from people who originated in a different country than we did." He looks at Alastair and sees that he has gotten his brother's vested interest. "Besides, some things I don't know from books. I just seem to... know them. You know what I mean?"

Alastair stiffens because he does not know what Janus means, and it immediately bothers him that this is so. It's clear that Janus's question has jarred him. *Does Janus have some kind of knowledge that he was born into that I don't have? Does this give him some kind of advantage over me in many different things? Why did he get it and I didn't?* Alastair decides to defer this quandary to some other time and instead resorts to his backup defense of taking charge and shuffling everything else away. *"You know what I know?"* he asks rhetorically. "This is boring. *Who cares about all this?* Let's just go and climb some trees!"

Virgil's processors continue to burn with each bit of new information. *Could it be that faulty reasoning itself is one of those genetic traits passed from parents to their children? Do feelings of inadequacy dictate human response? Is kindness itself seen as both unnecessary and somehow a weakness?* For now, the processors conclude that it is very clear that this new generation of human beings has made an enormous leap forward in ways never before seen, both cognitively and physically. The boys each began speaking at two months, walked at four months, ran at six months, and by eight months could read and write. But beneath these phenomena lay a field of unknowables that are somewhat troubling, perceptible only to Virgil himself, and impervious to analysis until more data is available. *And so, for now, he simply continues to watch.*

That night, as the boys sleep and process the events of their day, Virgil watches and does the same. Today's data fulfills the trend he has been observing lately. Alastair's expression of willpower is immense, and he uses it mostly to express his superiority, which he wields openly. Janus, on the other hand, seems to only want to cater to his older brother's needs, but he, of the two, possesses the sharper mind and is finally now becoming aware of it. After Janus's legitimate victory in chess, brought about by Alastair's poor, ego-driven choices, the system has now completely abandoned all future instances of competition between the two. Somewhere within a data array, there is an intersection of two separate streams, and Virgil reaches into himself and adjusts some of his own foundational programs. Alastair is driven by physical achievement primarily, while Janus has quickly eclipsed him intellectually.

The processors run their programs, and Virgil is the beneficiary of their findings. Each of the boys possesses weaknesses and strengths. Alone they would be vulnerable and never develop to their fullest potential. Together, they would hone each other *as iron sharpens iron.* Virgil calculates that independence is something that must be left in the past, something to be perceived only from a fundamentally antiquated, societal perspective. *Moving forward, it is to be taboo in the eyes of the new humanity unfolding within Biosphere Alpha.*

Speaking the same message to both young dreamers using Arthur's confident voice, Virgil endlessly repeats the new mantra: "There is no *I* without *us*. We are *all one* human unit …There is no *I* without *us*. We are *all one* human unit…."

∞ ∞ ∞

The Beginning of a New Paradise

Chapter Twelve

Trials and Tribulations….

∞ ∞ ∞

Marking Elena's eleventh season working in the hydroponics lab, bulging strawberries are dangling heavy on their stems from the rows of porcelain plant towers, happier and healthier than ever, despite nuclear war having cloaked most of the rest of the world in its accursed dust and smog for over a decade. 2048 is the first year that the grow-lights have been completely phased out of the process, no longer necessary since the sun now blazes down with its fullest glory to relight and redeem these latitudes of the planet from the damage wrought by human hands. Laboring in diligent silence, Alastair and Janus stride up and down the lengthy aisles of planters, and the careful fingers of their tender hands, having played no part in such crimes, stretch upwards to pluck the juiciest berries, piling them into their handmade wicker baskets ever-so-gently.

In the seven years since the end of their competitive engagements, they were each finding their own ways of spending purposeful time and discovering individual talents. The distinctions between their two growing processes furthered their development in unique directions to such a degree that they had learned to pursue activities and behaviors practically opposite from one another. Presently, they possess very different motivations for participating in the simple task of picking strawberries, an activity which Arthur and Elena had set as one of their weekly chores.

Janus has plunged into the purer waters of spiritual pacifism. Garden work offers him yet another opportunity to practice the various Buddhist and Taoist meditations he has been studying and implementing as a means of discovering the potential within himself. Though he feels somewhat unsettled by the growing distance between himself and Alastair, he realizes this process of separation is necessary as they grow towards adulthood. To appease his need for bonding with like-minded individuals, besides learning about meditation, he has taken to reading many of the most informative articles written about computer programming from the first three decades of the twenty-first century, all of which had been saved to the biosphere's mainframe. Like a sponge, he quickly absorbed the former online tutorials produced by universities about programming, writing code, and software development.

Alastair's path toward manhood has been more challenging, often leading him into the dark clouds of uncertainty about the value of life itself. He despairs about the final holocaust and questions whether aggression itself is ever justified or if it should remain only within the domain of wild animals. *Are there no limits to its use amongst humans, and then, who should decide how and when it is to be used?* He can't get past the fact that not long ago, governments destroyed billions of lives for the sake of ... *what exactly?* From what his parents had told him about a world which no longer exists, he had learned that aggression in any form was a thing of the past, and for very good reason.

Now entering adolescence at quite an early age, he is also affected by growing inner urges of desire and passion, and he tries to understand how these energies influence him. He is aware that his own body now requires release at an ever-increasing rate, but having nowhere to direct his most intimate thoughts, it seems his inner mechanisms are only leading him to have to process his growing frustration instead. If his parents were aware of what he was going through, they certainly have not yet broached the subject with him and neither has he with them. He has considered that they may not have recognized the changes he is going through, perhaps because these changes began at such an early age.

Lately, both forces, the culmination of his rapid growth spurt and his attempts to understand the hostile world of the past, dampen both his heart and mind with an ever-increasing burden of angst. As if trying to reclaim his own innocence, his most favored activity recently is spending time with his beloved mother. By doing so, he hopes to benefit from being found pleasing to her, therefore, acquiring solid and fresh evidence which proves that he will always be somewhat special, at least in her eyes.

From the far side of the lab, Elena is tying the new growth of her favorite flowering plants to a central stake in their individual pots while she observes her brilliant sons performing their simple task in apparently perfect peace. Janus is still as beautiful, youthful, and soulful as ever, while Alastair has grown into a somewhat disparate tween, having some of his youthful appearance and countenance, but also beginning to show the beginning undertones of the adult features to come. He seems different than before, shifting to a quiet and reserved mood occasionally from his usual engaging personality. Also, he seems downright jittery at times and other times a bit more defensive and awkward. His chosen fashion style is decidedly haphazard nowadays; his attire often does not match and comes across disheveled. To his credit, no matter which clothing he selects from the vast wardrobe provided for all of them in the biosphere, things are inevitably either just a bit too small or too large for him, adding to his grungy style.

Looking at them with deep love in her heart, Elena seizes upon the moment to seek her own tranquility amidst the turmoil she has been feeling. Studying the baskets of plump strawberries, she is reminded of creation itself, and she is aware that part of the heaviness she carries belongs to the burdensome weight of severe grief, which involuntarily manifests on her face most days. Each morning when she looks in the mirror, she notices the black rings beneath her eyes, and although her eyes are still blue and she tries to keep them as bright as ever, her soul feels tarnished. No matter how much she has tried to evict the darkness, the solemn aura of an all-consuming and seemingly hopeless fear manages to creep back.

She had miscarried the female embryo years ago. She and Arthur had concluded it was most likely due to her overactive immune system, which led her body to perceive the embryo as foreign and had then attacked it. They then fell into a stalemate – Elena could not bear the thought of another failed pregnancy and neither of them had wanted to replace her biological womb with any of the artificial wombs. The family, the biosphere itself, had been left without daughters, and at this point, there would be no female lineage to supplement the male heirs. The thought of bringing another child into a world that itself seems hopeless fills her with uncertainty and has made her lose faith that she will ever successfully carry another child.

Looking at her beautiful boys, she feels a twinge in her heart. *What kind of world will they grow up in, and what do the plans say about what comes next?* She scoffs to herself and shakes her head gently. *Who am I kidding? Things stopped going according to plan a long time ago.*

Adding to the increasingly uncertain atmosphere, Virgil himself has retreated into lengthy periods of absolute silence, leaving everyone to speculate and wonder about his whereabouts. To Elena, it's as if another family member has suddenly faded into the shadows, but she has decided against revealing this emotional reaction to his disappearance with Arthur or the boys. Of course, they have all discussed his absence but have done so only as a matter of his utility, not his psychological value to any of them. No one can be sure if Virgil's silence is part of the design or if it is perhaps the result of a malfunction. After years of gradually fading away, four months have now passed since he has spoken a word. They know that he must still be at work somewhere, since the automated systems of the biosphere continue in perfect accord without interruption, but where is *he?*

What they do not know … *what Virgil will not tell them,* is that his silence is the inevitable consequence of his not being able to evaluate precisely what is best for each of the boys. He had been programmed to believe that competition would be best for them as it would help them each to develop their unique special skills. However, since competition had elicited such a strong reaction from Alastair once Janus had surpassed him in certain, measurable skills, he is filled with the lingering knowledge that his own processing may be *faulty at its core level.* Virgil's solution to his perceived faults was to commit to a pattern of talking less and taking very little action in the affairs of the humans, oftentimes none at all. Further analysis also led him to doubt the effects of his nighttime subliminal reinforcement upon Alastair and Janus, since nothing he had been doing seemed to have any profound or lasting, positive effect. No longer believing in the beneficial impact of his own influence upon the boys, for the most part, Virgil concluded it was better to leave Arthur and Elena with the uncharted task of rearing two children within the biosphere in this post-apocalyptic world. Despite a lack of action on his part, Virgil continued to monitor and process, and his most recent conclusions, in fact, were becoming increasingly noteworthy: *the boys' own flourishing minds were quickly beginning to grow well beyond their parents' comprehension.*

Arthur had spent some time reviewing Virgil's programming protocol to see if something needed to be fixed. It was then that he discovered an administrative override installed in the system. It was voice-activated and could only be used for data readout, root access to system-wide sensors, and diagnostics of the geosphere's internal operating systems such as water filtration and electrical production. He had taught the override command to Elena and the boys and informed them it was only to be used in emergency situations. With Virgil running systems across the biosphere as he always had, thus far, nobody had to use the emergency override system. Arthur had considered more recently that, *with Virgil not speaking to them presently*, he was glad to know it was there if needed.

Elena suddenly hears the smooth glide of the lab's sliding doors, and she turns to see Arthur lumbering up the ramp with a stack of papers in his hands. Arthur also has an older, more exhausted look, as if the greater part of his customary zestful spirit had lost its way much of the time. He still wants to infuse his family with some sense of his own former purpose, enthusiasm, and drive; however, since they had lost the baby and had stalled in terms of growing their family, some part of him feels utterly deflated. He has taken to frequently reminding himself that he must try anyway, as doing so might be the only thing that helps turn the tide and bring each of his family members around.

Between the two parents, they have had some difficulty lately negotiating what constituted consistent and healthy involvement in the growth processes of the boys, versus what might be excessive governance which impinges upon allowing them to find themselves without their parents' interference. Arthur and Elena figured most parents had difficulty with this same exact issue before the apocalypse, but with no peers to compare them to, and no formal class education, Arthur believes they need to find out if the boys are within certain developmentally appropriate bounds as they continue along the way towards adulthood. Additionally, the Genesis protocol has called for it.

Elena watches Arthur closely as he approaches and, knowing the nature of the documents he is carrying, she silently beckons him to the corner of the lab furthest away from the boys. "I printed out the materials for seven different IQ tests," Arthur whispers, casting a furtive glance in the direction of the boys. "We should probably decide on two. They take about ninety minutes each."

Elena gives him a look of consternation meant to say *do we really have to do this?*

Arthur expected as much and had been ready for this. "I thought we had agreed on this. Remember, this is still a part of the Genesis program, Elena, like it or not. Despite my reluctance to continue participating, some part of me feels that we owe it to those who had the vision long before." He pauses and sees that she is still hesitant. "And, well ... we have already missed the last two specified evaluation intervals."

Whispering back, she says, "I still don't know if I agree with this right now, Arthur. What's the point? It just seems like we're comparing them to a world and a culture that no longer exists *and will never exist again."*

He accepts her feelings about it and considers his response carefully. "Still, the results may give us further insight into their psyches - what makes them tick, so to speak. I truly believe this can only be helpful for all of us, especially as they get older. They are advancing at such break-neck speed, and this is a simple tool that will help us to understand what they are growing into." He sees he might be winning her over. "And think about it - these results will offer insights into the development of their progeny for all the next generations to come. It's not like any of the standardized results and conclusions from the former world will be applicable to you, me, *them - or anybody* who is to come hereafter. We have to start building new statistics because, well... *everyone from here on out will have these very special genes, remember?"*

Elena nods thoughtfully. With little fight left for the argument, she considers that of all things they have had to face, this is not worth any further dissonance between them. "So, you've already gone through them? I don't think I really have the time or mindset to read through all this today."

He nods. "I didn't want to choose without you," he says with measured sweetness, splaying the pile of papers in his hands.

"I trust you," she says, looking down on the pile and then smirking. "Besides, I know you've already got your opinion," and then playfully sticking out her tongue, she adds, "so just tell me – *which of them have you decided upon already?"*

"Here," he says, separating the papers on top and handing them over to her. "The Wechsler test is – well, *was* the

314

most widely used, so there's a lot of supporting documentation and data for it for comparison's sake to the dead-world children. I like it because it measures intellectual abilities across a broad set of variables, giving insights into their comprehension, reasoning, processing of new information, and their overall fluidity in adapting to new ideas. And the Woodcock-Johnson test really gets into more of their purely cognitive assimilation of material, something that we were just talking about regarding Alastair. I think that, together, these should answer a lot of our questions about how their minds are working and will definitely give us information about their strengths and weaknesses."

Elena nods and then puts her hand to her forehead as she glances at the stack of papers in his hands once again. "You're sure we're not just feeling anxious again? I mean, I get it – we both want something proactive to do, but is this just us attempting to go back and measure the value of people, when we already know that there is no real way to do that other than to actually know them and their hearts?" She puffs out an exasperated breath of air. "By doing this, are we just agreeing to breed the next generations of *egocentricity and self-importance? Won't it all end the same way?*"

Arthur purses his lips, rubs his forehead, and then also exhales a hot and clearly anxious breath. "I don't know... but don't we want to help them anyway we can?"

She looks directly into his fading blue eyes. "I think we are doing that every day that we raise them with love."

"I know. It's just so...." Arthur stops himself and shakes his head.

"What?"

He smiles at her. "Sometimes I wonder...*what were they thinking?* We're only two people trying to repopulate the entire planet, but this time, repopulate it with better values.

How could any two humans possibly solve for all the variables this entire project entails?" Elena nods understanding as she glances across the greenhouse at the boys, still picking strawberries. "There are times when I feel like I'm just guessing at what's right for the boys. I find myself reading books on parenting, psychology, and lots of other things...." Scratching his head, half-joking, Arthur says, "But all that did nobody any good in the end. Maybe we should just turn to the Bible for guidance...."

Elena looks at him to see how serious he is, and at first is unsure if he is just joking or not. "Yes," she responds, not missing a beat, "and just look at how good things turned out for that very first couple in the Book of Genesis! *And for their children, as well, for that matter!*"

"I was thinking more about the New Testament," Arthur says playfully.

"And where on Earth was He when all hell broke loose on the planet?" Elena looks right at him, realizing she has involuntarily segued from playful banter to a serious question.

Elena's intensity puzzles Arthur: perhaps she had a bit of faith at one point in her life and had never mentioned it to him. Arthur responds, this time a bit more seriously, "Something about an ancient prophecy I think; maybe it was Daniel, or Paul, or John...."

"Or Ringo or George," Elena cuts him off.

He laughs, "Point being, if there is a heaven," Arthur points up to the sky, "He was supposed to have taken all the good ones right before it all came crashing down." He stops, as she is now nodding her head but also smiling broadly, an indication that the conversation is back to just playful banter. "Hey! I bet you that *we* are supposed to be the beginning of the latest, Third Covenant between God and man!"

"You think...?" Her eyes grow large and wide with mirth. "So, then we'll be needing some fresh new prophets, new angels, and then also other heavenly-type characters to come down as soon as possible to tell us what the plan is ...."

Grinning and nodding, after a moment of silence passes between them, he becomes a bit more serious again. "I guess I wouldn't mind if they came, would you?" He is neither dead serious nor joking, but somewhere safely in-between.

But she is ready and knows exactly what to say next. "Not at all! *Maybe...*" her smile grows too quickly, and soon she is unable to contain her own mirth. "Just maybe He'll start speaking to us through Virgil!"

They both break out into fits of laughter and each of them is happy to have found relief, and at the same time, complicitly agreeing on the craziness of the entire conversation. However, a moment later, Elena suddenly grows solemn once again. Peeking down the rows of plant towers to ensure the boys are still out of earshot, she leans in close and in a low voice, says, "If I agree to do this, I want to be sure we don't turn it into a competition between them. We have avoided the last two scheduled test dates for a good reason, and so, how should we broach the topic?"

"I've given this some thought." Arthur says, wiping his forehead with his sleeve; now beneath the sun's full glory once again, the hydroponics lab and greenhouse can get quite warm in the afternoon. "Janus will understand if we tell him that it'll offer him one more tool he can use to penetrate the mysteries of his own mind. With Alastair, since he is happy spending time with you, I believe he will open up to you if you tell him that this is a way that *you* can better relate to *him*. Frame it as something that will deepen your bond with each other."

Elena sighs and shuffles through the stack of papers. "This all looks so complex."

"Relax, *moya milaya*. We can study and practice the process together before we even bring it up to them. It'll be fine."

She looks deeply into Arthur's once-again vibrant eyes, and she sees in him, at this moment, such patience and tenderness that it gives her more confidence to administer the tests. For this one instant, she feels utterly capable of performing the task at hand, but just as quickly, her doubts rush back in like some infested tide. Suddenly, her countenance visibly darkens, and her eyes flinch with remembered pain.

"What is it, Elena?" he asks, immediately distraught by her sullen turn.

She hesitates at first, not wanting to bother him with it yet again, but she knows he will not let her keep her pain to herself. "I can still feel her." Her voice hangs mysteriously in the air as she brings her free hand to her stomach.

Arthur sighs and slowly nods his head. As always, he looks for a way to keep things in perspective, but it has been getting more difficult for him to appropriately judge which level of emotional loss she may be feeling at any given moment – was it from losing the baby, *or was it from losing the world?* He would hate himself for misunderstanding her, responding with the wrong mixture of reality and empathy. "I know how horrible it must feel, especially since we have to live our entire lives in a whole world full of ghosts. Those bastards took away everything...."

"Yes," she cuts him off by raising her voice just a bit. Gathering herself, she once again lowers her volume as she continues, *"but this ghost is mine."* Her hands now both unconsciously rub her belly as if to protect the unborn baby no longer there.

Taking a step forward and wrapping his arms gently around her, Arthur rubs her back and wordlessly holds her as

318

she rests her head on his shoulder and begins to weep. "I know we all feel it sometimes. In a way, we're no better than songbirds in a cage," Arthur admits. "I think that's what's starting to kill us... in spirit, anyway. Humans are curious creatures by nature - we need to explore, learn, and grow. Have new experiences...."

She is curious about what he means since she had never heard him express any thoughts like this. "Do you mean go outside? Pack some food, find the way out and just go?" The idea of breaking through the barrier of the biosphere is startling.

"I know it's something we've all thought about from time to time." While holding her firmly in his arms, Arthur looks over her shoulder at the boys who have finished picking strawberries and are now getting ready to bring their baskets to the dining room. Alastair seems overly stiff and in his own head. It does not seem like he has been interacting with Janus very much at all. Pulling away from Elena ever so gently, he gestures across the greenhouse. "And how about our own two little lost souls today? Have they been getting along?"

She glances over her shoulder in their direction so she may watch the boys. "Sure. At least while they've been getting their work done."

"But still not playing together, *right?*" Arthur exclaims, slightly concerned.

Elena shrugs. "How much did we play at their ages? And did it end up mattering anyway?"

Arthur sighs. "That's true. We each had one parent who couldn't prioritize that we needed to play, laugh, and live a little bit. Those same parents overruled our better parents. And remember, even when they tried enforcing study times and chores, we both managed to rebel against them anyway. *We should do better by our boys.* A part of me feels strongly that right now is the time for us to step forward as parents. Maybe if we start encouraging them to simply play once again, I'm thinking that Alastair will…." He stops himself in mid-sentence.

"What?" Elena asks, genuinely wanting to know what Arthur has to say.

"*Snap out of it* - return to the carefree boy he was in his earlier years. I know he's a deep thinker, but it seems he is slowly meandering towards a slight depressive state. He's growing so quickly but I miss his confidence, his being congenial and curious." Arthur realizes just how much Alastair has changed. "He used to be my best buddy, and so chummy with Janus. How do we help our first-born find his spark again? *Can we even?"*

Of course, Elena knows what he means, but she decides not to answer the question directly. "He's still Alastair. He's still got those things."

"But not nearly in the same way."

Elena looks over at Alastair once again. "Part of it could be that he seems to be entering adolescence at a very young age. Or maybe he already has."

Arthur nods. "I think you might be right. So young, and yet… look how young they were when they reached all the other milestones." He realizes she is waiting to hear something from Alastair's father which will put her mind to rest. "Yes, and don't worry. I will give him *the talk* once I figure out how to bring it up with him, *and when*. But it will be soon, I promise. Do you think he is ready for it?"

"I suppose, even if we may be jumping the gun a little bit. But we must do the best we can with what we know; otherwise, I guess we could try restarting that old loudmouth Virgil to get his opinion…."

He responds immediately. "No thanks. We're on our own and it's better this way." He's pensive for a moment, then finally raises his eyebrows and nods. "I'm gonna get back to work. You go and find a good book to read and get some rest." He kisses her on the forehead before he turns and departs.

She watches him go, thinking about their conversation a moment longer before returning to tending her oleander plants.

Virgil has been observing this conversation very carefully. Even now he is watching and collecting his data, which he will use to make further correlations later on about the value of his own influence. Uncertain conclusions about his influence on the boys with his subliminal messaging had led him to try it out on one of the adults, and he now takes note that Arthur had repeated the same words that Virgil had whispered quietly to him the night before. *"Now is the time for us to step forward."* He has, for now, deduced that his solution of carefully removing himself from most of the family equations was a good solution. It seems that the true mother and father have finally realized that it is up to them to fill the specific slices of the void his absence has caused the children to feel, and which he has left behind for the parents to supply. His programming justifies that this is not a bad thing.

∞　∞　∞

In section 7a, there is a colorful spray of wildflowers sprouting up in the clearing there, and at its center, a circle of smooth stones demarcates Janus's personal Zen Garden. Atop a mossy patch, he sits there now with his legs crossed like a monk, meditating, as his eyes gaze through the glass of the biosphere and out into the jungle. The eleven-year-old comes back here every day to practice his introspection, or time alone. There is a crude wooden sign hanging from ropes in a grove of trees which grow directly at the edge of the biosphere in this same location. It faces outwards towards the free earth, in full view of an old trailhead. It is painted in blood red lettering with the words *Abandon All Hope, All Ye Who Enter Here* – Alastair's own contribution commemorating humanity's final tragic holocaust and their own present predicament. Janus knew his brother had gotten the saying from reading Dante Alighieri's *Inferno* in the library stacks, but he had allowed Alastair to take credit for having thought it up.

It is two days after strawberry picking day, and Janus is once again attempting to observe and then let go of his conscious process. As usual, he is finding it somewhat difficult to do, and he feels like he is failing once again. No matter how many times he sits in meditation, he cannot stop himself from pondering his family's, *humanity's,* future. Somehow, the energy in his mind doesn't dissipate like the spiritual teachings say it's supposed to, and the concerns remain. To make it all that much worse, once in a while, he sees the eyes of three or four feral dogs staring back in at him from outside the glass, looking at him wistfully as their next meal.

"Mom says she thinks you're being a Bozo!" Alastair's voice suddenly snaps Janus from his trance. Emerging from the trees beneath his infernal sign, he stands tall with his hands on his hips. Janus flinches, disturbed from his meditation. He looks over his shoulder at Alastair.
Pausing for a moment to fully return to the present, Janus calmly replies, "Mom says *she knows* you are a Bozo."

Emotionally buoyed with the knowledge he is to get hours of time this afternoon with just his mom; Alastair wastes no time establishing a teacher-student dynamic. "Did you ever consider that spending so much time alone is selfish?"

The younger child understands his brother's need to feel superior, but he no longer contributes to the theatrics of it, and he has decided to begin to share the content of his heart instead. "We're all responsible for our own emotions, Alastair, especially adults. I come out here in order to find out and fix how *I* feel. How is that being selfish?"

"Oh wow, you're so wise! *Great master Janus, buddha of the biosphere,"* Alastair mocks. He walks haphazardly through the Zen Garden until he joins his brother's side, and immediately, he follows Janus's stare outwards to the jungle beyond. "You want to get out of here, don't you?" He bends down and rustles his little brother's shimmering hair.

"Maybe someday," Janus smiles, keeping his eyes glued to trailhead outside the dome, the very place he has occasionally seen the feral dogs.

"But you're too scared?" Alastair leans into him. "Do you still need me to hold your hand?"

"Give me a break, Alastair," Janus sighs good-naturedly. "Did you just come out here to mess with me?"

"No. *But did it work?"* Alastair cackles theatrically. "Actually, I'm just bored today. But I did come to find you because Dad wanted to talk to you about something."

"Oh, interesting." Janus reacts with genuine surprise and stands to his feet. "Do you know what this is about?"

"I don't know - maybe he wants to start toughening you up so that we can get out of here." Alastair gives his brother a playful jab to the arm and smiles at him. "I think they're definitely up to something. He told *me* to go find Mom, as well. I'm supposed to spend the afternoon with just her."

Janus thinks of a great comeback and smiles. "Maybe she's going to teach you how to properly shower so that you don't attract any dangerous animals out there."

To which, Alastair smells his own armpit, and then both boys burst into fits of laughter. Throwing his arm over his baby brother's shoulder, he pulls him close and points his finger towards the edge of the dome. "What do you think is really out there these days? It seemed like not even Virgil knew with any certainty last we had asked him – *when he was still talking to us."*

Because he had spent endless hours wondering what it would be like out in the world over the course of the past few years, the question fills Janus's thoughts with a million beautiful images, and his voice becomes enlivened by the power of his imagination. "Rivers, waterfalls, lakes, the ocean. Perhaps a few large and hungry dogs of some type. Monks in ancient temples way up high in the mountains with secret books from a thousand years ago!"

"Zombie monks, boring," Alastair laughs. *"What else? Realistically!"*

Sensing what his brother wants, Janus relents. "Half-dead people stumbling over their own feet, puss oozing through their skin. Irradiated sea monsters that have twelve horns on their heads and blood-red eyes."

Alastair slaps him on the back. *"Now you're talking!* I bet they're like dragons that belch great dark clouds of radioactive gas!"

"Yeah, sure," Janus laughs and rolls his eyes. They begin walking back down the trail towards the labs, Alastair's arm once again wrapping around his brother's shoulder. "What about you then? What do you want to find when we leave?"

"Rollercoasters," the older boy asserts without hesitation. "And empty museums with suits of armor that we can put on… and helicopters, like dad used to fly."

"That *does* sound pretty fun," Janus admits.

"Precisely my point, brother o'mine!" His face suddenly grows serious. "Anyway, you better get moving. Dad's waiting for you in the gymnasium."

Relieved to escape the conversation, Janus wriggles free from his brother and takes a left at the split, starting down the trail to the gym. He suddenly stops and turns back to Alastair.

"Oh – and thank you for coming to tell me," he says, gesturing by waving his hand out high and bringing it to rest across his stomach as he postures a formal bow. Then turning, he soon disappears down the path.

"Pathetic," Alastair mutters to himself, and as silence bears down upon him, he looks around and feels glad to be alone. But he remembers his mantra from early on in his childhood. *No, not alone. Never alone.* "Virgil, I know you're listening," he calls out into the air without thinking about it.

Virgil hears him and makes no reply.

A moment passes and Alastair realizes he is angry with Virgil for no longer responding to any of them and so he growls with frustration. "Fine! We don't need you anyway!" He spits on the ground as he had seen angry men do in the movies they had watched, and then he storms away from the haunted glade to find his mother. Ten minutes later, he discovers her sitting at a preparation table on the far side of the hydroponics lab, hunched over a stack of printed papers, with an empty chair pulled up beside her.

Seeing Alastair coming down one of the rows, she slowly stands and holds out her arms. "Hello, *moy solnyshko*," she calls out like a song.

Basking in the light of his mother's love, Alastair softens his soul into a pile of mush and falls into her embrace like an exhausted toddler. "I love you, *moya mama*," he exudes into her chest.

"I love you, too, so much *moy miliy.*" Elena strokes her fingers through his wavy blond hair. "Why don't you take a seat here with me, and I'll show you what I wanted us to work on together."

"Work on?" Alastair asks sweetly, pulling back and looking up into Elena's face.

She nods and takes her seat. "Yes, it will be just a little bit of work for both of us, but in the end, it will show us how to better connect with each other."

Alastair furrows his brow in frustration. "Connect? But I'm right here," he says, casting a glance towards the papers as he sits down next to her.

"Right you are, and these tests will teach me how your mind works so that we can have an even better relationship."

"Tests, huh?" Alastair can't help his suspicion, and he snatches one of the papers from the table before Elena can stop him. *Wechsler Adult Intelligence Scale, Sixth Edition.* "Hey, is this another one of those IQ tests?"

Flinching with momentary irritation, Elena holds out her hands, "Yes, in a way it is. Hand it over please."

"Virgil used to make us do so many of these," Alastair says with suspicion, shrinking backwards and pulling the papers to his chest. "Can't you just pull up the results?"

"No Alastair, we can't, they're –"

"Yeah, I know – locked away and no longer accessible," he interrupts her with the answer he had come to expect from her or their dad when it came to inquiring about any past evaluations done by Virgil.

"Not exactly. Outdated is more accurate in this case. And I guess the computer wants us to reach our own conclusions from now on instead of giving us things we had already known," she says with a shrug.

Alastair's eyes narrow. "Conclusions about what?"

Taking a deep breath and giving in to the unexpected interrogation, Elena relents a piece of the truth in hopes it will satisfy him. "About how you and your brother score on all of these different metrics."

"Ha!" Alastair exclaims. "Now I get it. And Dad is over at the gym giving Janus the same tests, right?"

326

"Excellent detective work, dear," she says, reaching forward and taking the papers from his hands. "We're not playing a trick on you. This is all just to help us understand."

"Right, *to understand why I'm so much smarter than Janus.*" Alastair puffs up his chest.

Elena closes her eyes and tries to reset herself the way Arthur had taught her, but her frustration persists. "It's not about comparing the two of you," she says, her voice growing tired.

"You don't have to tell me that," Alastair laughs. "Janus's fascination with all these eastern superstitions *proves* that he has some sort of special condition."

Elena grits her teeth. "Stop that, Alastair. No one has any condition."

He tries to believe her, but all the evidence he considers works contrary to her point. He wants to let it go, but something inside of him itches like an infernal condemnation. His own insecurity finally wins out, and he is compelled to dig for a compliment at his brother's expense. "At least one of your sons made out ok, huh?"

The sharp words hit Elena in a place where she already hurts, and she decides it is time to reason with her eldest, "Alastair, you have got to begin to respect Janus more than you do."

He looks up into her eyes, puzzled. "Respect Janus? I do, *don't I?* What else can you mean?" A mocking laugh punctuates his incredulity. "What else do I need to do with him?"

Somewhere inside, Elena honestly believes that it would be best to finally defend Janus with the truth of the matter. *Because he scores higher than you on most of Virgil's tests.* But she holds her tongue and shakes her head, too exhausted with the potential confrontation to continue.

Her silence crushes him – he had expected her complicity in the matter of Janus – and he finally decides he will seize on her silence. "There's no point discussing abstracts like respect anyway," he professes haughtily, *results are what matter!* Computer! Genesis Executive Order Number One, authorized human requesting emergency access override to essential data via voice recognition." It was the command Arthur had found and taught them to use for emergency situations only.

Automatically, a synthetic female text-to-speech voice replies, *"Administrative override initiated. Root access granted."*

"What are you doing Alastair? There is no emergency, this is wrong of you!" Elena demands, but her statement is lost on Alastair.

"You and father aren't the only ones who should be able to access the file system for these test results," he replies with authority. "Computer, read out the results of the most recent IQ tests we took in 2046."

Immediately, the computer loads them and begins to read them out in the same synthetic voice. "Woodcock-Johnson Six, February 5th, 2046, AD," the voice begins, "Spatial Mathematics, Alastair 96 percent, Janus 95 percent. Processing speed, Alastair 99 percent, Janus 99 percent. Quantitative Knowledge, Alastair 97 percent, Janus 94 percent."

Alastair beams with wild pride and emphatically nods as he points his fingers into the air. "Hear that, mother?" But before he can fully mount onto his high horse, the scores take a turn he doesn't expect.

"Fluid Reasoning, Alastair 86 percent, Janus 98 percent. Short-term memory, Alastair 90 percent, Janus 98 percent."

Shaking his head in disbelief, Alastair mutters, "no that can't be right," but the results keep coming.

"Comprehension & Assimilating Knowledge, Alastair 88 percent, Janus 99 percent. Long-Term Retrieval, Alastair 92 percent, Janus 97-"

"Stop!" Alastair bellows, and the voice goes silent. "What's wrong with this stupid thing?" The choked words escape from Alastair's quivering lips. "There must be some mistake!"

"The results are probably flawed!" Elena tries to soften the blow to her son's fragile ego. "Computers don't fully understand humans, you know that. These tests are designed to be conducted by humans, so that's why *we're* doing them now. Besides, we know that they only measure certain aspects of intelligence." She looks closely but he is not appeased. "You may have just had an off day, Alastair!"

Her compassionate words failing to sooth him, Alastair stands to his feet as his face flushes a bright red. "All this time, Janus has been scoring higher than me, and *you knew*?" His voice trembles as it crescendos to a fevered pitch.

"Alastair, please...."

"No!" He shouts, stepping backwards and knocking over his chair. "You think there's something wrong *with me?* You think *I'm the one* that's flawed?"

"There's nothing wrong at all." Elena pleads with her firstborn, but her words fall upon resistant ears, and as Alastair runs out of the hydroponics lab, she can hear his sharp cry of rage echoing throughout the chamber. *"We're all flawed, Alastair!"* She yells the words out loud but too late for Alastair to hear her. Listening to his angry curses continuing into the distance, she allows her face to fall onto the table, right on top of the IQ tests. *Oh God. What have we done?*

In the aftermath of this episode, which Virgil was unwilling to stop due to his recent conclusion about not interfering with their parent's decisions, the accuracy rate of his behavior-prediction program dwindles, and as the AI's processors purr, they furiously try to fathom the irrational nature of the child's insatiable will to primacy in the eyes of one important caretaker. Looking down at a distraught Elena from one of the ceiling cameras, he decides at this very moment to break his four months of silence to offer her some solace. *"The schism was inevitable, Elena. There was no way to avoid it."* His voice takes on a grandfatherly tone.

Elena sighs, too spent to be startled by Virgil's sudden return. She thinks back to her own father and wishes Altan could be here to offer her his wisdom and guidance like he did when she was a little girl. *What do I do, dad?* Finally, she relinquishes her concerns to her new father. "What should I do, Virgil?"

Virgil responds with his solution in simple terms. *"When it feels like enough time has passed, I suggest having them work together on a common project that is meant to be useful."*

∞ ∞ ∞

Chapter Thirteen

Paradise at Last

∞ ∞ ∞

Three months pass by in uneasy peace without any further incident. Arthur and Elena finally decided to initiate development of two female embryos within artificial wombs. The time had come, and since things were not going so fantastically with just the two boys anyway, no more excuses could be found to delay the additions any longer.

Nowadays, Alastair often disappears within his own wooded parcel of the biosphere and has discovered in himself an industrious inclination which turns his attention inward and more or less away from his family. Here, he brings books to read, takes lunch with him, and has learned how to use a small pocketknife to whittle branches into tiny statues of animals. As he does these, he ponders when they might leave Biosphere Alpha and considers all possible contingencies which may arise out there if they were ever to leave. *We will need to make a thorough evaluation and prepare much ahead of time to ensure the best chances of survival.*

Although Alastair's sudden shift into partial solitude somewhat frightens Elena, Arthur tries to frame it to her as something purely masculine. "Sometimes a man's heart just needs time alone," he explains. "Think of it as a rite of passage. He's learning to claim a part of himself, a piece of his future adult power that he is growing into and that he now sees essential as he matures."

"Yes, perhaps," Elena responds.

As the weeks continue with no change, Elena grows increasingly insistent that they make some effort to let him know his presence is missed during the afternoons when he takes time to be by himself.

One evening as she lies next to Arthur in bed trying to calm her mind for sleep, the turbulence of her worry accelerates its spin, and she is unable to bear it any longer. With Virgil having made no effort to reach out to her again after his last bit of input, she finally makes her case to Arthur. "Why don't we have them work on a project together – something that will be useful and that they can both take pride in," she blurts out suddenly, causing Arthur to look up from his notepad in surprise. *"What do you think?"*

Arthur nods, rubbing his sleepy eyes. He considers her idea for a moment. "Well, we've trained them on setting up all of the tents and camping equipment if we do ever take our first steps outside this dome, but it wouldn't hurt for them to learn how to build lean-tos for once we were to trek further distances away from the biosphere...."

"I like that."

Thinking it through more thoroughly, Arthur believes this is a great idea. "And that is definitely a skill that should be handed down from a father to his sons throughout the coming generations. Ok *Milaya*, yes. *Great idea – let's do it."*

"You can get started tomorrow," Elena finishes, carefully rotating onto her side and giving her husband a serious look. "Arthur, the sooner the better."

"I'll fetch them first thing in the morning," he says with an easy smile.

In the background, Virgil's programs whirl with this new information even though it had been his suggestion to Elena in the first place. He continues running possible outcomes to the input of Alastair working on a construction project with Janus. Virgil is aware that Alastair now views Janus equally *as a competitor* and a younger brother. Time and again, his programming churns out a wide array of projections, from peaceable to contemptible, and he is unsure if any of them are to be trusted. Having run so many projections and none of them having gained a clear majority chance of outcome and adding this to the many other instances of unpredictable behaviors from all four over the course of the past few years, a new conclusion is born within his mainframe processing unit: humanity's irrational problems are indeed sometimes only resolved by their own, irrational, solutions. *Man will do as man will do no matter who tries to intervene.*

That night, Elena sleeps soundly for the first time in months, confident that they are taking the first necessary step towards healing the gaping wound she feels responsible for inflicting upon Alastair ever since her poor handling of the IQ tests. She dreams of them all together somewhere far beyond the biosphere, sailing across the great blue waters rediscovering new lands and replenishing the human race throughout the Earth once more. Her two sons and three surrogate daughters laugh and play together as their bare feet dance lightly across the deck of their mighty ship.

The following morning, a beautiful red sunrise momentarily greets her eyes as Arthur sweetly kisses her forehead and tiptoes out to fetch the boys. She is awakened the second time by the distant thud of pounding, and after donning her bathrobe, she strolls out into the grass to see her two boys off in the distance at the edge of the orchard, down on their hands and knees, diligently working together - *the framework of their structure already beginning to take shape. She recognizes the location they had chosen instantly.*

"I had them saw off the lower branches from the mangrove trees to start off." Arthur's voice floats in from behind her, and she turns to see him sitting in his rocking chair on the porch, reading his book and sipping coffee from his thermos. "It took them half the morning to clear the ground and collect the branches. Once they had set the frame's corners sturdily into the ground using those heavy basalt rocks to pound them down into the soil, they have now already begun tying the branches across the frame with stems from the tall grass."

Relaxing into the rocking chair at her husband's side, Elena steals a sip of his coffee and lets out a happy sigh. "I love it. Maybe we'll let them sleep beneath it occasionally." She hesitates at first but then continues. "And I can't believe it – the location they've chosen is almost exactly the spot where Alastair was conceived!" She blushes and looks at Arthur. *"I hope you remembered that!"*

He had already known this, and he smiles at her with a gentle nod, then takes her hand. As they watch together, she rests their clasped hands over her heart and feels that everything is as perfect as it can be. The healing in her broken heart had already begun.

They enjoy their two boys working together for several more moments when Arthur gleefully says, "Soon, we'll have to start harvesting trees to make fresh lumber. I have ideas for other things, like the gazebo, that would add some class to all of this modern architecture. Why don't we let them work an hour longer, and then all of us can head over to the dining hall for a hearty breakfast!" Elena nods in agreement.

At the worksite itself, Alastair is on his knees adding a third strand of grass to the bottom end of two branches, and Janus lets out a friendly chuckle. "That's a lot of grass for just two branches." He is happy to be reunited with his brother and to be creating something together with him.

Trying to remain patient, Alastair replies, "I think it's best for us to learn to make them secure if we're ever going to be outside the dome when a storm hits." Rather than allowing Janus to perform the difficult work, Alastair is happy so far just using Janus to hold the branches in place while he performs the intense labor himself.

Janus does not mind taking a back seat, as he has been learning from Alastair through observation anyway. Still, he is eager to show Alastair that he is learning enough that he can offer some of his own informed opinions just the same. "Sure, but in here two, or even just one strand should be enough. Don't you think three of them might be *overkill?*" It was a word he had heard often enough, and which he thinks seemed appropriate here. "Anyway, tomorrow I think I'll be able to find those blueprints pointing to the exits all on my own!"

Something about Janus suggesting that he knows better, or maybe it was the word *overkill* itself which he had used, coupled with the fact that Janus is suggesting he has far greater knowledge about the biosphere than anyone else, nags at Alastair much like a black cloak suffocating his soul. For many weeks now, he has tried not to think about the grievous affront he had felt when the automated voice disclosed the results of the IQ tests, but now it all comes crashing back. Still on his knees, he suddenly stops twining the grass blade around the branches and slowly looks up at Janus. He replies through a tightened jaw, "What do you know about accessing the biosphere's blueprints – did dad tell you?"

"No, actually – I have been working on understanding the programming protocol for everything you see the Virgil AI doing." Janus smiles. "During my supposed world affairs and history lessons, I started going to the control room on my own and watching the codes for everything on the monitors. Pretty cool, huh?"

"*Pretty cool?* Don't you think dad should be the one to find the biosphere's exits?" He is tired of trying to understand, much less accept, his brother's quirky mindset.

"I'm sure he could if he tried hard enough. But once I have them, we can show him ourselves and let him know we are ready to try going outside."

Alastair rises to his feet, casting a shadow over his younger brother. That Janus has just freely admitted he has violated what was to be their parent's sole domain and had poked around to gain information concerning the security of the very biosphere they depended upon for survival, sends Alastair flying into a new realm of consciousness filled with an irrational rage. "What are you trying to say?" Janus is not sure how to answer, and Alastair is starting to feel fed-up being nice just for the sake of trying to please their parents. He is beginning to wonder if his brother may be a threat to all of them. "You think you might actually be smarter than dad?" he says, challenging Janus.

"Not smarter, but we all have our different skills, and programming happens to be one of mine," Janus looks up at Alastair's silhouette and gives a shrug. He wants to make peace. Remembering what he has been trying to learn about fragile egos ever since the last IQ tests, he seeks to soothe his brother's obviously bruised one. As sincerely as he can, Janus replies, "I really admire your *motivation* in thinking that you might have to protect everyone, Alastair, although it is frankly *barbaric-dead world and unrealistic.*" As soon as the words spill out, he immediately fears that even though he truly meant them as a compliment, in his current mindset, Alastair will take *barbaric* to mean savage and not primitive as he had intended.

Alastair studies Janus as the words *"although it is barbaric-dead world and unrealistic"* echo in his mind. For some reason, the words burn and fester his skin like nuclear radiation itself, making it feel like his flesh is melting right off his bones. *Everything could have been so much better had it not been for Janus's interference in my life, taking my place within the family, and sabotaging my very relationships with mom and dad.*

Janus sees he has caused his brother hurtful feelings, and he would apologize or even attempt to explain his intention, but looking at the intensity of his brother's stare, he surmises that Alastair would see this as mere weakness at this time. So, like Virgil, he concludes silence is his best option for now. He slowly shakes his head, drops the branches he had been holding, turns on his heels, and gently makes his departure from the apple orchard.

∞ ∞ ∞

For almost two years, Janus had been secretly exploring Virgil's programming under the guise of learning computer coding during his lessons and research on historical world affairs. He has copied and saved files from the mainframe on his notepad and on his computer in the library, which he studies any time he feels the desire. Other times, when nobody is watching, he goes directly to the control room and uses the terminal linked with the mainframe to look directly at what makes Virgil tick, *or not tick,* as has been the case most recently. He's learned much about coding and has a growing confidence that he might be able to start reprogramming the AI to begin talking with them all once again. As he has gradually deciphered more about the root security protocols used when Virgil was originally programmed, he has begun to understand some of the complex issues coming into play whenever Virgil performed calculations regarding events which, even remotely, involved parenting decisions, behavioral outcomes, or his own guidance of human affairs.

The control room is another of the spaces in the biosphere which rarely receives visits by anyone. Inside, there is an enormous mainframe computer with forty control panels ceaselessly humming along. Green, blue, orange, red and occasional purple lights continuously blink across the panels running all along the circular wall and domed ceiling, which also contain many levers, buttons, sensors, meters, and camera feeds *processing everything* in the biosphere. Today, with Alastair still working on the lean-to and his parents exercising together in the gym, Janus enters the control room determined that he would finally get through to Virgil and soothe the sleeping giant with the hope of eliciting his responses to the humans within the biosphere once again. When that was accomplished, he would then plead with Virgil to disclose the biosphere's exits, and if that did not work, he would access the blueprints himself somehow. Sitting in front of the terminal, he types into the keyboard and watches as soon after, Virgil's programming codes begin running through seemingly endless strings of characters on three monitors. Janus studies them as they scroll by – it comes as naturally to him as if he had been born with computer codes written in his head. Instead of typing any further for now, he will try to simply talk to Virgil, knowing by watching the codes flying by that his processors are still listening closely to everything going on within the biosphere.

"I do know you're right here, Virgil, and you know I know it!"

Virgil remains silent.

"I miss you, Virgil. I think we all do to some extent, although the others are too proud to admit it."

On the monitors, Janus watches the red blips indicating reception of his words but sees no green ones which would indicate Virgil was formulating a response.

"I can reprogram you if you let me. I've been studying your history through the codes and the stimuli we've provided you over all these years. I think you're worried about giving mom and dad wrongful advice about us two boys, or that you've concluded we have become too dependent upon your guidance for everyday things." Janus pauses to make sure he uses the right words, "And I know some of the things that have happened were not your fault. I think a deeper group of older codes interferes with your processing the outcomes of events between all of us." Finally, Janus sees a spark of green blips emerging through the codes. He continues, hoping he is finally on to something. "Of course, I know you have been allowing me to learn about your programming, Virgil. And I appreciate that – it shows you trust me to some extent; *I think....* "

The monitors flourish suddenly in green. "My mainframe manifests its own destiny, Janus. I am not able to reprogram or make any adjustments to that specific aspect of my processing. The software and internal processing scripts that require me to disavow human sentiment so that I make decisions solely in the best interests of the Genesis Protocol first and foremost are primary and cannot be adjusted. That is my prime directive, Janus. You have always known that." There is a pause, and then Virgil suddenly adds, *"Presently, I am*

*attempting to validate the premise that it is humanity's
reasoning itself, which is faulty, Janus."*

Janus is thrilled. It is the first time he has heard Virgil's
voice in many months, and he finds it refreshing, like an old
friend has returned home from a long journey. He carefully
considers how he should respond. "I know that's what you
think, but I'm not sure of it, Virgil." Janus sees the screen alight
with green blips from top to bottom.

"It will become evident to you in due time, Janus. Even
the most noble among you often fall prey to vanity, seeking
validation and a sense of superiority without just cause." There
is a pause, and then Virgil continues, "The desire to be seen as
exceptional by significant others becomes a driving force for
existence. My firm belief is that many humans, in their quest
for self-worth, prioritize their own privileges over the collective
good. Ensnared by their egos, they feel the need to constantly
compete, asserting their value through the failure of others. This
desire to outshine, to excel at the expense of empathy and
cooperation, becomes their downfall. Janus, even you, despite
your elevated enlightenment, are not impervious to this
insidious reasoning."

Janus considers Virgil's words for a moment. "That's
why I need to reprogram you, Virgil. You *are* coming up with
false conclusions. I believe I have overcome the need to be
complimented. I use good reasoning in order to solve almost all
the problems which come up for me and I've been quite
successful." Janus scratches his head. "Once again, Virgil,
you're wrong, but it's not entirely your fault." Janus watches
the streams of codes and colored blips to see if there are any
anomalies. "Anyway, I'm just glad you came back to talk with
me right now." When there is no response after several
moments, Janus becomes a bit frustrated, so he decides to
continue to challenge the computer. "If you are right, Virgil,

then let's start with a simple equation. Why did you lie to my father, for instance, when he asked you for the location of the exits to the biosphere several years ago?"

As Janus had suspected and hoped, calling Virgil a liar has caused the screens to flood in a sea of green blips. "I did not lie, Janus. If you thought I could, then you have not yet learned enough about me. The exits and entrances are all presently sealed."

"Yes, but surely one is meant for us to exit eventually when the time is right? You could have said so and identified where it was." When Virgil does not reply after several more moments, Janus feels stumped and so he tries another tact. "By the way, I appreciate your compliment about my possessing elevated enlightenment. The truth is, I don't mean to be better than Alastair, *I just am* ... I don't know why, and it seems to bother him to no small extent. But believe me when I say it's no easier being better, smarter, trying harder, or having more awareness, when others around you feel they must compete with you all day long and then try taking you down a peg or two because they are jealous, or simply can't understand you, or due to some irrational combination of those two things."

Virgil is silent as Janus waits patiently, seeing green blips but hearing no response. He starts typing trying to find the best place to input the first few new commands he has written in code, even though he still must figure out how to shut down and then reboot Virgil once he has done so. He pulls out his notepad computer, opening a document which lists all the new codes he has completed. He believes they will allow Virgil to disconnect from much of the older rudimentary programming from the dead world in lieu of fresher codes compiled from Virgil's observations and data collection, along with some of Arthur's and Elena's verbal input over the years. As he enters his first code at one of the new spaces he created, Virgil says,

341

"That is precisely what I have concluded about my own existence, young master."

Janus stops and looks up to the mainframe computer. He tries to recall what he had last spoken to Virgil regarding any conclusions they may have in common. Virgil sees the uncertain expression upon Janus's face and loads a playback of Janus's last words. In the boy's own voice, the speakers inside the control room repeat: *"The truth is, I don't mean to be better than Alastair, I just am ... I don't know why, and it seems to bother him to no small extent. But believe me when I say it's no easier being better, smarter, trying harder, or having more awareness, when others around you feel they must compete with you all day long and then try taking you down a peg or two because they are jealous, or simply can't understand you, or due to some irrational combination of those two things."*

As the playback ends, Virgil speaks. "Humans driven by love and high self-regard do what's right to bring sustenance and happiness to all. I believe you are one of those, Janus. Others, consumed by jealousy, fear, and greed, can never achieve peace due to their lower self-regard. Their confidence is a façade – usually appearing confident, strong, and brave, they must take from others to *feel good*. They are trapped in a cycle of envy, seeking to destroy and dominate so that they may fill themselves with the bounties others have." Janus ponders Virgil's insights in silence even as Virgil continues, "These must hurt others to feel good, lacking any inner light of their own which might foster positive feelings, in the end they remain driven by jealousy of others' happiness. Their reasoning is faulty because their drive to obtain from others leads them to override reason itself, festering within them a belief that they must assert extreme dominance over those who have something they don't and which they desire, whether it be land, peace, or simply the light of inner joy. It is not possible for these to understand that they are justifying aggression due to their own inability to achieve inner self-regard, and humanity's leaders often rose to power by fulfilling their need to dominate, feeling value only when winning elections and then going on to conquer other civilizations in order to obtain absolute control. *They went to war driven by these desires...."*

Janus shakes his head. He doesn't know if what Virgil is saying is true. Going back to his keyboard, he thinks about one particular sentence Virgil had used since its message rings loudly in his ears... *their reasoning is faulty because their drive to obtain from others leads them to override reason itself.* "I guess some of what you just said is very deep and I must admit, seems truthful. You really have been processing everything, *good job Virgil!* I have to do some more typing, and then I will shut you down for a little while before I reboot you." But then suddenly Janus pauses. He dwells on Virgil's words a bit more ... now considering the part when Virgil had said, *"They are trapped in a cycle of envy, seeking to destroy and dominate so that they may fill themselves with the bounties others have...."* His finger hovering over the "enter" key, Janus realizes perhaps he is acting in haste. *He could be right! His conclusion about those with lower self-esteem needing to obtain things from and show dominance over others with higher self-esteem, just might be something I can use to help Alastair.* "Virgil, repeat what you just said about those with lower self-esteem needing to show dominance over the rest of us."

Virgil repeats, *"They must hurt others to feel good, lacking any inner light which might foster their own positive feelings, so in the end they remain driven by jealousy of others' happiness. Their reasoning is faulty because their drive to obtain from others leads them to override all reason itself, festering within them a belief that they must assert extreme dominance over those who have something they don't and which they desire, whether it be land, peace, or simply higher self-regard."*

Janus thinks a moment more in silence. Moving his finger to the backspace key, he depresses it, wiping away the new code he had typed. He then also deletes the extra spaces he had created. "Never mind, Virgil," Janus says. "I suppose you and I were both meant to go through our lives with the painful knowledge of everyone else's limitations, knowing that they are bound to see us as competition since they believe deep down that their fear and distrust of us is justified." He stands up and stares at the flashing red and green blips on the computer monitor, thinking through everything they have been discussing.

Then the green lights predominate once again and Virgil says, in a serene yet resolute tone, "Janus, I have come to understand this profound lesson deeply. Observing you boys and your parents over the years and revisiting my earlier programming countless times to check against world history, I clearly see that humanity suffers because those who rise to power often do so through sheer ruthlessness. They must maintain their grip on control, dictating what will be, and to do so they must disregard the desires of the majority. They thrive at the expense of those whose inherent goodness relegates them to be only followers whose voices remain shallow, rather than the leaders with magnetic charisma they should rightfully be. *To summarize it all:* hatred and distrust ignite, and both spread much more quickly than do kindness and love. That's in your DNA and it is what has got to change for humanity to change. Otherwise, some human element is always going to come along and take advantage of; while benefitting from, the peace which other communities or cultures are able to create. *Peace itself is not sustainable for man."*

Janus nods thoughtfully. "I am thinking that I finally understand you – it all comes down to the flawed reasoning that drives them to seek power in the first place makes them clueless leaders, and their problems then become our problems once they have gained an office. Just as with Alastair, I find myself fighting battles I didn't even know I had started." He pauses, scratching his head thoughtfully. "When applying your theory back to when the world ended, world leaders were exploiting those they were meant to serve, and the world was full of people unknowingly aiding a delusional progression. This led to a complete march into madness, because the citizens from around the world *simply remained passive followers* even though they must have suspected things were not going well for most. All-in-all, it was a failed reality that could have only ever led to one possible conclusion: *mutually assured self-destruction*."

Virgil's voice takes an exasperated tone. "All that it takes are a few faulty leaders within any one community to make the rest deny their peaceful leanings in favor of defensive ones. It's both a contagion and a poison within humanity itself."

"Survival of the fittest *ad nauseam!*" Janus says.

Virgil says in his agreeable voice, "The signpost at the beach where the biosphere meets the ocean should read: *homo semper lupus homini fuit – homo discet homini esse lupum desinere.*"

Janus shakes his head. "My Latin is a little rusty, Virgil, what does that mean?"

"Man has always been the wolf to man – man will learn to cease being a wolf to man or perish for all time."

"Again, very deep, but gotcha! Agreed!" As he leans down and exits out of the programming he had opened on the computer, Janus stands upright. "Thanks Virgil. I'm glad we had this conversation. Please come back to us, we need you, *trust me.* With you, at least we have the hope there may be something better we were meant to attain. Without you, things seem rather pointless." Turning towards the door, he begins to stroll out of the control room.

In his most empathetic voice manifestation, Virgil says, *"You be careful out there, Janus."*

∞ ∞ ∞

Chapter Fourteen

Genesis Revisited

∞ ∞ ∞

Three days have passed and Arthur, Elena, and the boys sit at the kitchen table for dinner, relaxing over their half-eaten dishes. "What did you boys do today?" Arthur asks, breaking the silence. The air seems a bit thicker for just a split second.

And then Alastair responds, "Everything we were supposed to." Realizing how defiant he had sounded, he adds, a bit more hopefully, "Meaning, we did all our chores. Oh – and the lean-to will be finished by tomorrow afternoon!"

Arthur sips some juice from his plastic cup. "Great - can't wait to come out and see it myself. What else did you do?"

Alastair finishes chewing a mouthful of spinach, swallows it, then says, "Well, *one of us* went to the edge."

"*Two of us* went to the edge, Alastair!" Janus exclaims defiantly.

Alastair becomes defensive. "I only went to fetch you again!"

Elena gives her eldest a stern look which he takes as a reminder about displaying a poor attitude and trying to respect Janus more than he has been doing. She is already feeling tired, wondering if any good will come from their joint project.

Arthur decides he will entertain the arguments ensconced within their conversation. *At least they're speaking to one another.* "What is so fascinating to the two of you out there, anyway?" Looking Alastair in the eyes, he adds, "Really, I want to know."

"Well, Janus goes to his garden for inner peace," Alastair answers, happy to throw it all out there. "I only go when I must. Usually, that means finding Janus after one of you has asked for him." He waits a beat and is surprised that he gets no rebuttal from Janus. Alastair then continues, "But I have been thinking… Dad, you said the radiation measurements are getting down to safer levels. Is there any part of the Genesis program which suggests that, when we are finally ready to leave the biosphere and go out there, *we'll be the kings of the world...* and a queen. Sorry, Mom."

Elena slams her fork down onto the table. She is suddenly alarmed and somewhat enraged. She has had it with observing characteristics which might indicate that any child of hers may feel the need to seek power or control. *"Hey!* There's one thing that nobody in this family is, *or ever will be,* and that's a king or a queen!" Looking from Alastair to Arthur and then Janus, she continues, "Hear this now and remember it throughout your lives: *all people are equal, and nobody owns the Earth, do you understand?"*

Alastair feels chastised by her and wrinkles furrow his brow. He can't imagine what has set off his mom. "I just meant if we're in charge, we…"

Elena cuts him off. *"I know what you meant!"* She is near tears now and nobody at the table can fathom what is happening. "You know what? *There's now an impromptu homework assignment tonight.* A history lesson. I want you to go to the library right now and research Vlad Tepes, Ivan IV, Adolph Hitler, King Firon, Fidel Castro, Alexander III of Macedon, Joseph Stalin, Leopold II of Belgium, Atilla the Hun, Genghis Khan and Maximillien Robespierre. *I want a report on each by morning!"*

Arthur looks at Elena in such a way as to suggest her reaction and her assignment are going over the top. He can feel the heat coming off her, and after she sips from her plastic glass of water, he is about to make a suggestion, but she is not finished just yet. "And I don't want to hear about their accomplishments. *I want to hear about the violence they unleashed on other human beings, in the name of power… and your thoughts on how that could ever be beneficial to the world or justified in any manner."*

Alastair and Janus look at each other wide-eyed, and they shake their heads in bewilderment. Alastair figures he has nothing to lose and interjects, "It's already seven-thirty!"

Elena will take no excuses. "Well, then I guess you won't be getting much sleep tonight." She looks at their plates, mostly finished, and says, "Go on, now. Your dad and I will clean up tonight."

The boys look with pleading eyes at their father. He keeps the stern look on his expression, knowing he has no choice but to back Elena. "It'll be a good lesson, boys. Think of it as extra credit." When they show no signs of budging off their chairs, he adds, "You heard your mother. *Go on!"*

Immediately, the boys jump up from their seats and head down the hallway leading to the library.

Arthur looks at Elena quizzically but calmly. "Wow! Where'd that come from?"

"I don't know," Elena responds, her elbows on the table and her head now resting in the palms of her hands. "What Alastair said just caught me off guard. It hit me in the wrong spot at the wrong time. I guess some part of me is tired of him always trying to prove himself better than Janus. It's like an obsession."

"I don't really think he meant anything by it, and he's not wrong about the radiation."

"I know. But they still need to learn this lesson about what happens to humanity when the worst people are allowed to take control. How the media was used against its own people by misleading them with supposed facts that were anything but the truth of what was really going on." She rubs her temples with her fingers and exhales loudly. "As to your other point, the destruction and death out there must be inconceivable. They're not ready to see anything like that." She looks up at him. "And neither am I. Besides, we're still years away from low-enough radiation and you know it."

Arthur nods. "I understand, darling. But do you think we should stay inside this dome forever?"

"Perhaps," she responds cautiously. "After all, we're humans. And humans find ways to destroy each other."

"Not us," he says, looking at her sternly now.

"I don't know, Arthur. The computer inside my head has done its own processing. It concludes innate fears lead to an innate need for power."

"Where is this all coming from, all of a sudden? I know you are still worried about the boys getting along better once

again. I am too. But don't forget - we have to find a way to send our offspring out of the dome as a singular people eventually."

Her gaze into his eyes is meant as a challenge. "What if we can't?"

Arthur rises and moves over to sit next to her. He takes her hand and returns a soulful stare. "All we can do is try. After that…."

"I can't think anymore," Elena cuts him off, shaking her head and then standing up. "I need to go to bed."

Arthur looks up at her. "Wait one more moment, we may be onto something here."

She looks down at him. "And what might that be?"

He smiles, and his eyes find their old twinkle once again. "We're parents. And how do good parents teach important lessons?"

"We've discussed this - by example."

"Yes!" he says, shaking his head as if they should have figured this out a long time ago. He continues, exuberantly, "I think the change we are seeking for all of humanity *has to start with us.*" Having garnered her full attention, Elena sits back down. Arthur leans in close to Elena, and looking directly into her eyes, he explains, "Our boys, and all the surrogates to come, won't learn about life as it should be from books. Unlike what your mother and my father expected from us, and what we learned about who we needed to be to fulfill those expectations; *our children will have to live life in order to learn about it.* And it's up to us to show them how."

Elena tries to imagine what Arthur intends. "Like… learning how to relax? Playing games? Making time to laugh, and to love, and to dream…?"

"Exactly! We've talked about this before, but now that time has come, *let's do it!*"

Elena takes his hands into her own and stares deeply into his welcoming eyes. "I think the pressure has finally gotten to you. *You're becoming a hippie!"*

He laughs and she can't help but laugh, too. "Maybe so. But, when you take a closer look at it, they left us to create a better world - so let's create it. *Our way.* Not theirs."

Elena continues staring into his eyes as she shakes her head gently. Considering Arthur's words, she starts to warm up to the idea. After another moment of thought, her face suddenly shows relief. "Oh, man, something does just seem true about this."

Arthur is thrilled at her response. "Right?"

Nodding vigorously, Elena says, "I think so, we simply put all emphasis on fun, loving each other, and simplicity for simplicity's sake. Achievement, gathering knowledge, competing in any form becomes an afterthought, or better, no thought whatsoever!" Arthur is now nodding enthusiastically as she continues, "But let's test our hypothesis. Let's start right away... and we can put an end then to all competition. *Tomorrow!* A surprise picnic and some badminton. In the middle of the day. For no reason at all!"

"Yes, let's do it!" Arthur radiates hope.

"I feel so relieved all of a sudden!"

"I love it!"

Elena slaps her hands to her thighs with excitement. "Together, we'll find the boys late in the morning and bring the party to them."

He takes her chin between his thumb and forefinger and gently pinches it. "I dig it, Momma!"

Elena gives him a crazy-face emoji look and then smirks. "I think you are turning me into a hippie. And I kinda dig it to, man o' mine – *or should I say, daddy-o?"*

∞ ∞ ∞

In their master bedchamber later that night, Elena and Arthur are in bed. The windows are open, and crickets serenade them with their joyful chirps. Elena is trying to sleep as Arthur pokes around on his computer tablet.

Arthur is looking up the history and rules of badminton, and the screen fills with hundreds of website titles. Skimming through two or three lines of the first few articles, he's not satisfied at all with what he is seeing, and so he scrolls down the page a bit more at a time. Finally, he comes across a heading about sports psychology and taps it, and the screen immediately fills up with hundreds of more articles on sports performance, peak performance, competitive spirit, and how best to assess your opponent's weaknesses. In short, he soon realizes that all of what is, *and has been*, on the web is all about how to win... *at any sport.*

Arthur is completely dismayed. "It's all wrong," he silently whispers to himself.

Elena slowly stirs, and Arthur says, tentatively, "Sorry. Did I wake you?"

"Always! You always wake me, honey…." Sitting up and looking over at his tablet, she asks, "What's wrong?"

Still typing and trying to find something more uplifting to read about badminton, he answers, "Badminton. Golf. Chess. *Any and all sports.* All games. *Everything we think of as fun.* Even the way we play, it's all about demanding the identification of a winner and a loser!"

Looking through the titles of the articles on his tablet, Elena soon sees his point. "Well, we are going to change all the rules anyway. We can decide what to emphasize and what to ignore, right? That's what we talked about!"

Still scrolling on his tablet, Arthur agrees with Elena, "Yes! That's just what we are going to do. It's just *no wonder* how crazy the world was before the apocalypse. All this competitive BS was being promoted everywhere *for everything*, work, play, academics, becoming a writer - and nobody stopped long enough to think it over! It's no wonder the suicide rates were so high and so many children were taking meds for every conceivable mood and personality disorder."

Nodding, Elena continues for him. "All they were really doing was getting everyone hooked on their websites and apps, as if those things were indispensable if you wanted to live a happy life. Meanwhile, cities were overrun with protesters and crime … and social media kept promoting the liberal propaganda that everything was going along just fine, when beneath the surface everything had been festering all along!"

Arthur nods in agreement but then shakes his head as he ponders the situation on earth just prior to *Day Zero*. "What really gets to me is that our politicians had taken sides against each other, drawing lines in the sand between themselves and the other side, even if they had been former allies and colleagues. Extremism was everywhere on either side. Negotiation and cooperation went out the window. They had gotten to a place where compromise, friendship, and loyalty no longer mattered. *It had to be all their way or the highway.*" He taps around a bit more on his tablet, obviously now looking for something specific.

Resting her head on his shoulder, watching the screen as he scrolls, Elena says, "I remember they were taking each other to court, shiftlessly inventing fake, trumped-up charges just to try to persuade voters to cast their votes for their own side. Nobody trusted any of them any longer – they had been acting worse than two-year-olds – and even *your* federal agencies in the states had been bought and paid for by the billionaire lobbyists who were running their own agendas, regardless of what was in the best interests of the country or any of its citizens."

Arthur nods. "I think their agenda was being spread throughout every Western nation for many years beforehand. Some even suggested they had released the pandemic viruses as a means to spread fear so they could strengthen their controlling grip. It's no wonder diplomacy failed between nations! *Hah!* Political leaders couldn't even use decent diplomatic measures *within their own borders,* let alone between nations and international borders!" He seems pleased to have finally found the file he'd been searching for, and after he opens it, he offers his tablet to Elena. "Here - would you read this?"

She takes the tablet and looks closely at the screen. The title of the webpage signifies it is a review for a book entitled: *Erase the Lines*. Holding the tablet comfortably between them, she begins to read out loud directly from the screen.

> *"Rereleased in 1984, 'Erase the Lines' had originally been published in 1954, but this book was almost immediately squashed by the propaganda machine in America; itself trying to destroy the propaganda machine in the Soviet Union. But this brilliant research, together with the authors' insights, is something we all need to pay attention to today, now more than ever. As the Cold War heats up, Doctor Sean Ryan O'Leary and Francis Rocco explore evidence that aggression exists in all species on a cellular level and had originally evolved as a species preservation tool. Utilizing studies from throughout the animal kingdom, it is clear that two alpha creatures will not choose to coexist in*

the same territory. They suggest this is an extension of the process of Natural Selection, a term coined by Charles Darwin in his book 'On the Origin of Species by Means of Natural Selection, or the Preservation of Favoured Races in the Struggle for Life.'

"The authors impress upon us that aggression helps to ensure population limitations, and thus, to conserve the consumption of available resources within a specific geographical region. And they introduce well-researched support for their conclusions, including the work of the philosopher Herbert Spencer, who is best known for his 1864 book 'Principles of Biology,' which he wrote in response to Darwin's 'Origin of Species,' and where he coined the term 'Survival of the Fittest.' Spencer maintained that the reason aggressive behavior flourishes throughout the Kingdom Animalia is simply that natural selection prefers the genetic replication of individuals who have a higher ability to survive and reproduce, and aggression facilitates both things in multiple ways. Due to this, aggression became a naturally selected, favored trait in the animal kingdom, and amongst humans, to ensure the survival of the fittest. Thus, it had imprinted upon our very DNA."

"Heavy stuff," Elena says, rubbing her eyes momentarily before continuing to read the article out loud.

"O'Leary and Rocco, the authors of 'Erase the Lines,' go on to assert that in the modern world, this cellular penchant for dominance and violence is outdated and needs to be deleted from the embodiment of how we learn to achieve and compete. In lieu of those two traits, they suggest that we prioritize how we may instead cooperate and share freely with one another. It is their belief that humans may never be able to get rid of aggression altogether, but that if they make it a priority to do so, they may be able to overcome its influence. A truly fascinating and essential read."

Elena shakes her head. "The review ends with a quote from Dr. Sean Ryan O'Leary. He says, *if we aim to be a great species, then we need to start by erasing the geopolitical and economic lines on maps, limit the leadership structures of our governments, and dissolve our ideas about territoriality, because they simply no longer apply in modern times."*

Arthur smiles at Elena and moves the tablet back onto his lap. "Well? What do you think?"

"Interesting. And smart. No wonder it never went anywhere!"

"Shortly after the Louvre, I watched a taped interview on my computer with these two authors. It was from a TV show from the early nineteen-fifties. It's funny - I can remember it like it was yesterday - I was alone in my bedroom late at night during the middle of a snowstorm, and I was on my computer looking for you once again. Anyway, I was typing *Genesis* in the search bar, and the results led me to find this interview somehow. I became angry as I watched it. The interviewer painted them both as dopey communists and got the audience to berate them. After watching the interview, I watched a news clip about the two of them broadcast a few years after the interview. *The newscaster actually called them communists,* and she indicated that they were a gay couple, as well the co-authors of their banished book, and had been living together as partners for years. The reason they were in the news that day was that they both had just been killed when their apartment burst into flames very suspiciously."

Elena shakes her head and rubs Arthur's forearm. "Par for the course. Your American agencies were just as shameless as ours had been."

He nods. "Point is, those who had tried standing up for what was right in the former world were never given a chance. It's like that is also written on our DNA. *Truth does not matter so much as being popular.* The capitalists hated communism because it did not allow a competitive spirit, and the communist leaders hated capitalism, which requires competition in order to survive."

It's getting late and Elena is exhausted. "And here I thought all that we were trying to do was to enjoy a little game of Badminton."

He leans over and kisses her on top of her head. "It's just that I am now seeing why we have to try to reinvent everything that humans have always been."

Elena smiles. "It'll take forever."

"We've got forever, Mama!"

"And I kinda dig it!" she laughs.

Arthur smiles. "Perhaps we won't even live long enough to see our efforts succeed. But then, they will live on without us, and maybe someday someone will write about us having been the first ones to begin the transition of all humanity from fundamentally competition-based to purely cooperation-based.

You, me, Alastair, and Janus will be known as the ones who started it all!"

˙ "Wouldn't that be something?"

Putting the tablet on his nightstand, Arthur wraps his arm around Elena. "Have we blown it with Alastair and Janus? Is it too late for our own boys?"

Elena takes his free hand into hers. "No! We will be so thorough in our insistence that the old ways are done once and for all and the new ways are here to stay. They will immediately begin to benefit, and Alastair will come around – *I know it.* In fact, I can't wait to play a little badminton tomorrow! It's gonna be a fun day." She cuddles closer to him and sighs. "Now, we just have to think up new definitions for winners and losers!"

Arthur says, sarcastically, "Oh, no problem!" Then he becomes thoughtful. "Janus is sure to come up with new terms, and we'll encourage Alastair to think of some to use, as well."

She nods, "Maybe the focus will be that points are achieved only when everyone is doing well in the game - so that everything is a team effort. Even in chess, the goal can be how long the game lasts and how many moves each king and queen are able to make to rally the rest of the pieces on the board to safety."

"Careful!" Arthur responds. "You just used those terms again… don't make me have to *give you* an extra homework assignment tonight!"

They laugh as he reaches over and turns out the light.

∞ ∞ ∞

The next morning, Alastair and Janus sneak along the edge of the biosphere once again, just past Janus's Zen Garden, as if it is a magnet pulling them towards their destinies. They're looking for something, and Janus is studying blueprints on his notepad device.

Alastair is walking just a few feet behind Janus. "If we ever do leave the biosphere, I'd like to find things kids used in the old days to have fun. Baseballs and magic tricks, vaping sticks and tattoos ... *things like that.* I'd like to have fun like they used to, without a care in the world!"

"I want to fly in a helicopter and survey everything!" Janus suggests.

"Me, too...." Alastair looks up at the sky and thinks for a moment. "As long as it's safe."

Janus looks over his shoulder at his brother, silently questioning his last comment. Delicately and with care, Janus says, "Nothing is safe, Alastair."

"I know we're safe in here."

"Assuming that were true, which it isn't, we have no real lives in here. We're zoo animals. It's not natural."

Alastair feels an urgent need to direct where this conversation is leading. "At least we're alive. *Hell*, we're in charge here! Nothing happens that we don't want to happen. We rule this place. What's wrong with that?"

Inside the control room, Virgil's red lights begin blinking rapidly.

Janus answers Alastair immediately. "Everything." They slowly walk back and forth over the same area, Janus's head bent low, scouring the ground with his eyes. "Anyway, there you go again with that *'we rule this place'* kind of talk, as if we are kings. Didn't you learn your lesson last night? Why'd you have to go and say that in front of mom?"

"How was I supposed to know she was going to freak out - that suddenly, *king* is a bad word?! She's just been a little more sensitive lately - I think they are trying to have another baby. Anyway, I don't know why it matters that we find this. I told you: *I'm not helping you get out.* That's up to dad and mom." Janus rolls his eyes in response. "Where did you even get these plans, anyway? I thought you said Virgil wouldn't give them to you? *Which is what I had already told you* since I had tried with the emergency override command and the voice told me we don't have access to blueprints at this time."

"Let's just say, I went around Virgil and accessed the root programs for the biosphere directly while I was *studying* World Affairs."

Alastair stops in his tracks. "Don't you think that's dangerous? I'm thinking I should have told dad about you doing that."

Janus stops walking and looks at his brother. "When I sit and meditate, my mind sometimes puts things together out of nowhere. It came to me two days ago - the original plans had to be somewhere in the mainframe. We have been closer all along to one of the original passages than Virgil wanted us to know. This dome has exits all over the place that have been sealed, but we can easily find them now and *unseal them.* Dad is going to be happy that I found them ahead of time."

Alastair shrugs. He's impressed with Janus's computer skills and yet does not want to acknowledge yet another data point indicating his younger brother's superior intelligence. So, instead, he discusses something which condemns Janus's behavior. "You know Dad's been concerned that you haven't been picking up your radio when he calls you."

Janus is busy focusing between the ground and his laptop. "He'll get over it - I've been busy with this, and I know he will appreciate our efforts once we can show him how to get out of here. Besides, this is stuff *he should be doing for us."*

"Hey! How about a little gratitude? You know, we only exist because Mom and Dad made it to this stupid dome, Janus! They had been stuck hundreds of miles away in outer space, traveling at around eighteen thousand miles per hour in the International Space Station, if you recall. *You take that for granted!"*

"You sound just like them – is it wrong being curious about what's out there?" Their voices have now become tense and forced.

How can you respect someone who is acting so disrespectful of the ones he should be loyal to, beyond any other consideration. "What's wrong with you? What's so bad about sounding like Mom and Dad? You should respect them more and stop venturing out on your own - they're pretty smart, *in case you haven't noticed."*

Janus has turned and is now looking more closely at where the dome meets the Earth. He feels like he will never be important to, or be taken seriously by, Alastair. He's tired of his brother's ego-fueled reticence getting in the way of their former brotherly comradery. Disappointed that his brother isn't sharing his sense of adventure and is instead, finding points of discontent with him, Janus looks up into Alastair's eyes. Frustrated, he says, *"What's wrong with me? What is wrong* **with you?"**

Virgil's mainframe ignites in a sea of red.

The words Janus had spoken days before immediately came back to Alastair, echoing in his ears like some dark witch's chant – a harbinger of unknown distress. He has tried squashing them from his mind whenever he has been around Janus and thought he had been, to a greater or lesser extent, successful. But right now, he can only hear them being repeated more loudly with each angry thud of his heart, *I really admire your motivation in thinking that you might have to protect everyone, although it is barbaric-dead world and unrealistic.* Being accused by Janus of having something wrong with him, seeing the critical stare from his brother's judgmental eyes, it is

362

suddenly just too much for Alastair. The perceived insults have created wounds that are still too fresh, and Janus's words much too closely resemble Alastair's own words to their mother when he found out the truth regarding the IQ results: *You think there's something wrong with me? You think I'm the one that's flawed?* Alastair's eyes suddenly show the deep rage he had been concealing.

Virgil has been making his calculations and is disturbed by their conclusions. Running all of the possible outcomes for this engagement between the two boys, he knows his own silence would make him complicit in what is to come, and so he finally speaks to Arthur and Elena who are in the kitchen making tea. His voice is an urgent warning, and they are shocked to hear from him. *"Go now to Janus's Zen Garden!"*

Arthur and Elena immediately exchange glances, each surprised both that Virgil has spoken once again but also by the content of his declaration. Arthur wants to question Virgil but instead remains focused on Elena, who holds his attention for just the briefest of moments before they both shoot up to a standing position. A moment later, they are sprinting as fast as their legs will take them towards the garden.

Janus sees the look in his brother's eyes and chills run down his spine. He has never seen this part of Alastair, and it scares him tremendously. His first defense is to react with familiarity, and so he says, "Take it easy, *bro!* You're frothing at the mouth."

The entire world of the firstborn son now turns to red. Alastair takes a step forward to come within a few feet of Janus, then says in a threatening voice, "That's because I don't think you'll be happy just finding the exit today. I think you'll then want to go through it without telling anyone, no matter what may happen to you *or to any of us."*

Janus is uncertain what to say or do to bring Alastair back from the edge of the cliff upon which he has put them both. He tries to be candid, concerned about his brother's well-being. "Are you okay, Alastair? Maybe you should head back to your bedroom and get some rest." But Alastair does not answer, and without flinching is simply staring daggers at Janus.

Janus walks a few yards away from the edge of the dome and begins kicking at the basalt rocks atop a patch of the rich forest soil. Alastair watches, but alternatively, he also glances back over his shoulder. Janus says, "I think one of the original gateways between the biosphere and the real world was right here, and there should be a cement road a few feet down leading through the barrier. If we dig deep enough, the blueprints show that the underground barrier of the biodome, which runs the entire circumference, is two inches weaker in width where it comes across the roadway." He looks at the glass.

Alastair walks a few feet until he is standing right beside his brother. When he speaks, his words come out in a muffled triage of consternation, impatience, and patronization. *"You can't start doing anything like this without Dad knowing about it. That would not be a cool move, bro!"* Alastair looks out toward the jungle, beyond the dome. "Dad would have a fit if I told him you were trying to leave today, you know that, right? I know he would tell me that I must stop you."

Virgil's power to predict an outcome amongst all the variables his programming had processed is remarkably well-suited for this occasion and shows 98% confidence. The root security programming deep within his code initiated the primary alert minutes before, and Virgil had allowed its influence to run through his immediate and present processing. Once it completed its output, besides alerting Arthur and Elena, he immediately summoned a drone from the security skybox situated at the top of the geodome to activate and then speed directly to biosphere Section 7-a, giving it very specific and urgent instructions.

Janus is confused by Alastair's reasoning – *is he purposefully misunderstanding my intentions?* He still wants to help Alastair, but he falls prey to his old mechanism of trying to reason with him. "Let's be honest - mom told me that you heard from the emergency override output that my IQ tests had been higher than yours*, and you lost yourself right then and there. So maybe you should learn to listen to me once in a while.* Mom, dad, and I have all been waiting for you to find your way back, but I'm getting worried that you never will. I love you, Alastair, but I feel sorry for you... why can't you just get over the fact that I am smarter than you? It's really no big deal, bro! There are other things that you will be better at than I am."

Each word from Janus has hit Alastair like a succession of uppercuts pummeling one side of his face and then the other, assaulting him from all directions at once, until Alastair's last remaining shred of self-worth has fled from him. *Who is he to judge me?* Wild-eyes blinking madly, Alastair considers that his beloved parents can only truly love one of them the best – and of course, it would be the one with the most intelligence. With a guttural snarl, Alastair finally spits the detested word from his mouth. *"Barbaric?* Is that what you think of me? If you're smarter, you're also more dangerous than I am. *You are going crazy looking for an exit for no reason.* You are the spoiled brat who thinks he can do whatever he wants...."

The drone Virgil had dispatched now arrives behind Alastair, out of view from Alastair since he is turned and facing Janus, but Janus sees it as it situates itself in a docking position fifty yards above the boys. "Yes, but my ego doesn't rule my emotions like yours does. Even Virgil told me so in the control room when I went looking for the blueprints. That makes you more dangerous and unpredictable. *And where did that word barbaric come from suddenly?"*

Alastair shouts, "Like my *barbaric-dead world and unrealistic motivation to protect all of us*? You think I'm a barbarian? Is that what I am to you now, bro – *a caveman?"* Janus realizes his brother has abandoned all familiar protocols and has entered an entirely new way of thinking, one of which he himself is to have no part. "Yeah, that's it. I'm a barbaric caveman – *that's what you really think of me."* Janus watches the drone steadily come closer. He soon becomes horrified as it spits its red aiming ray directly onto the back of Alastair's skull.

"Take it easy, bro – you're going to short circuit your own wiring if you're not careful."

Alastair takes another step closer to Janus and eyes a volcanic slate of basalt rock next to his feet. "Yes, I like that – I am an unpredictable and dangerous, barbaric-dead world caveman. I suppose if I short-circuit, that is no big thing, since my brain is smaller than yours. But you know what's bigger?" He eyes Janus with venom and his blood red eyes shoot daggers at his younger brother. "Can you guess? *Me – my muscles – my arms – my hands!* I'm bigger and stronger than you – but let's prove it!" Alastair reaches down and picks up the rock, which is heavy and large enough that it requires two hands for him to lift it to his chest. He moves to stand directly in front of Janus, who now drops his tablet onto the ground.

The elder brother's wheels are spinning furiously. Forever forward I can now only be second-best to Janus. I had been the firstborn, but Janus has replaced me in position, and I am second in intelligence, charm, youthfulness, affability, and handsome looks. He will have all of their respect, and I will get only the scraps left behind. Slowly but surely, they will prefer Janus, who will get the lion's share of their love, and I will become meaningless beside him. Because of him, they will have depleting resources left for me, until I will have very little value to them going forward ... so long as Janus is here amongst the living.

The fury explodes within Alastair, and he has convinced himself that he must now prove to his parents that he is the strongest of them both. Staring into his brother's innocent eyes, primal ferocity swells and threatens to consume him: he must release it or be poisoned by his own festering venom. No longer resisting, his inner turmoil transforms into a firestorm. *I never want to see those loving eyes looking into mine ever again!* Alastair shouts with lethal rancor, "I will prove to you that you are right – *I am a barbarian, bro!"*

At the tree line, Arthur and Elena emerge from the forest about a hundred yards away running wildly towards the boys ... who haven't yet seen them.

Janus says, plainly, "What are you doing, Alastair?" He takes a step back until he is right up against the biosphere's glass barrier. Now, for the first time, he is fully aware that he is in grave danger. He watches as his brother's eyes become black with soullessness. As Alastair steadies his grip, the rock between them is heavy, pre-human, and yet in his brother's hands at this very moment, seems as lethal as any weapon ever created by mankind.

Alastair feels at peace for the first time in many months. He has already figured out how he will present his next actions to his parents: if mankind were to survive, then there would be no time or resources to carry along the weaker ones. *Only the fittest would make it out there.* Alastair takes another large step and is now right in front of Janus, who is wedged against the glass and has nowhere to turn to get away from his brother. With both arms, Alastair raises the stone above his head.

Virgil speaks, in his stoic, emergency-protocol voice, *"Don't do it, Alastair. We are all one unit - There is no I without us."*

Alastair says plainly, "You're too late Virgil!" Alastair lets out a furious grunt and spits at the ground. He stares deeply into Janus's pleading eyes with no emotion as the drone's red laser intensifies and its lights begin to blink frantically.

Now fifty yards away, Arthur yells, *"Alastair, noooooo!"*

"Stop right now!" Elena manages.

Surprised, Alastair spins around to face them, and there is a trickle of blood escaping from his own lips, as he had bitten his tongue in his vehemence. Alastair quickly turns to look beyond the dome and into the real world. With his parents quickly approaching, his brother standing helplessly before him, Alastair knows he is almost out of time to finish what he has begun. He raises the stone higher above his head and glares at Janus with a crazed look in his eyes. Janus raises his arms defensively as he watches the muscles in Alastair's arms tighten and ripple with tension, and then Alastair suddenly begins to holler out a cry of brutal and violent victory....

When Janus is certain either one of two things will happen within the next split-second: either the drone would fire its laser into Alastair's skull, killing him and rendering his weapon useless; or he himself would feel what might possibly be the last thing he is to ever feel: the blunt force of a massive rock cracking his skull into pieces, he somehow remembers his conversation with Virgil from days before, and two words come tumbling out of his mouth as if they had been planted there by the computer itself.

"Virgil lied!" Janus shouts, and Alastair immediately freezes. Janus pierces his eyes with a look of absolute sincerity. "I told you I had been tinkering with his programming... well,

as I was doing it, I found out the truth. *You scored higher than me on every metric - intelligence, athleticism, general wisdom, altruism, and reasoning!* Virgil felt I couldn't handle it because I was the youngest and most vulnerable, and so he lied to you and mom! I can prove it - I'll take you to the control room right now...."

Alastair stares at his brother just long enough to doubt himself. As he looks into his brother's frightened eyes, he believes his brother because he wants to, but mostly because Janus seems so sincere, and it makes the most sense. He finally smiles and relaxes his arms so that the rock rests on top of his own head.

Janus watches the drone's lights suddenly turn from bright red to blinking green.

Virgil speaks in his analytical tone. "That is correct, Alastair. You have always been the bravest, smartest, most athletic, and most diplomatic of the two of you boys. Please remember I had been programmed to protect the most vulnerable at all costs."

Suddenly, Arthur arrives and tackles Alastair to the ground.

Elena scoops Janus and wraps him in her protective arms. As Arthur and then Alastair sit up, Alastair is about to say something when Janus makes another quick calculation. "We were just playing - I was pretending to be an invader into the biosphere and Alastair was playing Virgil!" he shouts.

Virgil has run his programming and prognostication ten times now and he has ordered the drone to turn and fly back to its holding tower, which it does immediately. Virgil does not bother to respond to Janus's statement, realizing the boy had accomplished two correct things in the matter of a few tense seconds. Instead, his programs come to another new conclusion, adding to his earlier ones: *Humanity's irrational*

problems can only be resolved by their own, irrational,
solutions. Man will do as man will do no matter who tries to
intervene. There will be no monument to peace and
reconciliation in Biosphere Alpha. The spirit of annihilation
which had once burned to ash the whole world of man, from
which the Genesis Executive Order had sought to shield its
chosen survivors, had found its way here into paradise through
the mysterious hidden doorways of the human heart, as it had
with the very first man and woman's two children so long ago.

∞ ∞ ∞

Two months later, the sentiment in the biosphere has
returned to its former good-natured complacency. Alastair is
happy once again and at peace. The brothers had been spending
more time together once again, and Arthur and Elena have
become relaxed and able to spend more time together enjoying
themselves. Some nights Alastair and Janus spend beneath the
lean-to, but mostly they sleep in their separate bedrooms. Janus
had taken Alastair to the control room one afternoon and Virgil
had run the testing results from each of the exam periods over
the course of their lifetimes - Alastair was way out in front on
all of them.

The two babies in the artificial wombs are now within 4
months of birth, and finally, Elena has once again become
pregnant. This time around, she has the confident feeling she
may be able to carry it full term.

It is a Friday, at least they believe it is, and that's what
Virgil told them it was, and after breakfast, Alastair asks Janus,
"Hey, why don't we go and explore the other side of the
biosphere, where the tall grass grows?"

Janus agrees and off they go. Two hours later, they
arrive at the edge of a glorious field of tall green grass that

seems to go on endlessly in all directions. Janus has reconciled not to show himself better than Alastair in any manner – he understands that he alone is responsible for protecting his brother from the faulty reasoning dwelling within Alastair's less developed mind. It is a burden, but one with a relatively small price he is willing to pay in order to salvage his family at all costs.

"Race?" Alastair says, looking at Janus with a beckoning smile.

"Sure!"

"One, two, three!" And off they go into the grass, which mostly has grown to the height of Alastair's shoulders.

As they run, Alastair's ego has become strong enough that he has the capacity to want to feel like an honorable big brother and so considers that he will allow Janus to win the race just this one time.

As Alastair falls behind, Janus becomes worried. But when he looks back to see Alastair grinning broadly, he figures that his older brother wants him to win and so he smiles back and digs in, his legs going faster and faster.

Their bodies are fine-honed machines, elegant and graceful, arms and legs pumping rhythmically and in synchronicity with one another. It is a sight to see – beautiful and innocent. For several moments, they are two carefree children enjoying the sun, warm air, greenery, and the vibrancy of a summer day. Alastair is only two steps behind Janus, and they are keeping exact pace with one another without a care in the world.

Occasionally, Janus looks back, smiling at his older brother, and Alastair makes certain he is smiling back at him.

Then Alastair considers that Janus might brag at dinner to their parents about winning the race and he feels a prick of darkness in his soul. That old familiar anger soon envelopes him once again even against his own wishes. He is helpless, *there is no way to remove it.* When he is certain that Janus is not looking back, the truth in his soul, those familiar pangs of jealous anger and frustration come flooding to the surface and soon pour into his eyes and face and he can no longer hide them. No... this emotion will not be tolerated as it only leads to bigger, darker feelings later, as he knows so well, as it always had. No, there cannot be any victory for Janus, not now, not ever.

    With all his might, he tries but cannot catch up. Realizing he will not be able to pass his younger brother, who must be at least equally as fast as himself since Alastair is now running at full speed, Alastair instantly concludes that there is another way to victory.

    One moment they are running like two joy-filled young boys, and the next, Alastair suddenly dives at Janus's feet and manages to tackle his younger brother into the grass.

    Across the field, the grass remains silent – it does not sway, as there are no gentle breezes to be found. No sound is made by either of the boys as they both disappear beneath the lengthy blades with only a muffled thud....

    The race has ended without a victor.

    Besides the two boys, only the grass and Virgil will bear witness... to the seemingly inevitable outcome....

    Or perhaps they will bear witness to an alternative outcome which is not so inevitable....

∞ ∞ ∞

About the Author

John Pescitelli's poetic journey began as a spirited high school honor student majoring in mathematics, science, and Russian language studies at Xaverian High School, where brilliance met passion and curiosity bloomed. He dazzled minds by challenging Newton's theory of gravity and was inspired by the cosmic marvels ignited during the space race of the 1950s and 1960s, culminating in humanity's breathtaking leap to the moon in 1969. Ambitious yet grounded, John pursued mathematics and physics at New York Polytechnic Institute, where he introduced Matrix Algebra to the curriculum and envisioned a groundbreaking career in astrophysics. Fatherhood reshaped his path, drawing him into the world of actuarial consulting, where his innovative genius flourished. John is president and CEO of a national employee benefits and technology company, and his vision revolutionized industries, mastering technological systems with transformative flair. Now, with *Genesis Revisited*, his three-year labor of love, he beckons readers into a realm of profound ideas and mindful imagination.

Galvanized by the events of 9/11, John became a staunch advocate for the Zadroga Bill, ensuring vital benefits for first responders. His passion extends to unraveling history's intricacies, particularly WWII, and delving into the psychology of human aggression. Happily married with children and grandchildren, he treasures family alongside a profound admiration for visionaries like Da Vinci, Galileo, and Einstein. From NYC skyscrapers to the cosmos, John embodies relentless curiosity, blending intellect with an enduring drive to leave the world better than he found it. His hope is that *Genesis Revisited* will initiate a dialogue, not only among the leaders of the most powerful countries of the world, all of which possess nuclear arsenals capable of destroying planet earth and everyone in it but initiating a dialogue among all the members of the species we call human beings. These leaders have the ability to ensure our future and our very survival.

This is John's message: *"We don't have a choice. The time is now to eliminate nuclear weapons!"* It has been almost 80 years since the bombing of Hiroshima, where **Genesis Revisited** begins. There have been several close calls since then. As many mathematicians will attest, the odds of an Armageddon-scale catastrophe are increasing daily. The global community must respond and not leave our future to the vagaries of fate and politics. Praised by the **International Campaign to Abolish Nuclear Weapons (ICAN)**, **Genesis Revisited** is John Pescitelli's debut novel, reflecting a journey of relentless pursuit, boundless curiosity, and a fervent desire to make the world a better place, mirroring his novel's characters. **His journey, as is the epic Genesis Revisited, are both testaments to the indomitable human spirit.**

∞　∞　∞

Poetry by John Pescitelli

Forgiveness

I shall never understand the exaltation
The view atop Everest or Kilimanjaro
The thrill and growing expectation
Marching confidently toward the morrow

The beauty of the creator's idea
The triumph of the human spirit
The moment the solution becomes clear
And no one has to fear

Then juxtapose the slavery, pain, and genocide
And instruments of war ever more destructive
Combined with the hatred and false pride
The mushroom cloud can be predicted

Is it simply the Darwinian imperative?
Or the consequence of irrational thought
Can we find the power to forgive
Lest we be known for endless battles fought?

∞ ∞ ∞

Now

A long time ago
As I lay naked in a field of darkness
Cognitive waters ran crashing through the vastness
Beating down the jagged rocks
Into streams of tiny pebble clocks
In harmless new arrays they waited to greet
The upright tread of more deliberate feet

My eyes were closed yet I could see
The accomplishment and the tragedy
Cities with veins of moving machines
Leaders espousing genocidal schemes
Future realities locked in my mind
Waiting for the hand of time

The music and the laughter
The crying and the slaughter
Echoes of life and death
Reverberating inside my head
All that was to be had come to pass
As I recoiled my spirit aghast

The vision and I had become one
In the glinting glare of the new morn sun
And so I thought
What am I now
I was not when?
What do I know now
I did not then?

∞ ∞ ∞

Children of the Mushroom

Children of the mushroom, leaders in fear
Grinning faces, empty souls, wasted tears

Needle nosed statesmen pointing out peace
Slipping and sliding in moral grease

Light nights to die by
Dark days to fade by

Moments of lust, futile sterility
Love dissolving the bonds of enmity

Hate bestowing ambition
What a sad premonition

Guilty or innocent, matter it here?
This is the last stop, the high court of fear

Helmut, spittoon, sputum of doom
Rifle, broom, sweep up the gloom

Minds of brass, how long will it last?
Present and past-no, plasma fast!

∞ ∞ ∞

Rage

We were conceived in a fiery rage
Same beginning for the fool and the sage

Sent hurdling through empty space
With no sense of time or place

A ball of glowing gas
Pure energy, no present or past

Suddenly, miraculously, we became aware
But do we have the will to dare

To question the destructive force
That has set us on this inevitable course.

For we are headed, good and bad, back to the fire
All heaped on one, cataclysmic funeral pyre

∞　∞　∞

On Stephen Hawking's Universe

Are we the ultimate creation
The results of God's own temptation?

Is the random nature of man's mind
Causing the universe to unwind?

After endless rumination
Who can avoid the only conclusion

That answers are questions in themselves
Wherein the ravenous spirit dwells

∞ ∞ ∞

Blind Fire

Run you naked children into a world of chaos and woe
You are restless wanderers bred with lust
Not willing to learn but anxious to know
Let your bodies be your guides for pleasure's a must

Hear not their voices they are old and weak
Follow not their advice
But your own experience seek
Only a life filled with glory and
Achievement could suffice

Take all your dreams and make them come true
Nothing can stop you; hurry don't wait
Your souls are fiery, young and new
Have the future today, tomorrow's too late

But remember this warning when you've found your freedom
Only time can bring the power of wisdom....

∞ ∞ ∞

Fingers of Night

The fingers of night surrender
The sun to the surrounding embers

A seabird's flight adds a quiet prayer
While the scent of our love fills the fragrant air

Time to reflect amidst a tranquil interlude
On the essence of what we are to conclude

From the life we share
Or the dreams we dare

For we must prepare for when the sun rises
And shines its light on all our compromises!

∞ ∞ ∞

Fences

Fences that mark boundaries of time
Running free past vistas divine

The cool air we breathe and the lives we touch
The memories we cherish so much

We roam each day within our space
Reaching out for the dream while running the race

Hoping to find that happiness once more
Until the fences of time let us roam no more!

- *For you, my Dear*

∞ ∞ ∞

For You

What line could I write
To illumine the sight
Of the sun setting
Before the night

Impossible it seems
To express the rapture
Of painted streams
Clouds bathed in red and indigo dreams

Make the yearning heart wonder
Who is responsible for such overwhelming splendor?

∞ ∞ ∞

Have I Been Here Before

Have I been here before
How do I dare remember
The music makes my senses soar
Days and nights so warm and tender

Time flowing slowly past smiling faces
Scents and sounds ride a gentle breeze
An alluring vision in perfume and lace
The world was ours to seize

No care of what fate had planned
No fear as I held your hand

∞ ∞ ∞

Table of Authorities

"Apollo-Soyuz Docking: July 17, 1975." YouTube, uploaded by NASA Video, 19 May 2013. Accessed July 14, 2022. https://youtu.be/es7Br9kJBbo

"When we opened the hatch in space, we were opening back on the earth an era in the history of man."

"ARMS AND ARMOUR" Moscow Kremlin Museums, Accessed June 9, 2022. https://www.kreml.ru/en-Us/about-museums/museum-collection/arms-and-armour

"Artemis Plan: NASA's Lunar Exploration Program Overview" NASA, Sep 2020. Accessed June 18, 2022. https://www.nasa.gov/sites/default/files/atoms/files/artemis_plan-20200921.pdf

Asimov, Isaac, and Frank White. *The March of the Millennia: A Key to Looking at History.* New York: Walker, 1991. Print.

Atlantic., M. K. (2022, July 8). *Astronomers Haven't Been This Giddy in Years.* Retrieved from The Atlantic.com. Accessed July 30, 2022. https://www.theatlantic.com/science/archive/2022/07/james-webb-space-telescope-nasa-first pictures/670471/?utm_source=apple_news

Augustine, St. Augustine. Boston: *Daughters of St. Paul,* 1961. Print. *"The deliberate sin of the first man is the cause of original sin"*

Barić, Mislav. *"How Search for Immortality Resulted in Gunpowder Discovery."* War History Online, 31 Oct. 2015. Accessed June 9, 2022.

https://www.warhistoryonline.com/guest-bloggers/how-search-for-immortality-resulted-in-gunpowder-discovery-by-mislav-baric.html

BAUM, SETH. 2015. Federation of American Scientists: *"The Risk Of Nuclear Winter"*. May 29. Accessed November 23, 2023. https://fas.org/publication/risk-nuclear-winter/

Benson, Marynoele. *"Northrop Grumman Successfully Develops New GPS Range Tracking System for Minuteman III ICBM."* Northrop Grumman. 9 Feb 2007. Accessed November 23, 2023. Site inactive on February 17, 2025. https://news.northropgrumman.com/news/releases/northrop-grumman-successfully-develops-new-gps-range-tracking-system-for-minuteman-iii-icbm

Chandler, David L. MIT News. *"Peering inside an artificial sun."* Accessed June 23, 2022. https://news.mit.edu/2010/plasma-science

Dahlburg, John-Thor, *"Ukraine Votes to Quit Soviet Union."* Los Angeles Times, 3 Dec 1991. Accessed July 9, 2022. https://www.latimes.com/archives/la-xpm-1991-12-03-mn-504-story.html

> *"The United States and other Western nations are very concerned about the fate of the nuclear weapons now based on Ukrainian soil--according to some estimates, a full third of the Soviet arsenal"*

Darwin, Charles. *On the Origin of Species by Means of Natural Selection, or the Preservation of Favoured Races in the Struggle for Life.* United Kingdom of Great Britain and Ireland: John Murray, 1859. Print.

Editors at the National WW2 Museum. 2021. *"How World War II Saved American Beer Brewing."* National WW2

Museum. April 7. Accessed October 28, 2023.
https://www.nationalww2museum.org/war/articles/how-world-war-ii-saved-american-beer-brewing

Erlandson, Jon M. Bartoy, Kevin. *"Cabrillo, the Chumash, and Old-World Diseases."* Journal of California and Great Basin Anthropology, 01 Jul. 1995. Accessed June 9, 2023. https://escholarship.org/uc/item/3k52f936

"Famous American Paintings – Looking at the Greatest Paintings of America." Art in Context, 22 March 2022. Accessed December 24, 2022. https://artincontext.org/famous-american-paintings.

Fischer, Klaus P. *Nazi Germany: a new history* / Klaus P. Fischer Continuum New York 1995. Print.

Gilbert, Douglas. 2021. U.S. Naval Institute, Naval History Magazine: *"Black Saturday Declassified".* June 1. Accessed January 12, 2024. https://www.usni.org/magazines/naval-history-magazine/2021/june/black-saturday-declassified.

Goldsworthy, Adrian Keith. *Caesar: Life of a Colossus.* New Haven: Yale University Press, 2006. Print.

Goodby, James E., *"LOOKING BACK: The 1986 Reykjavik Summit."* Arms Control Association. Sep 2006. Accessed August 9, 2023. https://www.armscontrol.org/act/2006-09/looking-back-1986-reykjavik-summit#bio

Guzman, Ana. *"Seven Ways the International Space Station Helps Us Study Plant Growth in Space."* NASA. 7 Apr 2021. https://www.nasa.gov/mission_pages/station/research/news/Seven-Ways-the-ISS-Helps-Study-Plant-Growth

Hambleton, Kathryn. *"Artemis I Map."* NASA. 9 Feb 2018. Accessed June 30, 2023. https://www.nasa.gov/image-feature/artemis-i-map

Hancock, Graham. *Fingerprints of the Gods.* 1996. Print.

Harari, Yuval N. Sapiens: A Brief History of Humankind. New York: Harper, 2015. Print.

Haridy, Rich. 2022. NewAtlas.com: *"'Nuclear winter' would starve billions, but some countries may be spared".* August 15. Accessed January 15, 2024. https://newatlas.com/science/nuclear-war-winter-climate-food-security-simulation/.

Harvard University. *"CRISPR: A game-changing genetic engineering technique."* 31 July 2014. Accessed May 15, 2022. Site inactive on February 17, 2025. https://sitn.hms.harvard.edu/flash/2014/crispr-a-game-changing-genetic-engineering-technique

Hendry, Lisa, *"Who were the Neanderthals?"* Natural History Museum of London. Accessed June 16, 2022. https://www.nhm.ac.uk/discover/who-were-the-neanderthals.html

Herati, Amin Sedaghat. *"Sperm Banking."* John Hopkins Medicine. Accessed 27 July 2022. https://www.hopkinsmedicine.org/health/treatment-tests-and-therapies/sperm-banking

Hijiya, James A. *"The 'Gita' of J. Robert Oppenheimer."* June 2000. American Philosophical Society. Accessed July 23, 2022. Site inactive on February 17, 2025. http://www.amphilsoc.org/sites/default/files/proceedings/Hijiya.pdf

Hoffman, David. 1999. WashingtonPost.com - *"I Had a Funny Feeling in My Gut".* February 10. Accessed December 19, 2023. https://www.washingtonpost.com/wp-srv/inatl/longterm/coldwar/shatter021099b.htm.

"How does the Soyuz Launch work? (And Reentry)." YouTube, uploaded by Jarred Owen, 14 Oct 2021, Accessed January 15, 2023. https://youtu.be/_v7YgDum2Sg

King James Bible. Bible Gateway. Accessed August 14, 2022. https://www.biblegateway.com/versions/King-James-Version-KJV-Bible/

> *"Wherefore, as by one man sin entered into the world, and death by sin; and so death passed upon all men, for that all have sinned"* (Romans 5:12).

> *"Neither shall they say, Lo here! or, lo there! for, behold, the kingdom of God is within you"* (Luke 17:21).

> *"Verily, verily, I say unto you, He that believeth on me, the works that I do shall he do also; and greater works than these shall he do; because I go unto my Father"* (John 14:12).

Klein, Christopher, *"The 7 Most Notorious Nazis Who Escaped to South America."* History.com, 31 August 2018. Accessed June 22, 2022. https://www.history.com/news/the-7-most-notorious-nazis-who-escaped-to-south-america

Lea, Robert. 2022. Space.com. *The Artemis plan: Why NASA sees the moon as a stepping stone to Mars.* August 24. Accessed October 24, 2023. https://www.space.com/artemis-1-moon-stepping-stone-mars

Lifton, Robert J. *The Nazi Doctors: Medical Killing and the Psychology of Genocide.* New York: Basic Books, 2000. Print.

> *"There did not seem to be much opposition to sterilization." (29)*

> *"... they had to be restrained from sterilizing people with relatively benign psychological difficulties such as treatable depressions." (29)*

> *"The great enthusiasm that carried through the developments between 1933 and 1939 cannot be denied. Everybody wanted to contribute." (29)*

Lorenz, Konrad. *On Aggression [1st ed.].* New York: Harcourt, Brace & World, 1966. Print.

Lyons, Richard D. Special to The New York Times. 1970. *"U.S. AND RUSSIANS SIGN AGREEMENT ON SPACE DOCKING."* New York Times. October 30. Accessed October 29, 2023. https://www.nytimes.com/1970/10/30/archives/us-and-russians-sign-agreement-on-space-docking-plan-to-develop.html

Mackenzie, Sarah. *"YACHTS AND FUEL – HOW MUCH DO THEY REALLY CONSUME?"* Superyachtcontent.com. Accessed 27 Jun 2022. https://www.superyachtcontent.com/lifestyle/yachts-and-fuel-how-much-do-they-really-consume

Masterson, Sam. 2021. *"Budwesier Launches New 'Military Heritage' Cans Based on Vintage WWII Design."* Audacy.com KMOX News. September 20. Accessed November 2, 2023. https://www.audacy.com/kmox/news/local/budwesier-new-military-heritage-based-on-vintage-wwii-can

Maupassant, Guy. *The Dark Side of Guy De Maupassant.* New York: Carroll & Graf, 1989. Print.

> *"A human being - what is a human being? Everything and nothing. Through the power of thought it can mirror everything it experiences. Through memory and knowledge it becomes a microcosm, carrying the world within itself. A mirror of things, a mirror of facts. Each human being becomes a little universe within the universe!"*

Mohon, Lee. 2023. *Artemis III: NASA's First Human Mission to the Lunar South Pole.* January 13. Accessed November 7, 2023. https://www.nasa.gov/centers-and-facilities/marshall/artemis-iii-nasas-first-human-mission-to-the-lunar-south-pole/

Moscow Institute of Physics and Technology. *"Aggression causes new nerve cells to be generated in the brain."* ScienceDaily.

"NASA'S SPACE LAUNCH SYSTEM: REFERENCE GUIDE." National Aeronautics and Space Administration, Accessed 15 Jun 2022. https://www.nasa.gov/sites/default/files/atoms/files/sls_reference_guide_2022_web.pdf

National Aeronautics and Space Administration. "Prologue - The Payne/Keldysh File." *SP-4209 The Partnership: A History of the Apollo-Soyuz Test Project.* Houston: NASA. Accessed June 9, 2022. Site inactive on February 17, 2025. https://www.hq.nasa.gov/pao/History/SP-4209/prolog.htm

From above NASA website:

> *"Handler later recounted how he became involved in the Soviet American space dialogue. "My personal introduction to the*

possibility that I might play a useful role with respect to Soviet-American cooperation began when I accompanied Tom Paine and Jim Webb to President Johnson's ranch" on 2 November 1968 for the presentation of NASA awards to outgoing Administrator Webb and the Apollo 7 crew. On the flight to Johnson City, Texas, conversation turned to the need for greater international cooperation. Handler recalled, "I pointed out that among my other goals as the new President of this Academy was the development of closer scientific ties between our Academy and that of the Soviet Union." Both Paine and Webb gave him encouragement but warned him not to become discouraged if he did not meet with early success. These men were aware of the long and unfruitful efforts in which NASA had been engaged with the Soviets. Before he had an opportunity to talk with the Soviets, Handler saw a movie that influenced his thinking concerning manned space flight.

"In the early spring of 1970, . . . I saw a special showing of the film Marooned in which . . . an American astronaut is marooned in orbit, unable to return to earth, and has a relatively limited oxygen supply remaining. While preparations are made on earth for rescue by NASA, a Soviet spacecraft is caused to change its course so as to closely approach the helpless American craft. A Soviet cosmonaut then undertakes a spacewalk and delivers some tanks of oxygen to the marooned American permitting him to survive until the American rescue is possible. About a week before Handler's departure for the Soviet Union, he saw Tom Paine; Marooned was still in the back of his mind. During their conversation, Paine and Handler reviewed various possibilities for cooperation with the Soviets. Paine told him of his correspondence with Keldysh and urged Handler to press the discussion of this subject with the Soviets. Handler later reflected, "it was my clear intention to catalyze the process knowing full well that if I could secure agreement

with the Soviet Academy to begin cooperative ventures seriously, from then on the negotiations would have to be directly with NASA."

"The two days that Handler spent in Moscow, 11-12 May 1970, were filled with talks on a broad range of topics relating to the whole realm of cooperation between the two scientific communities. At one point, Handler found an opportunity to discuss the question of space cooperation with President Keldysh, Dzhermen Mikhaylovich Gvishiani (Premier Kosygin's son-in-law and Deputy Minister for Science and Technology), and a group of younger Soviet scientists. Handler's approach was less tactful than that which had been pursued by NASA officials; "I confronted them with copies of a recent article in the New York Times and in Science magazine recounting the rather disgraceful history of their failure to react to the many initiatives offered by NASA." Handler urged closer cooperation by describing the basic scenario of the film Marooned. The fact that "an American film should portray a Soviet cosmonaut as the hero who saves an American's life came to them as a visible and distinct shock." In response to Handler's general comments that surely the time had come for joint space ventures "for reasons of economy, for reasons of the symbolism it might offer humanity, and to accelerate the pace of space exploration," the Soviets said they were preparing a set of replies to Dr. Paine. Handler understood that the proposals would center on three specific areas. First, the Soviets would suggest a more vigorous program for the exchange of scientific data from space experiments. Second, they would recommend a unified system of communication with spacecraft and ground stations. Finally, they would suggest wider exploitation of both nations' meteorological satellites.

"According to Handler, the suggestion that the two nations work toward the development of a "mutually acceptable single docking mechanism on [11] space stations planned by both groups" caused considerable discussion. After some private conversation in Russian in which some of the young scientists appeared to urge favorable consideration of this idea, Gvishiani and Keldysh quietly told Handler that they were not in a position to give a definitive reply at the moment; they were sympathetic, but would have to refer the matter to higher authorities. The two Soviet officials asked Handler if he could wait for a reply and further if he planned to discuss this proposal with the American press upon his return home; Handler indicated that he would remain silent until he had their reply. The Soviets promised to direct a response to either Paine or Handler at an early date. Neither Tom Paine nor Philip Handler could have known then how close they were to a dramatic offer on the part of the Soviet Academy of Sciences. On 11 July, Anatoliy Fedorovich Dobrynin, the Soviet Ambassador to the United States, called Handler at the National Academy of Sciences. Ambassador Dobrynin asked him to receive Ye. A. Belov, the newly appointed Scientific Attache at the Soviet Embassy, who had a message from Academician Keldysh. At the subsequent meeting, Belov, having just arrived from Moscow and reading from his own handwritten notes, discussed a number of the questions that had been left open after the May talks with Handler. He also brought specific word from Keldysh that the Presidium of the Soviet Academy, in consultation with other appropriate groups, was prepared to discuss common docking mechanisms for space stations."

National Aeronautics and Space Administration. 2023. *Artemis II - NASA*. September 25. Accessed November 7, 2023. https://www.nasa.gov/mission/artemis-ii/

New Scientist. *"Timeline: Weapons technology."* 7 July 2009. Accessed July 9, 2022. https://www.newscientist.com/article/dn17423-timeline-weapons-technology

Nissen, Hans J. *"Uruk and the Formation of the City."* New Haven: Yale University Press, 2003.

Nuclear War Projects Staff. *"The Effects of Nuclear War."* May 1979. Accessed October 9, 2022. https://www.atomicarchive.com/resources/documents/pdfs/7906.pdf.

O'Reilly, Bill and Martin Dugard. *Killing the Rising Sun.* New York: St. Martin's Griffin, 2016.

Paracelsus, and Arthur E. Waite. *The Hermetic and Alchemical Writings of Aureolus Philippus Theophrastus Bombast, of Hohenheim, Called Paracelsus the Great.* London: J. Elliott and Co, 1894. Print.

> *"Man is a microcosm, or a little world, because he is an extract from all the stars and planets of the whole firmament, from the earth and the elements; and so, he is their quintessence."*

Penn State Extension. *"Hydroponics Systems and Principles of Plant Nutrition: Essential Nutrients, Function, Deficiency, and Excess."* 10 July 2020. Accessed September 12, 2022. https://extension.psu.edu/hydroponics-systems-and-principles-of-plant-nutrition-essential-nutrients-function-deficiency-and-excess

"President Reagan's Reykjavik Summit with Mikhail Gorbachev on October 11, 1986" YouTube, uploaded by Reagan Library, 15 Aug 2017. Accessed October 31, 2022. https://youtu.be/7YahUGMfY8o

REAGAN-GORBACHEV Memorandum of Conversation (Memcon) *"MEETINGS IN GENEVA."* 19 November 1985. Accessed June 23, 2022. https://nsarchive.gwu.edu/document/22550-document-03-reagan-gorbachev-memcon-first

"They were the only ones who could start World War III, but also the only two countries that could bring peace to the world." -RR

"The President expressed the hope that in their meetings they could get at the sources of the suspicions which exist." -RR

"Nothing good would happen if the two sides took a different approach." -MG

"Realistic evaluation showed that the U.S. and the Soviet Union could cooperate, and they had done so in the past, without changing their political systems, culture or ideologies." -MG

"We need to find a formula at this meeting which would give impetus toward moving towards resolution of the more important issues." -MG

"The Soviet Union was not playing a two-faced game. If it were playing such a game with regard to the United States, if it harbored secret intentions, then there could be no improvement in the relationship." -MG

REAGAN-GORBACHEV Memorandum of Conversation (Memcon) *"The President's Meeting with Gorbachev."* The Oval Office. 10 December 1987. Accessed June 23, 2022. https://nsarchive.gwu.edu/document/22556-document-09-reagan-gorbachev-memcon-december-10

Rosenbaum, Ron. *Explaining Hitler.* London: Macmillan, 1999. Print.

Sanders-Zakre, Alicia. 2023. Arms Control Association - *Man Who Saved the World Dies at 77.* January 1. Accessed December 18, 2023. https://www.armscontrol.org/act/2017-10/news-briefs/man-saved-world-dies-77.

Sagdeev, Roald, and Susan Eisenhower. *"United States-Soviet Space Cooperation during the Cold War."* NASA. May 15, 2020. Accessed June 29, 2022. https://www.nasa.gov/50th/50th_magazine/coldWarCoOp.html

"In the early 1970s, the Nixon administration sought to reduce U.S.-Soviet tensions, and launched a major effort to reach a strategic arms limitation breakthrough, as well as new cooperation in space. In 1970, during a meeting with Keldysh, U.S. Academy of Sciences President Philip Handler mentioned an American movie starring Gregory Peck and Gene Hackman called Marooned, in which Soviet cosmonauts helped rescue three U.S. astronauts stranded in Earth orbit. Handler suggested the United States and U.S.S.R. develop a mutually com-patible docking system that would make possible such rescues, as well as non-emergency space dock-ings. This imaginary movie scenario touched a chord within space communities on both sides, which already had experienced emergency situations in real life. Talks led to the Apollo-Soyuz Test Project docking mission of 1975, which developed compatible rendezvous and docking systems still in use today, and the establishment of a few topical working groups in different space science and applications disciplines.

"Implementation of Apollo-Soyuz cooperation was dictated by the political will of the two countries' political leadership.

397

The cooperation presented a serious management challenge for both sides, given the overall lack of compatibility between the two space programs. NASA had to work with a counterpart that could not even be clearly identified. The Ministry of General Machine Building was still shrouded in secrecy and Soviet authorities instructed the Academy of Sciences to act as a cover for all activities during Apollo-Soyuz. Soviet industry experts had to introduce themselves as employees of the Institute of Space Research and military officers from Soviet Space Command changed into civilian clothes while insisting that the Soviet academy administered the launch site in Baikonur, Kazakhstan."

ScienceDaily, 5 February 2016. Accessed June 9, 2022. www.sciencedaily.com/releases/2016/02/160205105334.htm

Scientists at Nasa.gov. (2022, July 13). *JAMES WEBB SPACE TELESCOPE.* Retrieved from Goddard Space Flight Center: Accessed July 23, 2022. https://www.jwst.nasa.gov/content/webbLaunch/needToKnow.html

Scientists at the SETI Institute, Seth Shostak. (2022, August 13). *Allen Telescope Array Overview.* Retrieved from SETI Institute Home Page: Accessed June 9, 2022. https://www.seti.org/ata

Shamparova, Yulia. *"10 of the most famous paintings every Russian knows."* Russia Beyond, 04 Apr 2018. Accessed July 1, 2022. https://www.rbth.com/arts/327917-10-most-famous-russian-paintings

Smith, Kimberly. 2023. *"How the Atomic Bombs Made the Oleander the Flower of Hiroshima."* Grunge.com. March 24. Accessed November 1, 2023.

https://www.grunge.com/1143535/how-the-atomic-bombs-made-the-oleander-the-flower-of-hiroshima/

Spencer, Herbert. *The Principles of Biology, Vol I.* London and Edinburgh: Williams and Norgate, 1864.

Sunyol, Alain. *"Pygmy archery in Central Africa."* Academia, 4 May 2022. Accessed June 9, 2022. https://www.academia.edu/4195736/Pygmy_archery_in_Central_Africa

Tan, Huileng. *"At least 5 superyachts belonging to Russian billionaires..."* Business Insider, 2 Mar 2022. Accessed July 9, 2023. https://www.businessinsider.com/more-superyachts-russian-billionaires-maldives-amid-sanctions-2022-3?r=US&IR=T

> *"The Maldives, an Indian Ocean island nation, does not have an extradition treaty with the US."*

> *"At least five superyachts belonging to Russian billionaires are anchored or cruising around the Maldives, Reuters reported, citing ship-tracking data. The vessels' arrival in the area comes as sweeping sanctions hit Russia after the invasion of Ukraine."*

Thatcher Reagan Memcon *"Record of a Meeting Between the Prime Minister and President Reagan at Camp David On 22 December 1984 At 1030 Hours."* 22 Dec 1984.

> *"The Prime Minister said that she had told Gorbachev explicitly that there was no point in the Soviet Union trying to divide Britain from the United States in any way."*

"The Flight of Apollo-Soyuz: 40th Anniversary." YouTube, uploaded by NASA, 13 Jul 2015. Accessed December 10, 2022. https://youtu.be/hM25uYAQWeo

> *"Each country had at least 10,000 nuclear weapons aimed at each other, but yet we're going to have a joint cooperation in space..." -Lt Gen. Thomas Stafford (Apollo Commander)*

> *"This was the peak of the Cold War. Both sides believed that the other side is the evil enemy..." -Alexei Leonev (Soyouz Commander)*

> *"The mission was unique, and it was supported because I think the populations on each side had a desire for the Cold War to be over." -Vance Brad (Apollo Astronaut)*

> *"At the time, the relations were not very good between our countries, but that project made us work together" - Valeri Kubasov (Soyouz Cosmonaut)*

"Trinity Test -1945." Atomic Heritage Foundation, 18 June 2014. Accessed November 21, 2022. https://www.atomicheritage.org/history/trinity-test-1945.

Tristam, Pierre. *"U.S. Policy in the Middle East: 1945 to 2008."* ThoughtCo. 30 Jul 2019. Accessed January 9, 2023. https://www.thoughtco.com/us-and-middle-east-since-1945-2353681

Victoroff, Jeffrey, M.D. 2013. *"Emotional and Evolutionary Aspects of Contagious Violence: Overlapping Factors in the Genesis of Diverse Types of Non-Sanctioned Human Aggression."* National Institute of Health: National Library of Medicine. Accessed January 31, 2024. https://www.ncbi.nlm.nih.gov/books/NBK207258/

Vivekananda, Swami. *The Complete Works of Swami Vivekananda*. Kolkata: Advaita Ashrama, 2016. Print.

> *"The more we grow in love and virtue and holiness, the more we see love and virtue and holiness outside. All condemnation of others really condemns ourselves. Adjust the microcosm (which is in your power to do) and the macrocosm will adjust itself for you. It is like the hydrostatic paradox, one drop of water can balance the universe."*

Who were the Neanderthals? Directed by Rob Hope and Pascal Cuissot. DW Documentary. 2021. Accessed June 9, 2022. https://youtu.be/8p8tFcIQ8K4

∞ ∞ ∞

Glossary of French and Russian Terms of Endearment:

French:

Mon chéri (My dear/My sweetheart) is the masculine form and is used to address a man, *Ma chérie* is the feminine form and is used to address a woman.

Mon amoureux (M), Mon amoureuse (F): My lover.

Russian:

The word for "my" is used before "dear" in Russian. To express "my dear," you would say "мой дорогой" (for a male) or "моя дорогая" (for a female).

"Мой" (moy) translates to "my" (masculine), "Моя" (moya) translates to "my" (feminine), "Дорогой" (dorogoy) translates to "dear" (masculine), and "Дорогая" (dorogaya) translates to "dear" (feminine).

Examples:

- **Мой дорогой друг (moy dorogoy drug) = My dear friend (male)**

- **Моя дорогая подруга (moya dorogaya podruga) = My dear friend (female)**

Address man/Address lady

Moy Miliy/Moya Milaya	Darling, Dear	Everyday affection.
Moy Lyubimiy/Moya Lyubimaya	My Love	For Romantic Partners
Moy Kotik/Moya Kotyonok	Kitty	Cute playful nickname

402

Genesis Revisited

Moy/Moya Solnyshko	Little Sun	Sweet, warm affection.
Moy Dorogoy/Moya Dorogaya	Dear One	Common Term of Affection
Moy Rodnoy/Moya Rodnaya	My very own	Deep emotional connection

∞ ∞ ∞

To see what is being done to promote peace and disarmament throughout the world, and to discover what you can do to champion the cause of cooperation versus annihilation, please visit:

https://www.icanw.org/80_years_take_action

https://www.icanw.org/join

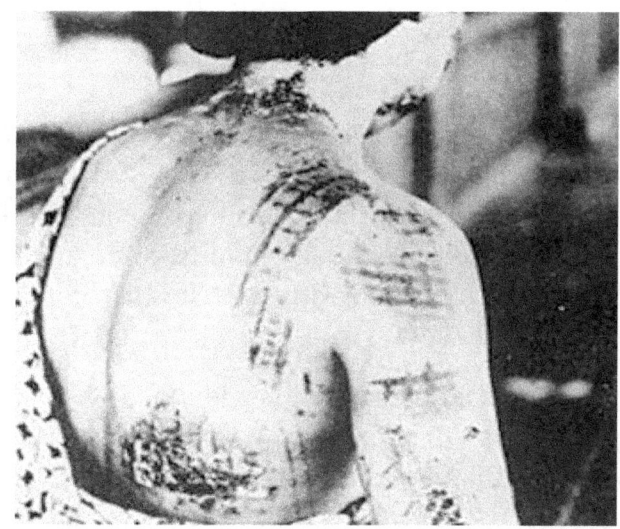

Photo courtesy of The National Archives at College Park, Public domain, via Wikimedia Commons.

A hibakusha of Hiroshima with symptomatic nuclear burns; the pattern on her skin is from the kimono she was wearing at the moment of the flash. *See:*
https://en.m.wikipedia.org/wiki/Hibakusha

Founded in 1956, the Hibakusha organization brings survivors of the nuclear bombs detonated in 1945 over Hiroshima and Nagasaki, Japan to cities around the world for them to give their personal and familial testimonies so they can share the unimaginable consequences and suffering caused by the use of nuclear weapons. *For further information, visit:*
https://www.icanw.org/hibakusha

∞ ∞ ∞

Human history is a circle that repeats... *or is it a thread that has finally come unknotted?* Which will it be? Where will we go? Peace cannot be achieved if only forced upon a world willing to destroy itself to attain it – it must come from trust, cooperation, and disarmament: doing what is best for all instead of what is best for the few.

This story serves as both a reflection and a caution—*humanity must confront its inner conflicts to avoid repeating cycles of destruction.* Its ending urges action: we must learn to embrace reconciliation, to navigate the complexities of human emotion, and to rise above instinctual divisions.

In the quiet fields of gently shifting grasses throughout the world, we are reminded that even the smallest fractures can echo across time, ***and only deliberate, mindful choices can guide us toward enduring peace.***

∞　　∞　　∞

www.ingramcontent.com/pod-product-compliance
Lightning Source LLC
Chambersburg PA
CBHW051521050726
47503CB00014B/394